I0638404

All he wanted was the truth about his mother's death, but his quest had now endangered the woman he love...

At that time of night, Trinity was dead quiet, no traffic to speak of, no pedestrians out walking. All the shops and businesses were closed and their windows were dark. Grant slid behind the wheel of his car and slowly made his way through Trinity's small business section. Keeping his head on a swivel, he glanced up and down the town's side streets but saw no Celica.

He decided to cruise down to Pete's Crab Shack on the off chance Carrie went there with friends for an after work dinner. However, her keys laying on the asphalt didn't portend well for that possibility. Visions of Lori Spelling flashed through his head.

Turning onto the river road, he ventured along the river, window down, breathing the fragrant salty air. The road was devoid of traffic, he was alone. At the restaurant, it too was closed and its parking lot empty. He turned around and headed back to Carrie's apartment where he found a note tacked to her door. It was short and to the point.

Your girlfriend's life is in your hands! She will die unless you leave town immediately. Get out of Trinity before you both die! This is no idle threat! Your friend will be released unharmed but only if you obey these instructions. If you value the woman's life you will do as we say. We mean business! Leave and never return! Do not call the police. Just leave.

Grant's pulse skyrocketed. The note was typewritten on what appeared to be an old typewriter for several of the letters had parts missing. Now, he had really messed everything up. And Carrie was the new victim.

Grant Collins is a man tormented by his past and it may get him killed. Returning to his hometown of Trinity to attend his mother's funeral, Grant finds himself drawn into the local politics. A large corporation is attempting to bring a nuclear power plant to the town. And the stakes are high—including the murders of a number of citizens opposed to nuclear power. As Grant begins to unravel the mystery behind his mother's unfortunate accident, he finds himself a target in the life-and-death struggle for wealth and power in Trinity.

KUDOS for *Trinity*

In *Trinity* by Richard Edde, Grant Collins is a soldier wounded in combat and sent back to the US for medical treatment. When his mother dies in his hometown of Trinity, he goes home to the funeral and discovers that his mother's death might not have been an accident. In fact, a number of people opposed to having a nuclear power plant in Trinity have fallen victim to mysterious accidents recently. Like most of Edde's books, the story is intense, thought-provoking, well written, and hard to put down. You won't want to miss this one. ~ *Taylor Jones, The Review Team of Taylor Jones & Regan Murphy*

Trinity by Richard Edde is the story of greed, corruption, and the struggle for political power with a wounded hero caught in the middle. All Grant Collins wanted was to attend his mother's funeral in peace. Her death is just another blow after his being wounded in combat in the Middle East, returning home to struggle with both physical and emotional scars, and finding that he doesn't really fit into civilian life anymore. But when he tries to get closure by finding out more about his mother's fatal car accident, he is pulled into a dangerous web of intrigue as he discovers that opposing a nuclear power plant in Trinity is bad for your health—in more ways than one. Trinity is both a mystery and a thriller, combining intrigue, suspense, and fast-paced action that will keep you on the edge of your seat from beginning to end. ~ *Regan Murphy, The Review Team of Taylor Jones & Regan Murphy*

Trinity

Richard Edde

A Black Opal Books Publication

GENRE: MYSTERY/THRILLER/SUSPENSE

This is a work of fiction. Names, places, characters and incidents are either the product of the author's imagination or are used fictitiously, and any resemblance to any actual persons, living or dead, businesses, organizations, events or locales is entirely coincidental. All trademarks, service marks, registered trademarks, and registered service marks are the property of their respective owners and are used herein for identification purposes only. The publisher does not have any control over or assume any responsibility for author or third-party websites or their contents.

TRINITY
Copyright © 2017 by Richard Edde
Cover Design by Jackson Cover Designs
All cover art copyright © 2017
All Rights Reserved
Print ISBN: 978-1-626947-99-3

First Publication: NOVEMBER 2017

All rights reserved under the International and Pan-American Copyright Conventions. No part of this book may be reproduced or transmitted in any form or by any means, electronic or mechanical, including photocopying, recording, or by any information storage and retrieval system, without permission in writing from the publisher.

WARNING: The unauthorized reproduction or distribution of this copyrighted work is illegal. Criminal copyright infringement, including infringement without monetary gain, is investigated by the FBI and is punishable by up to 5 years in federal prison and a fine of $250,000. Anyone pirating our ebooks will be prosecuted to the fullest extent of the law and may be liable for each individual download resulting therefrom.

ABOUT THE PRINT VERSION: If you purchased a print version of this book without a cover, you should be aware that the book is stolen property. It was reported as "unsold and destroyed" to the publisher, and neither the author nor the publisher has received any payment for this "stripped book."

IF YOU FIND AN EBOOK OR PRINT VERSION OF THIS BOOK BEING SOLD OR SHARED ILLEGALLY, PLEASE REPORT IT TO: lpn@blackopalbooks.com

Published by Black Opal Books **http://www.blackopalbooks.com**

DEDICATION

To my mother, Jeanne.
Her love and devotion will never be forgotten.

Chapter 1

The phone call came out of the blue and the voice on the other end told him his mother was dead. It was a call that forever changed his life.

Grant Collins woke in a cold sweat. It was the same nightmare. The one that haunted him since Iraq.

He sat on the side of the bed, rubbed his temples. His palms were damp and his pulse pounded in his head. He reached for the bottle of water on the night table and swallowed several large gulps. The apartment was dark, quiet. Only the ticking of the regulator clock in the living room pierced the silence.

Tick, tick, tick.

Like the time bomb in his head ticking away the time before the inevitable explosion.

Grant sauntered to the small living room and stared out the window that overlooked Bethesda and the Potomac River. In the far distance, beyond the lights of the city, was the black void of the river, and he could barely make out the lights of traffic along the George Washington Parkway. He wiped his forehead with the back of his hand and collapsed in a chair, trying to calm his racing pulse.

In the dream, he was back in the town of Nasiriyah,

located along the banks of the Euphrates River 200 miles southeast of Baghdad. He was a member of the Second Marine Expeditionary Brigade and had seen sporadic fighting as his unit pressed toward the capitol. When his unit missed a turn, they suddenly found themselves involved in a nasty firefight.

Grant's nightmares began that day.

The marines found themselves stranded on what became known as Ambush Alley, being attacked on all sides by Iraqi forces using small arms and mortar fire with RPG and Iraqi tank support. It was a fight they hadn't expected, at least not there. Through the smoke and haze, Grant saw a car full of small boys heading in their direction. It looked like a dilapidated Ford but he couldn't be sure.

He saw the driver clearly. The car slowly approached the convoy in the midst of sporadic gunfire. He shot a glance up and down the column but nobody noticed the approaching car. Grant yelled a warning but no one seemed to hear.

The car was closer now. There were guns sticking out of all its windows. The boys looked as if they were ten to twelve years of age, it was hard to tell in the smoke and confusion. No one had stopped the car, it kept approaching at a crawl. He could tell there were no uniformed Iraqi soldiers within the car. So why did the boys have the guns? What were they doing here? Were they combatants? He had no way of knowing.

He tried to yell a warning, command them to turn around but the warning died in his throat. *Please stop! You don't belong here! What kind of parents would allow their children in a war zone?*

But the car kept advancing on the column. Now their rifles were pointed at Grant's Humvee.

Without another thought and using a reflex more out

of fear and training than anything, he fired his grenade launcher at the vehicle. It disintegrated in a ball of fire with a thunderous explosion.

They continued fighting that day after receiving reinforcements, eventually subduing most Iraqi resistance. But the faces of the children haunted Grant for the rest of his deployment. What were they doing on that road? Why were they fighting?

Slowly his heart rate returned to normal, his breathing became more regular. He took another drink from the water bottle. It was all he needed—no sleep before his drive in the morning. He didn't relish going to a funeral. Especially this one.

It was his mother's funeral.

The phone call notifying him of her death still echoed in his memory. It was difficult to put it away.

He glanced at his watch. Four a.m. He was awake now, sleep was impossible. He decided to shower and pack for the trip to Trinity. His therapy sessions at Walter Reed Medical Center would have to wait a few days until he returned.

ↄ⁖ↄ

The road alongside the Dogwood River mirrored the river's serpentine course through the fertile southern flatland as it paralleled the Savannah River before finally joining it northeast of the city of Savannah. Dominated by spreading live oaks, towering cypress and tupelo trees in the Lower Coastal Plain, the surrounding woodland stretched for miles on both sides of the river.

There were other river-swamp species including such canopy trees as green ash, overcup oak, swamp black gum, and water hickory, and such understory flora as saw palmetto, swamp dogwood, and swamp palm. The vegetation was verdant and lush. It was an overcast day, threatening rain—a perfect weekend for a funeral.

Hoping to make Trinity before dark, Grant's foot kept a steady pressure on the accelerator of his rental car. After leaving Savannah Hilton Head International Airport earlier in the afternoon he crossed Interstate 95 then watched as dark clouds billowed lower, matching his mood. He wasn't happy about missing his therapy sessions, for he had made remarkable progress since leaving the Marine Corps. His large frame had been pressed uncomfortably into a narrow seat on the flight down. Now he was tired, hungry, late.

And stressed.

Grant hated funerals. He had seen plenty during the Gulf War when his buddies were honored before their bodies were shipped back home to their relatives. Those helmets resting on their rifles were skeletal reminders that they had paid the ultimate price. This funeral was particularly distasteful for it was his mother's. Her death was unexpected, the result of a freak car accident a week earlier. A police sergeant made the phone call and he had arranged the details by phone with the funeral home. According to his mother's wishes she was to be buried next to her husband, Grant's father. It would be a simple graveside affair.

Helen and her husband Herbert settled in Trinity shortly after the Second World War. Located on the banks of the Dogwood River northeast of Savannah, Trinity was a small rural community, its only claim to fame was the community college where his father had worked. His parents raised two boys, Grant and his younger brother, Eric, who at the age of eighteen, had died of a heroin overdose. That left Grant to carry on the hopes and aspirations of his parents. Herbert was a quiet man with almost no sense of humor but his saving grace was that he believed in work and taking care of his family. The man worked in the maintenance department at nearby Trinity Community College and earned enough to send Grant to college. Herbert had a fatal heart attack at age fifty-seven leaving Grant and his mother alone. Life insurance provided by the college allowed Helen the luxury of not having to work so for the past ten or so years Helen lived the life of a comfortable widow. She kept the family house as always, bowled in her ladies league on Wednesday evenings. She went to the Presbyterian Church every Sunday.

It had taken Helen a long while to adjust to life after Herbert's untimely death. Even though there had been admirers during the following years she was never romantically involved with any other men. And that was the extent of her life after his father died until around a year ago. In one of her letters she mentioned she had become active in a group protesting the development of a nuclear power plant outside town.

Grant visited his mother several times a year and at Christmas but he never really liked returning to Trinity, for it never seemed to grow, in spite of the college and influx of new students each year. The town had its share of eccentrics and busybodies like old Mrs. Parsons, a widow who lived in a big two-story house close to the river and Newell Quisenberry who served as the town's village idiot. He chased young boys off his lawn with a pitchfork someone said he stole while a patient in the state sanitarium. But most folks were harmless enough and Trinity was a slow-moving, easy-going Southern town with very little crime. Still, with all its Southern charm it had an air of backwoods affectation that made him feel uncomfortable. So it had been in his youth and so it had remained during the ensuing years.

Speeding along the two-lane road, Grant noticed the

river on his right and through the cypress trees he saw a large flock of egrets take flight from the far shore and head southeast toward the Savannah. He was weary from his flight and the drive seemed to never end. He hoped his mother's best friend, Mrs. Bullock, would be waiting at the house and give Grant a key. Before leaving DC, he called her and the woman cried for a while but said she would be there when Grant arrived. Staying in the family home was a sight better than any motel in Trinity.

Mrs. Bullock had only sketchy details of his mother's accident. It seemed that Helen ran off the road and hit a bridge abutment killing her instantly. Her car was an old Ford so there was no air bag to save her. She was dead at the scene. He hoped there would be time to go by the funeral home and say goodbye to her. The thought produced foul-tasting bile to creep into the back of his throat and burn his tongue. He grabbed for the bottled water nestled in the center console and took a long gulp.

He switched on the car radio and pushed through the selector buttons in search of some relaxing music but finding none, turned the radio off and allowed his mind to wander. High school in Trinity was a monotonous time for Grant with him playing basketball and the clarinet in the band. It was funny, he thought, that during those days he never gave much thought to what he would become when he grew up. His parents didn't provide much guidance on the subject, just go to college and study something, anything. Mostly, he enjoyed fishing with his friend, Billy Weaver. During the summer months they would fish, camp, and swim, not caring about the nearing responsibilities of adulthood. After graduation, Billy went to Vo-Tech in Savannah and Grant enrolled at the local college.

Grant's father usually sat in his easy chair after work, silently reading his newspaper, rarely saying more than a few words to the family. He wasn't abusive, just not interested in what Grant and Eric did in school. In retrospect, Grant now realized his father was clinically depressed and his condition worsened after Grant entered college and Eric had become addicted to heroin when he was sixteen. His brother always seemed to have the wrong kinds of friends around. When Grant tried to tell him he was heading for trouble, Eric blew up and lashed out at him. It was his first indication that something was seriously wrong with his brother. They didn't have much in common as Eric wasn't scholastically or musically inclined. He just hung out with his friends. Where he obtained the drugs, Grant never learned but one night his brother didn't come home. The police arrived at the house with the sad news. Eric, his happy-go-lucky brother, had been found dead in an abandoned cabin on the river north of town. After that, his father took to his room, rarely making an appearance, even for supper. He died of a heart attack while at work as he neared his fifty-seventh birthday.

When his father died, Grant quit college and got a job. He told Helen that college was wasted on him. He worked as a laborer, a carpenter, an electrician's helper. Then one day he up and enlisted in the marines. After leaving Parris Island he was trained in advanced infantry at Camp Geiger then shipped to Iraq during the US-led invasion.

He came home a changed person.

However, Trinity hadn't changed much. He pulled onto Trinity's familiar main street, a narrow affair with diagonal parking in front of the various shops. It was late afternoon and most of the stores were closing, people leaving downtown and heading home. Grant drove through town and headed east toward the river for two blocks then turned on Elm Street. The houses were fifties style and all looked similar while large elm trees shaded the street. A dog barked in the distance.

The family home was near the end of the road on a cul-de-sac. It was a whitewashed affair with wooden steps that led to a large covered porch. Two tall windows bordered the front door. A detached garage stood to the house's west side and Grant noticed the lawn needed mowing.

He parked his rental car in the driveway, sauntered up the steps with his overnight bag, and was about to knock when the door opened.

A short, plump woman wearing an apron greeted him. She wore her graying hair pulled into a bun behind her head. Dark eyes looked him over.

"Grant?" she said from behind the screen door.

"Yes, ma'am," he said, squinting through the screen.

The woman opened the door and stepped aside.

"Come in, son," she said. "It's your house. "I'm Hazel Bullock, your mom's friend. We talked on the phone."

"Yes," Grant said, stepping into the living room. He gave the room a quick once over, satisfying himself that everything looked the same as during his last visit a year earlier. "Thanks. Mom spoke of you often."

"It's a shame to meet a son of Helen's under these difficult circumstances. I really liked your mother. I moved here ten years ago and she befriended me. Would you like to look around the house or just relax? The funeral parlor is open until nine tonight. There's no hurry in getting over there unless you want to go now."

"I'd like to wander around the house for a while, if you don't mind. Then, maybe eat something, I'm awfully hungry. Then go over."

"I understand," Mrs. Bullock said. "I fixed some stew and it's on the stove so you can eat anytime. Unless you prefer to get a hamburger or something. "I can just sit here and read. You take your time."

"The stew sounds good, Mrs. Bullock. I'll just have a look about the house."

"And please, young man, call me Hazel."

Grant nodded. He dropped his bag near his father's worn easy chair and walked from room to room, his mind a flood of memories as he did so. In his parent's bedroom Helen's vanity was crowded with pictures of him, Eric, and his father and mother. The frames were old, covered with dust. He picked up a picture of Eric in an antique pewter frame. He was dressed in a Little League baseball uniform and it brought back memories of his brother's love of the game. There was a photo of his father when he was a young man. Wearing a suit, he looked much the successful businessman. Who would have known he worked maintenance at the college?

The wallpaper was faded, decorated in the floral design he remembered from childhood and how his father detested it. The man always threatened to put up new wallpaper but his mother wouldn't hear of it, she loved the design. He ran a finger along the antique cherry wood bedstead where his mother slept for over forty years. Grant sat on the bed while he continued to look about the room, remembering times past. Now that his parents were gone they were times never to be reclaimed. They were just ephemeral memories. He felt his eyes moisten, a lump formed in his throat. Scenes from his younger years came flooding into his consciousness, the smells of supper that greeted him after school, the sight of his mother cleaning and polishing the furniture, his father reading the paper.

When he returned to the living room, Mrs. Bullock was in the kitchen putting the finishing touches on supper. He sauntered past the tattered easy chair that was his

father's favorite—the man rarely got out of it after work.
He had given him and Eric many a stern lecture while
sitting in that chair. It had been a distant awkward relationship and Grant wondered why the man couldn't have
been more the father some of his friends had. Grant
moved to the small dining room, sat in a chair at the
square table, while Mrs. Bullock ladled large bowls of
the aromatic stew. There was a platter of cornbread and a
large pitcher of iced tea on the table. Sitting opposite
Grant, she smiled, said grace, then passed the cornbread
to him.

"I hope you like it," she said. "I didn't know what to
fix and stew was something that could keep warm until
you arrived. No matter what the time."

"Tastes great," he said, after a mouthful. He poured
them each a tall glass of tea and the two ate in silence for
a few moments.

"Mrs. Bullock, I'm sorry, Hazel, is there anything
more you can tell me about the accident? The circumstances surrounding it? Where did it happen? Where
mother was going? What was she doing?"

The woman shook her head. "No, not really. It was
pretty bad when she hit that bridge. Strange thing was,
your mother never drove anywhere very fast. And she
was an excellent driver. I ought to know, I rode with her
often enough."

"She drove her car often?"

Hazel nodded. "Helen was a real dynamo," she said.
"Always going somewhere and checking on her friends.
You know, seeing to it that they had enough groceries or
needed a ride themselves to a doctor's appointment or the
like."

"I remember my mother always worrying about me
and my father," Grant said. "It's hard to believe she's
gone. You think she suffered?"

"No, Grant, I don't," Hazel said, pushing the plate of cornbread toward Grant. "I heard she died instantly. Such a tragedy. Such a tragedy." Grant saw her eyes moisten and heard her voice almost break as she spoke.

"Did a lot of damage to the car?" Grant said.

"I believe it did, but you would have to ask the police. It happened at the bridge over Cottom Creek. You know where that is?"

Grant nodded.

Hazel stood and gathered the few dishes. "I'll just wash these and get out of here, Grant. I left the house keys on the lamp table next to her chair. I'll check on you tomorrow."

"Thanks for being here, Hazel. And thanks for being a friend to my mother."

"Nonsense, young man. It was my privilege."

After the woman left, Grant found the house keys and drove over to the funeral home.

Chapter 2

After talking with the funeral home director, Grant learned that his mother had prepaid her last expenses and wished to be buried in Trinity. It was a heart-wrenching hour. Sitting next to the casket, he noticed how the wrinkles on his mother's face were gone, replaced by relaxed serene features. It was as if all Helen's trials had been laid to rest with her.

Helen's graveside service was a simple affair. The day dawned overcast and the threat of rain hung on the low dark clouds. A small group gathered under the awning at the cemetery, none of whom Grant recognized except for Hazel Bullock. The minister, a short fat man who wore a rumpled black suit, declared to the small gathering that Helen Collins was a fine lady, an asset to their small community, and in her later years, became a devoted environmental activist.

Following a brief prayer, the service concluded and the few Trinity residents who attended walked hurriedly back to their cars. A brisk wind sent small swirls of dust parading among the headstones heralding a threat of rain. Grant shook hands with the minister, thanked him, slipped an envelope of money into his palm, then ambled toward his rental car. As the last of the attendees left the gravesite, a young woman approached Grant. She had blonde hair, blue eyes, and wore a dark blue dress.

"Grant?" she said, as she approached.

Grant stopped and turned.

"Hi," the woman said. "It's me, Lori. From high school."

"Lori?" Grant said, getting closer. He smiled when he faced her. It took a few moments before he remembered. "I didn't recognize you during the service. I'm sorry."

Lori smiled back, her white teeth glistening. "You do remember me, Grant. Don't you? Lori Spelling? We dated a few times."

"Of course, Lori. It's been a long time and my, you've changed. But I guess we all have, right? What's it been, fifteen years?"

They walked together back to Grant's car and stood by the passenger door. They were alone in the cemetery.

"Yeah, about that. But you don't seem so different, Grant. Just as handsome as ever."

Grant felt himself blush. "I don't know about that, Lori," he said.

"I'm sorry about your mother," Lori said, touching Grant gently on an elbow. "I didn't know her very well, except during the past year. What have you been doing with yourself? I vaguely remember your mother mentioning that you live in Washington, DC, now."

"Been there since I got out of the marines, Lori. So, yeah, I live in DC. What about you? Married?"

"I was," Lori said. "Divorced three years ago. No kids. I work as a secretary for the Dean of Students at the college." She laughed and smiled again. "It's a living, as they say."

"Say, Lori, I was going to grab a hamburger for lunch. Do you have time to have lunch with me? I won't keep you if you have to get back to work soon."

She glanced at her watch. "No, I have the time and I would love to. We can catch up on what the years have done to each of us." She pointed down the cemetery road toward town. "There's a hamburger joint just down the road here."

After getting into his rental car, Grant followed Lori to the *Trinity Diner* where they took a booth in the corner of the room. The place was noisy and looked full of people, some of whom he recognized as having attended his mother's funeral. An auburn-haired waitress with a mustard stain on her blouse took their order and brought iced tea. When the burgers came they ate in silence for a while until Lori cleared her throat.

"You married, Grant? I'm sure some beautiful woman has taken you out of circulation by now."

"Not yet, Lori," he said, between mouthfuls. He laughed at her remark. "Right girl hasn't come along, I guess."

"I thought I had found the right man, but alas, it was not to be. I wanted a family, he didn't. We went our separate ways."

"I'm sorry to hear that, Lori."

"I've made my peace with it," she said. "I'm just going to be more careful next time, that's all. I guess you have to kiss a lot of toads before finding that prince."

They made small talk for a while, eating and sipping iced tea, while Grant studied her. She was thin, with wavy blonde hair, a perky upturned nose that sat between the bluest eyes he had ever seen. When she smiled the corners of her eyes wrinkled. There were a few aging lines on a face that she obviously tried to hide with makeup. All in all, she was still quite easy to look at.

"Back at the cemetery," he continued, "you said something about not really knowing mom until a year ago. How was that?"

Lori smiled again and shrugged. "Well, she got me involved in this group that's trying to keep the nuclear plant out of Trinity. You've heard of it?"

Grant shook his head.

"Oh well, let me see. Where to begin? There's a big corporation in Tennessee I think, which wants to build a nuclear power plant here in Trinity. Why, no one seems to know. Possibly because they can't get it done in Savannah or up near Augusta. But, anyway they want to build it here. Your mother was against it. Well, we bumped into one another at the grocery store where she was handing out pamphlets and getting signatures on a petition to try and block them coming here. One thing led to another and now I'm part of the group. Citizens Against Nuclear Power."

"I see," Grant said. He wiped his mouth with a napkin and pushed his plate aside. "Mom's friend, Hazel Bullock, mentioned last night how active Mom was. That she was always on the go."

"She was," Lori said. "And now she's gone. I don't know how the committee will go on without her. Her energy kept everyone motivated."

"Mrs. Bullock said her car was badly damaged. She was probably killed instantly."

"I wouldn't know. I never saw her car after the accident. I haven't been able to bring myself to drive over to where it happened."

"Was it dark? Raining? Poor visibility?"

"No," Lori said. "It was late in the afternoon. Your mother spent the afternoon testifying before a hearing on the plant. She was on her way home when she apparently hit the bridge abutment."

"You think she was speeding?"

"Oh dear, no. Your mother never drove anywhere very fast. I used to tease her about it all the time."

"But Mrs. Bullock mentioned her car was badly damaged."

"Again, Grant, I wouldn't know about that.

"You said something about a hearing?"

"Yes, that's right. The mayor, who is all for the plant locating here, scheduled the hearing and various citizens showed up and gave their opinions."

"I see," Grant said, taking a gulp of his tea. "And how is opinion running would you say?"

"I'd say the town is about evenly split either way. Tensions are pretty high right now because the city council is going to vote next month. It would mean more jobs, cheaper electricity. But a lot of folks are worried about another Three Mile Island incident. Don't think the risks are worth it."

"Who's the company that wants to build the plant?"

"DynaTech. They have a contract with the local electric COOP and as soon as the council gives them the go-ahead they will start construction. They say it'll take three years to complete. And they have been running ads on TV saying how wonderful life will be with nuclear power. How many good-paying jobs they'll provide."

"Never heard of them."

"DynaTech is mostly north in Kentucky and Tennessee, I believe."

Their waitress refilled their tea and left the check that Grant picked up. Most of the lunch hour traffic had left leaving only a few customers in the diner. Its over-taxed air conditioner wheezed and the ceiling fan chugged.

"I don't know the first thing about nuclear power or nuclear plants," Grant said.

"Currently, approximately seventeen percent of electricity worldwide is produced by nuclear power plants, but in some countries, like France, over seventy-five percent of their electricity's produced by nuclear power. The

United States, on the other hand, only produces about fifteen percent of its electricity from nuclear power."

"Lagging behind the rest of the world, eh?" Grant said, smiling.

"Nuclear power plants use pellets to fuel the plants. A pellet contains approximately three percent U-two-thirty-five that is encased in a ceramic matrix. That's the isotope of uranium. The pellets are aligned in linear arrays or fuel rods that are interspersed with moveable control rods. The control rods act to dampen or stop the nuclear reactions so that the nuclear reactions do not get out of control. The whole assembly, called the reactor core, is submerged in water to help keep the core cool. A modern power plant might have as many as 13 million pellets in the reactor at a time, and they stay there for three to four years. To optimize power production, between one third and a quarter of the fuel rods are changed out every twelve to eighteen months."

Lori took a sip of her tea, laughed. "I sound like an expert, don't I? I learned this stuff since joining the group."

"You sound very knowledgeable," Grant said, noticing the sparkle in her eyes.

"Well, nuclear fission produces heat, and this heat is used to heat water and make steam. The steam powers turbines that turn generators. The generators produce electricity. Nuclear power generates electricity much like coal- or diesel-powered plants. What is different from the other two is that nuclear doesn't produce greenhouse gases like the burning of fossil fuels. It does produce spent nuclear fuel that's radioactive and this has disposal problems. Other than having a major meltdown of the reactor core like what happened at Chernobyl, what to do with the nuclear waste is the other enormous issue facing Americans."

They sat quietly while they finished eating. Grant felt drawn to this woman who had been close to his mother.

"I've heard the bad press concerning nuclear waste," Grant said.

"The waste, sometimes called spent fuel, is dangerously radioactive, and remains so for thousands of years. When it first comes out of the reactor, it is so toxic that if you stood within a few meters of it while it was unshielded, you would receive a lethal radioactive dose within a few seconds and would die of acute radiation sickness within a few days. Hence all the worry about it.

"In practice, the spent fuel is never unshielded. It is kept underwater for a few years until the radiation decays to levels that can be shielded by concrete in large storage casks. The final disposal of this spent fuel is a hot topic, and is often an argument against the use of nuclear reactors. Options include deep geologic storage and recycling. The sun would consume it nicely if we could get into space, but since rockets are so unreliable, we can't afford to risk atmospheric dispersal on lift-off."

He smiled as he listened to her chatter on, almost without regard for his patience. "Lori," he said, "I'm flying back home the day after tomorrow so I'm not doing anything this evening. How about dinner later? You can show me the rest of Trinity."

She laughed and her eyes twinkled. "Not much to show you. The town's essentially unchanged since you left but sure, I'd love to. The only good restaurant is Martin's but they have pretty good seafood and steaks. That okay?"

"That sounds fine, Lori. Seven o'clock, then?"

"Why don't I meet you there, Grant. I've got a few errands to do and I can just meet you. Then after we eat I'll show you Trinity."

"Fine."

Grant paid the cashier and the two of them found their cars. Grant watched Lori head back toward town. He drove back to his mother's house and let himself in with the key Mrs. Bullock gave him.

After slouching in his father's chair, he surveyed the darkened room. The curtains were drawn allowing the afternoon light to filter weakly through the gauze-thin curtains. The clouds were lifting and an afternoon sun peaked through gaps in them casting rays of golden light into the house. He wandered into the kitchen and made a pot of coffee. While it perked, he went back into his mother's bedroom, looked through a stack of papers on the nightstand.

There was a pamphlet published by Citizens Against Nuclear Power decrying the evils of a nuclear accident. There was a list of names that Grant surmised were members of the group for Lori's name was near the top. At the bottom of the stack was what looked like a legal document, some sort of proceeding. Looking closer he saw that it was a cease and desist request naming DynaTech that had been denied by a judge in Atlanta. *My God, Mom was serious about this stuff.*

Back in the living room he found a petition with over several hundred signatures on it. He ambled to the kitchen, poured himself a cup of coffee. Returning to the easy chair, he pursued the petition, page by page. There were certainly a lot of signees against the power plant. If Lori was right and the town was divided then emotions must be running high. The mayor, she had said, was a proponent of the plant coming to town, and his opinion surely, carried a lot of weight. In a clash between big business and citizens, the people usually lost out. Especially if the politicians were aligned against them. But it wasn't his problem. He was leaving soon. Probably needed to sell the home place, as he had no use for it. He would need to

return and pack up some stuff of his parent's that he
might want to save. Too bad that his father had been an
only child and his mother had one sister who had been
too ill to come to the burial. So, there was no other family, except him. The son that had not been very reliable
about visiting in recent years. He took a shower in his
mother's bathroom and put on fresh clothes then took a
short nap.

Upon waking, Grant wondered about the matter of his
mother's estate. Did she have a will? If so, where was it?
Did she even have a lawyer? He doubted it for his mother
never seemed that organized. She might have had one
drawn up years earlier but he had no idea if she had done
so or where it might be. He would have to search the
house later.

And a decision would have to be made about the
house, to sell it or keep it. He was going to have to make
another trip to Trinity to haul stuff he wanted to keep
back to DC. He made a mental note to check on the
whereabouts of a will and if his mother had a lawyer.
Trinity couldn't have but a couple of attorneys.

ഗ്ദേ

Lori Spelling took a long shower, wrapped a towel
around herself, and sat in front of her makeup mirror,
thinking back on the funeral and her lunch with Grant.
How interesting that, after all the years, she should see
him again. They had dated only a few times but she
wished it had been more for she remembered his sense of
humor and he made her laugh. In fact, she hadn't been
able to get serious with him for they were always laughing together. He was quite the comedian. She had known
Grant's brother, Eric, and wanted to mention to Grant
that the boy was headed for big trouble—doing drugs in

junior high—but never could bring herself to interfere in something she thought was none of her business. To tell the truth, she couldn't deliver such bad news. After Eric's funeral, she wanted to reach out to Grant but he had moved on to another girlfriend. She stayed in Trinity after graduation and attended the local community college while Grant went off to the University of Georgia. After getting her degree she found a job in the Dean's office and occasionally saw Grant's father who worked on the plumbing or light fixtures. She would say hello and inquire after Grant and Mr. Collins would smile and chat for a while. But that all changed, the man becoming increasingly somber and morose. It seemed to Lori that he was grieving his son's death for he rarely smiled and never said much when she tried to engage in conversation. She felt sad for the Collins' household.

Her marriage lasted two years to a man who worked all the time and had little left over for her. He provided a good living but that was as far as it went. It turned out they had different wants and expectations from their marriage. He wanted a partner who stayed home and cooked his meals, did his laundry. She wanted a lover and children. In retrospect, she could see that, from the start, the marriage was destined to fail.

Periodically, over the following years, she thought about Grant Collins and wondered what had happened to him. Had he graduated college? Was a successful businessman somewhere? Or a scientist teaching at a university? She had dated a few men since college but none of them possessed Grant's sense of humor, the idea that everything in life was funny. His personality had charmed her, to be sure, and she had doubted if she would ever see him again. Then she saw him at Helen's funeral. What serendipity. Certainly a sad time for Grant but it was grand talking with him over lunch and now it seemed like old times, their having a date. She wondered if the years had spoiled his humor.

She finished with her makeup and chose a floral casual dress with a modest neckline. After checking her lipstick, she grabbed her purse, and headed out the door.

Chapter 3

The dark clouds had moved on and the sun was low on the horizon as Grant steered his rental car to the restaurant to meet Lori for supper. An azure sky melded with a reddish-orange glow that was a welcome sight after the two days of overcast weather. He drove slowly through town and noticed that most of the diagonal parking spaces were empty, the stores closed, the sidewalks devoid of people. *Town closes up early*, he thought. Nothing had changed. At the gas station at the end of Main Street a police car sat parked in the shadows, its lone occupant speaking into a microphone. As he cruised past, their eyes met for a moment. The officer didn't smile. Grant found Martin's Restaurant right across the street from the patrol car and pulled into an empty parking space. He didn't see Lori's car so he went inside to wait for her.

He was ushered to a table covered with a white tablecloth and set the menu aside. He ordered a scotch on the rocks and looked around the dark dining room. A few patrons were sitting at tables, drinks in hand, talking and laughing. A few of the men looked up from their talk as he sat at his table sipping his drink. One of the men already had had too much to drink for he was regaling his

party with loud, boisterous talk. He looked at his watch—
seven o'clock. Lori should be walking through the door
any minute. He looked through the menu and saw it had a
fair selection of the usual steaks and seafood, shrimp and
lobster. At the far end of the dining room was a long salad bar. He looked at his watch again. Seven-oh-five.

Grant finished his drink but refused another when the
waitress offered, deciding to wait until Lori arrived. The
loud man was filling a plate at the salad bar, still talking.
He was getting antsy. Having spent most of his life alone
he wasn't use to waiting for someone to show up for supper. The occasional dinner with his bosses usually started
with him arriving late so he could avoid the small talk
with the senior partners. They talked endlessly of the
market and making money which was fine with Grant
while he was at work but when the workday was over he
wanted to unwind. He usually did that by playing video
games on his home computer. Air combat, mostly.

He looked at his watch.

Seven-fifteen.

Still no Lori.

He got up and told the waitress he wanted to look
outside for his date but her car was not in the parking lot.
Back at his table he ordered a cup of coffee and continued to wait. Now and then the loud man glanced over his
shoulder at Grant and nodded ever so slightly. He raised
a finger in reply. He thought about Lori. Had she been
stalled in her errands? If so, why hadn't she called the
restaurant? Maybe she had second thoughts about seeing
him. But she seemed genuinely happy to see him again.
He remembered their dates as being nothing special, just
a movie and a burger afterwards. After a few dates, Lori
started dating another guy in the class below them. That
was about all he could recall.

At seven-thirty, he paid for his drinks and wandered

outside into the humid night air. Crickets and tree frogs sang from down by the river, a few short blocks away. Lori was not there. He was hungry so he decided to drive to the diner where they ate lunch and eat something there. Along the way he noticed again how empty the streets were and that the police car was no longer at the gas station.

The parking lot at the diner was almost empty, the place obviously did most of their business at noon. Inside, the air conditioner still moaned and wheezed, and he took a seat in the booth he and Lori used at lunch.

He ordered a steak sandwich and fries and a beer, then settled back in his seat. When the waitress brought him his beer he smiled. "Excuse me, but I used to go to high school here years ago. I was supposed to meet a classmate for supper at Martin's but she never showed. Maybe you know her."

"What's the name?" the waitress said, wiping his table with a damp cloth.

"Spelling. Lori Spelling," Grant said.

"Miss Spelling? From the college?"

Grant nodded.

"Sure, I know her. I used to go to school at the college a few years ago. She was the Dean's secretary back then."

"Yes, that's her. Happen to know where she lives or anything? I'm kinda worried that she didn't even call."

"Stood you up, eh?" The waitress smiled. Her shiny auburn hair hung in curls over her ears. "Well, she probably got tied up somewhere. You know women. You're from around here?"

"I grew up here," Grant said. "I moved away after high school. How about you?"

"I'm just here, a working girl."

Grant thought that was a mysterious answer but maybe the girl didn't want anyone prying into her affairs. He decided to not press the issue.

"This place always this busy?" he said.

"The lunch hour always is, yes. Dinnertime not so much. It's a living as they say."

Grant nodded and looked at the menu.

"My name is Carrie. I get off at ten. Maybe we could grab a beer, if you want some company."

"That's a possibility. But I'd like to find my friend. If she just didn't want to see me that's one thing but if something happened, that's another."

"I believe she lives in the apartments south of town. The only apartments in Trinity. She comes in for lunch pretty often with her girlfriends and I think I overheard her say that's where she lived."

Carrie brought his steak sandwich and slid into the seat opposite Grant. Her white uniform still sported a mustard stain on its front.

"What's your name, if you don't mind me asking," she asked.

"Grant. I came back for my mother's funeral."

"Yes," Carrie said, "I knew there was a big funeral today. It was your mother?"

"Yeah. And I met an old high school friend, Lori, and we were supposed to have dinner. I'm just worried that she didn't show up."

"Not used to being stood up, eh?" Carrie's eyes sparkled and she sported a grin.

"I can stand the brush-off, if that is what it was," Grant said. "I'm kinda worried."

"I can understand," Carrie said. "Miss Spelling was pretty."

"I think I'll drive over to the apartments you mentioned and see if her car is there." Grant sauntered to the cash register and paid Carrie for his dinner.

"I get off work at ten," she said. "That is if you don't find her."

Grant found the apartment that Carrie mentioned but Lori's car was not in the parking lot. He found an *L Spelling* on the communal mailbox so he figured he was at the right place. He didn't know which apartment was hers but if she wasn't there it didn't matter. He didn't see her car anywhere. He waited with the air conditioner running until after nine then drove back to the house. He didn't pass Lori's car on the way home. He read magazines and drank leftover coffee until nine forty-five, then drove back to the diner and waited for Carrie to get off work. When she emerged into the night, he honked once.

She climbed into the passenger seat and buckled the seatbelt.

"Where to?" he said, starting the car.

"We can get a beer at *The Shrunken Head*," Carrie said, using the car's rearview mirror to straighten her hair. "It's our only bar. They have pool, if you play."

"*The Shrunken Head* it is, then. Point the way."

Carrie gave directions. The bar was located outside town on the shore of the Dogwood River. It was a rustic affair with a large deck that extended out over the water. Cars were packed all around it and the noise from inside boomed into the parking lot.

Carrie led the way to an empty booth at the rear of the bar, weaving her way among a crowd of partiers, each holding a longneck beer. Country music filled the smoky room. At the bar's other end, Grant noticed the pool tables were all being used. They ordered beer and tried to talk over the din.

"She wasn't at her apartment," Grant said.

"What?" Carrie said, obviously having difficulty hearing.

"She wasn't at her apartment," he repeated. "Her car

wasn't there, either. I waited awhile but she never showed."

Grant took a long pull at his beer. The jukebox music had stopped and the noise level was more bearable.

"That's odd, isn't it?" Carrie said. "You have strong feelings for this Lori?"

"Not really," Grant said. "We had a few dates in high school and she was at mother's funeral this morning. We had lunch at your diner and planned on having supper together, that's all. I return to New York tomorrow afternoon."

"I thought I remembered you. I served you both lunch today." Carrie brushed a lock of hair from her eye. "You both got burgers."

Grant laughed. "You can remember that?"

"It's a hazard of the job, I guess. I have a hard time with faces but can remember orders. Weird, right?"

"Yeah."

"Would you want to drive around Trinity and see if we can locate her car? It might make you feel better. I don't mind driving. I'd like to drop by my place and shower first, though."

"Are you sure you wouldn't mind? I'd feel better if I found her. Just to say goodbye if nothing else."

"I don't mind. Besides, the pool tables are busy. You seem nice enough. We can use my car."

Carrie had a Toyota Celica and Grant wormed his way into the passenger seat while she started the car. The night had a heavy feel to it and a musky smell filtered from the river.

"Mind stopping by my place so I can take a shower?" she said.

"Not at all."

"I've got beer while you wait, if you'd like."

She pulled her car into the driveway of a small house with stairs on one side.

"I have the garage apartment upstairs," she said and led Grant up the wooden stairs, fumbled with some keys, and let them in.

"Make yourself at home," she called over her shoulder as she disappeared through a door. "There's beer in the icebox."

Soon he heard water running. The small living room had a few pictures placed on a lamp table next to a recliner. The apartment smelled of potpourri, a woman's variety. Maybe cinnamon. There was a flat screen TV against one wall and a bookshelf full of paperbacks. Grant took a look into the kitchen where there was a small table and three chairs. An ancient refrigerator stood next to an even older-looking stove. A waitress salary was not very large. He sat in the recliner and tried to relax. Soon Carrie emerged, clean and fresh, smelling of perfume. She wore shorts and a low-cut blouse that revealed an ample cleavage. Her eyes sparkled and her hair seemed brighter, if that was possible.

"How's this?" she said, doing a pirouette in front of him."

Grant stood.

"My," he said. "What a remarkable metamorphosis. You look fine."

"Then, let's go."

She removed keys from her purse and locked the door behind them. Grant climbed into her car and she drove down Main Street.

"Did you grow up here, Carrie?" Grant asked. He looked at the few cars parked in town but Lori's car was not among them.

"No. I moved here three years ago from Atlanta. I had dropped out of college and was tired of all the crime in the city. One Sunday I took a drive just to get out of town for a while and stumbled onto Trinity. It seemed like a nice enough town."

"You been happy here?"

"For the most part, yes. The only job I could find, however, was at the diner, so I've been working there. I'm keeping an eye open for something at the college."

"Tired of cleaning mustard stains, eh?" Grant said and laughed.

"Isn't it the truth?" Carrie said.

She continued to drive through the streets surrounding Trinity but they had no luck in locating Lori's automobile.

"You grew up here," she said after a while.

"I did, yes. Graduated high school with Lori. Did a bunch of odd jobs until a friend introduced me to the Marine Corps."

"Wow," Carrie said. "You're a marine, then."

"Not anymore. I was in the Gulf War, saw some action, then got out. I've had some problems since."

"What kind of problems?"

Grant hesitated. He didn't really want to get into all the bad stuff in his life with perfect stranger. He smiled. "Let's just say I've had some issues with all the killing," he said.

"I can understand that," Carrie said, glancing over at him. "Your mother just passed away?"

"Days ago. Had the funeral and burial this morning. My father died a number of years ago."

"Any brothers or sisters?"

"I had a brother. He died a long time ago."

"I'm sorry," said Carrie. She turned eastward toward the river. "There are a few houses down this way. We might as well look."

The riverfront houses were well spaced and of newer

construction. Near the end of the road was a black wrought-iron gate with a small guardhouse inside. A light was on in the guardhouse.

"Wow," Grant said. "Whom does that belong to?"

"The mayor. Bruce Baxter. Built this place about five years ago I hear tell."

"Where's the house?"

"The driveway meanders back into the trees and the house overlooks the river. It's quite a big place."

"How did this Baxter make his money?"

Carrie thought for a minute before answering.

"From what I've heard no one really knows. Came here ten years ago with money and opened the local radio station. Then, right after I moved here, he ran for mayor and won. Word was he used a lot of his own money during his campaign."

Carrie drove her car back onto Main Street and headed back to the *Shrunken Head.*

"Well," she said, "you've seen Trinity. I guess you didn't see this Lori's car."

At the bar the place was still hopping, the music still loud, people going in and out. She pulled the Toyota behind Grant's rental car and stopped.

"Care to come by for desert? I baked a chocolate cake yesterday." She put a hand on his arm. "I'd like to talk if you're not too tired. It's not often I get the chance. I don't have many friends."

"Sure, Carrie, but I can't stay long."

He followed her back to her apartment and into her living room. She went to the kitchen and returned with two pieces of cake. She placed the plates on the table beside the recliner.

"I put coffee on. I'll see if it's ready."

Later, after the cake had been eaten and they were sipping the coffee, Carrie went into her bedroom and closed the door. When she returned she was wearing a bathrobe only. She moved across the room and sat on the arm of the recliner.

"I thought maybe we could do something else before you left," she said. She put a hand to his cheek then bent down and kissed him. Grant put a hand inside her robe and felt her skin tingle under his touch. She stood, took him by the hand, and led him to the bedroom.

Chapter 4

An alarm pounded in Grant's head and he was suddenly awake. Sunshine billowed in the strange window and he sat up in a strange bed. Then he remembered. Carrie, of course. He rose and pulled on his pants and stumbled into the kitchen where he found Carrie laboring over her antique stove. He smelled coffee and bacon.

"Good morning," he said, startling her.

She turned and gave him a peck on the cheek. "How do you like your eggs?"

"Cooked," he said.

"Very funny."

"Any way is just fine."

She broke two eggs into a frying pan. She wore the bathrobe she briefly wore the night before.

"Coffee cups are in that cupboard there."

Grant poured himself a steaming mug and sat at the small table and watched while she fried the eggs.

"I enjoyed last night," he said, after a small sip.

Carrie shot him a quick glance then returned to the eggs. "I did too. What time you going to start back?"

"I thought I would stop by the police department and see if I can get any more details regarding Mom's accident. For some strange reason I'd like to look at her car. After that, I thought I'd find you and say goodbye. Do you go to work today?"

Carrie plated his bacon and eggs, set two plates on the table, and joined him. "I wasn't going to do much today but do some housecleaning and some laundry. So I should be here when you are through. I don't have to be at work until this afternoon. I work until closing tonight. I am going to miss you, Grant. Any chance you'll be down this way again?"

"I hadn't planned on it but now," he smiled and touched her hand, "now, I may just have to find a reason."

Finished with his breakfast he dressed and kissed Carrie. He returned home, showered, shaved, and put on clean clothes. As he was getting ready to leave there was a knock on the front door. It was Hazel Bullock. She had a dish in her hand.

"I just knew you need some food, young man," she said. "If you're like most men, you don't think about food until it's time to eat. I brought you a cake."

"How nice, Hazel," Grant said, stepping aside and allowing the woman entrance. She sauntered into the kitchen and set the dish on a counter. She looked at Grant with a twinkle in her eye. "I learned that Helen had been to some hearing about a power plant," he continued. "You know anything about that?"

"Unfortunately," Hazel said and eased her plump frame into the easy chair in the living room. "Your mother was on a mission. A mission at her age, can you believe it? At a time when most seniors are content to relax on their porches and watch the sun go down, your mother, bless her soul, had discovered a new calling. The nuclear power plant that the mayor and his cronies want to build here your mother campaigned against."

"Yes, I have heard about the citizen's group she was involved with."

"Really, where?"

"A woman I met at the cemetery who was on that committee with Mom."

Hazel nodded. "Anyway, there was a public hearing earlier in the day. The day of your mother's accident. Well," Hazel continued, "she had just come from a hearing at the courthouse and was heading home. I don't understand how it happened but it did. Maybe she fell asleep or something. I think the car was going pretty fast. It was just so sad that it had to be her. She meant so much to me. She was a dear lady."

"She mentioned you often in her letters," Grant said. "She was so happy having a close friend."

"I moved here after Ben died. Ben, he was my husband. We were married for forty years before he went to be with our son who was killed in Vietnam. Massive stroke."

Grant noticed a tear form in Hazel's eye, how her voice wavered but the woman continued. "Helen and I would get together several times a week, sometimes here, sometimes at my house. We'd cook, gossip, and laugh together. I'm going to miss her."

"You know anything about this citizen's group she was involved with? Citizens Against Nuclear Power."

"Yes, she had become deeply involved in our local politics. It's a situation that is big news here in Trinity. Some corporation wants to build a nuclear power plant outside of town and she was part of a group that is actively opposing it. They were stirring up support against the plant coming here. Trying to educate everyone on the dangers of nuclear power. You know, Three Mile Island and Chernobyl. Like I said, your mother and several members of the group testified at a hearing earlier in the day. They don't want the plant built in Trinity. I must say, I don't blame them."

"It's a big deal, then?"

"Oh, yes. Got the town all fired up. Citizens Against Nuclear Power. Your mother had been working with them, circulating petitions, speaking at small groups and the like for the past year. They have got a lot of folks worked up about nuclear safety, especially using Three Mile Island as an example of what can happen."

"I didn't know," Grant said. "She never seemed the orator type when I was a child."

"Oh, Helen turned out to be quite the crusader. She had found a cause, she said, a cause to get her up each day. A reason to live, so to speak—a new direction in her life. She told me that after your father died her life became pretty monotonous and the power plant issue got her blood moving. She discovered a new energy. Tried to get me involved but I was never interested in politics. But gracious sakes, look at the time. I need to be going. I hope you enjoy the cake."

"I'm sure I will," Grant said.

So Mom's been protesting, he thought.

After Hazel left, he drove into town and found the police department. It was a small red brick single story building that had a number of patrol cars parked in front. The sun shone bright and the morning temperature was rising. He entered through the small front door and was greeted by a uniformed female officer behind a large gray metal desk.

"Good morning," Grant said.

"How may I help you?" the woman officer replied.

"Yes, my mother was killed in a car accident here earlier in the week. I was wondering if I could speak to someone about the investigation."

"Name?" the woman said, looking at her computer screen.

"Collins," Grant said. "Helen Collins."

The woman used her mouse to search the computer, then looked up.

"That would be Sergeant Brady. Down the hall, last door on the right. He should be in."

"Thank you," Grant said, and ambled down the tiled hallway until he found a door with *Sgt. Brady* stenciled on its frosted window. He knocked and opened the door.

"Come in," said a man seated behind a desk and dressed in a brown suit. He looked up as Grant walked in.

"Sergeant Brady?"

"That's me. What's up?"

"My mother, Helen Collins, was killed in an accident earlier. I was told you might give me the details."

"And you are who?"

"I'm Grant, her son. I'm down from DC for her funeral yesterday."

"Any ID?"

Grant produced his driver's license and showed it to Brady who then retrieved a manila file from a desk drawer. He opened it and thumbed through its pages.

"Yes, yes," he said. "She may have had a heart attack or stroke. Her car ran off the road and into the bridge abutment over Cottom Creek east of town. She was dead at the scene. I'm sorry."

"My mother never drove anywhere very fast. How fast would you say she was traveling at impact, sergeant?"

"Well, from the way the front of her car looked, I'd say fifty miles an hour."

"Fifty? I don't think so, Sergeant. She would never drive that fast around town, never."

"From the looks of her car," Brady said, producing

several photographs, "she was a reckless driver." He tossed the pictures to Grant who thumbed through the photographs. "You can see how caved in the right front of the car was."

Grant stopped at one photo. It was of the rear of Helen's car.

"What is this here?" Grant said pointing to damage to the rear bumper and trunk.

"It has obviously been damaged in a prior accident. Must have backed into something or someone."

"Or someone rear-ended her," Grant said and handed the photos back to the officer.

"Hard to say. There were no marks or paint residue on her rear bumper. No telling how old that damage is."

"Were you at the scene, Sergeant?"

Brady nodded. "Yep," he said.

"How bad were my mother's injuries? Was she banged up pretty bad?"

"From what I could tell," Brady said, "she had a severe head injury. There was blood over her face and down her front. She wasn't moving or responding."

Grant's stomach rolled at the police sergeant's description. He could picture his mother sitting in her car, dead.

"Where is the car now?" he said to Brady.

The policeman eyed Grant through narrow eyes. He lit a cigarette and blew acrid smoke into the air above Grant.

"It was towed to the local salvage yard and, if I know Buck, it's been taken to the auto auction in Atlanta. You might check, however. It might still be in town."

"Did the Medical Examiner examine my mother's body?"

Brady thumbed through the file and found a sheet of paper. "Doc Witherspoon didn't do an autopsy, if that's what you mean," he said. "Didn't have to. But yes, he examined your mother at the scene."

"And?" Grant said in a tone that belied impatience.

"Doc thought your mother had a heart attack or stroke. He pronounced her dead. Cause of death was accident. We closed the case after that," Brady said. He inhaled deeply on his cigarette.

"Dr. Witherspoon? Does he have an office here in town?"

Brady stared at Grant for a moment then nodded. "Dr. Samuel Witherspoon. And yes, his office is right off the downtown intersection. Can't miss it. You going there?"

"I might. You don't think her car could have been pushed from the rear into that bridge?"

Brady took a deep puff and exhaled before answering. "What are you trying to say, Mr. Collins?"

"I dunno. Just that in the absence of an autopsy how can anyone be sure she had a fatal heart attack? Maybe there are other possibilities."

"Like reckless driving?"

"Well, for starters, I understand she was active in protesting a nuclear power plant whose owner wants to locate here in Trinity. Maybe she had enemies."

The officer took another deep puff on the cigarette then snubbed it out in an already full ashtray. "Oh, come now. There's no reason to think that. And certainly nothing that even remotely points in that direction. No, I'm afraid it was an accident, simply an accident."

"But—"

"No buts, sir. This is a quiet, friendly town, Mr. Collins. You can't just come waltzing in here throwing wild theories around. Not after a police investigation has closed the case. What you are suggesting is unthinkable. And impossible."

Grant took a deep breath, tried to calm himself. "One

last thing," he said in a low voice. "I have been looking for a friend of mine from high school. We met at my mother's funeral and were to have supper but she seems to have disappeared. I can't find her car anywhere in or around town."

Brady put down a pencil and looked at Grant. He raised both hands. "All right, what's the name?" he said.

"Lori Spelling."

Brady dropped his pencil and stared at Grant. "Mr. Collins, take a seat there, will you?"

"Why?"

"Well, for starters, we just fished a dead woman out of the river. The name on her driver's license was Lori Spelling."

ↄↄↄↄ

Mayor Bruce Baxter sat in his expansive office at City Hall that overlooked Main Street and the park behind it. The mayor was a man of sublime tastes and the office was decorated with accoutrements of his many world travels. On the wall next to his ornately carved desk hung a replica of the huge black marlin he caught while on vacation in Costa Rica. There was a shield and spear from Africa and numerous photographs of Baxter with various rich and famous people. Since becoming the mayor of Trinity he had put down plush carpet, brought in Italian leather chairs, and hung expensive art on the walls. He relished the power of his office, the bending of people to do his bidding, how they came to him in bended knee for favors. Ensconced in his little fortress he ruled over a small kingdom and he did so with an iron will. Sure, it was a comparatively small kingdom when compared with Savannah or Atlanta but it was his kingdom. And it was certainly a decided step up the food chain from where his life began but that was a story no one in Trinity was ever going to know. Not if he could help it.

He gazed out the large window onto the park's green lawn surrounded by azalea bushes in blooms of red and yellow. Several mothers pushed baby strollers along its walkway. The town was waking up.

Baxter came to Trinity after making a small fortune in a pyramid stock market scam that left many investors penniless and him with a large bank account. He managed to escape prosecution by utilizing an expensive lawyer who was able to work out an undisclosed agreement with the Manhattan US Attorney. He used part of his small fortune to finance his mayoral campaign. When he ran for mayor, his opponent raised questions about where he had come from and what his past had been but he deftly sidestepped them and turned the tables on the man, making the campaign about the man's business dealings.

He was able to convince the voters of Trinity that his past belonged in the past and was unimportant to the present. Baxter was a lucky man, born with a natural gift of gab, an ability to sway people with his naturally good looks, charm, and old-fashioned double-talk.

He had gotten fat and sassy in Trinity, his large frame requiring an oversized chair to support him. He traveled frequently to New York to buy his suits from Brooks Brothers. He drove the only BMW sedan in Trinity and folks said hello when they passed him on the street. His hair was thinning and turning gray and he needed reading glasses but life had been good for Baxter. Kickbacks from construction projects of all kinds resulted in money flowing like a river into his Cayman Island account.

But all was not a bed of roses for Baxter. He did have one major problem—the proposed nuclear power plant facility. If he couldn't push it through, he stood to lose millions. His secret alliance with the owner of DynaTech was buried deep within pages of legal documents. His principal role was to sway public opinion, get the city council's favorable vote. Only then, would he realize the wealth that was promised. But he knew the members of the council, and they wouldn't back the plant unless their voters wanted it and that meant the citizens of Trinity. The thought of strong-arming the council was an attractive one, he certainly had enough dirt on some of them to possibly sway their vote but he balked at using such tactics. Only as a last resort if the polls didn't turn his way. He had been using his radio station to run ads extolling the benefits of the plant and what it would mean to the town in more revenue and jobs. The polls, he knew, were about even. The group called Citizens Against Nuclear Power was waging a people's campaign and it seemed they were slowly turning the town's opinion in their favor. His phone calls with Winston Conway, the president and owner of DynaTech, always ended with the man making the same veiled threat—produce the votes or lose the plant and the money.

Ahead of a favorable vote, Conway had bought a sizable tract of riverfront land and was building a large home on it. The frame of the large house was already up and it promised to be the largest in the county. The construction crew lived in two trailers on the property. Baxter didn't know what the man planned to do with it if the vote was against him. He knew it was his job to not let that happen.

He picked up the phone and dialed Conway's private line in Savannah. The man's gruff voice answered.

"Conway here."

"Mr. Conway? Bruce Baxter. How are you this morning?"

"Up to my ears in federal regulations, Mayor. And you?"

"Pretty good. Just wanted to give you the results of the latest poll down here."

"And?" came the gruff reply.

Baxter looked out onto the park that now was filled with children kicking a soccer ball. "We're up three points. So, I think the tide may be turning."

"Well, that's some good news, at least. If you can keep the momentum up, things might turn around for us."

"I think the radio ads are having an effect on people's opinion. But that citizen's committee is putting up some stiff competition. They're out in town every day drumming up signatures on the petition they've got going.

"Any chance they can force a city-wide vote on this thing, Mayor? If that would happen, we could lose everything we've been counting on. I wouldn't like that."

Baxter didn't like the way the man said the last sentence. Sounded a little ominous. "Nor would I, Winston. We just need to keep pushing, that's all."

"I do hope you're right. What about the woman?"

Baxter noticed that the children were on the far side of the park still kicking the soccer ball. "Police found her yesterday. A tragedy, her falling off the bridge like that. Papers said she was full of cocaine."

"Yes," Conway said. "Another tragedy in the world of illicit drugs. Young people like that die every day. Well, I wouldn't play up her death too much on the radio. Just cause people to start wondering unnecessarily."

"I understand," Baxter said and hung up.

Chapter 5

Carrie finished her housecleaning and showered. After putting on jeans and a red blouse she settled into her chair with a book and waited for Grant to return. She hadn't expected the previous night with a relative stranger but the experience left her with warm feelings for him. He was self-assured in a quiet way, self-confident, besides good-looking.

When Carrie moved to Trinity from Atlanta seeking a quieter life away from the city's crime and drugs, she soon realized that the number of eligible men in town were few in number. There weren't many jobs available for a young woman with two years of college and the diner was hiring so she talked to the owner and was hired the same day. She enjoyed the work, meeting new people as well as having a regular clientele, and now was the senior waitress at the diner. She was almost married once to a man in Atlanta, a man several years older, but he hit her a few times so she left him. After that he kept turning up, pestering her so she obtained a protective order against him. She hoped that, by moving to Trinity, he was out of her life for good. But she knew her time was running short, not that she was thinking of marriage with Grant, but she was beginning to sense her biological time clock ticking away. Now another man in her life wouldn't be so bad.

She put her book down and went to the bathroom to put on her makeup. As she did, she worried that the few lines and wrinkles were beginning to show in spite of the powder she applied to her face. She brushed her auburn hair and arranged the curls so they hung on her shoulders. She wished her dark eyes were lighter and her nose a little straighter but there was nothing she could do about them.

She got the morning paper from the porch below the stairs and returned to her chair and opened the *Trinity Eagle.* Its headlines hit her like a load of bricks.

LOCAL WOMAN FOUND DEAD IN RIVER
A Trinity woman, identified as Lori Spelling, was found yesterday floating in the Dogwood River near the Euclid Street bridge. The woman was entangled in some brush and was found by some boys playing in the area. Sheriff spokesman, Dan Whitlock, told the Trinity Eagle that an autopsy was pending but it appeared to be a drug overdose for the residue on the victims fingers tested positive for cocaine. It is Trinity's first drug-related death.

Carrie put the paper aside, her heart suddenly racing. *Has Grant seen these headline*s, she thought? Probably not for he was going straight to the police department so they surely have told him. *Why hasn't he called?* She couldn't believe that they were just looking for her last night. But Grant said she was a no-show for their dinner date so what could have happened? Cocaine overdose? She doubted it. Anyone who worked for the college underwent random drug testing and any positives meant immediate termination for an employee. Besides, the times she had come to the diner for lunch she just didn't appear the druggy type. She was always dressed in the latest fashions and well groomed. She knew that wasn't a guarantee of no drugs but in Trinity it usually was as close as it came to one.

What was keeping Grant? She thought about going to the police station to see if he was still there. If so, he might welcome a friendly face. But, she thought better of it and returned to the paper. Lori Spelling. She even knew the woman. Not well, but knew her on sight, knew who she was. She had seen her passing out leaflets at gatherings against the power plant. Such a shame that a young, beautiful young woman was now dead. But a drug overdose? Carrie didn't think so.

Trinity didn't have a drug problem, or at least that was the official line. Sure, they had they occasional weed smoking parties on the river among the high schoolers or college crowd but the hard stuff was almost nonexistent. The few serious dopers that found their way into town were quickly locked up and told to move on. Parents kept a tight rein on their children in Trinity. Most of the activities centered on the sports and arts of both schools and the town's residents went to football games or band concerts long after children had left home. It was the thing Carrie valued about Trinity—quiet, peaceful, idyllic. Almost too good to be true.

Until last night and this tragedy with Miss Spelling.

Until this morning when the town woke up and read the headlines of the paper.

Carrie looked at her watch. What was keeping Grant? He was going to have to return soon to Hilton Head if he was going to catch his flight home. What would he do when he learned the latest news? She wanted a chance for an unhurried goodbye. Would she ever see him again?

લ૭લ૭

Grant stood speechless while hot, bitter bile rose in his throat. Sergeant Brady stared at Grant and motioned to the chair beside his desk.

"Mr. Collins, please take that seat, there. I've got a few questions."

"What did you say?" Grant said, still standing. Bright sunlight beamed in Brady's office window flooding the office in warmth. A photo of a woman and child sat on the sergeant's desk.

"I said we just fished a body from the river by the name of Lori Spelling. At least that's the name on a driver's license that was in a purse found nearby. The medical examiner will make a positive ID in a day or two."

"My god," Grant said, falling into the chair next to Brady's desk. His heart raced. "I just had lunch with her yesterday."

"That's when you saw her last, then? Yesterday at lunch?"

Grant nodded.

"What did you talk about?"

Grant glanced around the office, noticed its spartan furnishings, cleared his throat.

"Nothing much. She had come to my mother's funeral and we went to the diner for lunch. She mentioned the power plant possibly coming to town. That's about all."

Brady took a cigarette from a pack on his desk and lit it with an antique Zippo lighter. He toyed with it for a few silent moments, his gray eyes seemed to study Grant. "You sure about that?" he said.

Grant felt suddenly nervous as if he was a possible suspect in Lori's death. He wondered if he should ask for a lawyer but he didn't have anything to hide. He glanced at his watch. He still had time to catch his plane.

"Sure, I'm sure. There was some small talk about Mom then Lori mentioned DynaTech and we talked about how the town was divided over the plant coming to Trinity. We made a date for dinner at Martin's Restaurant later in the evening and that was the last time I saw her."

Brady wrote on a notepad as Grant related the facts of his lunch. "Okay, thanks. Anything else you wish to add?"

"What kind of car was it?" Grant asked.

"Haven't located her car as yet."

"She didn't seem the druggy type, Sergeant. I remember her from high school. She never did drugs back then, and I don't think she was doing drugs now."

"The tests don't lie, Mr. Collins. Maybe you supplied her with them."

"You've got to be kidding," Grant said, his voice clipped, showing irritation. "So, that's it? Drug overdose, pure and simple. Kinda like my mother's accident. You sure are quick to make determinations on how people die here in Trinity."

"Mr. Collins," Brady said, "I'll overlook that comment as coming from a distraught son. Anything else?"

"Nothing, except that I ate dinner alone at the diner, made friends with my waitress, and after she got off work she drove me around town while we searched for Lori's car. But we didn't locate it."

"Where did you spend last night?" Brady said.

Grant squirmed in his chair. "With Carrie," he said after a while.

Brady blew smoke into the air and took another puff. "Carrie. The waitress?"

Grant nodded.

Brady smiled a small smirk as he wrote on the notepad. After finishing his writing, he looked up. "Okay, Mr. Collins. You can go. But don't leave town just yet."

"I have a plane to catch this afternoon. I have things to do in DC."

Brady snubbed out his cigarette and stood, signaling the end of the interview. "Cancel it. And call your work and tell them you'll be delayed. You can say police business if you care too. I'll inform you when you're free to return home."

Grant left Brady's office and stumbled, dazed, into the parking lot, and into bright sunshine. He found his rental car and climbed in, headed back to Carrie's.

ତ৩ତ৩

She answered the door before he knocked.

"I was watching through the window," she said, as he fell through the door. "Come in. I was getting worried."

Grant sat in the living room chair and shook his head. He rubbed his temples.

"Well?" Carrie said, "what happened? Get any information about your mother's accident?"

"I did, and more. Guess what? Lori is dead."

"I know. Look at this." Carrie sat on the chair's arm, while Grant read the newspaper article on Lori.

"Brady said some boys found her in the river and that she had cocaine on her hands. They're doing an autopsy."

"My, my," was all Carrie could say. After a moment she said, "You just never know about some people."

"You believe it? That she was sitting down on the river shooting cocaine?"

Carrie shook her head. "No, of course not. But the test—"

"Look, Carrie. The cocaine could have been planted on her. Brady said there'll be an autopsy so we'll know for sure then."

Carrie put a hand on Grant's shoulder, smiled at him.

"Grant, please don't take this the wrong way," she said, her voice soft. "But you've been in town only two days and you're seeing conspiracies everywhere. First your mother. Now Lori. Are you sure you're not overreacting?"

"I dunno. Dunno." He exhaled a long breath. "It's possible, I guess."

"Did the police say anything else? You were gone quite a while."

"The police sergeant questioned me about how I knew her, where I was last night, what she and I talked about."

"Are you a suspect? Surely not." She rose off the chair and headed toward the kitchen. "I made some iced tea. Would you like some?"

Grant nodded and smiled. Carrie looked nice and smelled even better.

"Thanks," he said. "Brady, that's the sergeant's name, didn't indicate I was a suspect, but who knows. He doesn't want me to leave town, just yet however."

"But you have a plane to catch," Carrie called from the kitchen. She returned with two large glasses of tea.

"I'll stay at Mom's if I'm not going to leave for a while."

"Nothing doing, Grant. You can stay here."

He took her offered glass and took several large gulps.

"Thanks. I don't get it, Carrie. I just saw her yesterday. What could have happened?"

Carrie dropped into the sofa opposite Grant and hung a leg over its arm. "I have no idea. But I can tell you this, I don't believe she was doing drugs. She always seemed well dressed, went to work every day. I didn't know her except from a distance but working in a diner, you get pretty good at judging people by appearances, and she just didn't have the looks of a druggy. I ought to know, I've seen my share."

"Yes, I know. But people can get awfully good at hiding that stuff from everyone, including family." Grant took another sip of tea and set his glass on the table next to his chair.

"I just don't think she was the type. Call it woman's intuition if you want."

"So, if she didn't overdose, then she was killed. Is that what you're saying?"

"I dunno. What other explanation could there be?" Carrie said and brushed a lock of hair from her face. "Maybe she was taking a walk along the river and stumbled, fell in, and drowned. An accident. Especially, in the unlikely event she was stoned on cocaine. Have they found her car?"

"An accident is certainly possible, Carrie. Brady mentioned that they haven't found her car but it shouldn't be that difficult if it's along the river somewhere. But it's something we could do today. Continue looking for her car."

"I have to go to work later, Grant, but you can use my car today, if you like, then pick me up when I get off."

"I've got my rental. Let's say it was an accident and she wasn't on drugs. She was walking along the river's edge for some unknown reason then slipped and fell in. Is the river around here bad enough to cause her to drown? I haven't seen rapids or anything like that."

"You're right, Grant," she said. "The river around Trinity is usually pretty gentle except during periods of excessive rains that happen in the spring. We've had a few drownings but always when the river level was high."

"So, an accident seems unlikely. We're back to drugs or—"

"You're saying she might have been killed." Carrie shook her head as if pondering the impossible. "Why would someone wish to kill her? She didn't appear to have enemies."

"If her death wasn't due to drugs then we're left with only one alternative. We'll just have to wait on the autopsy."

"What about your mom's accident? Anything there?" Carrie said.

"Apparently there was damage to the rear end of her car also but the police can't say when that happened. They don't believe it figured in the accident. The car is at a local salvage unless it's already been sold or taken to Atlanta. I want to look at her car just to satisfy my curiosity."

Carrie stood and put an arm on Grant's shoulder. She bent down and kissed him softly on his cheek which stirred memories of the previous night. He looked into her deep blue eyes and saw a woman of genuine caring. He marveled that there was no man in her life and wondered if she had been hurt deeply in some past relationship. Her slender fingers brushed through his hair and she kissed him again.

"Here," she said, producing a set of keys from her purse, "is a key to the apartment. I have some chicken salad in the fridge so what do you say to some lunch before I go to work. I get off at nine."

"Sounds fine," he said. "But are you sure you trust me? After all, we just met yesterday."

Carrie laughed and ambled to the kitchen. "We've done more than just meet," she said over a shoulder. "Besides, you have trustworthy eyes."

Grant wondered what *trustworthy eyes* were, exactly, as he followed her to the kitchen.

Chapter 6

After Carrie left for the diner, Grant drove back to his mother's house. The curtains were drawn and the living room was dark. He didn't bother turning on a light, but instead, found a bottle of water in the pantry, then sat, turning the events of the last twenty-four hours over in his muddled brain. He made a mental to-do list. First the salvage yard, Buck's, if he remembered right, pick up a newspaper for any news, then scout the town for Lori's car. Then there was Carrie. She was friendly enough but was this just a fleeting passage of two ships in the night? They seemed to have hit it off but should he keep it on that superficial level? He really knew nothing about her. Maybe later he could get her to open up about herself. There had to be a reason why a pretty young woman, single to boot, would settle in a small town with few eligible men.

The damage to the rear end of Helen's car puzzled him. His mother never mentioned being in any accident during their phone conversations, a fact strange in itself. Not like her to keep quiet about something like that. It wasn't like her. The fact that Brady said she had hit the abutment going fifty-five miles per hour also did not sound like his mother. Helen drove like the proverbial little old lady and she would never drive that fast on a road close to town, never. He had to get a look at her car himself, that was for sure.

Lori's death was an unexpected shock. He had to agree with Carrie—the woman didn't appear the drug-addicted type. But looks could be deceiving. He knew that from personal experience. So, if drugs weren't involved, how did she wind up dead in the Dogwood River? An accident was certainly possible. Hopefully, the autopsy would provide some answers, if he was still in town to hear them. Two deaths in Trinity within a week, surely that didn't happen often.

A small town like Trinity couldn't have more than a few thousand residents so things like automobile accidents and people floating in the river had to happen infrequently. Another item on his mental list—go to library and research old newspapers and check for previous deaths. Why not, he didn't have anything to do until time to pick Carrie up at the diner.

He found *Buck's Salvage* two miles south of town on the road that paralleled the river road but slanted off in a somewhat southwesterly direction.

A small faded sign directed him onto a narrow lane where there must have been over a hundred rusting, dilapidated car bodies aligned in rows on two acres of dirt and crab grass. A small, ramshackle office stood in the center of the salvage yard and when Grant came to a stop, an overweight man dressed in greasy coveralls and sporting a John Deere baseball cap emerged through the office door. Grant stepped out of his car.

"You Buck?" he said.

The man eyed him for a moment, then flashed a smile that sported two black teeth. "Yep," he said. "Junk's my game."

Grant shot a quick glance at the man's soiled hands,

thought about not shaking hands, but extended his right anyway.

"I'm Collins. Grant Collins."

"Well, Mr. Collins, what can I do for you? Not from around here are you? Car break down? Looking for a part? I got plenty." Buck spit tobacco juice onto the ground.

"No, nothing like that. But, you're right, I don't live here; however, my mother did. Helen Collins. She died in a car accident earlier in the week. Hit a bridge abutment. We had her funeral yesterday, that's why I'm in Trinity. The police said you had her car. I wanted to take a look at it if I could."

Buck removed his baseball cap and ran a hand through unkempt hair that hung over his ears.

"Yeah," he said. "I remember that car. Little job. But, I'm afraid it ain't here. Went to the Atlanta auction this morning."

"I was afraid of that," Grant said. "The police said she hit the bridge doing fifty-five."

"I doubt that," Buck said and spit more tobacco juice.

"Why do you say that?"

"Well, for one thing, the road curves right before the bridge. It would be almost impossible to take that curve at anything over thirty or thirty-five. Not enough road after it straightens out to get speed up. Unless you're in a race car or something."

"Any pictures taken of her vehicle?"

"Police should have taken photos at the accident scene. They usually do."

"Thanks, Buck." Grant strolled to the driver side of the car and opened it. He stopped, looked at the man who appeared as if he starred in a redneck movie. "Listen, Buck," he said. "You've loved in Trinity a while?"

"Fifteen years," the man said.

"I've heard there's a big fuss over a nuclear plant coming to town. Know anything about that?"

Buck spat tobacco juice again onto the ground. "Well," he said, "I do hear tell a lot of folks are stirred up about that. I don't rightly care one way or the other, myself. The rich folks will get their way. They usually do."

"I only ask because my mother was involved in trying to keep them out of town."

"I see," Buck said.

"Did you happen to notice the damage to the rear end of her car? The police said there was damage to the rear of mother's car."

Buck smiled, nodded. "Actually, I did notice where the rear had been damaged. Like someone rear-ended her."

"Think it could have happened the day of the accident? She got rear-ended and was pushed into the bridge?"

Buck rubbed his chin. "I suppose so. Couldn't say for sure, though. The police lab could tell you. I'm sure of that."

"Too late for that," Grant said. "Thanks for your help."

"Come back if you need car parts," Buck said. "Got plenty. Business has been kinda slow here lately."

"Will do," Grant said and he crawled into the car and headed back into town.

At the first intersection he turned east and headed to the river road. The blacktop road was lined with dogwood and oak trees with a dense layer of underbrush. The sun was high and there were a few billowing cumulus clouds scattered in the white sky. As he neared the river a definite musky odor reached his nostrils, the smell of swamp water and algae.

He turned north on the river road and noticed that it

was markedly narrower that the one he left. The blacktop was in a state of disrepair with numerous potholes on its faded surface. No shoulder and the road edge was crumbling in sections. He slowed and kept an eye toward the river fifty yards below to his right. The ground sloped down to the water gently in most places but now and then it dropped precipitously to the river. There were occasional pulloffs into the brush that Grant surmised were perfect spots for high schoolers or the college crowd who wanted nighttime privacy.

As he inched his way along the river road he kept looking on both sides of the road for Lori's car but did not see it. At the north edge of town he turned on Euclid, wound around a sharp curve, and drove down to the bridge his mother had hit. He stopped, got out, and walked around the bridge abutment. There were no marks on it, just a small divot of concrete broken away. As he stood there, it hit him—this was where his mother had died. Right here. Less than a week earlier. What was it Buck said? No way a car could be doing much over thirty? But Sergeant Brady said they estimated her speed at fifty-five.

Grant got back his rental car and resumed his search of the town. When he had seen nearly every square inch of Trinity, he stopped at the gas station, bought a paper, and headed to the ME's office. He had not seen Lori's car. It was not in town.

დონდ

Winston Conway had the blueprints of the proposed nuclear plant spread out over his large conference table and was bent over them, in studious thought. Seated opposite him was his project engineer, William Talbot. The engineer chewed an unlit cigar while Powers held a drink in his hand. The hour was late and the room was otherwise empty, the two men were alone. A laptop computer sat to one side of the blueprints. Both men were in their shirtsleeves having doffed their suit coats hours earlier. The room smelled of pipe and cigar smoke and the remains of a catered supper. The hour was late.

"I don't think it can be done, Mr. Conway," said Talbot pointing to section on the blueprint. "Too dangerous."

"But Bill. It would cut construction costs dramatically."

"But you can't make the walls of the reactor vessel or the containment structure any thinner. It's part of the redundancy of the system in case of a meltdown. There's a certain thickness one cannot go below. It's the law."

"Who determines these specs, Bill?"

"The Nuclear Regulatory Commission. It regulates commercial nuclear power plants that generate electricity. There are several types of these power reactors. Of these, only the Pressurized Water Reactors and Boiling Water Reactors are in commercial operation here in the States. They can close us down in a heartbeat if they don't approve these blueprints. And trust me, the NRC will go over these blueprints in minute detail."

"The whole process fills me with distress, getting the damn thing running, I mean. Too much can go wrong. The building of it is easy. Getting it approved is a huge hurdled we have to overcome and once the enriched uranium gets here, things really get dicey."

Talbot nodded. "The water is heated by the nuclear reactions, but because the water is pressurized, it doesn't boil. The water in the reactor heats the water in the steam generator side, but it is on a different loop so they do not mix. In the boiling water reactor, the water comes to a boil due to the heat produced by nuclear fusion. The water from the reactor powers the turbine. In both systems, the water is reused.

"As I was saying, the reactor vessel and containment structure need to be built according to specifications. That is, if you want to have a power plant down in Trinity."

"I don't seem to have much of a choice, do I, Bill?"

Talbot shook his head. "Can't fight the government, sir. Besides, you can't afford the bad publicity if the public perceives you have cut corners and compromised safety."

"You're right, of course," Conway said. He took a folder and opened it. "This DynaTech reactor has an electrical production capacity of more than 1650 megawatts, which places it among the most powerful reactors in the world. A direct descendant our previous models, the DynaTech pressurized water reactor is based on tried-and-tested technologies and principles. It is classified as an advanced generation reactor due to the level of safety obtained and the economic savings that it achieves in relation to the earlier models. From a safety point of view, this reactor ensures an unequalled safety level thanks to a drastic reduction of the probability of severe accidents as well as of their consequences on the environment. In addition, the DynaTech reactor is designed to resist severe external impact loads such as airplane crashes, floods, that sort of thing.

"Economically, it achieves an unrivaled level of competitiveness because electricity production costs are reduced by ten percent, compared with current plants. It also produces less waste."

"No doubt about it," Talbot agreed. "If we get this plant up and running DynaTech will be the envy of the industry."

"Where will we be getting the uranium?" Conway said.

"From the United States Enrichment Corporation's plant in Kentucky. They do the enrichment there."

Conway shook his head, a frown formed on his face. "I've never quite understood the process. Seems so much a mystery to me."

Talbot looked up from the computer monitor and smiled at his boss. He took a piece of paper and a pencil and began drawing.

"Not really," he said. "Uranium is an element that is similar to iron. Like iron, you dig uranium ore out of the ground and then process it to extract the pure uranium from the ore. When you finish processing uranium ore, what you have is uranium oxide." He drew a diagram outlining the process. "Uranium oxide contains two types or isotopes of uranium: U-two-thirty-five and U-two-thirty-eight. U-two-thirty-five is what you need if you want to make a bomb or fuel a nuclear power plant. But the uranium oxide from the mine is about ninety-nine percent U-two-thirty-eight. So you need to somehow separate the U-two-thirty-five from the U-two-thirty-eight and increase the amount of U-two-thirty-five. The process of concentrating the U-two-thirty-five is called enrichment, and centrifuges are a central part of the process.

"U-two-thirty-five weighs slightly less than U-two-thirty-eight. By exploiting this weight difference, you can separate the U-two-thirty-five and the U-two-thirty-eight. The first step is to react the uranium with hydrofluoric acid, an extremely powerful acid. After several steps, you create the gas uranium hexafluoride.

"Now that the uranium is in a gaseous form, it is easier to work with. You can put the gas into a centrifuge and spin it up. The centrifuge creates a force thousands of times more powerful than the force of gravity. Because the U-two-thirty-eight atoms are slightly heavier than the U-235 atoms, they tend to move out toward the walls of the centrifuge. The U-two-thirty-five atoms tend to stay more toward the center of the centrifuge.

"Although it is only a slight difference in concentrations, when you extract the gas from the center of the centrifuge, it has slightly more U-two-thirty-five than it did before. You place this slightly concentrated gas in another centrifuge and do the same thing. If you do this thousands of times, you can create a gas that is highly enriched in U-two-thirty-five. At a uranium enrichment plant, thousands of centrifuges are chained together in long cascades.

"At the end of a long chain of centrifuges, you have uranium hexafluoride gas containing a high concentration of U-two-thirty-five atoms. Not all that complicated, the actual process."

Conway shook his head.

"Well, Bill, you do make it sound rather complicated. Who dreamed up this process, anyway?"

"Well, it is a complicated chemistry but in practice it turns out to be a simple process. Now you need to turn the uranium hexafluoride gas back into uranium metal. You do this by adding calcium. The calcium reacts with the fluoride to create a salt, and the pure uranium metal is left behind. With this highly concentrated U-two-thirty-five metal, you can either make a nuclear bomb or power a nuclear reactor."

"Quite a process."

"The creation of the centrifuges was a huge technological challenge. The centrifuges must spin very quickly—in the range of one hundred thousand rpm. To spin this fast, the centrifuges must have very light, yet strong, rotors, well-balanced rotors, and high-speed bearings, usually magnetic to reduce friction. Meeting all three of these requirements has been out of reach for most countries. The recent development of inexpensive, high-precision computer-controlled machining equipment has made things somewhat easier. This is why more countries are learning to enrich uranium in recent years."

"And once you get the enriched uranium you can make a bomb instead of a power plant," Conway said.

"That's the fear, sure. In this country, the industry is highly regulated by the NRC and there are a lot of checks and balances. But in another country, who could say."

"You've convinced me, Bill. Let's wrap this up for tonight, what do you say. We can continue to go over these plans in the morning."

"Whatever you say, Mr. Conway."

After Talbot had left the building, Conway sat in his office, a tumbler of scotch before him on his antique cherry wood desk. It had been a trying evening attempting to assimilate all the facts and figures his engineer had thrown his way. And this was after a meeting with his comptroller who brought bad news. DynaTech was in trouble, financially. The man had pleaded with him to go public with a stock option but he had resisted, wanting to keep total control of DynaTech himself. Getting a seat on the stock exchange might mean an influx of capital but it would also mean less control, he would have a board of directors who would oversee every operation. It would no longer be his sole company. He needed cash if DynaTech was to survive after the Trinity plant but where it was to come from he hadn't a notion.

There would be revenues from the electricity produced by the plant sure, but not nearly enough to cover DynaTeah's debts. He had greatly overextended the company building the last plant in Tennessee and he was hurting. Some of the business decisions required the infusion of capital. A lot of it. Money was tight and he didn't want to get a loan. The revenues he hoped would come from those decisions never materialized, leaving only debts. He thought he had the money to cover it but he was in a cash flow bind. The stock offering seemed the logical choice. But damn, he didn't want to do it.

Conway had grown up in the South, Alabama to be exact, at a time when the civil rights movement was hitting its climax. He remembered the separate bathrooms, one labeled *colored*, the other *white*, and the separate restaurants in his hometown. He never understood his father's rantings about *those damn people*, as if they were all that different. His mother would tell him it was just skin color, otherwise they were just people like everyone else. If that was so, why all the fuss? He was in junior high when the march from Selma to Montgomery occurred and Bloody Sunday happened. He remembered watching on television as swarms of police, state troopers, and deputized citizens brutalized the marchers with clubs and tear gas, leaving many severely wounded.

Conway had no siblings and was thankful of the fact. He received all his mother's affection. His father, he would later learn, was a bigot and a racist, always ranting about people of color. In the south, the man's ideology had a lot of support but as Conway continued to grow, he and his father drifted apart, mostly on account of his father's overt racism.

He spent two years at Emory University, leaving early to join the navy so he could see the world as the advertisements claimed. His parents died while he was deployed in the Pacific. While in the navy, he became friends with Jake Milburn, a fellow seaman. Jake was bright and resourceful and ran a numbers racket aboard ship. He always had money. After the navy, Conway and Milburn started several businesses, all of which failed, and he eventually took a job with Georgia Power and becoming first a lineman, then a supervisor, finally a project engineer. Jake Milburn went his own way. It was his experience with the power company that gave him the idea to start his own company and he had carved out a niche in the growing field of water-driven turbines used in dams for electricity. Now he was branching out into nuclear power. He had searched for and found Jake and convinced him to join his company and now Milburn was his chief of finance and it was Jake who had delivered the bad financial news. The Kentucky plant had been highly successful but the construction delays and cost overruns on the Tennessee plant had left DynaTech in a financial hole that was going to be difficult to climb out of. The company had used up every penny of its multi-million dollar line of credit and the bank wanted its money.

Conway never married. He preferred to pay for his sexual gratification. It was easier and less complicated in the long run. No personal entanglements to get in the way or detract him from his main obsession - making money. He saw women as objects for sexual release, nothing more. It was the way his father had treated his mother and it seemed to be a good way to run one's life. Fewer problems.

Not that there hadn't been a close call. Wanda. She had waltzed into his life while he was at Georgia Power and working in Macon enlarging the grid there. He was having a beer after work with a few co-workers and he bumped into her on the way to the restroom. He spilled her drink and offered to buy her another one. That began a six-month relationship that ended when her boyfriend returned from the army. Conway had been devastated. He remembered the day she told him, sitting in his truck in the parking lot of a grocery store. He had been a momentary diversion, nothing more for a woman he thought of asking to marry him. Well, it would never happen again.

Conway downed the last of the scotch and turned out the office light. He was weary, worn out. On the way to his Savannah condominium his thoughts returned to the meeting with Jake Milburn. *Was this the beginning of another of his ventures that would fail?* As he drove to the Ardsley Park neighborhood south of the city, traffic thinned. Savannah's first suburb, Ardsley Park was a district of plush lawns and four- and five-bedroom mansions and Craftsman bungalows built in the 1920s. Ardsley Park was the place to find ancient live oaks dripping with Spanish moss over streets lined with stately mansions. It was far enough away from the touristy bustle of downtown to be peaceful and residential. Children walked or rode bikes to school, and residents had easy access to downtown and the Southside shopping malls.

Driving southeast into the city a full moon rose over the Savannah River causing the water to glisten like tony diamonds. Where was he going to get the money to pay off his debts? He was tired of starting over and didn't think he had the energy to do it again. And he was getting too old to work for someone else, having to ask when he wanted a day off or was ill. No, the future seemed bleak at the moment but maybe he could find a way out. He had to.

As he slipped into bed he thought of Wanda. He wished she was lying next to him once again and longed to feel the warmth of her body next to his. She could make the night seem brighter. If she was only here.

Chapter 7

The office of Dr. Samuel Witherspoon was located in a converted white frame house on the backside of Trinity's downtown area. Grant parked his car between a jacked-up pickup and a SUV. Patients obviously. Tall stately cypress trees framed the office as in a Gothic painting.

The doctor's waiting room was empty except for a young woman who sat reading a magazine. Grant smiled at an older woman with graying temples who sat behind a small window. She smiled at his approach.

"May I help you?" she said. The wrinkles at the corners of her eyes deepened.

"I'd like to speak with the doctor," Grant said in a low even tone.

"Name?" the woman said. "I don't remember you being a patient of Dr. Witherspoon."

"I'm Grant Collins. No, I'm not a patient. I came to talk about my mother, Helen Collins. He was the ME on her car accident. He signed he death certificate. I don't know but she may have been a patient of the doctor's."

"Oh my," the woman said. She retrieved a pen and looked up at him. "Mr. Collins, you said?"

"That's correct. Like I said, he might have even attended my mother before she died. She lived here in Trinity for many years."

"Let me check," the woman said and she went to a filing cabinet behind her desk. She returned with a file in her hand. "Actually, Mr. Collins, your mother was a patient of the doctor. If you would like to have a seat I'll tell Dr. Witherspoon you are here."

Grant took a seat and thumbed through a sporting magazine. He glanced up and noticed the other woman waiting was looking at him. She returned to her magazine when she saw Grant looking at her. A nurse in bright blue scrubs called the woman and she disappeared into the belly of the medical office leaving Grant alone in the waiting room.

It was late in the afternoon and he figured the office hours were just about over for the day. Ten minutes later the woman reappeared and left the office. Grant noticed she got into the jacked-up truck.

The nurse in the bright blue scrubs led him to the doctor's private office and he took a seat across a cluttered desk. The small office, filled with medical journals and books, had a faint musty odor. A small television occupied a corner behind the desk.

A man in his sixties breezed in and extended his hand. He had a thick head of white hair and wore wire-framed spectacles that were perched low in his nose.

"Mr. Collins?" he said, shaking Grant's hand. "I'm Dr. Witherspoon. Wilma said you are Helen Collins' son."

He indicated a chair and took his seat behind his desk. He cleared some files out of the way and looked at Grant.

"Yes, doctor. I wanted to talk to you about her accident."

"Of course," Witherspoon said. "So sorry about your

mother. She was a pillar of our community for many years. It was so tragic."

"I understand you were at the scene of the accident," Grant said.

He watched the doctor straighten his white coat and adjust his tie. He removed his stethoscope from a pocket and set it on the desk.

"Yes, I was."

"The police told me you signed her cause of death as accidental. Is that right?"

The doctor squirmed in his chair obviously not comfortable with someone questioning his actions. "It was an accident," he said. "Fairly obvious."

"How so, doctor?" Grant said.

"Well for one thing there were no obvious signs of foul play. She had suffered a severe head injury. There was bruising and blood on her face as well as the cracked windshield. For another thing I attended your mother for a number of years. She had high blood pressure. It's a risk factor for heart attack or stroke. Finally, the police determined that she left the road at a high rate of speed and hit the bridge abutment. I believe she was already dead when she hit the bridge."

"But an autopsy could easily have determined whether or not she died as you believe. Why not do one and be sure?"

The doctor fidgeted again and peered at Grant over his glasses. A furrow formed between his eyebrows.

"Like I said, Mr. Collins. I believed she died of natural causes and signed her death certificate, indicating that professional opinion."

"If you had simply done an autopsy there would be no questions as there are now," Grant said, the tone of his voice sounding much harsher.

"What questions? I was well within the scope of my

duties in doing so. One doesn't always need an autopsy to determine a cause of death."

Grant smiled. "Any way I can see her medical file?"

"Not without a court order," Witherspoon responded. "There's not a signed release of information in her file."

"But she was my mother," Grant protested.

"Like I said, not without a court order."

"Well—" Grant said.

"I'm pretty busy, Mr. Collins. Unless you have other questions—"

"No, that's fine." Grant stood. "I thank you for your time."

ↄ∙ↄↄ

It was a busy evening at the diner. For most of the evening dinner rush hour the place was packed with patrons. While Carrie waited tables her mind was occupied with thoughts of Grant. She went about the business of waiting on customers with methodical efficiency but mentally she was elsewhere. Grant had become important to her and the hurt he was living through touched her heart in a way quite unexpected. He was different than most men she knew in Trinity, calm and serious, not at all the shallow personalities of most of her acquaintances. She wanted to hold him, comfort him, be a part of his life. He seemed to need her companionship and for now, that was enough for her. It hadn't taken but a few days but she thought of him often, especially now that he was at the library, searching for previous deaths in Trinity.

She couldn't understand how the woman Miss Spelling had wound up in the river, the victim of a drug overdose. The woman came to diner frequently for lunch and Carrie never suspected that she was on drugs. It was a mystery for the woman didn't look the type. She knew

Lori worked at the college. She would come to the diner
with a few of her friends and the group always seemed
cheerful, with them laughing and talking animatedly.
Carrie didn't know the woman any better than that but
felt she could tell things about her customers. She could
spot a creep, a man who wanted to see her after work,
and a the immature college kids who dropped in from
time to time. The few women that ordered lunch wearing
their diamonds and other fine jewelry she knew were the
banker's and other businessmen's wives. They acted
condescending and left small tips. So, she didn't understand the newspaper article describing Lori's death as
one related to drugs. It just didn't figure. Or at least that's
how Carrie saw it.

She was supposed to meet Grant after she got off
work when the library closed. Maybe they would go to
her place for a beer or drive down by the river and listen
to music on the car radio. She cleaned a table and placed
menus in front of an elderly couple in the rear of the diner. The place was busy tonight.

ℰℭℭℭ

Grant looked at his watch. Eight-thirty. Close to closing time, there was only one other person in the library.
Beside him on the table there was still a tall stack of
Trinity Eagle newspapers. He had been looking through
back issues of the papers but as yet not come across any
accidental deaths or murders. There were a few deaths by
natural causes of some of the town's senior citizens but
nothing suspicious. At nine he would pick up Carrie. He
pulled another paper off the stack and began thumbing
through it. It was from three weeks ago.

On Page two there was something—a short article
under a small headline

WOMAN DROWNS IN HOME POOL

A forty-two year old Trinity resident drowned in the family swimming pool Sunday. Police stated the woman, identified as Cybil Nottingham, had been drinking prior to falling in the pool. Family and friends had gathered at the home for an intimate party and no one saw the woman fall into the pool. She was unable to be revived by paramedics.

Grant took a notepad from his hip pocket and copied the article along with the date of the newspaper. On the surface the woman's death seemed like just another tragedy in a world full of tragedies. The woman's family were probably the only people still mourning the loss of their loved one. He checked the time. Eight-forty-two. He still had a few minutes.

He browsed through three more papers until someone announced that the library was closing.

So there it was. Another death in the past six to eight weeks, three if you included Lori and his mother. It seemed like a lot of accidental deaths for a small town. Two drownings and an auto related death. Well, Lori's drowning might have occurred another way—the autopsy report should be out in the next day or two. At the moment it was impossible to say anything more about the deaths other than that they occurred. But still it belied statistics that a town the size of Trinity would have three accidental deaths in so short a time. He would be interested in what Carrie had to say about them.

He checked the time again. Eight-fifty-seven. Returning the notebook to his pocket, he sauntered out of the library into the warm night. The last rays of the sunset were fading in the western sky and the sweet scent of honeysuckle wafted on a gentle breeze. Grant eased himself into his car and headed to the diner. There were only two cars in the parking lot and he pulled into the slot next to the front door and waited. Soon Carrie emerged and slid into the passenger seat. She had put on fresh lipstick.

"Hi," she said, touching his arm. "Take me home, I'm glad today is over."

"Rough day?" Grant asked as he pulled the Celica out of the parking lot.

"Busy dinner hour. The usual rush was worse than normal. How has your day been?"

"We need to talk. But Mom's car is gone. It wasn't at the salvage yard."

"You talked with Buck?" Carrie said. She rolled down her window and took a deep breath of the humid night air, a heady mix of river and dark earth.

Grant chuckled. "Yeah. Good ole Buck. He wasn't much help."

"What about the title? Can you just get rid of a car without its title?"

"If no one is around to claim the car you file a lost title claim and there goes the car. Simple. And no one knew how to contact me."

"No luck with Lori's car either, I take it?"

"None. But there has been another accidental death that needs explaining. That's what I want to show you."

Grant pulled up at Carrie's garage apartment. Inside, she brought out two beers from the fridge and they sat together on her sofa. He produced his notebook.

"First of all, there is a woman who drowns in the family swimming pool. Cybil Nottingham."

"Yes, I think I remember that," Carrie said.

"Is it an accident? It appears to be. Then there's Lori's death and finally, my mother. Three deaths, Carrie, all in a relatively short period of time. Is it just coincidence? Were these all just simple accidents that happened to unlucky people? It seems like a lot of accidental deaths in a short time span for a town no larger than Trinity. What do you think?"

"First, Grant," she said. "I need a shower. I feel slimy. I'll think about it while I'm bathing then we can discuss it. Finish your beer and I'll be right back. There's more in the fridge."

Carrie disappeared into her bedroom before he had a chance to say anything and he soon heard the water running. When she returned fifteen minutes later she was dressed in jeans and a tee-shirt. Her damp hair smelled of roses.

"Have you eaten? I'm starved. Care for a sandwich?" she said from the kitchen doorway.

"Golly," Grant said. "I totally forgot about eating. I am hungry. A sandwich sounds great." He followed her into the kitchen and sat at the small table while she worked. "Didn't eat at work?" he said.

She shook her head. "No, too busy."

"So," he said, "what do you think?"

"Well, you certainly have been a busy boy today. For starters, I agree that it appears too coincidental, those deaths in a short period of time."

"Know anything about this woman who drowned in the family pool?" Grant said.

Carrie brought two plates to the table and set them down. "I hope ham and Swiss is okay, it's all I had."

Grant nodded and she handed him another beer and continued.

"Not really. But now that you mention it I do remember when it made the news. I didn't know the woman but the owner of the diner did. I remember him saying the woman was a good swimmer and there was no reason she should have drowned."

"Did the police investigate?" Grant began munching his sandwich.

"Dunno. I presume so, but don't know for sure."

"Did she work here in town?"

"Don't know that either. Grant, I can ask Deke if he remembers anything more about the woman if you want."

"Deke?"

"Yeah, he owns the *Trinity Cafe*. Has for years."

"If you don't mind, it might help shed some light on her death."

"But your mother. That was an accident, pure and simple. An unfortunate one, to be sure. I'm sorry."

He swallowed a mouthful of his sandwich and took a gulp of the beer. "What makes you say that? I'm not so sure, Carrie. An autopsy was never done. I've been thinking about the damage to the rear end of her car Sergeant Brady mentioned. Someone could have hit her from behind and shoved her into that abutment. That's why I wanted to look at the car myself. Mom never told me she had been rear-ended or bumped into something. It doesn't add up."

"Maybe your mother was embarrassed about bumping into something and didn't want to mention it to you. I would think the police would have pictures." Carrie talked between bites of her sandwich. "Don't they usually take photographs of an accident scene?"

"Sergeant Brady showed them to me. Not much to go on there."

"But, if those deaths, including your mother's, were anything but accidental, what would that mean?"

"That they had happened on purpose."

"Caused to happen?"

"By someone, or someones, yes."

"But why? If there was anything suspicious about the accident I'm sure the police would have investigated." Carrie took the empty plates and placed them in the sink and returned to the table. Her gentle smile caused Grant's heart to skip a beat. Gosh, she was lovely to look at. She took his hand in hers across the table and gave it a gentle squeeze. "Why?" she repeated. "Why would someone cause these deaths?"

"I dunno. That *why* would be a big question if they weren't accidents. Maybe I'm just grieving over mom's death a little too much and am trying to put blame somewhere it doesn't belong. It's just that—"

"Grant, no one grieves *too* much. It's natural that you look for answers. Hers was an untimely death which makes it even more likely you'll question the how and why of it. Don't berate yourself for asking questions."

"It's just that the damage to the rear of her car is suspicious, that's all. If it weren't for that, things might look different. And when I spoke with the Medical Examiner, a Dr. Witherspoon—"

"Yes," Carries said. "He's been a doctor in Trinity for many years.

"When I spoke with Dr. Witherspoon, he hadn't done an autopsy. Just ruled it an accident without so much as any evidence. You know the man?"

"You mean have I been to him as a patient? No, I haven't. If I need a doctor I go to Savannah."

"Know anything about him?"

"Only that he's been in practice here for a long time."

"He was Mom's physician," Grant said, taking a swallow of his beer. "And when I asked if I could see her medical record he said not without a court order."

"Well—"

"Well, it's odd, that's all. Why would he care if I looked through Mom's medical chart? She's dead now. Unless—"

"Unless what?" Carrie said between mouthfuls of sandwich.

"Unless there was something in it that he didn't wish me to see."

"I suppose. You gonna ask the police if you can see the pictures of her car again?"

"First thing tomorrow, you bet.

"Grant, don't take this question the wrong way but you mentioned earlier that you hadn't been to see your mother very often over the last few years." She waited and he nodded. "Well, isn't it possible that you're feeling guilty over that and if her death wasn't an accident it might dispel some of that guilt? That you're seeing conspiracies where none exist?"

Grant looked her for a long silent moment. A lump formed in his throat as he considered the possibility that Carrie suggested. "I don't think so. I guess it's possible but I don't think so. You just said I shouldn't berate myself for these questions. The two drownings seem innocent enough. But Lori's death has really knocked me back. It came out of the blue."

"You were having feelings for her?"

"Not in the way you are implying," Grant said. "It's just that we had lunch, talked a while. We dated a few times in high school. Then suddenly, she's dead. Kind of a shock."

Carrie stood, put an arm around him, and kissed his cheek. "Hey now. I know what you need. Come to bed and let me make you feel better. A good night's sleep and you'll be a new man."

℘℘℘

Mayor Bruce Baxter sat alone in the darkened study of his house on the edge of town. A bottle of Kentucky bourbon was on the desk, half full, for he had downed several drinks since his wife had fallen asleep. However, he could not sleep, so after hearing her rhythmic quiet snoring, had risen and went to his study. His deal with Winston Conway would realize him a huge fortune if he could push the power plant through the city council. And doing that depended on public sentiment, which at present, was only slightly in his favor. He needed something, a new slant on the campaign or an incident, which would sway public opinion decidedly toward the plant's construction. The recent hearings had gone against DynaTech and the Collins and Spelling women's articulate denunciation of the plant had made the evening edition of the *Eagle*. If he threatened the few council members in order to get the vote passed and the public was actually against the plant, it could be bad.

Baxter poured himself another generous shot of the bourbon and settled back in his leather chair. The Citizens Against Nuclear Power group that had formed in Trinity certainly had the local paper on their side. The elderly Collins woman, although a widow and not earlier known for environmental activism, had become a dynamic spokesperson against DynaTech and its proposed power plant. From what his aides told him the Spelling girl had come under the woman's spell and joined the group only a month earlier but her diatribe at the hearing was passionate and might be convincing. He had not known either woman personally but they seemed genuinely concerned about Trinity's future. But in a way, their deaths were good news to him. Two less voices in opposition to his financial future.

What kind of incident could be manipulated to push the town's sentiment toward the building of the plant? More rallies? Get the governor involved with a personal visit? Better still, possibly an electric blackout or brownout that would silence the critics once and for all?

As Baxter sipped the liquor he felt its satisfying burn

down his throat and pondered the possibilities. Something had to happen, that was for sure. The stakes were too high, his future too unsettled, to let the power plant project fail. In his mind, the CANP's environmental objections were based on inexact science and emotional fear mongering. Their concerns over another Three Mile Island accident were unfounded in these days of better construction methods and governmental oversight. People were nervous about nuclear power in the wake of the disaster at the Japan nuclear power plant, questioning whether nuclear power was a sensible option for energy production in light of the perceived risks.

In fact, the disaster showed how safe nuclear reactors actually are. Reactors designed half a century ago survived an earthquake many times stronger than they were designed to withstand, immediately going into shutdown, bringing driven nuclear reactions to a halt. But the radioactive products in the reactor kept decaying, producing heat, so they had to be cooled.

The real problems began when the tsunami took out all the back-up generators that were meant to provide power to circulate the coolant. Loss of site power was the worst-case scenario for a nuclear power plant, so for Fukushima this was the worst crisis imaginable. New reactors had improved safety features, including passive systems that allow cooling to take place without power.

From what Winston Conway had told him in their meetings together modern nuclear power reactors were safe and efficient and used all over Europe. There were too many built-in safeguards that would prevent a meltdown and leakage of radiation into the atmosphere. Currently, nuclear waste created in the US was stored underwater in spent fuel pools near nuclear power plants. Assuming the DOE eventually licenses the Yucca Mountain repository in Nevada, this waste would eventually be stored deep underground. Since Yucca Mountain was on a Nevada test site, and since the area is geologically stable, the location is suitable. However, the repository was designed to a certain capacity of nuclear waste. If it ever opened, it would fill quickly thanks to the build-up of waste throughout the last few decades and another repository would need to be constructed. But he wasn't enough of a science person to really understand the details and that fact concerned him. He needed to get some quick education if he was going to be an advocate for DynaTech. And maybe along the way an incident might just happen in his favor.

Chapter 8

The sky was overcast with flat gray clouds allowing the sun to filter weakly through them. It was a depressing morning. Grant parked his rental car in the police station parking lot and found Sergeant Brady drinking coffee in his office.

"Come in, Mr. Collins," he said, blowing steam off the coffee's surface. "To what do I owe the pleasure of this visit?"

"Two things," Grant said, taking the seat in the chair indicated by Brady. "First, I would like to again look at the pictures taken of my mother's vehicle. Especially, if you have any I have not seen." He waited while Brady took a sip of his coffee.

"I think we could accommodate that request. What else?"

"Has the autopsy been completed on Miss Spelling? If so, I was wondering if you would share the results."

Grant shifted in his chair, his palms damp.

"Actually, Mr. Collins, the report was faxed from Atlanta just this morning. I have it right here."

Brady shuffled through papers on his desk, producing a document that he scanned briefly.

"Says here her system was full of cocaine and other drugs. Take a look for yourself."

Brady handed the report to Grant who saw the critical passage highlighted.

Toxicology results: Blood: Ethanol, 0.261%, Cocaine 0.043 mg/L, Cocaethylene 0.092 mg/L; THC, Not Detected. Urine: Ethanol, 0.241%, Cocaine 7.549 mg/L, Cocaethylene 7.749 mg/L, THC, Not Detected

"I'm not a medical person, Sergeant. Translate, please."

Brady took the report from Grant and studied it for a moment.

"All too typical of mixed overdose and intoxication death with cocaine and alcohol. The victim used cocaine within a short period prior to death. There was no marijuana in her system."

"I can't believe it," Grant said, stunned at the revelations. "She didn't seem like that sort of woman. I understand she worked at the college. My friend, Carrie, says she saw her at the diner often. Never acted or looked like a drug abuser."

"Well, Mr. Collins, you never know about people's private lives."

He returned the report to the stack of papers on his desk and lit a cigarette.

"I suppose that's right." Grant's voice weakened. "Did you know her?"

"Nope, sure didn't."

"What about the autopsy? The results?"

"An autopsy wasn't performed," Brady said. "Doc Witherspoon certified the cause of death based on the toxicology report."

"He examine the body?" Grant was becoming quite irritated at the circular discussion.

"Yes. I believe I mentioned that on your last visit here."

"Yeah, I spoke with him. Got rather irritated when I asked to see Mom's medical record.

Brady chuckled. "Old Doc can be exasperating at times."

"If he didn't do an autopsy, then how did he get the blood for toxicology testing?" Grant's voice had an edge to it.

"Can't say. The body was taken to his office for him to do whatever and then it was released to the funeral home."

"Sergeant, I can't believe this. No medical examiner worth their salt would run a toxicology screen after a death such as this without doing an autopsy as well. What kind of place is Trinity?" Grant was breathing hard, his pulse pounded in his head. It sounded like gross incompetence.

"Mr. Collins," Brady said, "you're treading on thin ice now."

"Has her car been found?"

"Not as yet. We've put a tracer on her tag so it's just a matter of time before it turns up."

"What about the pictures of Mom's car?"

"I showed them to you once," Brady said and retrieved them from a manila folder in his filing cabinet. "But here they are." He tossed them on his desk.

"Any I haven't seen?" Grant asked, looking through the familiar photos.

There were four photographs of Helen's car, two showing the front and two showing the rear. Three of them he had not seen before. The left front part of the small car was pushed into the driver's seat, the twisted metal causing Grant's stomach to churn. The one he hadn't seen before was of Helen's rear bumper and it was crumpled severely, more than what he thought should happen in a simple rear end accident. Part of the car's trunk was mangled as well.

"The rear of her car looks more damaged than a simple accident would render, Sergeant. Don't you think? Look how the trunk is even pushed way in."

He handed the photograph back to Brady and pointed to the car's rear.

The man nodded. "That is possible but there was no paint residue on the bumper to make any conclusions possible. It looked like an old accident to me when I was at the scene."

"But it is possible someone could have pushed her from behind into that bridge abutment, right? You will have to agree with that."

"I suppose it's possible, Mr. Collins. But is it probable? I don't think so. Who would want to kill your mother? Any ideas there?"

"No, but that does not mean there wasn't someone. I haven't visited in a while so I don't know that much about her life here in Trinity. Maybe I should have been closer to her but it's too late now."

"If you turn up anything, be sure and let me know. And I don't want you to leave town just yet, not until we close the Spelling case. Maybe in a day or two."

Frustrated, Grant left the police station and drove to Carrie's and picked her up, then headed to his mother's house. Along the way he brought her up to date.

"So that's it. Lori's body was full of drugs and the police are calling it an overdose but they still haven't located her car. Mom's car could have been pushed from the rear but there's no evidence to support that theory. I'm about ready to give up and go home when the sergeant gives me the go-ahead. I need to get back to DC soon."

"Where to now?" Carrie said.

"I want to drop by Mom's house, see if I can locate Mrs. Bullock. She's a friend of mother's and had the key to the house. I'd like to talk to her, again."

"Have you looked through the house?" Carrie said. "I mean really searched the place? There might be something there that would help ease your mind about her death."

"Not really. I did find a brochure from her action group but haven't searched the house. Can you help?"

"Sure," Carrie said.

Together they began a systematic search of his mother's house beginning with the living room and ending with the two bedrooms. All they found were her the usual family knickknacks and a few jewelry items.

And a key.

In her jewelry box.

With the number one-one-seven stamped on its side.

"What do you suppose it is?" asked Carrie as Grant held the key in his hand.

"My guess would be a safe deposit box," Grant said turning the key over. *Trinity State Bank* was stamped in small letters on the reverse side.

Next to the telephone, Carrie found a small notebook with phone numbers. In it was Mrs. Bullock's number. When Grant talked to her, she said she would be happy to see him again and to come right over. She was baking cookies.

Mrs. Bullock's house was located on the eastern edge of town a few minutes' drive from Helen's and the woman answered the door with the first ring of the bell.

"Oh, come on in," she said, glancing at Carrie and smiling.

Grant closed the door and took Carrie's elbow.

"Mrs. Bullock, this is my friend Carrie." The two women smiled and nodded at each other. "As I said on the phone, I was hoping you could fill me in on my mother."

"Please," Mrs. Bullock interrupted, "let's sit in the dining room where I can keep an eye on my cookies."

The gray-headed woman wore an apron and led Grant and Carrie into a dining room that seemed reminiscent of a previous era. Knickknacks lined every horizontal surface and there were pictures of whom Grant surmised were of her family. A large portrait of a man hung on the wall over an antique credenza and Grant hesitated in front of it.

"My husband, John," Mrs. Bullock said. "We were married for fifty-one years before he died. He's been gone three years now and I still miss him."

"I'm sure," Carrie said from Grant's side. "He's a handsome man."

They each took a seat around a polished walnut table and after Mrs. Bullock returned from the kitchen, Grant continued.

"What was mother's life like, the last few years?" he asked. "Did she seem happy? Were the two of you very close?"

"Oh my, where to start. Helen, your mother, was a very gracious lady and a friend to everyone. She attended church every Sunday. Helen always mentioned how proud of you she was but wished you would come to see her more often."

"I was never very good about visiting," Grant said, ruefully.

"Before she became involved with the power plant ordeal," Hazel said, "Helen and I would spend several days a week cooking together and chatting. Mostly about family, past remembrances, life in general, our eventual deaths. She was very pragmatic about dying, hoped her own death wouldn't hurt. In a way, I think she looked forward to seeing Herb and Eric again. She read her Bible every day."

"I don't remember mother being overly religious," Grant said.

"This past year she was very busy campaigning against the power plant. For a woman of her age she was extremely active and dedicated to keeping nuclear power out of Trinity."

"Yes," Grant said, leaning forward on the walnut table. He could see his reflection in it. "Tell me more about her involvement with the citizen's group."

"Not much to tell, really. She had the hope that a petition signed by most of Trinity's residents would sink the power plant. So, this past month she was totally consumed with it. She spent almost every day going door-to-door trying to get signatures on her petition or organizing anti-nuclear rallies here in town. I think she had been to every neighborhood in Trinity. She spoke at the several town hall meetings the mayor had convened regarding the plant. She was a real dynamo."

"It's hard to picture Mom as an activist," Grant said. "A protestor."

"Yes, I know. Before all the fuss over the plant Helen spent most days reading her Bible and watching television. She loved *Wheel of Fortune*."

"What got her interested in nuclear power?" Carrie interjected.

"That's a good question. She never did say. It was as if it just came to her one day, like an epiphany."

"Did she have any enemies because of her activism?"

Mrs. Bullock rose and went into the kitchen and returned with a plate of warm cookies.

"Fresh out of the oven," she said. "Help yourselves."

Grant and Carrie each took a cookie. Carrie nodded in appreciation.

"I don't know about actual enemies but I'm sure there were folks who would rather have seen her stop all her campaigning. The mayor, for one. He's for the power plant coming to town. It wouldn't surprise me if some people were pulling some fast ones in order to get the plant passed by the city council. But killing your mother? I don't know about that."

"Lori Spelling, the girl found in the river, worked with mother, right?"

"She did, yes, and now the poor child is dead. Poor dear."

"Did you know her, Mrs. Bullock?" Carrie said, her mouth full of cookie.

"Only slightly through Helen's work against the plant. The past months the two were almost inseparable."

"And now she's dead," said Grant, repeating Hazel's description.

He removed his notebook from a hip pocket and turned to his notes on the recent deaths in Trinity.

"The woman who drowned in the family pool—"

"Cybil Nottingham? Yes, I was acquainted with her. She worked on the citizen's committee with Helen."

Grant shot a glance at Carrie who frowned and took another cookie. She stared at the old woman.

Mrs. Bullock put a hand to her mouth then left the table for the kitchen, leaving Grant and Carrie staring at each other in quiet disbelief. After a moment, Grant spoke, his mouth dry as a cotton ball in the desert.

"Did you hear that?" he said. "The woman who drowned in her swimming pool worked on the Citizens Against Nuclear Power committee. Each of Trinity's last three deaths were committee members. That can't be a coincidence. Tell me if I'm wrong." A wave of nausea coursed through Grant, his temples pounded.

Carrie shook her head. "I don't think you're wrong. And you need to go back to the police and give them this information. I'm sure they will want to know what you've uncovered."

When Mrs. Bullock returned from the kitchen, Grant and Carrie excused themselves and headed to the police station. Sergeant Brady was not there and the officer at the desk did not know when he would return.

"There's a cafe south of town on the river," Carrie said. "Care to grab something to eat while we discuss these latest developments? They have great fried catfish."

"Sure," Grant said. "Sounds good. Point the way."

The clouds were beginning to dissipate, revealing a sun high in the sky. The air was warm and pleasant so Carrie rolled down her window and let the sounds and smells of the river drift into the car. The narrow road ran a winding course along the Dogwood River and as they left the town behind the houses became fewer in number. They passed an abandoned lumber mill that Carrie said had closed up years earlier when the owner murdered his wife then committed suicide by ingesting rat poison. The structure rested on a natural cove in the river, the dilapidated office building and sawmill having fallen into disrepair. Through large holes in the buildings Grant got glimpses of the river.

Pete's Crab Shack stood on a pier that jutted out into the Dogwood River and was built of logs and aging lumber. Grant pulled into the tiny parking lot and he and Carrie walked into a near empty restaurant and were seated at a table overlooking the river. The log rafters combined with the wooden floors and gave the place the look of southern charm. Over a lunch of catfish and fries they chatted about the recent turn of events.

"The whole thing is weird," Carrie said. "I don't know what to make of it all."

"The coincidence angle is too much to overlook," Grant said. "It can't be coincidence. With all that's riding on the power plant coming to Trinity, these happenings can't be coincidence. Here's what I'm beginning to think. A vote on a nuclear reactor is coming up soon on the city council and certain antagonists to the plant, members of a citizen's committee, have turned up dead within weeks of the council vote. What does that suggest to you?"

"Any uninterested party would say there's a relation-ship somewhere there."

"Well, those same uninterested parties would say these people were murdered to get them out of the way so the vote would go through the city council. Let's not mince words. That's what we're talking about in a roundabout way, isn't it?"

"It's not a very nice word, Grant. Murder. I can't be-lieve we are sitting here talking casually about this. Hel-en was your mother, for god's sake."

"I know, I know. Let's get out of here, okay? I've kinda lost my appetite."

The two of them sat in silence on the drive back to Trinity.

Chapter 9

Winston Conway studied the man across from him and wondered how Trinity could have elected the man its mayor. Bruce Baxter seemed to Conway to be a few shovelfuls shy of a full load and now, sitting in the man's office and listening to him, Trinity's mayor confirmed that impression. He had arrived in Trinity to check on the status of the upcoming council vote on his power plant and he wanted Baxter's firsthand analysis of how everything was going. The man's incoherent ramblings left him unsure if he could trust the man's opinion. The furnishings of the mayor's office were luxurious to be sure and Conway had settled deep into a tufted leather chair near a window. He sipped a cup of coffee from a large ceramic mug.

"So, Bruce, what's the breakdown on the council? We got the votes or not? Time's is getting short." He toyed with his silk tie as he spoke and observed Baxter's reaction. He needed the man to focus on the task at hand.

The mayor shifted in his chair, seemingly uneasy in Conway's presence. He cleared his throat. "There are four councilmen and myself on the city council, Winston, and as yet I don't have a handle on how two of them are leaning. One of them is Hollister McLain, who was friends with the Collins woman, so he might be a problem. The other is Bob Bennett. He is a progressive thinker so he'll likely be in favor of the plant, but I don't know for sure."

"The McLain could mean trouble? If he votes against the plant and the other man votes for, then the vote would be tied, right? You would cast the deciding vote. Doesn't sound all that worrisome to me, Bruce."

Conway took a gulp of his coffee and set the mug on a nearby table stacked with magazines. Talking with Baxter was always a trying affair, usually a circuitous one leading to confusion. The man fidgeted in his chair as if worried. He sensed something was troubling the mayor and he was determined to find out what it was. He continued.

"Unless you know something you haven't shared yet."

"Well," Baxter said. Conway thought he detected a nervous tick in the man's voice. "Bob Bennett isn't a lock for our side, Winston. I mean, I think he's on board with the plant but I don't know for sure. I haven't spoken to him about the deal."

"You what?" Conway blurted out. "The vote is almost upon us and you say you haven't talked to the man? Even bothered to do a little old-fashioned cajoling or arm-twisting? Christ, man."

Baxter was visibly shaken by Conway's sudden outburst and lit a cigarette with trembling hands. He took a deep breath as if to calm himself.

"I've been busy with other mayoral duties, Winston, and have been meaning to get around to doing just that. I think we half to consider public opinion. If it's against us it will be a long haul to get the plant up and running."

"I really don't care about public opinion, Bruce. You should know that by now."

"Well, there's another thing. The Collins woman's son is in town and is poking around, asking questions."

"What kind of questions?" Conway emptied his mug and leaned forward in his chair.

"Asking the particulars about his mother's accident and death. He's been to the police. And the library."

"The library?" said Conway. "Whatever for?"

"I dunno. Research, I suppose.

"I don't like it, Mayor. Is it possible he could uncover something to derail this project?"

"Possibly. I don't know."

"Not good, Bruce. Not good at all." Conway leaned forward and gave Baxter a solemn look.

"Yeah," Baxter said. His hand twitched visibly.

"Time is running out," Conway said, his voice still showing irritation. "What's more important than a few million in your pocket, Bruce?"

Baxter was silent and puffed his cigarette nervously.

"Nothing, of course," he said.

"Listen up, Bruce. If this deal falls through it's going to be your head. Understand? I've got a fortune tied up in this thing already so you've got to deliver on your end. If you don't I'm going to come looking for you."

"Well, two of the town's most vocal opponents are no longer with us, so that helps. A nice coincidence."

Conway stared at Baxter through narrowed eyes.

"Coincidence? What makes you so sure it was a coincidence? Things don't always happen by chance."

A long silence ensued as Baxter looked at Conway, a shocked expression on his face. "Are you saying—"

"I'm not saying anything, Mayor, except this. This nuclear plant is important to me and if you screw it up, there's going to be hell to pay. I've got a ton of money tied up in this thing and if it all goes down the drain..." His voice trailed off for a moment, allowing his words to sink in. "Now, I suggest you get busy and get the council behind us."

Conway stood to leave and Baxter walked him to the office door. As he walked to his car he wondered if the mayor was up to the task.

୧୬୧୬

Grant dropped Carrie off at work and continued on to the police station. He found Sergeant Brady closing the door to his office.

"Can I have a minute, Sergeant?" he said, approaching the officer.

"Just leaving," Brady said. "Got some field work to do."

"On my mother's accident?"

"No," came Brady's short reply.

Grant stood in the hallway of the police station, hoping to slow the officer's departure. "I was hoping," he said, "to show you a headline I found in the local newspaper. I thought you might find it interesting. It will only take a few minutes."

"Look, Mr. Collins. It might just interest you to know that your mother's accident and unfortunate death aren't the only things going on in Trinity that requires my attention at the moment. So, if you please."

"Miss Spelling? Anything new on her?"

"Mr. Collins, I don't have time for this. I'm in a hurry and you are interfering with police business at this very moment. Now, excuse me."

Brady stared at Grant for a moment, his eyes fixed in an intimidating gaze. With that, the police sergeant pushed past Grant, bumping his shoulder in an aggressive way, and exited the building. Grant stood, wondering why the sudden change in the officer's attitude.

He decided to drive back to the scene of his mother's accident. He turned on Euclid and made his way to the bridge crossing. At the edge of town he glanced in his rear view mirror and noticed a black jacked-up truck behind him with two men inside. He continued on to the bridge and pulled his rental car to the side of the road, stopped, and got out. He strolled over to the abutment and looked at the bridge. A concrete and steel trestle affair, it spanned the Dogwood River some thirty feet below and connected Trinity with the farmlands east of the river. The ground broke sharply next to the bridge and contained boulder outcroppings all the way down to the water that ran slow and deep on its course to the Savannah. Dense underbrush grew among the rocks while oaks and poplars towered above. A harsh bright sun caused Grant to sweat. As he headed back to his car, the black pickup pulled in behind. It had orange and red flames along its sides. Two men dressed in jeans and wife-beater shirts climbed out and sauntered toward him.

Grant's pulse quickened. "Hi," he said, trying to sound nonchalant.

The men continued to approach.

"What can I do for you?" he continued.

When the men were closer, Grant could see the grease-stained jeans, their unkempt hair. One of them had both arms covered with tattoos.

"Mister," the tattooed one said. "What are you doing round these parts? Stranger, ain't ya?" he snarled, revealing black teeth. His nose was bent to one side, the obvious result of previous trauma.

"My mom was killed at this bridge," Grant said, warily. His pulse quickened. "I was just checking it out. Hope you fellas don't mind."

"Oh, but we do mind," said the second man. He sported a faded ragged baseball cap with a logo that was unrecognizable to Grant. "We don't like you in our town."

Grant had the funny feeling this was not going to end well. He deplored fist fighting but was taught hand combat skills in the marines. "Sorry," Grant said. He started for his car but the two men blocked his way.

"Not so fast, bud," the tattooed man said. "I don't think you heard my friend here. He said we don't want you in Trinity. Didn't you understand that?"

Grant quickly tried to size up the situation. There was going to be a fight ,and he was going to lose, that was plain enough. But if it were to happen he would make them earn it. His combat self-defense training in the marines would see to that. He stepped back several paces. The tattooed man was the leader, the instigator, so he would have to hit him first and hope the other man didn't react too quickly. There was no point in talking, no point in arguing. The sooner it was over the sooner he could get back to town and Carrie. He just hoped it wasn't going to hurt too much.

The tattooed one took several steps in his direction while the other held back. They circled each other for a minute while Grant glanced back and forth between the two men. Grant took a deep breath and rushed the man hitting him in the stomach and knocking him to the ground. He tumbled on top of the man and landed a punch directly on his bent nose. Blood gushed forth and spewed onto the man's wife-beater shirt. He pitched Grant off of him, sent him rolling. When he regained his feet, the other man grabbed him from behind, spun him around, and head-butted Grant's forehead. For a moment he was blinded by a sudden flash of white light then his own blood running into his eyes.

The tattooed man got up and stumbled toward Grant who again rushed the man. After locking arms, the two of them went sprawling into the dirt with the tattooed man punching away at Grant's head. Each time he connected, it sent a shower of sparks through his brain.

Somehow Grant managed to get to his feet just as the second man hit him from behind. Grant collapsed to the ground and, out of the corner of his eye, he saw the tattooed man charge. He struggled to his hands and knees and grappled the man about his waist and dug in with his toes and pushed off. The man toppled onto his back with Grant miraculously on top of him. A few quick blows to his face caused the man to grunt in pain. The man had a large, soft face and blood stained his blackened teeth. For a moment, Grant thought the man had been a professional wrestler for his arms were as big as his own thighs. The man grabbed Grant by the throat with powerful hands. Grant gasped for air. Bringing his hands up between the man's arms, he smashed his nose. The big man howled in pain.

A blow hit Grant from behind when the tattooed man pounced on him rolling him off his buddy. Grant struggled to his feet, his head reeling from the successive blows. His knees buckled, his vision blurred. The tattooed one stood directly in front of him but the second man was nowhere to be seen. Then Grant felt those powerful arms close around him from behind pinning his arms to his sides.

No amount of struggling could free Grant from the man's grasp. The tattooed man limped toward him, seething, fists clenched.

"Here's where you go down, buster," he hissed. Then he hit Grant in the head with something hard. As the lights went out, Grant felt the blows reigning into his midsection until there was nothing but blackness.

ℰↃℰↃ

It was dark when Grant regained consciousness, rolled onto his back. His mouth tasted like metal, his body howled with each move of his limbs. He touched his eyes and winced. He looked around. The fuzzy outline of his rental car stood next to the bridge where he left it. Only the bleating of tree frogs and the occasional splash in the river pierced the quiet of the night. A yellow moon rose over the valley east of the river casting enough light for him to stumble to his car. He leaned on the hood, chest heaving, with every sinew and joint aching. Especially his knuckles.

It took a while fumbling with the door handle but he got it open then fell into the driver's seat. After starting the car, he sat for a moment, looked at himself in the rearview mirror. A bruised and battered face stared back. He flinched at the sight. His watch read nine-thirty-three so Carrie would have already been off work for a half hour. Was she still waiting at the diner, angry at his not showing, or had she walked the half-mile back to her apartment? He decided to drive to the diner first.

The diner was dark, the parking lot empty. Carrie was not there so he drove on to her garage apartment. It took effort but he struggled up the stairs. She must have heard his halting, clomping steps for as he reached her door it was flung open and she stood in the doorway, staring.

"My god!" she exclaimed, seeing his condition. "What happened to you?"

She took him by an arm, led him to the sofa.

"I was jumped by a couple of thugs," Grant blurted out.

"But why?" Carrie was still in shocked disbelief.

"I dunno. Just lucky I guess."

"Oh, sweetheart. You're beat to a pulp. Let me get some ice on those bruises." She left for the kitchen and soon returned with ice wrapped in a towel. "Here," she said. "Put this over that eye. It'll help the swelling. I can't believe this happened. Why would anyone do such a thing?"

"Two thugs who didn't want me in Trinity, that's for sure."

"You going to report this to the police?"

"Well," Grant said, holding the towel to his face. "That's a another story."

Chapter 10

While Carrie showered, Grant lay on her sofa, holding the ice pack on his face. He lay there thinking about had just happened. He had not gotten a good look at either of the men so reporting the assault to the police would go nowhere. It was doubtful he would be able to return the favor but the more he thought about it, the madder he got. Those goons were probably sitting in a bar somewhere regaling their buddies how they worked over a stranger half their size. Buying beers for everyone in the place. Patting each other on their backs. But they hadn't got away without a scratch. He had inflicted some damage of his own, if only minor.

However, as he continued to think about it, those oversized morons might still be in town, in fact, they might even live somewhere in Trinity. If that were the case, it would be a real stroke of luck if he could locate them or their truck. Payback might ease the pains in his head and face. There couldn't be many places in town where they could be. Later, when he felt better, he would take a drive around the town.

Carrie returned and checked the swelling on his face. She shook her head, kissed his cheek.

"You're going to have quite a bruise, there," she said, replacing the icepack. "Tell me again what happened."

Grant spent a few minutes retelling the story of his meeting at the bridge with the two men. He described them as best as he could.

"Never seen anyone like those two around here," Carrie said after listening to the men's description. "I've never seen anyone with that many tattoos in Trinity."

"You sure? People come through the diner all the time."

"Mostly regulars, Grant. We rarely get strangers eating at the diner. Once in a while someone or a small party of people might stop. People taking the scenic route on the way down to Savannah or Hilton Head Island. Otherwise, mostly just locals." She smoothed his hair with a soft caressing hand.

"Well," he said, "after I clean up, I'm going to try and find those goons. This time—"

"Grant," Carrie said, interrupting him, "don't do it. You could get really hurt. Please."

"No, this time will be different, I promise. I'm not going to let a couple of jerks get away with this."

"Just go to the police. That's the best option. File a complaint and let them handle it."

"You don't know me very well, if you're asking that of me. They're going to pay, one way or another."

"I don't understand why they jumped you like that." Carrie went into the kitchen and returned with two beers and plopped down next to him.

"They said something about not wanting me here but they didn't elaborate."

Grant gulped his beer hoping it would ease the throbbing in his head.

"If that police sergeant won't help, maybe you need to see the police chief. Go over the sergeant's head."

"I've thought of that."

"Maybe what happened has something to do with these deaths you've uncovered. And the power plant."

"But why?"

"I dunno. I'm sure there's a lot of money to be made if the plant goes through. Maybe someone doesn't want you snooping around, asking questions."

"Like who?"

Carrie got up off the sofa and paced about her small living room. "Well," she said, her hand rubbing her forehead, "I know the mayor has been campaigning in favor of the plant coming to town. Whoever owns DynaTech, the company who wants to build it. There's two right there."

"They would stoop to violence, you think? How well do you know the mayor?"

Carrie sat in her easy chair and thought for a moment.

"Not well at all. But you can't be naive, Grant. Surely people have done such things with a lost less at stake than this."

"No, I understand. I just don't know the politics or dynamics of your town. I'm sure there's millions to be made with the plant."

"Grant, I don't think this wasn't a random act of violence. We don't have that sort of thing here. Someone has targeted you for a reason and wants you out of town. You, a stranger, show up, ask a lot of questions about your mother's death, uncover some other deaths that appear to be related, and are assaulted. Follow the dots. It's logical that they are all related. And now I'm frightened for you."

"Don't be, I can take care of myself. But I'm going to find these guys and make them pay. I promise you that. Is there more than one bar in town?"

Carrie walked over and put her arms around his neck,

kissed him again on the cheek. "The popular one is down near Pete's Crab Shack. You can't miss it."

"Thanks," Grant said as he headed toward the door.

"Please, be careful," she said.

ↀↀↀ

Grant cruised Trinity in his rental car going up and down its side streets searching for the jacked up truck with flames along its sides. Before leaving Carrie's apartment he took a paring knife from a kitchen drawer and found the tire tool in the rental car's trunk. They lay on the passenger's seat next to him.

There wasn't much to the town's residential sections, a smaller subdivision of later model homes to the east expanding down to the river and an older addition to the south that was filled with mostly '50s and '60s style houses. He didn't expect to find the truck in the newer section and sure enough, he didn't. It was largely an up-scale neighborhood, probably business owners in Trinity and college professors, he figured. Single story homes with well-manicured lawns.

He headed toward the bar near Pete's. It was a rustic affair a block from the restaurant. A Dixie flag hung from a window and as he pulled up he heard the country music blaring all the way into the parking lot.

The bar was even more unrefined inside than its exterior suggested with bare rafters and a couple of ceiling fans. He squinted through the dim interior, figured it must be early for there were only a couple of patrons sipping longnecks at the bar. A large heavy-jowled man cleaned glasses behind the long polished counter while the men drinking eyed him with suspicion as he ambled to the bar. Grant motioned to the heavy-set man who returned his smile with a scowl.

"I'm looking for a couple of friends," Grant said. He smiled but it was not returned.

"Haven't seen you in here before," the bartender said. "What ya need?"

Grant glanced around the room and noticed that the other patrons were looking at him. It was hard to hear and talk over the blare of the music.

"Like I said, I was supposed to meet these fellas down at the Crab Shack but they haven't showed. I thought they might be in here."

"What they're names be?" the bartender demanded, still wiping the glasses, not looking at Grant.

"Well, that's a funny thing. I don't remember their names. Just met them, in fact. But one of them had both arms filled with tattoos and one of them drove a jacked-up pickup with flames in the side."

The bartender acted like he was listening and nodded. He continued to wipe the glasses.

"Know who I'm talking about?" Grant said. He didn't like the way things were shaping up. A couple of the patrons had moved closer to where he was standing.

"You just met them but you don't remember their names?" the bartender said.

"Well," Grant said, "I'm not too good with names. Know them?"

"I might," the big man said. "But then again I might not."

"Well, I can see you not going to be very cooperative," Grant said, turning and heading toward the door.

"You're in the wrong place, cowboy," the bartender called after him.

At the bar's doorway two men blocked Grant's exit. They smiled at him. He walked up to the men, stopped.

"Excuse me," he said.

The men stepped aside and as Grant passed, one of the men spoke.

"Like ole Jake says, mister, you're in the wrong place."

Back in his car, Grant headed back toward town, thinking. *What creeps*, he said to himself. He turned into the older neighborhood, slowed his speed. As he kept an eye out for the truck, he pondered what he would do if he found it. A plan had only partially formed in his mind and it didn't include another confrontation. That's why he brought the tire tool and knife. And Carrie had a point, a good one—why was this happening to him? When he had learned what all the deaths had in common was environmental activism against the power plant he realized that coincidence was out of the question. Those people had been murdered, plain and simple, and their deaths made to look accidental. Were the police complicit in a cover-up?

The brush-off he had been given by Sergeant Brady could be construed as not wanting to discuss anything further. Carrie again had pointed a finger at the two obvious persons with motive to eliminate all obstacles to the nuclear reactor coming to Trinity. The mayor and the owner of DynaTech, whoever he was. Grant hoped he could uncover that piece of information.

He turned left and drove down a narrow street. The houses here were definitely older, more rundown. Most had detached garages and the trees were taller. In a few places the oaks arched over the street touching each other creating a canopy, a tunnel of trees. The sun was on its downward arc and the air was humid, heavy, sweet. Bright azaleas bloomed in front of the houses and lent their fragrance to the air.

Was it possible his mother had been murdered? He dared not believe something so sinister but the facts were starting to point in that direction. He thought back on the times when she came to his room and sat on his bed and they talked. Mostly about school and girls he liked. She was always interested. When Eric died, something in his mother died along with his brother. By then he was in college or working and those times spent with mother became fewer and fewer. But to murder a sweet old woman? He was having a difficult time getting his mind around that.

On the surface, Trinity appeared to be a small quiet town in rural Georgia, a town where people were peaceful and neighborly. It had been years since he lived here so it could have changed—nothing was as he remembered it. With the possible coming of the nuclear power plant, the town's citizens were being dragged into the twenty-first century whether they wanted it or not. When pushed to the limit people were capable of all sorts of dirty things. He had seen that in Iraq. But murder, multiple murders, seemed too much even for this otherwise quiet town.

Turning right at the end of the block, Grant immediately saw the truck. It was parked at the end of the cul-de-sac, a black truck with flames down the side. Jacked up. He slowed then stopped, fifty yards away. The truck was parked in front of a garage that stood next to a ramshackle house. The house's shutters were askew and the paint cracked. Weeds poked their heads from holes in the driveway. The place appeared quiet, no one was about.

Grant eased his car to just behind the truck and stopped. He grabbed the tire tool and knife and eased himself out of the car. He stood motionless for a moment and listened, his eyes darting from the house's front door and the garage.

Still, no movement.

He walked to the truck's far side, bent, and stuck the

knife into the front tire. Air shot out with a loud hiss. He moved to the rear tire and did the same. Another loud hiss.

No one emerged from the house.

Grant quickly punctured the remaining two tires and soon they were totally flat, sitting on rims. He took the tire tool and commenced to batter the truck, first over the hood, then its far side. He smashed the windshield until it was nothing more than a mass of splintered glass.

No sight of the goons.

He walked to his car, got in, and drove off, keeping the truck in his rearview mirror.

ೲೲ

Grant was back at the police station and eyed the directory in the lobby. An Alexander Paley was the chief of police and had his office on the second floor. Grant trudged up a flight of stairs and found the man's office, knocked on the door, and entered. A uniformed policewoman sitting at a desk greeted him. The woman looked up and sneered.

"Yes?" she said in a tone that sounded confrontational to Grant.

"I'd like to see Chief Paley," Grant said. He smiled and tried to appear as mild-mannered as possible.

"He's not seeing anyone," the policewoman said and returned to her work.

"I think he'll want to see me. You see I'm a disabled veteran and my mother died in a car accident in this city. Two weeks ago. So yes, I think he'll want to see me."

Grant had dealt with her kind all over the Marine Corps and he wasn't about to be put off by her condescending attitude.

"Now if I have to, I can call my friends at army CID

but I'd rather not. I just want some answers to a few simple questions." Grant took out his cell phone and waited.

Finally, the policewoman disappeared into an office and returned with a portly man in his fifties following her. He glanced at Grant. The man's vest was open and his tie was loose about his neck. His face contained numerous small scars as if he had been a boxer in a former life.

"I'm Chief Paley," the man said as the policewoman resumed her seat. "Amy here says you're threatening to call Washington. Whatever for?"

"Can we talk, Chief?" Grant said taking a conciliatory tone. "Just a few minutes."

"In here," Paley said and escorted Grant into his office where he to the procured chair. "Now what's this all about?" the Chief said when they were both seated.

"It's in regards to my mother, Helen Collins. She died several weeks ago out by Cottom Creek."

Chief Paley nodded. "I remember."

"It seems that not much of an investigation was done into the cause of her death," Grant said. He hoped his tone was not going to aggravate the man. "I talked with the ME—"

"You talked with Doc Witherspoon?" Paley said.

"Yes. He didn't do an autopsy or anything. More like, he refused. He just pronounced her dead and went on about his business."

"Old Doc knows his business, young man," the Chief said. He toyed with the stub of s cigar he retrieved from an ashtray. "We don't have too many accidents in Trinity, especially the kinds that result in a death. I remember that accident. It was pretty much an open and shut case. Doc agreed. Sergeant Brady, I believe was the investigating officer."

"In all honesty, Chief," Grant said, trying to strike a

conciliatory tone, "he hasn't been very helpful, either."

"Well," Paley said, rolling his cigar in the ashtray, "these things sometimes are pretty simple, really. Not a lot of extensive investigation required."

"I could get a court order and have Mom's body exhumed. Have the state Medical Examiner do an autopsy."

Paley chuckled. "I doubt you'll be able to get that order in Trinity. You would have to go to Savannah. Then you'd have to find a judge to hear your case. Then hope he'd rule in your favor. And you would have to have some sort of evidence. Do you have such evidence? No, I don't think you do. We don't take too kindly to busting open graves down here, sir. But you're sure welcome to try."

Grant sensed an undercurrent of hostility in the man's demeanor. This town didn't like outsiders coming in and asking questions. "You're telling me I can't count on you for any help?" Grant said.

"Son, you come here with some concrete evidence that your mother died as a result of foul play, then sure, you can count on my help. Otherwise, I'm up to my neck in other business." Paley shuffled some papers on his desk, eyed Grant through narrow eyes. "I'm saying that without more evidence, something more to go on, I'm not going to override an investigation that has been completed and closed. That's all. Surely, you can understand that." The police chief smiled, his pock-face expression remained dour, however.

ℰℑℰℑ

"Okay, gentlemen, listen up."

Winston Conway stood before the conference table surrounded by a few men in suits. Before him on the table was a yellow legal pad and a pen.

"We need to come up with a list of what are the objections to our Trinity power plant so we can develop a closing campaign here during these last few months. I want to hear what we are likely to encounter by these environmentalists in the days and weeks ahead."

A man in a gray suit and yellow tie raised his hand.

"Yes, Sam?"

"Mr. Conway, one of the biggest objections is that they are prohibitively dangerous. There have now been four grave nuclear reactor accidents. Windscale in Britain in 1957, Three Mile Island in the United States in 1979, Chernobyl in the Soviet Union in 1986, and now Fukushima. Each accident was unique, and each was supposed to be impossible. Without the filters installed at the last minute by Nobel Prize-winning scientist Sir John Cockcroft, the effects of the radioactive dust blasted into the air would have been much more devastating. Radioactive dust did escape, but the filters caught about ninety-five percent of it. With Chernobyl, by the time that the operator moved to shut down the reactor, the reactor was in an extremely unstable condition. A peculiarity of the design of the control rods caused a dramatic power surge as they were inserted into the reactor. The interaction of very hot fuel with the cooling water led to fuel fragmentation along with rapid steam production and an increase in pressure.

"The design characteristics of the reactor were such that substantial damage to even three or four fuel assemblies can result in the destruction of the reactor. At Fukushima, the earthquake itself did not damage the reactor but the following tsunamis damaged the seawater pumps for both the main condenser circuits and the auxiliary cooling circuits, notably the Residual Heat Removal cooling system. They also drowned the diesel generators and inundated the electrical switchgear and batteries, all located in the basements of the turbine buildings. So there was a station blackout, and the reactors were isolated from their ultimate heat sink. In other words, nuclear power stations are viewed as being so dangerous that no insurance company will undertake to pay the total costs of a disaster or a terrorist attack."

Conway was sitting at the table now as the man spoke and wrote rapidly on the legal pad.

"Anybody else have ideas?" he said, looking at the men at the table.

"Nuclear power stations use the same technology as that required to manufacture nuclear weapons. Any country that purifies uranium for use in nuclear power stations can also use its purification plant to manufacture weapons grade fissile material. Already nuclear power development has been used repeatedly as a cover for developing nuclear weapons. Of the ten nations which have developed nuclear weapons six did so with political cover or technical support from their supposedly peaceful nuclear program—India, Pakistan, Israel, South Africa, North Korea and France."

"That's a very big objection and one the press likes to play up," said a man at the far end of the table. "At the lowest level of sophistication, a potential proliferating state or subnational group using designs and technologies no more sophisticated than those used in first-generation nuclear weapons could build a nuclear weapon from reactor-grade plutonium that would have an assured, reliable yield of one or a few kilotons. At the other end of the spectrum, advanced nuclear weapon states such as the United States and Russia, using modern designs, could produce weapons from reactor-grade plutonium having reliable explosive yields, weight, and other characteristics generally comparable to those of weapons made from weapons-grade plutonium."

"Yes, I know," said Conway. "Anything else? Yes, Mark?"

The man named Mark took off his horned-rimmed glasses. "Since nuclear waste will be dangerous for thousands of years we are dumping our energy problems on future generations instead of using the benign methods of creating energy which are available to us. The currently favored solution of burying the waste in bedrock and sealing off access forever is a desperate and irresponsible one. And the transportation of such wastes poses an unacceptable risk to people and the environment."

Conway wrote. "I like these ideas," he said. "Any more?"

Sam spoke again.

"Because of their destructive potential nuclear power stations are a major target for terrorists. The Nine/Eleven atrocities would be tiny by comparison. If a large plane were flown into a nuclear power station the disaster would be immeasurably worse than Chernobyl. Studies inform us that over two thousand pounds of the highly radioactive and long-lasting isotope cesium-one-thirty-seven would be released into the atmosphere, contaminating most of the United States and making swathes of the country uninhabitable and causing more than two million cancers. If terrorists were able to detonate a crude nuclear weapon built with materials they stole or bought on the black market, the catastrophic consequences could easily include the deaths of tens or hundreds of thousands of people, the wide-scale destruction of property, the disruption of global commerce and restrictions on civil liberties worldwide."

Conway looked up from his pad. "Christ, Sam. Are you sure?"

"That's what I've read, sir. It's what our scientists are saying."

"Okay men," Conway said, standing. "I want this group to take these four major objections and develop an ad campaign combating and refuting them. And I want it done over the weekend. So get to work and let me hear from you when it's finished."

Chapter 11

Grant drove south of town on the river road to the turnoff that Carrie had mentioned. The road wound in serpentine fashion through the oaks and poplars on its way to the Dogwood River. He was beyond the few riverfront homes interspersed along the river leaving nothing but empty space all the way to Pete's Crab Shack. He came to an intersection where one lane continued on toward the river and another angled southward parallel to the water. He stopped, let the car idle while he contemplated which direction to continue. Straight ahead looked like the road headed directly to a bluff overlooking the river and was a dead end. He turned right and continued slowly, scanning through the trees on his left. The road turned in a slow left turn and went up a short rise. At its top he stopped again. Beyond he saw what looked like a huge house under construction.

A tall chain link fence extended on both sides of the road and it appeared to extend quite a ways in both directions. Next to the road stood a small guardhouse and a gate blocked entry onto the property proper. Using binoculars that Carrie loaned him, he scanned the area without getting out of his car.

In the distance he could make out a large clearing

with the beginnings of a two-story house in it. Mostly frame and roof. A few yards away was a large travel trailer and next to it was what looked like a construction trailer. The kind Grant had seen on many a construction site. There were a few men walking in the clearing and he could make out several on the roof with nail guns. Occasionally, the sound from a power saw would drift up to his car.

Putting the binocs aside, he inched his day to the gate and stopped. A man in a security uniform stepped from the guardhouse and walked over to Grant's window.

"Yes?" he said in a gruff, inpatient voice.

"I'm here to see Mr. Conway," Grant said. The guard was an overweight man with a walkie-talkie on his hip.

"Got an appointment?" said the guard.

"No. I was hoping to catch him here."

"Well, he ain't here."

"Know when he will be? It's important that I speak with him."

"Sure don't."

The man's curt answers implied to Grant that he wasn't welcome.

"Okay. Thanks."

He backed his car up enough to turn around and drove off. In his rearview mirror he noticed that the security guard watched him until he disappeared from view.

He really hadn't expected Conway to be on the construction site. Fat cats rarely are. They entrust the menial tasks of their lives to underlings. But it was a chance worth taking. He really wasn't sure what he would have said to the man if managed to meet him. He couldn't accuse him of anything.

Back in town, Grant noticed the jacked-up pickup with the flames in the side parked at the bar. His two friends from their earlier encounter stood next to the truck, talking. Only one other car in the parking lot. Grant pulled in next to the men and got out. The one with the tattooed arms looked up and grinned. Neither man looked like they had bathed.

"Hey, Billy," the tattooed one said. "Look who we have here. Back for another session, asshole?" Both men snickered.

"I dunno," Grant said. He eyed both men. There were no clubs or weapons in sight. "I thought I might stop and return the favor. I see where you morons got new tires for the truck."

"You do that, asshole?" the tattooed one said, stiffening. "We figured it was you. Time for a little payback, eh Billy?"

The other guy smiled again, nodded.

Grant walked slowly toward the pair, keeping his eyes on their hands and shoulders. Where the shoulders went, the rest followed.

The goon with the tattooed arms moved first, lunging at Grant who deftly sidestepped the man and drove an elbow into the side of his head. The man grunted, stumbled.

The second man came at Grant full force but, before he got close, Grant roundhouse kicked the man's face, shattering his nose sending spurts of blood onto the ground. Blinded, the man cursed loudly, grabbed his face, fell to his knees.

The tattooed man swung a muscled arm but Grant blocked it with his left arm, hit him with a right. The man stumbled awkwardly. Grant grabbed the man's shirt, pulled him close, then head butted him, sending a shower of blood down the man's front.

He stepped to the man on the ground and kicked him in the groin. Grant then pulled him to his feet and brought a knee up into the man's bloodied face. The man shrieked and fell back to the ground moaning.

"Goddamn you!" the tattooed one bellowed as he came at Grant again. This time he had a knife in his hand.

Part of Grant's marine training was hand-to-hand against a knife-wielding adversary. He knew the drill well. The man lunged again at Grant with the knife. Grant stepped aside, grabbed the man's wrist, and, in one quick motion, twisted the man's forearm back on itself over his own arm.

With an audible *crack* the big man fell to the ground holding his broken arm, wailing and cursing. He peered at Grant through the blood then closed his eyes. Grant took a step and kicked the man's head with his shoe. After a grunt, the man didn't move.

"Peckerheads," he muttered as he returned to his car.

He stopped at the Trinity State Bank. Inside, he presented to the receptionist the safe deposit key he found at his mother's.

"I'd like to open this box," he said. "It belonged to my mother. She died recently."

"This way," the receptionist said and Grant followed her to another desk. "What is number?"

"One seventeen," Grant said, producing the key.

He watched the woman open a card index file and thumb through the cards. She stopped at one-seventeen. She looked at Grant. "Helen Collins?" she said.

"That's right."

"I'm sorry," the woman said. "Mrs. Collins is one of two names on the signature card. Hers and one other, a Hazel Bullock. I'm sorry, Mr. Collins but I cannot grant you access to the box."

"But I have the key," Grant protested.

"You also have to have a signature on file, I'm sorry. Otherwise you will need a court order."

Grant returned to his car. He was getting tired of hearing about needing court orders.

ɞɞɞ

Grant woke and found the bed empty. He rose, put on his pajamas, and stumbled into the kitchen where Carrie was cooking bacon and eggs. A pot of coffee was on the counter. She smiled and gave him a peck on the cheek then returned to the stove.

"Coffee's ready," she said. "Help yourself."

He poured himself a mug and sat at the table and noticed the *Trinity Eagle* lying unfolded in front of him. "This today's paper?" he asked, picking it up and scanning the front page.

"Uh-um," she said, over her shoulder.

"This is getting to be a habit. Me sleeping in your bed and you fixing my breakfast. It's been four days now. I shouldn't be mooching off you like this. It isn't manly."

"I'm not complaining. You hear me complaining, Grant? And you're not mooching."

She set a plate of Canadian bacon in front of him and continued to stir the eggs.

"I need to get back to my therapy. I usually have a session twice a week. I don't want to go home but I'm going to have to very soon. Carrie, what's going to happen with us when I finally have to return to DC?"

"Can't we still see each other? You can come down here when you can and I can go up there on my days off. I don't want to stop seeing you. How do you feel?"

"Of course I do but seeing you only occasionally after getting to know you will be difficult. I don't relish the thought of waking up in an empty bed each morning."

Carrie brought their eggs to the table and sat next to him. They ate in silence for a while as Grant studied the headlines of the paper. After several minutes, he shoved the paper under her nose.

"Look at this!" he said in an excited voice.

Carrie took the paper and saw the headlines he was talking about.

TRINITY NUCLEAR PLANT TO HAVE FAIL-SAFE SECURITY

Underneath the headlines was a story outlining how advanced the security system of the proposed power plant was and the numerous backups that would prevent a terrorist attack. The last paragraph extolled the virtues of cheap electricity the plant would bring to the region.

"Wow," she said.

"The ad wars are heating up over this plant," Grant said. "I wouldn't be surprised if an editorial against the plant didn't appear in tomorrow's edition. You mentioned that the paper's owner is against the plant."

"Yes, he is. This has all the possibilities of an all-out war, actually. You ever see any more of the creeps that worked you over?"

Grant blushed, felt his face tingle. "Well, yeah, actually."

"How come you haven't said anything?"

"Didn't want you to worry. But I met them in the parking lot of the bar down on the river. I don't think they'll bother me again."

"Christ, Grant!" Carrie said. "What happened?"

Grant ate his eggs for a moment before speaking. "I left them moaning on the ground, each with his nose bleeding like stink."

Carrie ate and shook her head. She stared at Grant for the longest time. He was immediately sorry he told her.

"And today?" she said as she carried the empty plates to the sink and refilled their coffee mugs.

"Today, I'm going to see Sergeant Brady again, if at all possible. I want find out if they ever located Lori's car. My chat with your town's police chief was unproductive."

"I've got the day off so I thought I do some housecleaning. You might consider going to see Hollister McLain who owns the hardware store and is on the city council. He has been openly opposed to the plant coming to town. Will you swing by here when you're finished with the police sergeant?"

"Sure," Grant said and ambled off to take a shower and dress.

Later, at the police station, he found Brady in his office. "Can I come in?" he said after knocking on the door and sticking his head in.

The police officer was thumbing through a stack of papers ion his desk but he looked up and waved Grant into a chair across the desk. He continued to rifle through the papers.

"Mr. Collins," he said, without looking up. "What can I do for you? I thought I made it plain that I'm done with your mother's accident. That case is closed."

"Lori Spelling's car—did you ever find it?" Grant said, his voice showing a slight irritation.

"Not yet," Brady said. He still had not met Grant's gaze.

"I guess that's it, then. But I wanted to show you something. May I?"

"Mr. Collins, I am very busy and—"

"It won't take but a minute," Grant interjected. "Please. I think it's important."

Brady looked up from his work and shrugged then sighed. "Shoot," he said.

Grant retrieved a paper from his pocket and handed it to the officer who took it and studied it.

"Three deaths, sir. A woman drowns in her swimming pool and it is labeled an accident. Miss Spelling dies and it is ruled a drug overdose. My mother dies and you claim it was an unfortunate accident. All these people have died recently."

"So?" said Brady.

"The interesting point that connects each of them is they all were active campaigners against the nuclear power plant. The one lobbying to be built here in Trinity."

"And your point is, Mr. Collins?"

Grant was starting to lose patience with the condescending attitude of the officer. "Don't you see?" He wanted to say *don't you see, stupid,* but bit his tongue. "They all were on the citizen's committee against the plant and now they are dead. Each one looks like an accident but I'd bet good money they weren't."

"Mr. Collins, we've had this discussion before, I believe. You think you've uncovered a conspiracy here in Trinity. Well, there's no such thing, trust me. No sinister goings on in our little town. You may have them all the time up North but down here we're just quiet southern folk living in a quiet southern little town. Get my drift, Mr. Collins? You waltz in here and calmly state that there have been three murders committed in my jurisdiction without a single shred of evidence. Actually, you are beginning to irritate me. Now, I'm extremely busy and don't have the time for you any longer. Don't come back here with these wild, strange accusations that have no merit. Good day."

With that, the sergeant returned to his paperwork, leaving Grant sitting, feeling as if the world had just fallen onto his shoulders. He rose, stood for a moment in the doorway, but Brady never looked up from his work so Grant left feeling utterly dejected. He understood the part about evidence—he had to admit there was none but he had expected the police to at least hear him out. The town of Trinity was beginning to have the feel of the Southern hamlets characterized in movies and television and he didn't like the feeling. Good ole boys running law enforcement didn't bode well for Trinity's future.

He parked in front of the hardware store. It was located in the main part of town where businesses were located in a long block of brick buildings connected together like so many other small town Main Streets Grant had seen. The interior of the hardware store was cool, providing a welcome relief from the sweltering humidity. Row upon row of shelves with every item a person could want, from electrical and plumbing fixtures to gadgets of all sorts and sizes filled the store. A tall, older, balding man wearing glasses and a denim apron stood behind a counter talking to a man whom Grant surmised was an employee. As he approached the counter, the man looked up and smiled.

"May I help you, sir?"

"I'm looking for a Mr. McLain. Hollister McLain," Grant said.

"I'm Hollister," the man said, still smiling. "How can I help you? Looking for something?"

Grant shot a glance at the other man and hesitated. McLain nodded at the man.

"Okay, Sid, go ahead and order those gaskets. That'll be all for now."

The man called Sid turned and disappeared behind the rows of shelving.

"Is there somewhere we can talk, Mr. McLain? My name is Collins, Grant Collins." He held out his hand and McLain took it with a firm grasp. "It's about the proposed nuclear power plant that may be coming to town. I understand you are opposed to it. My mother was also."

"Collins," McLain said, scratching his nose and adjusting his glasses. "Your mother Helen Collins by any chance?"

"Yes sir, that's her."

"I was sorry to hear about her accident and death. You have my sympathy. Your mother was a small dynamo."

"So I've heard. Can we talk in your office? I feel awkward standing here."

"Surely. This way."

McLain led Grant to the back of the hardware store into a small office that was piled high with boxes and old trade magazines. He dusted off a wicker chair and offered it to Grant while he sat behind a wooden desk that had seen better days. Once settled, Grant spoke.

"I don't really know where to begin, Mr. McLain," he started.

"Please," McLain said, "call me Holly. My friends do."

"Thank you—Holly. I came down from Washington where I live to attend mother's funeral. While here I learned she was involved with a group who called themselves the Citizens Against Nuclear Power."

Grant paused and McLain nodded.

"Yes," McLain said, "your mother was the driving force behind their work. Tireless campaigner. I was ill the day of her funeral and couldn't make it. I'm sorry."

"Anyway, after the funeral, I met a former high school classmate and we made a date for dinner. The only thing is she never showed. I searched the town but there was no sign of her car. The next day she was found dead in the Dogwood River. Then I learned she worked on the committee with mom. Lori Spelling."

"Yes, I know her. She's—she's dead?"

"Blood tests showed she was full of cocaine and other drugs but people who knew her said she didn't do drugs."

"My, my," said McLain, rubbing his eyes. "Although I wasn't on their committee, I was an outspoken opponent of the power plant coming to Trinity. As a council member I said so repeatedly. I really don't know why DynaTech has chosen this area to build their plant. I knew Miss Spelling only vaguely but I knew your mother very well."

Grant removed a paper from his shirt pocket.

"I went to the library and looked at old newspapers and found another death recently in Trinity." He handed the paper to McLain. "And guess what? All three of these people worked on the citizens committee."

Grant waited while McLain looked the paper over. He removed his glasses, took a handkerchief from his pocket, and wiped his eyes.

"I remember the Nottingham woman's death," McLain said. "It was in the paper. But I didn't know she was on the committee against the plant." McLain shook his head, sighed. "Damn," he said. "It's worse than I thought."

"Excuse me?" Grant said. "What's worse?"

"You're not going to believe this."

"What? What?" Grant's pulse suddenly shot skyward and his mouth turned to cotton. McLain rummaged in a desk drawer and produced several faded newspaper clippings. He held them in his hands for a moment. Grant thought he saw fear in the man's eyes.

"Look at these," he said, handing the clippings across the desk. Grant took them. Looking at them he understood McLain's expression. He felt lightheaded, almost as if his head was floating.

MAN ELECTROCUTED
A fifty-three year old Trinity man was electrocuted while attempting to fix a broken generator at his home on the Dogwood River. The generator was apparently standing in a puddle of water when the man connected it to a heater. Funeral arrangements are pending.

The last article was dated seven weeks prior to the first.

HIT & RUN FATAL TO WOMAN
A twenty-seven year-old woman was killed yesterday when she was hit by a car as she was jogging on the Dogwood river road. Police are asking residents with any information concerning the hit and run to call them. The woman was airlifted to Augusta where she died during surgery.

"Are you kidding me?" Grant said after jotting the articles in his notebook. He handed the clippings back to McLain.

"I didn't know these people," he said. "I knew your mother well and had got to know Miss Spelling only recently."

"What do you think?" Grant said.

"These other two folks were on the citizen's committee as well. Now that makes five people altogether that served on the committee who are now dead. Certainly appears suspicious, doesn't it?"

"So if their deaths are related to the power plant, who could be behind it all?"

McLain wiped his nose with the handkerchief and shifted in his chair. "Well, the owner of DynaTech is a man named Winston Conway. Has his office in Savannah. But he is building a mansion south of here on the river and has a large trailer parked there where he stays when he comes down to inspect the construction. I've never met him but I can't believe someone with his reputation would stoop to something as low as murder to get his power plant. On the other hand, millions of dollars are at stake here."

"Yes, I drove out there. The security guard turned me away."

"I don't doubt it. The man's somewhat of a mystery. I've never seen him, personally. The other main player is Trinity's mayor, Bruce Baxter. He's a sleazy man who likes fancy clothes. How he got elected mayor, I'll never know. But he has lots of money. Baxter doesn't appear to have either the brains or the fortitude to be involved in something like murder."

"You never know, Holly," Grant said. "If they were involved, it was probably from a distance. I doubt they would stoop to dirty their own hands."

"Conway supposedly has a yacht on the East Savannah River. Likes to eat at the upscale restaurants on River Street. Cruise up to Hilton Head, that sort of thing."

"I wouldn't know, Holly. I don't have that kind of money."

"I can relate to that. Listen, if I can be of any help, let me know. Right now public sentiment against the plant is lagging a little behind the sentiment for it. If you can uncover something incriminating, it might just turn the tide for us."

Grant stood and extended his hand. "I appreciate your time, Holly. You're the first person in Trinity who even listened to me. The police sure didn't."

"The police?" Holly said with a laugh. "Ha! They're a joke here. Don't do much except hand out parking tickets. Fortunately, we haven't had much crime."

"Thanks again," Grant said.

He decided it was time to visit the mansion again.

Chapter 12

That evening Grant disclosed to Carrie what he had spent the day mulling over. He sat on her sofa and talked while she was in the kitchen.

"Trinity's police seem to be a joke," he said. "I bet they don't do much more than hand out parking tickets. Hollister McLain told me as much. Why do you think that is, Carrie?"

"I dunno," she said.

"You bet your sweet ass they don't. Someone has the police department of this town all wrapped up in their hip pocket. And I bet I know who."

"Who?" Carrie said.

"Who has the most to lose in all these power plant politics? Tell me that."

"DynaTech. They're the ones who are pushing for the plant to go through. They will build it."

"And who owns DynaTech?"

"A fellow named Conway, I think," answered Carrie, now on the sofa's edge.

"Winston Conway, to be exact. I was by his home site earlier. It's surrounded by a fence and has a guard. The man wasn't very friendly."

"I knew he was building a mansion around here."

"Dollars to donuts he's involved in this. And I'll give even money that somehow he's tied up with all these accidental deaths of the citizen's committee."

"Gosh, Grant," Carrie said, her voice suddenly wavering. "You really think that's possible?"

"Yes, I think it's possible. Do I have any proof? No, I don't. But I hope to get the proof. Tonight."

"What do you mean?"

"I mean I'm going back to Conway's construction site and see if I can get into that trailer of his. He may have some very interesting information stashed away in there."

Carrie stood and put her arms around Grant's neck. "Oh, please don't do that. It's dangerous and you could get hurt. Remember your beating the other day?"

"The damn police aren't going to do anything," he said, kissing her on the nose. "I'll be careful, I promise."

"I dunno. Breaking and entering, that's a serious crime. If you get caught—"

"I don't plan on getting caught," he said. "I'm going to need a flashlight. Do you have one?"

Carrie nodded.

"I'm glad we drove into Savannah the other day and picked up some sneakers and other clothes," he said. "Gonna come in handy tonight."

"Tonight? Does it have to be tonight? Can't it wait a few days?"

"I'm pissed as hell, now. Whoever is behind these deaths, including Mom's, I'm going to make them pay. If it's the last thing I ever do."

Carrie fixed them a supper of chicken fried steak and mashed potatoes while Grant changed and donned his sneakers. While she labored in the kitchen he took a nap on the sofa.

When she called him to eat it was getting dark outside with only the faintest orange coming through the kitchen window.

After they finished eating, they watched TV until almost midnight. Grant took Carrie's flashlight, kissed her on the cheek, found his car keys and left. Fortunately, the moon wasn't up yet and clouds obscured most of the stars. As he pulled onto the river road he realized that what he was about to embark upon might get himself killed. He followed the route he had earlier and stopped at the top of the rise and scanned the area with Carrie's binoculars.

All seemed quiet.

No lights glowed through the trees.

No movement could he see.

Grant eased the car down to the gate and guardhouse. He half-expected the security guard to jump out from the shadows but all remained quiet.

He opened the car door and slipped quietly to the ground and made his way to the chain link fence. In an instant he was over it and on the other side.

❧❧❧

Grant made his way into the closest copse of trees and waited. The only sounds were the prattle of tree frogs, the incessant chirping of crickets, and the occasional owl hooting down by the river. The road beyond the gate that led into the construction area was a narrow, rutted dirt affair that disappeared into the trees. After a quick reconnoitering of the area, Grant stumbled along trying to remain concealed in the shadows. His heart pounded in his ears with each pulse and his mouth was as dry as a sand pile in August. He wondered what he would do if he happened onto a watchman, what excuse he could give. There was none, of course, as he was trespassing, which was certainly a crime in Trinity. And he had no doubt that Sergeant Brady would take great pleasure in filing the charges against him. When he was within shouting distance of the house he stopped and scanned the area. The dense forest opened to a large clearing revealing a partially built structure that consisted of two stories of a lumber frame enclosure topped by a plywood roof. At the house's backside there was a massive stone fireplace and another stood at the far end. A framed-in area for a large bay window faced what would become a circular drive in the front. To the house's north side was an expensive-looking travel trailer, obviously belonging to Conway. Across from the clearing where Grant stood was a smaller trailer that must be used by the construction crew.

Both trailers were dark.

Grant stood at the edge of the trees, alert to the sounds of the forest and river, heart pounding, palms wet. Satisfied that no else was about, he inched his way to the travel trailer's side and jumped behind it, hiding himself from being seen by anyone who drove up. Then a thought struck him. He had left his car parked at the gate so if someone did drive up they would certainly notice he was on the property. Too late now to worry about it.

At the rear of Conway's trailer he found a door and tried it. Locked. Should he break in? Someone would discover his unlawful entry, which would alert the man that someone was poking around in his business, put him on guard. No, better not risk it. He tried several windows and found they were locked as well. Going back to the door, he shined the flashlight on its latch and studied it. It was a brass affair with a combination lock so he punched in 0-0-0. No luck. He tried 1-2-3 and again, no luck.

A twig snapped in the distance.

And another.

Grant froze.

Someone or something was walking among the trees in the distance.

He had nothing with which to defend himself except the small flashlight and it wasn't going to be of much help in a confrontation. He heard tales of animals that lurked Georgia's swamps and rivers at night and wondered if such an animal was prowling the construction site. Surely there was enough construction activity during the day to ward off any animals that might hurt him. He hoped so. But he knew that alligators sometimes found their way into these rivers only to prowl their banks at night. All he needed to do was stumble onto a sleeping gator. Or worse, Bigfoot.

He wished he had brought a bottle of water for his mouth was dry with a bitter taste. As he stood in the dark, listening, the thought struck him as to how foolish he was for getting involved in Trinity's local politics. What did he care if a power plant came to the town or not? What difference did it make? None, except he suspected his mother died because of her involvement. And he couldn't just let that pass without an investigation.

He peered into the night, searching for any movement, but saw none. The noise stopped. Grant returned to the door latch. This time he tried 3-2-1, and *voila*, he heard a click.

Opening the door, he glanced over his shoulder, then stepped into the trailer. It was pitch-black inside so he switched on his flashlight. It was a luxurious affair with plush carpet covering the main cabin. One side was a leather sofa while against the opposite wall set two recliners. At the rear of the main cabin was an electric fireplace with a large flat screen television over its mantle. To the immediate right of the fireplace a short series of steps led to what Grant surmised was the bedroom. He stood in the kitchen that, along one wall, contained a bank of stove, microwave, and fridge. He stepped into the main cabin and found a desk that sat between the two recliners. Holding the small flashlight between his teeth, he began rummaging through the desk drawers and quickly scanning the papers in each.

As he thumbed through the desk's contents he periodically glanced over his shoulder toward the door. Besides a file folder-containing contracts pertaining to his home construction there was nothing of interest in the desk. Some canceled checks and a few blueprints of an unidentifiable structure were all that occupied the desk. Grant closed the draws and stepped up into the bedroom. The small room was mostly wall-to-wall bed but there was a row of cabinets along one wall. He rifled through the cabinets that were filled with underwear and other clothing items. But in a bottom drawer were more documents.

One was a series of emails to and from someone named Sergei. They seemed to indicate that Conway was going to sell something once the reactor was functional. A small black book contained a list of phone numbers, including Sergei's, was included in the small stack of documents as well as what looked like safety and environmental reviews of the proposed facility. Grant replaced the items and made his way back to the trailer's door.

Back outside, he closed the door and hurried to the trailer's front and the safety of the trees next to it. A yellow moon rose just above the trees and the frogs were quiet. The only sounds were the continuous chirping of crickets. A sweet earthy fragrance tickled his nose. What was it that Conway planned to sell? The question nagged him. Grant edged his way through the trees until he arrived at the gate, which he vaulted easily. He climbed into his car and headed to Carrie's apartment.

On the way he passed a dark sedan heading the opposite direction before reaching the river road. Did its occupants know he was at the construction site? Were they coming to take care of him and he had just managed to escape trouble? He watched the sedan in his mirror until he turned onto the river road and was heading back to Carrie's apartment. The road was deserted for it was almost two a.m. He never saw the sedan behind him. As he reached the outskirts of Trinity, he glanced again in his rearview mirror. Nothing. He breathed a sigh of relief and drove to Carrie's.

♥♥♥

Winston Conway sat in the posh salon of his sixty-three foot yacht, *Sandpiper*. Moored at his private dock on the East Savannah River the boat was a technological marvel. The *Sandpiper* included vacuum-infused epoxy sandwich panels with fiberglass and carbon reinforcements. Its hull and deck structures were made from CNC lathed female molds for lightness, perfect surface finishes, all optimal in terms of stiffness, performance, and reliability over time. Advanced resin-infusion techniques were used on the yacht and delivered strength with significant weight saving. On board, the luxury liner housed five suites, able to accommodate up to twelve guests, each with an accompanying bathroom, living room and double bedroom. Conway had two VIP rooms for himself. The yacht included an on-board cinema, sun deck, as well as outside bars, Jacuzzi and a range of water sports equipment. In addition, mirrored surfaces were featured extensively throughout the interior while furniture, glassware and tableware were French crystal. Above the deck, the yacht housed a helipad. Conway was proud of the *Sandpiper*.

From his easy chair he could see a silver moon sparkling on the river and out beyond the Tybee Island light, the Atlantic. His steward had brought a silver coffeepot and set it on an antique table to Conway's side. Across the salon sat a man with a dark complexion with a large gold chain around his neck. The man puffed on a cigarette while Conway studied him carefully.

"Care for some coffee, water?" he said. "I appreciate you getting here on such short notice."

The man blew smoke into the air above Conway's head and chuckled.

"It wasn't far," he said.

"I need you to handle a few grisly details for me," Conway continued. "I no longer can count on our mayor to carry out some simple tasks without measurable fallout."

"I am at your service, Conway," the man said. "For the right price, of course."

"Of course."

Conway didn't like the man who sat opposite him nor did he especially trust the man. But business made strange bedfellows as the saying went. He couldn't remember when or where he first met Cain but he had used the man in the past to change the minds of difficult or obstinate clients. He never asked what methods the man used, he didn't much care. It was results that he was after and Cain always got results. The scar down his left cheek gave him a most terrifying appearance.

"Like I said," Conway continued, "I can no longer count on our mayor's help in obtaining the necessary votes at the upcoming council meeting. In addition, there is a man here in Trinity asking a lot of questions. Goes by the name of Collins. Has a girlfriend. Her name is Carrie and she works at the diner."

"You want me to dispose of them?" Cain said. He snubbed out his cigarette and lit another.

"Not just yet," Conway said. "Scare the hell out of them, yes. I will pay well."

"It has always been a pleasure, Mr. Conway, to do business with you."

Chapter 13

She let him in on his first knock and kissed him softly on the cheek. Grant slumped into the sofa and rubbed his temples.

"Well?" she said, after waiting for him to speak.

"Nothing really," he said. "Couldn't find anything in his trailer. Pretty nice trailer, though."

"How'd you get in?"

"I just jumped the fence. By luck the lock on the door was a combination thing and I guessed at the code and opened the door."

"I was so worried, Grant. I couldn't go to bed until you returned." She took his head in her arms and massaged his forehead. There was a worried look on her face.

"You shouldn't worry about me. I can take care of myself."

"Like you did with those two thugs? No, Grant, something's going on in this town—something sinister, evil. You don't need to get mixed up in it."

He sat up and looked into Carrie's eyes that were filled with tears. "Look," he said, "my mother died last week. And I'm not sure that it wasn't orchestrated. By whom, I don't know but until I do I'm staying in Trinity and looking into it."

"What about DC?"

"I'll call Walter Reed. Postpone my appointment again."

"You can still stay here, you know."

He nodded.

"Conway is planning to sell something once the power plant is up and running."

"How do you know?" Carrie said.

"I found an email in his trailer. Whatever it is, it's big because the figure twenty million was mentioned."

Carrie looked stunned. She got up from the sofa and paced about the living room.

"Wow," she said. "What could be with that much in this town?"

"I have no idea. But whatever it is, it's tied to getting the plant here. It may be why Conway is pushing so hard."

"You think it's possible that he's behind these deaths?" She had taken seat in the easy chair opposite Grant.

"Who else stands to gain by having all the plant's opposition removed? Yes, I think it's not only possible but also highly probable. If not directly, then he had someone do it. But I also think he's way too smart to leave a trail directly to his doorstep."

"Mrs. Nottingham, the woman who drowned in her family's pool—how could that have been a murder? How could Conway have done that? There were family and friends at the house and no one saw she had fallen into their pool."

"Yeah, the paper said she had been drinking but do we know that for a fact? Was an autopsy done? The newspaper article didn't mention one. Maybe the Trinity police just took the family's word that she had been drinking. Law enforcement in this town isn't the best, I've decided."

"What we need is an independent investigation, Grant. Someone outside Trinity who would take a careful look at these deaths and the politics surrounding them."

"*We*, Carrie? I don't expect you to get involved in this. This isn't your fight."

"But it is. I live in this town, remember? So I have a stake in what happens, too."

"Okay, so how do we get an independent investigation? I don't have the money to hire a private investigator."

"How about our mayor?"

"He's on the side of the reactor coming to town. I don't think we could count on him being impartial. What about going to the Bureau of Investigation in Savannah? They might have some ideas."

"It's an idea, Grant. They would at least give you an honest opinion."

"Unless they're in Conway's hip pocket as well," Grant said.

"It would be worth a try at least."

"I suppose we could drive down there on your next day off from work. If no one wants to listen to us, all we have wasted is our time."

"That's the day after tomorrow. My day off. We can go then."

"Tomorrow I'm going over to Lori's apartment and see if I can search the place. I might find something of value."

"You mean break in? Grant you can't." Carrie sat on the sofa next to him, placed a hand on his arm.

"I'm getting nowhere. And it's driving me crazy. I've got to do something, you know. Sitting around here just waiting is not for me."

"I don't want you getting into trouble." Carrie pulled him close, kissed his ear. "You're too nice a guy to get into trouble in this town."

"You don't know me, Carrie," Grant said, pulling away. "If you did, you'd feel different."

"What do you mean?"

"Nothing, just trust me. I've got a lot of problems."

"Who doesn't?"

"When I was in the marines—"

Carrie nuzzled closer. "Okay, so you were in the marines. And?"

"Something happened when I was in Iraq. Something bad."

"Care to talk about it?"

"I dunno," Grant said. "But you have a right to know. It's why I'm not—not—well."

"Go on," Carrie said.

A lump formed in Grant's throat making speech difficult. Acid shot into his chest. "It happened during the Iraq invasion. Our assault amphibian battalion was advancing toward Baghdad when we began taking small arms fire along with RPG, mortar, and Iraqi tank fire. We were on a road that was later called Ambush Alley. There were explosions and fire all around. Suddenly—" Grant stopped, glanced at Carrie who was frowning. He smacked his lips before continuing. "Suddenly, through the smoky haze I noticed a car approaching our Humvee. It was an old ramshackle Peugeot full of small boys. I couldn't see who was driving. There were guns sticking out of all the windows. Aimed at us. It kept coming right toward us. I didn't know why, couldn't understand why boys would be fighting in this war. I yelled at them to stop but the car kept coming. Kept advancing. I yelled again. Carrie, as God is my witness, I yelled at them to stop, to turn around. But they wouldn't. They wouldn't."

Carrie kissed him on the cheek. "It's okay," she said. "It's okay."

"Dammit, it's *not* okay. Those boys—they should have turned around. They had no business being there. But they didn't. They kept coming toward us. Something clicked inside me. Maybe it was training. I don't know. I grabbed a grenade launcher from my buddy riding shotgun and aimed it out my window. And I fired. The next thing I know the car disappears in a huge fireball. The explosion hurts my ears. The car is gone. The boys are gone."

Sobs come quietly, Grant's shoulders shaking. Carrie held him close for a long moment.

"Don't you see, Carrie? I killed a carload of kids! I killed them. Me, Grant Collins. Boys. They died because of me."

"They were combatants, Grant," Carrie said softly, tears streaming down her cheeks. "You said so yourself."

"I couldn't fight after that," Grant said. He wiped his eyes with a sleeve. "They sent me to a field hospital after we secured Baghdad. The doctors there shot me full of antidepressants and stamped me good for more fighting. But I couldn't do it, so eventually they shipped me home. I've been going to therapy at Walter Reed."

Grant slumped back on the sofa, exhausted.

"I—I don't know what to say," Carrie said, obviously shaken by Grant's revelation. "I've never known anyone who fought in a war. But, Grant, that's what you were doing—fighting in a war. You were expected to kill the enemy. No way you could have known you were going to face boys."

"I used to be a happy-go-lucky guy, Carrie, before Iraq. I used to have a sense of humor, used to laugh at most things. You can ask anyone who knew me back then. I don't do those things anymore. I'm different now."

"If the Iraq government chose to send boys into battle, they are the morally reprehensible ones. In the confusion of battle the bastard Saddam put those kids in harm's way. It was a tragic, unfortunate accident of war."

"Maybe," Grant said, his mouth dry. "Maybe."

"Come to bed, sweetheart," Carrie said. "Come on."

❧❧

A warm drizzle fell on the abandoned lighthouse situated on Cockspur Island in the mouth of the Savannah River. Clouds had formed at dusk and now, at midnight, the rain fell in a quiet steady drizzle. It was in 1958 that the United States Air Force lost an 8,000-pound nuclear bomb east of the island when a fighter collided with a B-47 bomber carrying the bomb. In order to protect the crew in the event of a crash the bomb was jettisoned and repeated attempt to locate it were unsuccessful. It was presumed lost near Cockspur Island.

A man sat alone in the lighthouse, its dim interior lit only by a kerosene lantern. Out beyond the rocky point the Atlantic moved and swelled like a giant amorphous black ameba.

As night fell the man had arrived on the island using a Zodiac rigid-inflatable boat or RIB that he had piloted down the Savannah River. He unzipped the waterproof duffel and removed the laptop and handheld VHF radio and set them on the table before him. He laid his Turkish Kanuni nine millimeter pistol and Mil-Tac stiletto beside the laptop.

Outside the abandoned lighthouse, the wind picked up, buffeting the single window and hurling the raindrops against it. It was a raw night outside in spite of the balmy temperature. The man shivered and removed his wet parka.

He opened the laptop, clicked it on, and waited for the screen to boot up. When it did, he typed his password and the desktop screen popped into view. He clicked on the email icon and waited for his mail to download. While he waited, he lit a cigarette and retrieved a thermos of coffee. He found the flask of brandy, poured it into the coffee, took a long gulp, watched his emails flutter onto the screen.

The man had come a long way to get to Cockspur Island. Born in Yugoslavia after the end of World War Two his family suffered under the dictatorship of Josip Tito. When the student protests in Belgrade failed to produce any meaningful reforms, the man traveled to Angola and fought with mercenaries in the country's civil war. It was there he learned and honed his skills of espionage, torture, and murder. When Yugoslavia disintegrated, he had no desire to return. He found his skills were much in demand all around the world and he had become a wealthy man in the process. It was difficult to believe but from Indonesia to the Middle East to Europe and the States the man never lacked for work.

There was a time when was a younger man that he longed for a family. A wife, children, house with a picket fence. These things filled his dreams at one time. Her name was Katya and he met her in Bucharest. She was from the Ukraine and she was beautiful. Long black hair with penetrating dark eyes, she had helped him find an apartment. They became lovers almost immediately. But Katya had a jealous ex-boyfriend, a muscled boy who worked in a steel factory. One night in a jealous rage, he beat her to death with his hands. The police, the *Politia Bucuresti,* couldn't find the man. But he tracked him down after several days of searching, gave the man something to remember in the afterlife. As the boyfriend lay dying from his assault, he finished him off with a piano wire garrote.

It was the last intimate relationship he had.

The man returned to his laptop and studied his emails, one in particular. He removed a small notebook from a shirt pocket, copied the information. Satisfied, he switched off the laptop, found a blanket in his duffel, turned the lantern down low. Lying on the wooden floor, he covered himself with the blanket and listened to the drizzle beat against the window.

And dreamed of Katya.

Chapter 14

Grant asked Carrie if she wanted to eat supper at Martin's Restaurant and she agreed. After they left her apartment and approached downtown, sirens pierced the evening air. When they were closer to town a fire truck rumbled past, its lights and siren flashing and wailing. As Grant turned onto Main Street, they spotted the commotion coming from in front of McLain's hardware store. A crowd of people was gathered on both sides of the street.

"What's happening?" Carrie said as Grant slowed the car's progress. Besides two fire trucks, there were two police cars and an ambulance parked in front, their emergency lights flashing.

"Looks like something is on fire," Grant said. A policeman waved them past. "It's the hardware store," he said when they had past all the emergency vehicles. "Christ, Hollister McLain's store is on fire."

Grant parked the car and he and Carrie hurried across the street to join a small crowd of onlookers who were gawking at all the activity. Smoke billowed from the store's front. Soon, several firemen emerged wearing their helmets and oxygen masks. As they worked pulling two fire hoses from the store, two paramedics entered pushing a stretcher. Grant craned his neck to get a better look and wormed his way to the head of the crowd just as the EMTs returned. They pushed a stretcher containing a body, covered with a blanket.

Carrie asked, "Who is that?" but Grant only shook his head.

"Is he dead?" someone asked.

"How did it happen?" came a question from another onlooker.

"Who was that?"

Carrie took Grant by the hand and led him to the ambulance. They watched while the paramedics loaded the body into it.

"It's old man McLain," a man said who had come to stand beside Grant.

"Hollister McLain? The store's owner?" Grant said.

The man nodded. "Never made it out. Apparently got caught in the back and couldn't get through the flames. The back door was stuck or something. Anyway, he couldn't get out through the back."

"That's terrible," Carrie said, her voice cracking.

"Yes," the man said. "He was such a nice fellow. His wife is nice, too. It's a loss for the city council, that's for sure."

Grant took Carrie by an arm and pulled her toward the car.

"Let's get out of here," he said. "I've seen enough."

Back at Carrie's apartment, Grant exploded. "Can you believe this shit? Goddammit! I was just at the man's store not more than a few hours ago. He showed me newspaper clippings on two other deaths around here. They were both on Mom's citizen committee against the power plant. And now the poor bastard is dead. Think the cops will rule this a suicide? Or an accidental fire?"

Carrie sat on her sofa and watched Grant pace the

small living room while he ranted. He didn't wait for her to answer. He found his notebook and gave it to her but continued ranting while she read his copy of the newspaper articles shown him by McLain.

"You bet they will. Just hide and watch. Someone's got this town and its police department all wrapped up. They won't get off their ass to investigate the poor man's death."

"I can't believe this is happening in my town," Carrie said, after examining the notebook. "These are two more people, both dead."

"Running out of options, dear," he said.

"How about calling the Georgia Bureau of Investigation? They would be independent of Trinity's law enforcement."

"Not a bad idea, Carrie. But I think tomorrow I'm going to find Hazel and see if she would go with me to unlock Mom's box at the bank. Might be something interesting in it."

They both had lost their appetite so spent the evening in quiet contemplation of what was happening in Trinity.

The following morning Grant found Mrs. Bullock at home and she graciously consented to go to the bank. She signed the signature book and Grant used the key to unlock the box.

Inside he sorted through a number of papers, a few gold coins, some more jewelry. At the bottom of the box and hidden for a cursory view he found a small black journal.

"Look at this," he said to Hazel.

"What's in it?" the woman said, as she pressed closer. "And why would Helen keep it in her bank box?"

Grant thumbed through the journal. In it were handwritten notes, looking like a diary of sorts. By dates. And times. Descriptions of Arab-looking men coming and going in Trinity late at night. Meetings with Mayor Baxter. What it meant, he had no idea.

"It appears to be a diary," Grant said. He handed the journal to Hazel and waited for her to peruse its contents. "Know anything of what she writes about?"

Hazel shook her head. "No, Grant, not really. She didn't confide in me where her power plant activities were concerned. I was never that interested in politics so she just never said much. Now I wish she had."

Grant put the journal into his pocket and the two of them drove back to Helen's house. After Hazel left he called Carrie and she came over. Together they looked through the journal trying to make sense of its contents.

"Hazel said Mom didn't go out much at night," Grant said. "Yet here are all kinds of notations made at night. Why? Had she uncovered something here in Trinity and was documenting it? If so, what could it have been?"

"Grant," Carrie said, "Trinity has been a pretty quiet town until recently. Nothing goes on here, especially after dark. And most folks like it that way. The college always has sporting venues or music concerts, plays and the like but the students, by and large, are a pretty quiet lot. I say until recently cause this thing with the nuclear plant has divided the town. Tempers are heating up. Trinity is becoming polarized. And I don't like it."

"Is the college involved in any way?"

"Not really. They have sponsored some seminars on nuclear power in the hopes of educating people but that's all.

"So why would my mom be staying up late spying on people?"

"You're asking the wrong person, Grant," Carrie said.

The following morning it was Grant's turn to fix breakfast. A sleepy Carrie stumbled into the kitchen where he had a platter of bacon cooked and a pot of coffee brewed. She plopped into a chair, Grant brought her a cup of coffee.

"Thanks," she said. "I can use this."

"How do you want your eggs?"

"Cooked," was Carrie's reply.

"I deserve that," he said, laughing. "You seem to be feeling better this morning."

"Much better. The demons of the other night are gone. At least for now. I'm sorry I unloaded all my personal problems on you."

"No problem. It was probably good that you spoke about it."

Granted plated their breakfast and brought them to the table. "I haven't told anyone about that except my shrink and group back at Reed."

"I'm glad," Carrie said. She dove into the breakfast Grant set before her.

"Still, I shouldn't have unloaded on you. It's my problem."

"I was glad you did. It made me feel—well, needed. No one has ever really needed me before, Grant. Bless you for that."

"I know I'll have to answer for my sins one day," he said, taking a sip of coffee. He looked her directly in the eye. "When that day of judgment comes, I pray I'm man enough to confess and ask for mercy. I know I have already many times over."

"I believe that's enough, sweetheart. I believe God understands. My heart grieves that you're still suffering."

"Well, enough of this depressing talk," Grant said, sipping his coffee.

"Did you know Lori's funeral was yesterday?" Carrie said.

"Oh gosh," Grant said. "I totally forgot. I've been so

wrapped up with this entire affair that it slipped my mind completely. And I wanted to chat with her parents. Do you know if they were there?"

"No, I don't. Yeah, we should have remembered."

"I wonder what their thoughts were concerning Lori's blood tests? Surprised? Not believing?"

"Probably madder than hell," Carrie said. "Especially not having any answers. I can't imagine the stress they are under right now."

"We going to Savannah?"

"Your idea to talk to the Georgia Bureau of Investigation was a good one but first I want to check out Lori's apartment. Then we can go."

"You sure you want to break into her apartment?"

"Yes, definitely." Grant noticed the look on Carrie's face. "Look, I'll be careful, I promise."

He kissed her goodbye and drove to Lori's apartment building. An inquiry at the office led him #142, an apartment at the rear of the small complex. The parking area next to the building was devoid of cars. Everyone must be at work, Grant thought.

The door was locked, of course. He wondered if Lori's family had been here and removed her belongings. If so, there might not be anything of note that would cast light on the recent deaths.

Grant scanned the courtyard. No one about. He removed a lock pick from his pocket and began jimmying the lock. His pulse pounded in his head. After a number of tries, the lock clicked open and he entered the dark apartment. The large living room had that lived-in look— clothes strewn over a sofa, magazines laying about. He wandered into the kitchen, opened the fridge. It held only a few items. Nothing unusual.

He crossed the living room to the bedroom. It was darker, the shades being drawn. He clicked on the bedside lamp, went directly to the closet. Lori's clothes were arranged in an orderly fashion by type and color, dressed, then pants, then blouses, all hanging neatly. He rifled through the clothes but found nothing of interest.

Along a far wall stood a small desk with a laptop resting on it. Grant opened the computer, turned it on, and waited for the screen to come to life. While waiting he rummaged through the desk's drawers. A drawer on the right held a few documents that he removed. Thumbing through the pages he saw that they were mostly articles from the Internet on the perils of nuclear reactors and the Three Mile Island incident. He laid them aside when the computer screen blinked on.

But there was nothing on the computer to be any help. He went through Lori's files, finding only an address book, a few articles she had written decrying the evils of nuclear power, bank statements. He closed the laptop, returned to the living room, dropped into a chair next to the telephone.

Grant noticed a notepad next to the phone so he picked it up. On it was written a single line: *River Road—eleven p.m.*

So Lori had an appointment on the River Road late at night. When was this? There was no date on the note so it was probably the same night she wrote scribbled it on the pad. The night she died? Who could she have been meeting so late? In a secluded area away from town? He tore the note from the pad and stuffed it into his shirt pocket.

Time to be leaving.

Grant stood for a moment at the front door, thinking, wondering about Lori's life. What sort of woman was she? What secrets, if any, did she hold? Was the late night meeting what got her dead? Was her death a clue into his mother's untimely death?

He opened the door to leave and was confronted by

Sergeant Brady and two uniformed police officers. Grant jumped at the sight of them, startled.

"Mr. Collins," Brady said. "May I ask what you are doing in Miss Spelling's apartment"?

"I—I—" Grant stammered.

"Breaking and entering is against the law, even in Trinity. You are under arrest. Officer, cuff him up."

Chapter 15

Carrie finished her shower and lounged on her sofa with a novel and wishing Grant was with her. He had driven to Lori's apartment with the intent of breaking into it. He was doing it against her wishes but the man was headstrong and intent on uncovering what happened to his mother. She had gotten used to him being around and wasn't looking forward to him returning home.

She thumbed through her book not really interested in it wondering what was keeping Grant. He had been gone two hours. More than enough time to search Lori's apartment.

She was worried. Something must have gone wrong.

Too bad he didn't have a cell phone so she could call or text him. Carrie got up and paced a while before sauntering into the kitchen to fix some lunch. While eating a sandwich she decided if Grant hadn't returned when she was finished she would drive over to the apartments and check. Grant's outpouring of emotion the previous night along with his revelation concerning the cause of his PTSD left her unnerved. It was a revelation she hadn't expected although she was glad Grant trusted her enough to reveal his deep-seated problems. He was a sweet man, she could sense that. His easygoing demeanor had taken her by surprise so now she found herself caring deeply for him.

She was living in Atlanta when her father died, leaving her mother having to find work to support herself. Carrie had just graduated from high school and was working as a secretary for a construction company. When her mother's salary needed supplementing, Carrie, after cashing her paycheck, would stop by her mother's house and give her a little money. Enough to help with groceries.

But when her mother remarried a year later, Carrie and her stepfather didn't get along so she left Atlanta behind. Left the drugs and crime and moved to Trinity. She loved the river and the solitude.

That is until recently.

As she was putting her dishes in the sink the phone rang.

It was Grant.

"Grant, where are you!" she exclaimed. "You should have been here an hour ago!"

"I'm at the police station," he said in a monotone. "Can you come down?"

"Whatever for? You been arrested?"

"Not yet. I think they're still trying to figure out what to do with me. But they have impounded my car so if you can come down—"

"Sure, you bet. I'm on the way. Don't worry. I'll be there shortly and then we can figure this out."

On the way to the police station, Carrie's mind was in a whirl. I warned him to not go over there, she bristled to herself. *Why couldn't he have listened?* She parked her car, rushed into the station, was directed down the hall to Brady's office where she found Grant sitting in a chair. He was obviously angry at his situation.

The police sergeant looked up when she entered.

"You Carrie?" he asked. He sat at a computer terminal typing.

"Yes," Carrie said. She went over to Grant and put a hand on his shoulder.

"Your friend here broke into Miss Spelling's apartment earlier. He hasn't said much."

"Are you going to arrest him, Sergeant?" Carrie said, still standing next to Grant.

"I haven't decided. I don't know if it's a crime to break into a deceased person's apartment. Probably is but Mr. Collins has been concerned about her whereabouts. At least up until her death."

"I'm sure he meant no harm, sir." Carrie left Grant's side, went over to the man's desk, and stood.

"He's been badgering me regarding his mother's death. Seems to thinks there was foul play involved."

"Yes," Carrie nodded. "We both think the same thing about that."

Brady looked up and smiled. "You too? Jesus, some people can find conspiracies almost anywhere." He went back to typing. Finished, he slid his chair back and shook his head. "All right, Mr. Collins," he said, lighting a cigarette. "I'm giving you a break. Nothing was stolen, apparently, and you had no items from the apartment on you as you were leaving. So I'm letting you go with a warning. Don't let me catch you doing anything in Trinity again or there'll be hell to pay. Understand? I don't even want to hear that you spit on the sidewalk. If you do, you'll be seeing me again and you won't like me then, I assure you. Now get out of here."

"What about my car?" Grant muttered.

"Pick it up tomorrow. Pay the towing fee and it's yours."

Carrie took Grant's hand and led him out of the station to her car. Once on the road she questioned him.

"Find anything?" she asked.

"Yeah," he replied. He reached in his pocket and retrieved the paper. "This was written on a pad by her phone. It says, River Road, eleven p.m. She was meeting someone, Carrie. Probably on the night she died."

"Who?"

"Don't know. If we can learn the answer to that we might know who killed the others."

☙☙☙

Mayor Bruce Baxter couldn't believe his good fortune. Never one to gloat over someone's death, he nevertheless realized that the politics of the nuclear power plant had been handed a gift-horse and he wasn't going to complain. Hollister McLain's death in the fire that consumed his hardware store, tragic as it was, provided him with an opportunity of turning the council vote his way as he would be the person to appoint an interim replacement until the next election cycle. Conway would be calling soon wanting to know whom his appointment was and when the vote was going to take place.

Baxter knew McLain to be an honest, hardworking man whose wife had been treated for some sort of cancer. They had been a childless couple so there wouldn't be many mourners at the graveside except for the few townspeople who loved him. He had been an ardent critic of the power plant from the very beginning and his eloquent denunciations frequently made the editorial page of the *Eagle* or were repeated at local rallies.

It was his and Helen Collins' enthusiastic opposition that had galvanized half of Trinity's Citizens Against Nuclear Power in spite of the promises of cheap and plentiful electricity. Now that both of them had met with

an unfortunate demise, things should move along
smoothly.

He picked up the phone and called the Chief of Police
Alex Paley and waited impatiently while the chief's secretary found him. A gravelly voice answered.

"Chief," Baxter said. "Mayor here. What's the word
on the hardware fire?"

"Don't know yet, Mr. Mayor" came a gruff reply.
"Won't know anything until the investigation is finished.
You in a hurry for answers?"

"Was it accidental or was it arson? That's what I need
to know. Give me your assessment at this point."

"Fire department's been over there doing their thing.
So far, nothing's turned up to indicate the fire was pur-
posefully set. Looks like some oily rags in a storeroom
ignited and caused the fire. Certainly a tragedy for old
man McLain."

"Where's his body, Chief?"

"Over at the funeral home. I think there's plans to
cremate him as I have heard that is the wish of his wife."

"No medical examiner?" Baxter was surprised that
there was not going to be an autopsy.

"No need. At this point all signs point to an accidental death."

After hanging up, Baxter breathed a sigh of relief.
The less law enforcement complications the better and
the sooner he could make his replacement for Hollister
McLain. He would wait a respectable few days then hold
a press conference notifying Trinity of his decision. He
had a person in mind. He knew Archibald Martin, the
owner of Martin's Restaurant, was in favor of the plant
for it meant cheaper power for his business. He would
talk to the man and convince him to take a seat on the
city council.

His secretary buzzed his intercom.

"Yes?" Baxter said, still preoccupied with Archibald Martin.

"There's a man here to see you, sir. He is Helen Collins's son. Do you have time to speak with him?"

A nervous tick ran through the mayor's body and he shuddered at the thought of a confrontation. But he was enough of a politician to know it wouldn't look good if he refused to see the young man. "Send him in," he said and stood to greet the man who entered the office and extended his hand.

"Thanks for seeing me, Mr. Mayor. I'm Grant Collins. My mother was Helen Collins. She died in an automobile accident here, recently."

"Yes, I know, son. A tragedy to be sure. Here, have a seat." Baxter offered Grant a chair to the side of his desk and took a seat himself behind it. "Your mother was such a lovely woman. A sad loss for Trinity."

"You knew my mother, then?" the man said.

"Unfortunately, not very well. But she was a champion of environmental issues in our town."

Baxter surveyed the man who wore dark slacks and a white shirt open at the neck. Collins's gaze seemed to peer beneath the surface with a calm steely resolve that unnerved him.

"I am here, sir, to find answers to her death and the deaths of several other Trinity residents in the past year."

"Yes?" Baxter said, starting to become annoyed. He didn't like the man's direct approach to problems. As a politician, he was skilled at dancing around issues. His mind quickly began calculating possible responses. He squirmed in his chair.

"Well, sir, the people I am talking about and who have died all worked on the Citizens Against Nuclear Power committee. Their deaths, including my mother's, have all been ruled accidental by the local authorities here."

"I am not aware—"

"Including most recently my classmate, Lori Spelling and Mr. McLain of the hardware store, whom I just saw the day of his death."

"Yes, it was a tragic fire, Mr. Collins. The fire investigators are doing their investigation as we speak but so far it looks like an accident. I just got off the phone with our police chief."

"My friend, Lori, wasn't a drug user, sir. Of that I am convinced."

"Yes, I am aware of the toxicology report on Miss Spelling. Our young kids these days..." Baxter looked out the window onto the park below. It was empty at the moment.

"These weren't accidental deaths, sir. Of that I am convinced. These people were against the nuclear power plant coming to town and now they are dead. It's not just a coincidence.

"Mr. Collins, I appreciate your concern and zeal in this but I can assure you that if there was anything to what you are implying our law enforcement would be all over it. Since they obviously don't think there's a connection, I don't see how there's anything I can do. Do you have anything in the way of proof of what you say? If you do, I'd like to see it."

Baxter was rapidly losing his patience with the direction the conversation was going. And this brash young upstart was beginning to ruin his day.

"No, sir, I don't. But I don't understand why no one here in Trinity can see the relationship of these deaths except me and Carrie."

"Who?" Baxter said. "Carrie?"

"Huh, just a friend," Helen Collins' son said. "No one in particular."

"I would be interested in who this friend of yours is, Mr. Collins. Maybe she has information the police could use."

"Not really. I appreciate your time, Mr. Mayor." The man stood and extended his hand. "I'll let you get back to the city's business. Sorry to have troubled you."

After Grant Collins left, Baxter phoned Winston Conway. The man needed to know that someone was snooping into their business.

Chapter 16

They were on the eastern side of the city. Their objective, two bridges, lay ahead. They needed to push north through Ambush Alley.

The incoming small arms fire was irritating but not devastating. The convoy crawled along toward the bridge at a snail's pace, sitting ducks for Iraqi RPGs and mortars. Their Humvees stopped in the road behind M1 tanks mired in a sewer. He was exhausted, not having slept for over thirty hours. They were low on fuel.

The radio squawked. Several Humvees approaching the convoy from the north. Their vehicles were smoking.

Suddenly, they were moving again through the eastern edge of the city.

Then, his world exploded.

Incoming rocket and machine gun fire erupted on his front, left, and right. Iraqi fighters in civilian clothes emerged from seemingly every window and doorway to fire rifles and rockets. Some ran into the streets to fire their rockets at point blank range.

It was chaos. Explosions everywhere, tanks and other vehicles going up in fireballs and heavy smoke. Wounded and dying marines screaming.

He tried to steer their Humvee around a disabled armored personnel carrier but was hemmed in by the narrow road.

Out of the corner of his eye he saw it.

The car slowly creeping toward them. Full of young boys. With rifles.

It kept coming.

What the hell are you doing here? Don't you know there's a war going on? Get back to your mothers!

The marine sitting next to him shouted and pointed at the car. His buddies in the rear compartment begged Grant to do something.

Anything. Just don't get them killed.

The car kept advancing. He could see their curly heads, their wide dark eyes. One was pointing at their Humvee. The marine next to him screamed in his ear. Grant's head pounded. He hadn't been trained for this.

He grabbed the grenade launcher, aimed it at the car.

Please stop. God, please stop.

It didn't.

He fired the weapon and an instant later the car exploded in an orange flash, the sound deafening, rocking their Humvee. When he looked the car was gone. Not even a mass of burned wreckage remained behind. It was simply gone.

Grant jolted awake, his body drenched in a cold sweat. It was the nightmare again. *God, when would it ever end?* He sat and rubbed his face as if trying to push the images from his brain. But it was to no avail and he knew they would never leave him.

Carrie was asleep beside him. In the pale moonlight that filtered through the curtained window she looked at peace, even beautiful. By her own admission, Carrie wasn't a looker, wasn't endowed with a model's beauty but over the past week Grant was able to see beneath the physical and glimpse into her soul, her character. She possessed a quiet maturity, something he found lacking in many women her age. A calm approach to whatever life handed out. He was beginning to rely on her, need her nearness, her kind words. He couldn't believe that some man hadn't snatched her up and made an honest woman out of her. Maybe it was time he thought of making a home for himself. Would she go for it? Even with his issues? Even with this heavy baggage he carried? Was it even fair to ask it of her?

He doubted it.

He eased himself quietly out of bed and wandered into the kitchen. He fixed coffee and sat at the table while it perked. Out of the blue he thought of his brother, Eric. Growing up the two of them were inseparable though Grant was three years older. Eric was headstrong as a child, leaving older brother Grant constantly working to keep him out of trouble. Eric had a lot of friends, mostly ones whom their parents disapproved. Trinity back then was a small rural town in the shadows of Savannah but some of the less desirable elements moved up along the Dogwood River to carry on with their nefarious activities.

After Grant left home and Eric was in high school, his brother became infatuated with Savannah's drug scene, driving there frequently to buy his drugs. At first it was just weed but soon he had moved to cocaine. When Grant discovered how deep was his brother's addiction, he spent one weekend screaming at Eric and his stupidity. That he needed to get help.

But Eric didn't listen. Soon he had moved on to his terminal drug—heroin. Bigger bang for the buck. By the time the boy was eighteen he had a hundred dollar a day habit and no job or income to support it. As his debt to his supplier mounted he began selling for the man to satisfy the debt. But what he owed kept growing until it reached a sum that was impossible to pay back. He began making demands of his supplier. One night to uncomplicated his life, the seller supplied Eric with uncut heroin and he died of an overdose in an abandoned cabin on the outskirts of Trinity.

The coffee was ready so Grant poured a mugful, returned to the table.

Their parents were devastated of course. His father, Herbert, took his son's death as a personal failure. He became quiet and morose, rarely speaking at dinner. He went to work, came home, read his evening newspaper, then we went to bed. After Eric's death, Grant didn't have much of a relationship with his father, spending most of his time either at school or at work. It wasn't that his father was a bad father, the man just seemed preoccupied with the death of his son and he had no energy left for the one who remained.

When his father had a fatal heart attack at work, the paramedics couldn't revive him. He was dead by the time they reached the hospital in Savannah. His mother fell in a deep depression after Herbert's death.

It took several years for her to regain her mental health but after that she never expressed an interest in the men that came calling on her. Finally, all the eligible men ceased their courting leaving Helen to herself, her books, and her knitting.

When she wrote Grant about meeting Hazel Bullock he was delighted that Mom was starting to get out and meet new people.

Carrie stumbled into the kitchen rubbing her eyes.

"You're up early," she said.

"Couldn't sleep," Grant said, pouring her a mug of coffee. She looked at it for a moment as if not fully awake, then took a gulp.

"Nightmare again?"

"Yeah. I keep hoping that one day they'll stop. But it may be a fool's hope."

"You wanna drive down to Savannah today? There's a Bureau of Investigation Field Office there. I checked. The Special Agent in Charge is a woman, Samantha Wilder. We wouldn't have to drive all the way to Decatur to see someone."

"Fine," Grant said. "I want to try and speak to McLain's wife too. See if she might know something."

"Good idea. You mentioned that Lori had an appointment on the River Road the night she died."

"Don't know if was the exact night but she was going there to meet someone. Who, we don't know."

ɾᴐɾᴐ

A bright blue sky dawned over the field office of the Georgia Bureau of Investigation in Savannah. Located in a suburb on the southern fringe of the city near the Little Ogeechee River, the field office was a single story structure with a red tiled roof. Special Agent in Charge Samantha Wilder was at her desk early, thumbing through the active files, making sure her fellow investigative agents were covering all bases. Two of the active cases involved white-collar crimes of corporate embezzlement, one case of an unexpected death in the Springfield jail, a rape case whose suspect was a prominent Savannah attorney, and a two year-old Savannah murder. The victim in the two-year murder case was a dockworker who apparently stumbled onto something he shouldn't have. He had three nine-millimeter slugs in him. One to the head, as in a professional hit.

Wilder jotted a few notes onto a legal pad, points she intended to make at the afternoon agent's meeting. She sipped her soft drink, a way of getting her caffeine level to a functional one as she clicked through the computer files. She smiled at the thought of the upcoming meeting. After her predecessor's retirement six months earlier, she had been appointed Special Agent in Charge much to the consternation of several agents who thought women shouldn't be allowed in the Bureau. At least those who carry weapons. But she had worked hard to win them over and though it was a slow, tedious process, she thought she was winning on that front. One of them, thinking she might be an easy love conquest, was given a stiff lecture with a threat of transfer. He behaved himself after that.

She was divorced with a ten year-old daughter. Luckily, she had found Maria, her housekeeper, who lived with them, got Jessica up each morning, dressed and ready for school, fixed her breakfast, then took her to the bus stop. Maria was a jewel. Wilder couldn't do this job without her. Wilder tried to be a real mom on the weekends.

She took a break from the computer and gazed out the window. In the distance the sun was creating dancing reflections on the dark water of the river. She could barely make out river birds swooping low looking for their breakfast. She leaned back in her chair and watched them soar while behind her she heard the sounds of her coworkers filing into the office. She turned at the knock in her door. Her secretary, Julie, stood smiling, a small sack in her hand.

"I brought you donuts, ma'am," she said, entering the office. "Chocolate cake with chocolate icing. Your favorite." She set the sack on Wilder's desk.

"Thanks, Julie," she said. "You're a godsend. I need some sugar to go with this caffeine."

The secretary turned and started for the door, paused, turned. "Let me know if you need anything else."

Wilder nodded and Julie closed the door behind her. She switched the computer screen to her daily schedule noticing that she had a full morning. Seems like crime never stops, she thought.

ℰↄℰↄ

The man in the lighthouse woke and fixed his breakfast of oatmeal and coffee on a small propane burner. His stiff joints ached from spending the night on the floor. He stared out the lighthouse window as he ate, saw nothing but water. The channel and Atlantic beyond were placid this morning, a far cry from their angry rolling during last night's storm. Now the sun shone bright rendering the ocean a pearlescent blue-green.

Finished with his breakfast, he rinsed the dishes in cold water and set them on a thick rag to dry. It was eight-seventeen. He needed to make contact at nine sharp so he sat at the small table and dialed channel three on the marine band handheld radio.

Waiting for the time to pass, he wondered about his contact, who it was, what they were going to be willing to pay. He had been contacted on his encrypted email server as to the possible nature of the contract but the details were sketchy. Killing a public figure in the States was always risky but he had done it before. Numerous times.

He kept those instances locked away in the basement of his mind and had thrown away the key. Kept all the evil, the ugly, locked away. He refused to go down to that room, there was no need. Once, with Katya, he wanted to give her the key, and say, *Here it is—come in and see for yourself.* But he hadn't the courage. With her, he had thought about giving it all up but, after her death, he no longer cared. She with the wide curious eyes, the laughter that came from a deep spirit, and her moments of quiet when they were together. But that ended with her brutal murder. She had called him, frantic. Her ex-boyfriend was on his way over. Please hurry! But he had arrived too late. Katya's bloodied battered body lay askew on her apartment floor. He briefly considered drowning his sorrows in alcohol. But instead, he allowed himself to be carried down the vortex of inhumanity until it no longer mattered if he lived or died. He adapted. He had gotten even with a bullet to the man's head.

The man glanced at his watch. Nine o'clock.

He picked up the radio, pushed the *TALK* button, and called his contact.

Chapter 17

Wilder's intercom buzzed. It was Julie. "There are two people here to see you, Special Agent Wilder," she said in a clipped monotone. "A man and a woman. They don't have an appointment."

"Tell them I'm busy," Wilder said.

"I did, ma'am but they were insistent. Said it has to do with some deaths up in Trinity. I have them waiting in the outer office."

Wilder breathed an exasperated sigh, looked at the clock on the wall. "What time is my next appointment?"

"Nothing until the agent's meeting at one-thirty."

"Oh, all right, Julie. Send them in but tell them to make it short. I want to try and make lunch at home with Jessica today."

She clicked off the intercom and soon Julie was standing in the doorway alongside a couple. Both bore serious expressions.

"Come in, won't you and have a seat? I'm Special Agent in Charge Samantha Wilder. How can I help you?"

The man spoke first, fidgeting in his chair as he did. "My name is Grant Collins," he began, "and this is my friend Carrie. We come from Trinity, just a short drive northeast of here."

Wilder nodded. She knew the town. "Yes, go on," she said.

"Well," the man continued, "now that we're here, I don't know exactly where to begin. You see, my mother was killed recently in a car accident, only we don't think it was an accident. Her name is Helen. Helen Collins. Anyway, she was on this citizen's committee trying to block the nuclear power plant from being built in Trinity. And she wasn't the only person on the committee to have died recently, either. I have a list here—"

The man removed a sheet of paper from his pocket and handed it to Wilder. She glanced at it. It appeared to contain newspaper articles outlining the deaths of several people.

"Yes, please go on," she said.

"The people on that list were on the Citizens Against Nuclear Power. Have you heard of it?"

Wilder had not.

"The committee," the man continued, "was lobbying against a nuclear power plant that DynaTech is wanting to build. The town's council is supposed to vote in the plant in the near future. Most of the committee members are now deceased."

"I see," said Wilder. "And your point, Mr. Collins?"

"Ma'am, their deaths couldn't all be coincidental. Anyway, that's what Carrie and I think."

"Were these deaths investigated by Trinity's law enforcement?" Wilder asked. She noticed the young woman seemed nervous.

But then she cleared her throat. "If you want to call it that," the woman named Carrie said. "Trinity's police are a joke. It's common knowledge."

"Have you approached them with your suspicions, Mr. Collins?"

"A couple of times. All I've received for my trouble are smiles and excuses that they have more important things to do."

"Like hand out parking tickets," interjected Carrie.

Wilder smiled at the woman's brashness. She warmed to her frankness and buzzed for Julie. When the secretary entered, Wilder handed her the paper with the articles. "Make a copy of this, Julie," she said.

The woman took the paper and returned to her desk.

"Now," Wilder continued, "do either of you have anything in the way of evidence that might support your contention that these deaths were anything other than tragic accidents?"

"My mother's car," Grant said, "was supposedly struck a bridge abutment and that killed her, due to a high rate of speed so she lost control of her car. But Agent Wilder, my mother never drove anywhere very fast. Her close friend, Mrs. Bullock can testify to that. My mother was in her seventies. She knew better than to take that road doing fifty-five. In addition, there are police photos showing the rear of mother's car dented in. Severely. The trunk was mashed pretty good. The police said because there was no paint on the rear of her car there was no reason to suspect she was rear-ended and pushed into the abutment from behind."

"But you don't think so?"

"Like I said, my mother was a careful driver. I suppose she could have had a heart attack or stroke but there was no autopsy to rule them out."

"No coroner?"

"Trinity's medical examiner was at the scene and certified her death was accidental. He didn't think an autopsy was necessary."

Wilder, who had been taking notes during the discussion, stopped and laid her pen aside. For a quick moment, she studied the pair before her. They looked like frightened young people with a genuine concern. Her grandfather, who had been a longtime police detective, always told her that cops were sworn to protect everyone. It didn't matter one's color, economic class, situation in life. Every citizen deserved the best from law enforcement. It was a mantra she attempted to live by, one she demanded from those under her. Could she send this couple away without a word? Hardly.

She smiled and drummed her pen on her desk. "All right," she said. "You've intrigued me. Tell you what— I'll type up your report so we'll have it on file. I'll assign an agent to look into your concerns. All my agents are busy as hell right now, but we'll look into it, I promise you." She took a business card from a holder and passed it to Grant. "That's the number here. My cell phone number is at the bottom. If you think of anything else or if new developments occur, please do not hesitate to call."

With that she stood and watched the pair stroll out of her office.

Seem like a nice couple, she thought.

※※※

Back in the car heading back to Trinity, Grant spoke first. "What do you think?"

"She seemed nice enough. Professional as well. I hope she can help."

He steered the car first onto State Highway 21 then turned onto the narrow road that paralleled the river. When they neared *Pete's Crab Shack* they stopped for lunch.

"You know McLain's wife?" he said over a fried crab sandwich.

"No," Carrie said. "Mr. McLain ran his hardware store for many years but I never saw his wife." She laughed. "We didn't run in the same circles."

"If I could talk with her, maybe she could shed some light on these deaths. She might have known some of the people. I'll drive by later, see if she will give me a few minutes. I can't help but think that someone somewhere has the goods on DynaTech and Conway. That someone in the committee did their research and knows what's really going on here."

"Like you," Carrie said, "I think there's more to it here than what's on the surface. I mean why would it be worth it to Conway to murder these people who stand in his way? What would be the point in that? Why risk it when all you have to do is move the proposed site of the plant to somewhere else. Surely, there's a town somewhere whose citizens would be behind it a hundred percent, unlike Trinity."

"All the more reason to chat with Mrs. McLain."

Carrie nodded. "It's worth a try. But tell me something, Grant. How much do we know about this committee? The Citizens Against Nuclear Power? I think we ought to find out more about them. Who they are, what their motives are, what kind of activities they've been involved in. That sort of thing. What do you think?"

"What good would that do?" he said. "We know they were planning to thwart the plant from coming to Trinity. What else do we need to know?"

"We wouldn't know till we checked them out, would we?"

"Are there any other committee members? No one has spoken out recently. The committee members may all be dead now."

"I'm saying we need to find that out. If there are any still living, we ought to find them, talk to them. Even if there's only one left, that person may have the same suspicions as us and is not speaking. Possibly out of fear."

"Laying low, eh?"

"Possibly even hiding out. Afraid they might be next. We ought to try and find out."

"Quite the little investigator, aren't you?" Grant said, finished with his sandwich. He wiped his mouth with a napkin.

They both laughed at his remark. Grant paid for their lunch and drove back to Carrie's apartment.

℮ɔ℮ɔ

The *Sandpiper* was moored in a shallow channel next to Bird Island in Caliboque Sound south of Hilton Head. It was an isolated place for a meeting, far from prying eyes or other traffic. The human kind. Conway had picked the spot himself due to the island was uninhabited and there was nothing near it for miles. After the boat's pilot dropped anchor, Conway's steward brought him his dinner and a bottle of scotch. Then the steward and the pilot retired to their respective cabins for the remainder of the evening.

Finished with his meal Conway climbed the short stairs to the main deck and slouched in a chair. He tried to focus his gaze on the dark nothingness beyond but ocean and sky blended into one amorphous mass. He couldn't make out the horizon. Above, the stairs were out, clear and brilliant, undeterred by Savannah's city lights. A beautiful night, he thought. A night fit for lovers not the business he was about to conduct.

He thought back to Wanda. They had such a good thing going while it lasted. He remembered when they sat out under these same stars, made love on the beach, held each other. When she left him he was devastated. He made a decision never again to let a woman get to him like Wanda. He drowned himself with hard work and soon she was only a distant memory.

But now his CFO Jake Milburn had delivered the bad news. DynaTech needed capital and lots of it. The company was floundering from overextension to the point where the Trinity plans had been compromised. He had enough cash reserves to hold out for a year but after that the company would be insolvent. Once the city council gave them the green light it would be easy to negotiate the needed capital to stay afloat. And once the plant was up and running the money would come pouring in.

However, Trinity's mayor had become an impediment to his plans. The man was an imbecile. He was sitting on a potential gold mine and hadn't the fortitude to act. Sure, the citizen's committee was now less formidable than it was a few short weeks ago but there were still a couple of member's on the council who needed swaying. Baxter was losing control of his end.

And now there was this man going about Trinity asking questions. Questions about his mother's death. Baxter had said the man had been to the police and the chief demanding action, threatening to get a court order for an autopsy. He had threatened the ME. *What next?* Conway thought. The man was a loose cannon. Baxter couldn't contain him.

In the dark distance, Conway heard the approaching sound of an outboard motor. It was off his port beam. He strained his eyes but saw nothing. Over his shoulder Bird Island loomed as a dark knoll.

The sound was closer now but still, he saw nothing. It was steady, probably a twenty or twenty-five horsepower motor.

Conway picked up the handheld floodlight and flashed it three times in the direction of the sound. He waited. And then—three flashes in return.

His contact.

Soon the Zodiac RIB appeared out of the gloom and its pilot cut back on the motor, allowing the boat to drift alongside the yacht.

The man in the RIB threw Conway a line and he secured it to a cleat. Clad in black clothes, the man climbed aboard, removed his gloves.

"Conway?" the man said.

Conway nodded and escorted the man below to the salon where both men sat.

"You've been informed of the target?" Conway asked, eyeing the man through narrow eyes.

"Yes," said the man.

"Good. How much?"

"I am not accustomed to dealing directly with whoever pays me," said the man, sitting back in the leather chair. "This is highly irregular. It can lead to—complications."

Conway winced at the man's suggestion. "I thought a courier for this part was unnecessary. I don't like trusting my money to strangers."

Now it was the man's turn to look dour. He sat and looked at Conway for a long moment. "It's done all the time, all over the world. I'm no amateur, Conway. But it's your funeral should something go wrong. I'll be long gone."

Conway twitched in his chair. He wasn't used to someone addressing him without the title *Mister*. The man obviously wasn't afraid of him. "I understand," he said.

"The money?"

"Yes. Shall we say fifty thousand now and another

fifty when the job has been completed? Sound satisfacto-
ry?"

The man nodded. "That was the initial agreement."

"Payment?"

"The courier will contact you by the previous method. He will give you instructions. Once he has confirmed
to me the money has been deposited you can expect
completion within a week."

Conway nodded, sipped his scotch.

"It must be done quickly, efficiently," he said.

"But of course. That is why my services are in such
demand all over the world." The man gazed about the
salon as if admiring its beauty.

"I will see to the deposit in the morning," Conway
said.

Now the man in black nodded. "I must go."

The man stood and Conway led him back to the deck
and his Zodiac. As Conway watched the enigmatic figure
motor away into the gloomy darkness, a chill shuddered
through him.

There was no going back.

Chapter 18

Sergeant Brady and two officers were waiting at Carrie's apartment when she and Grant pulled up. As they approached the police officers, Brady sauntered over to them shaking his head. "You just can't stay out of trouble, can you, Mr. Collins?" he said. The other officers spread out, stood alongside each of Grant's shoulders. He shot a glance at Carrie who was visibly troubled.

"What's going on, Sergeant?" Grant said, moving toward the apartment stairs.

"Hold it right there," Brady said. "I'll tell you what. Two acquaintances of yours filed an assault and battery complaint against you."

"What?" Carrie screamed. "They beat him up!"

"That's not the story they tell. They said you stalked them and started a fight. You proceeded to beat them both severely."

"Listen, Sergeant," Grant said, his voice filled with venom. "Those goons jumped me first. Why, I don't know. I just evened the score."

"You ever in the military, Mr. Collins?"

"Yes."

"What branch?"

"Marines. But I don't see how—"

"Get training in hand to hand combat?"

"Of course, but—"

"Your acquaintances thought you were using some sort of judo or something on them. They were beaten pretty severely. Still had the bruises and each had a broken nose. One had a broken arm."

"My heart bleeds for them," Grant hissed. "Like I said, the bastards hurt me bad first. I just got even. Should I swear out a complaint on them?"

"You can if you want. But for now I'm taking you down to the station to file a report. Let's go."

Carrie kissed Grant on the cheek as the two officers led him to the police cruiser. He looked back at her.

"Come and get me later," he said.

He watched her from the cruiser's rear seat as they drove away. Her fists were at her mouth.

❧❧❧

Standing on McLain's porch about to ring the doorbell, Carrie had second thoughts. She thought that while Grant was giving his statement at the police station she could run by the hardware owner's house and speak with his wife before seeing if she was going to have to post bail. But now she wished she had not made such a brash decision. But she was here so she pushed the doorbell and waited.

A slender woman with well-coifed gray hair opened the door.

"Yes?" she said through the screen.

"Mrs. McLain, my name is Carrie and I would like to speak with you about your husband's involvement with the committee trying to keep the power plant from coming to Trinity."

"I don't want to talk to any reporters," the woman said, turning away.

"I'm not a reporter," Carrie said. "Please, it will only take a moment. My friend, Grant Collins, his mother served on the committee with your husband. She died in a car accident last week. It would help a lot if I could talk. Just a few minutes, please."

"Helen Collins?" the woman said, now back at the screen door.

"Yes, ma'am. Her son, Grant, is my friend."

"Oh my, yes, Grant. I haven't seen him since he was a young boy. Where is he?"

"He is busy at the moment or he would have come with me. May I come in?"

"Sure," she said. She opened the screen door, stepped to one side to allow Carrie to pass. "Have a seat there." She indicated a worn upholstered straight back chair while taking a seat in a rocker next to Carrie.

Mrs. McLain was a woman near sixty, Carrie surmised, had remarkably smooth pale skin. Her green eyes were set wide apart on her face. She wore a plain cotton dress.

"I was sorry to hear about your husband," Carrie said. "I know it was such a shock."

The woman looked out the front window then down at her folded hands. "It was," she said. "I still don't understand how it happened."

"Did the police and fire departments investigate?"

"They said they did. Some oily rags or something. But Holly was too meticulous a man to be that careless."

"I've lived a long time in Trinity, Mrs. McLain, and the police have always been weak. Grant is finding that out."

"You mentioned the citizen's committee that Mrs. Collins was on."

"Yes, Grant's mother."

"Holly said she was very active. Going all over town handing out pamphlets. But Holly wasn't on that committee. However, serving on the city council, he was sympathetic to their cause. He sided with their point of view."

"Were you familiar with the work of the committee, Mrs. McLain?"

"Of course. Most people were. They were all over town, talking and handing out their pamphlets against the plant coming to Trinity. And I believe Grant's mother was one of their members."

"She was. Until her accident. But, Grant and I don't think it was an accident. We think it's possible that her death was orchestrated in some way."

"Orchestrated? You mean murdered? You really think she was murdered?"

"We think her death was beyond mere coincidence. Right now if defies explanation."

The woman stood and smiled. "I was just about to have some iced tea. Would you care for a glass?"

"That would be nice," Carrie said, standing. She followed Mrs. McLain into her tiny kitchen and watched as the woman fixed the tea.

"Holly and I lived in this house for thirty-two years. For all that time he never said a cross word to me." She handed Carrie a glass and the two found their way back to the living room. "We raised our two boys right here in this house. We don't see much of them or the grandchildren. They're very busy."

"You have many grandchildren?"

"Four. Two boys and two girls. They could do no wrong in Holly's eyes. He looked forward to their infrequent visits. Took the boys fishing."

They sat and Mrs. McLain took a napkin and dabbed her eyes. Carrie's heart skipped a beat at seeing the woman's tears. "Mrs. McLain, is there anything you can tell me about your husband and the citizen's committee? Or the power plant? Anything that you haven't told anyone before? It might help."

The woman thought for a moment, sipped her tea. "No, not really.'

"I mean if there was something out of the ordinary or something your husband said, it might go a long way in helping Grant."

"But—"

"Yes?" Carrie said, leaning forward in her chair.

"If those people who were on the committee—if their deaths weren't accidental then that means that—that Holly's death might not have been an accident either."

"Can you think of anything?"

This time the woman thought for a longer moment. She got up and went to the front window. Carrie thought she was on the verge of crying but then the woman turned and looked directly at her. There was a resolve in her voice that wasn't there earlier. "A week before he died, Holly seemed troubled but he didn't want to discuss it. I asked him numerous times but he put me off. He was quiet for days afterward, preoccupied. I baked his favorite cake but it didn't help bring him out of his mood. I was beginning to think it was me or that he had been to the doctor and received bad news. Come to think of it, it was right about the time Grant's mother was killed. How strange."

"Go on, please, Carrie said.

"A couple of nights before the fire, he spent the entire evening at his desk in the other room. I don't know what he was doing but I remember thinking how odd it was for him to be doing that. He hardly ever spent any time at that desk. He paid our bills at the breakfast table not at that desk. But he spent several hours there. He got irritated when I asked him if he wanted anything. He just waved me away."

"What was he doing?"

"Writing, I think."

"Did he ever say what it was he was writing?"

"No."

"And he never said anything about what it was he was doing all that time at his desk?"

"No. But—wait, my dear. I think he may have kept it in his desk. He has a locking drawer in which he keeps some important papers. He might have kept it locked away—whatever it was."

"Could we go look, Mrs. McLain? I know it's a bother but it might lead to something."

"Hon, I haven't gone through Hollie's things since he died. I've sat here and wondered why it had to happen. Maybe now is a good time to find out what was bothering him."

She stood and Carrie followed her into a room containing a love seat and an easy chair. A floor lamp stood beside the chair. A few family photographs hung on the walls.

"This was the boys room when they were young," the woman said, stopping at a worn roll-top desk that stood against a wall. Mrs. McLain switched on the banker's lamp at one end of the desk. She began opening the draws until she found one that was locked.

"He had the key somewhere," she said, still looking through the pigeonholes and drawers.

Carrie's mouth was dry and her heart pulsed in her throat. She silently wished the woman along, impatient to look inside the locked drawer. She thought of Grant, hoped he wasn't in big trouble at the police station, kept her eyes on the woman searching for the key. If she could uncover something that would help him put closure in his mother's death maybe he would consider staying in Trinity. He had captured her heart and it would be difficult to watch him drive away.

"I think this is it," Mrs. McLain said, withdrawing a small bronze key from a pigeonhole.

"Hopefully," Carrie said, impatiently.

The woman's hand trembled as she inserted the key into the lock in the drawer and turned it. An audible *click* was heard and she opened the drawer.

Inside, the drawer was filed with numerous papers and nestled among them, a small black journal. Both women stared at the little book.

"What is that?" Carrie said.

"Looks like a journal," Mrs. McLain said, thumbing through the journal.

"Is that what he was writing in?"

"I don't know. I suppose it could have been."

"Let's look through it, can we?" Carrie noticed that the woman's hands trembled as she held the little book.

"I dunno if I can. What if there's something in there I don't want to know." She handed the journal to Carrie. "Here," she said. "You look through it. If there's something bad, don't tell me."

Carrie sat at the desk and looked slowly through the book, page by page. The first few pages Holly had jotted musings about his fellow committee members and some of their activities—rallies, distributing antinuclear literature, council members for and against the plant and the like. As she scanned the pages Carrie thought how lucky Trinity was to have committed, educated group of men and women concerned about their town's welfare.

A few pages more and she saw it. Almost jumping off the page. It was more musings by Holly but this time it had a sinister, onerous bent.

I have been thinking about this for quite a while but now I'm nearly certain. I didn't want to believe it at first but I can no longer ignore my suspicions.

My suspicions were confirmed with the Spelling girl's death. I have known Lori all her life, watched her grow up, was joyful at her marriage, tearful at her divorce. In all those years, I never knew her to use drugs of any kind. The poor woman was afraid to take an aspirin let alone something like the police are saying she did. Cocaine? Never.

As member after member of the Citizens Against Nuclear Power committee members died I became more and more suspicious that their deaths were not accidental. That many people do not die from accidents in a town the size of Trinity.

In the years I have lived in this town, I have never experienced a police force as ineffectual as ours. I don't know if they are simply incompetent or just downright corrupt but their investigations of these deaths have been atrocious. Bordering on deceit and fraud.

Helen Collins was a woman of the highest integrity. Her death was completely unexpected. She was such careful driver that there was no way her death was accidental. I don't know how it was orchestrated but it was definitely not an accident. Of that I am sure. Mayor Baxter is not above suspicion in all this. The man has a past that is dark and murky. There are certainly signs that he made his money illegally and may have left bodies in his wake prior to coming to Trinity.

My own investigation has led me to believe our mayor might have dirty hands. My friend, John Jacobs, is an attorney in the state Attorney General office. Once the store's inventory is completed in the next day or two, I am going to pay him a visit and outline my fears. I pray he listens.

After reading the paragraphs, Carrie handed the journal to Mrs. McLain who took it with trembling hands.

"You need to read this," Carrie said. "I think it explains a lot."

Chapter 19

Carrie drove to the police station after leaving behind a stunned Mrs. McLain. On the seat next to her was the hardware store owner's journal. After reading what he had written, his widow peppered Carrie with questions. *What was this about? Why hadn't he gone to the authorities with his suspicions? Who could be behind all these deaths?* They were questions to which Carrie had no good answers. But the journal seemed to confirm hers and Grant's suspicions that someone had orchestrated the deaths in Trinity. But who? The obvious answer was the people who had the most to gain from the building of the power plant, which would be the mayor, and the owner of DynaTech. But would such high profile men stoop to dirty their hands to get what they wanted? Possibly, when there were millions at stake.

Mr. McLain had mentioned something about his own investigation. What was that? Had he accumulated any evidence to support his suspicions? If he had, where would it be? Or was his journal writings merely musings of an elderly, frustrated man? Carried worried there was no way of knowing the answers to any of these questions.

Mrs. McLain seemed genuinely concerned that there was more to her husband's death than the police investigation indicated. Her worry lines etched deeper into her face as she and Carrie talked about the journals cryptic words. Her heart ached for the woman who now, in addition to mourning her husband's death, was now facing the very real possibility that he had been murdered.

She found Grant as before, sitting in Sergeant Brady's cramped office. He looked haggard and tired. It had been a long day beginning with the Bureau of Investigation that morning. Now it was evening and Carrie was as exhausted as Grant appeared.

Brady looked up at her approach.

"Finally," he said, exhaling a long breath of smoke from his cigarette. "Now I can get some peace."

"Why?" Carrie said, puzzled at the sergeant's remark. "Has Grant been arrested?"

"Arrested, processed, and now out on bail," Brady said, snuffing out the cigarette. "He's all yours now."

"How?" She was mystified.

Grant looked at her with eyes that were sunk deep in his head. They had dark circles under them.

"I used my car in DC as security for the bail," he said. "Five hundred dollars."

Brady pushed a sheet of paper toward Grant and offered a pen.

"Sign in the last line, Mr. Collins, and then you can go. Your court date is in two weeks. I suggest you be there. Don't make me come looking for you."

"I wouldn't dream of it, Sergeant," Grant said, scrawling his signature on the paper. He stood.

"One more thing," Brady said, eyeing Grant, a frown etched on his forehead. "I wouldn't make any trouble for the men who filed this complaint. It wouldn't look good. Our judge here in Trinity doesn't care for witness intimidation. Got my meaning?"

"Loud and clear," Grant said. He took Carrie by the arm and hurried out of the station.

Once in Carrie's apartment Grant exploded.

"Those bastards! How dare they file a complaint against me? And how dare that asshole Brady believe them? I'm telling you this whole damn town is corrupt."

They sat in the kitchen and Carrie placed cold chicken on the table along with two beers. She watched as Grant devoured his meal in a matter of minutes. She shook her head, reached out and patted an arm.

"You don't know the half of it," she said. "I have some news. I went to see Hollister's widow earlier while you were at the police station. Talked with Mrs. McLain. We found something locked away in her husband's desk."

"Yeah?" Grant said, now attentive and sipping his beer.

"Mr. Hollister was keeping a diary, a journal of his thoughts. It was all spelled out. How he connected the dots with the committee member's deaths. Grant, he had the same suspicions as us." She reached in her purse and retrieved the small black book, handed it to Grant. "You can read it for yourself. He places Baxter in the same league with Conway."

Grant took the journal, opened it, and began reading. Carrie left him to himself while she cleaned the dishes, put them away. She sauntered into her living room, picked up a magazine, thumbed through it. It was upsetting to her that he had been arrested, as if his description of events did not matter to the police. After witnessing Sergeant Brady's attitude and body language she realized that Hollister's characterization of the Trinity law enforcement was an accurate one.

She placed the magazine down, unable to concentrate on its pages. She thought about clicking on the television but knew Grant would be through reading soon and she wanted to get his ideas. It wasn't soon before he ambled into the room.

"Well?" she said, making room on the sofa for him.

He plopped down beside her, the journal in hand. "For starters," he said, "our fears have been substantiated. We haven't been alone in thinking these deaths were more than coincidental."

"I believe you're right," Carrie said. "And our men who have been sworn to serve and protect—don't think we can count on them."

"For all we know, they may be part of the problem. I've certainly come to believe that Trinity's law enforcement is a fraud. They may even be in collusion with whoever is responsible for these killings. Holly obviously thought so. Whether or not he has any actual evidence has yet to be determined but at least we know something is amiss here."

"If we're right, Grant, then there is an evil in Trinity. An evil greater than anything I've known before. The city council may still have a quorum so if the mayor decides to hold a vote on the plant there may not be enough votes to stop it from passing."

"I think that's the idea," Grant said. "Once the council gives DynaTech the green light there's not much that can be done to stop them. And I fear the plant is only the beginning. Who knows what would be next?"

"So what can we do? How do we stop these people?

Grant looked at her, shook his head.

ༀ

Bruce Baxter sat alone in his study. His great house was quiet. His wife was away visiting her sister in Orlando, the maid had the evening off. After fixing himself a sandwich he settled in his easy chair to eat. A newly opened bottle of bourbon sat on the hand-carved mahogany table next to him. A sandwich and bourbon—not the most healthful menu for a man in his fifties. His wife had left strict instructions for the housekeeper for his evening meals but tonight he had sent her away. He wished to be alone.

He picked up a legal pad and jotted the names of the remaining council members. There were five members left. Fortunately, a quorum. A vote could go forward. But the outcome was still far from decided. He took a long pull on the bourbon, feeling the burn in the back of his throat. He lingered on each name, trying to decide if their vote was a lock. There were several that weren't.

He stopped what he was doing. *Was that a noise in the rear of the house?*

Baxter listened. I guess my mind is playing tricks, he thought. Returning to his list he tried to think what Conway would say to the present state of affairs. The man was a stickler for details and for micromanaging every aspect of his company. He fully expected the man to call and harangue him about how the vote was stacking up. Although definitely turning his way, the outcome was still not inevitable.

There it was again.

The noise in the rear of the house.

This time Baxter wandered out to his kitchen and into the laundry room where the rear door was located. He checked it.

It was unlocked.

I thought I locked the damn door.

He clicked the lock and wandered through the back part of the house, finding nothing amiss. He returned to the study and to the list. It was obvious to him that Conway wasn't pleased with the way things were going on his end. He should have already called a council vote but he had kept postponing it since the outcome was in doubt. But getting things back on track would be difficult.

The floor creaked.

It sounded as if someone was in the house. But he had just checked. It couldn't be. Baxter turned his attention back to the list of remaining council members. Now that there were only five members, with him making the sixth, if the vote was evenly split there would have to be a delay until another council member could be elected. And Conway would be pissed.

Once again the floor creaked. This time somewhat louder.

No, someone is definitely in the house.

Baxter's pulse quickened. His mouth felt as if he was chewing cotton. A bolt of fear shot through him. Was it a burglar?

He crossed quietly to his desk and found the revolver he kept for security. It had been years since he had fired the thing—it felt strange in his hand. Cool. He checked the cylinder, noted it was loaded, then proceeded toward the back of the house.

Leaving the study, a sudden thought struck him. He had never shot anyone. Would he be able to pull the trigger if confronted by an intruder? His heart banged away in his head, his eyes watered, his legs felt like jelly.

He crept down the short hallway to the living room and peered around the corner. Nothing. In the dim light from the study the living room was as his housekeeper had left it.

Gripping the revolver tighter, he moved on toward the kitchen. He held the pistol in front of him, pointing at nothing in particular as he made his way closer toward the back door.

At first, it was just a vague shadow moving toward him. A large dark mass getting closer by the second. Baxter turned. Too late.

Out of nowhere, a muscular arm grabbed his neck from behind. Whoever it was, he was strong, capable. Baxter lurched to one side, caught a blurred glimpse of a man dressed in black. But the stranglehold was a strong one.

He struggled against the man's powerful grip, falling against the kitchen table, sending dishes crashing to the floor.

Baxter fought for air. He couldn't get air into his lungs. His face burned. A dark haze began to encompass his world. The intruder's death grip was weakening him. In a frantic attempt to free himself before he lost consciousness, Baxter thrust his free hand into his assailant's face and managed to turn until he had loosened the chokehold enough for a gasp of air.

Then he saw it.

The faint light glinted off the steel of a long thin blade.

A stiletto!

Baxter summoned what little of his strength that remained and the two men fell to the floor. Locked in a struggle for his life, he cried out for help.

But none came.

With his free hand he clawed at the man's face, shoving a finger deep into an eye. The intruder growled in a language Baxter didn't understand. The stench of the man's breath lessened. Lying on his side Baxter swung at the man but his blow missed its mark. The pair grappled on the kitchen floor with Baxter thrashing his legs, trying to escape the man's grasp. But, the intruder's large powerful hands had a death hold on him making escape impossible.

Baxter attempted to roll onto his side but the man's weight held him down.

He felt the man's hand pull his head back exposing his neck.

In a flash the stiletto moved and Baxter felt a searing pain across his neck. Warm liquid gushed from the wound soaking his clothes. He felt himself getting weaker. The man's grip never wavered.

Baxter knew he was dying.

One thought shot through his rattled brain—*Why? Why?*

The darkness enveloped him.

ల౸ౡ

The man lay in the floor clutching his victim in a death grip until Baxter's breathing ceased and his muscles stopped twitching. Breathing hard, the killer relaxed, then pushed the man aside. He struggled to his knees, surveyed the kitchen. A large pool of dark blood spread over the tile floor, glistening in the weak light. A strong smell of iron filled the room. He staggered to his feet.

It wasn't supposed to go down this way. He was a professional, known for his clean kills. His plan had been to lure the man into the hallway, attack him from behind with a quick thrust to the neck. Very little blood. No struggle.

But his target hadn't cooperated, turning the fight into a dirty struggle. He didn't like that. As a professional who took pride in his work, he had no stomach for botched assignments. The only thing he could salvage was that the target was dead, mission accomplished.

He found a towel next to the sink, wiped the stiletto, replaced it in its sheath. With a gloved hand he felt his cheek where the victim scratched him. *Good, no blood.* It wouldn't do to be leaving his DNA behind. The man took a quick look around the kitchen then let left by the rear door.

It was a dark, balmy night.

Chapter 20

Grant was back in Samantha Wilder's office. He had given her Hollister McLain's journal and waited while she read through it. The woman seemed too young to be in charge of a Georgia Bureau of Investigation field office. Seated behind her desk, she leaned back in her chair, thin black spectacles perched on a perky Greek nose. Her dirty blonde hair fell in loose curls over her ears while her dark eyes narrowed as she read. He wondered if coming here was a good idea since Brady warned him against leaving Trinity. But it was a gamble he thought worth taking and besides he ought to be back at Carrie's apartment in a couple of hours.

Wilder closed the black book, laid it on her desk. She smiled. Grant's heart skipped a beat.

"Where is the young woman who was here with you on your last visit?" she said.

"Carrie is back in Trinity. She had some things to do so I came on along. We felt it was important that you see the journal."

"Mr. Collins, this is quite a read, I must say," she said. "This McLain obviously went to a lot of trouble thinking and putting it all down on paper."

"He was one of a number of people fighting against

DynaTech, Ms. Wilder. His widow is naturally heartbroken over this turn of events."

"I understand completely. However, I have a small problem. And that is that Mr. McLain offered nothing in the way of proof here. His apprehension and mistrust of the local law enforcement is clearly evident, but his suspicions are just that—deductions. They are conclusions for which he offers nothing in the way of facts to support them. I have no reason to doubt what he says. It's just that I need something more concrete than his hunches before I can act. He very definitely points an accusing finger at your mayor but that's not enough. That is why you're here, right? You want me to do something?"

Wilder sat forward, elbows on her desk. She possessed a pleasant way about her, one not condescending nor hurried. Grant knew what she said was correct but he needed more. An assurance that her office would look into the happenings in Trinity.

"I suppose so," he said. "I really don't know. I *do* know that something is wrong in Trinity, something evil is transforming the town. Killing its solid residents. All for what? The almighty dollar. You mentioned at our last visit that you would assign one of your agents to this case. I was wondering if that has proved fruitful."

"Like I said, Mr. Collins. I do understand. If you could just supply me with something more to go on. Something I could use to kick start an investigation. It would be most helpful. At this juncture we have not turned up anything concrete. Nothing more than a few worrisome facts about Mayor Baxter's business dealings but nothing on which to base an arrest or indictment."

"I'm sorry," Grant said. "At present I wish I had more to give you but I don't. I shouldn't waste any more of your time. I appreciate you seeing me."

Grant stood, extended his hand. As he shook hands

with Wilder, her phone rang. Grant stood while she listened on the receiver. As she did, her eyes widened, she motioned him back into his chair and continued talking in a hushed tone, barking a few orders with a clipped voice. Hanging up, she sported a wry smirk.

"Well now, Mr. Collins. It seems that Trinity's mayor has been murdered."

ℯↄℯↄ

Late that afternoon Carrie put dinner in the oven while Grant sat and watched her. Arriving home from his trip to Savannah and the Bureau of Investigation, he filled her in on Wilder's position and the bombshell she dropped on him.

"When I was coming back from the market," she said, "I passed by the mayor's house. There were all sorts of police cars out front and a string of satellite news trucks on the road nearby. I wondered what was happening."

"Now you know," Grant said, tossing McLain's journal in the table. "The man was murdered in his own home."

"Wilder have any ideas as to who might have done it?"

"She didn't say. I believe she just got the news while I was in her office. We may never know with Trinity's finest in the case."

"The Bureau not getting involved?"

"I dunno, but probably. I certainly hope so. Their current investigation hasn't been very fruitful. The only way we're going to get to the bottom of all these deaths is for her to become involved, start her own investigation. Maybe Baxter's murder will add impetus to that necessity."

Carrie went into her living room and switched on the TV. Together she and Grant watched the local late afternoon news. The mayor's death was the main focus of the program; there was even a live remote reporter at the scene. The young woman stood with Baxter's mansion in the distant background, the grounds surrounded by yellow crime scene tape. She told her audience that the mayor was found dead in his kitchen, lying in a massive pool of blood. There had been a violent struggle prior to his demise. Whoever was the perpetrator had used a knife and slit the poor man's throat, nearly decapitating him.

Carrie switched the television off, sat on the sofa.

"I heard enough," she said. "Don't need all the grizzly details."

Grant sat, quiet, seemingly lost in thought. He doodled in the legal pad he had earlier used to jot down his ideas.

"Penny for your thoughts," she said.

"I was just thinking," he said, continuing to doodle. "Special Agent Wilder said she needs something concrete on which to act. All she has right now are our suspicions and McLain's journal. Which, although enlightening, is not enough for her to dedicate assets. So, it's up to us, Carrie, to get the needed evidence for Wilder. I don't know how or where, but you and I are going to have to do it. There is no one else."

"All along we've thought that DynaTech might somehow be behind these deaths. But it was well known that Mayor Baxter was in favor of the power plant coming to Trinity. How does his death push that agenda forward? Doesn't it actually stall the council vote? There's going to have to be a new election isn't there? For a new mayor."

"You're assuming DynaTech might be responsible for the mayor's murder also, Carrie," Grant said, laying aside the legal pad. "You're right, that doesn't make any sense. But what if it was the work of someone opposed to the plant coming to town? Someone we haven't considered. Then it *would* make sense, to stall the proceedings. Or stop them temporarily."

"I see what you're saying. I hadn't thought of that. And it needn't be a person on the committee, could be anyone opposed to DynaTech."

"That's right."

"Oh my God, Grant," Carrie exclaimed. "Then the mayor's murderer could be almost anyone."

"Anyone," he said. "Although, if that be the case, it doesn't help solve mother's death or the death's of the committee members. It would be just a diversion. But what about this. What if the mayor was having difficulty putting together a winning vote for DynaTech? His efforts stalled by all the committee's efforts. What if Conway decided to rid himself of Trinity's mayor and start afresh? A new mayor and council members—all of whom he could buy through rigged elections. It might take longer in the long run but he would be assured of success. In the end, the delay might be worth it to him."

Carrie thought on the idea while Grant doodled on the legal pad. When she spoke her eyes were narrowed, her face in a scowl.

"What can we do, Grant?"

"For starters, we need tangible evidence that these deaths weren't accidents. Something, anything to tie DynaTech to them. Right now all we have are shadows. And we need more, a lot more. Then maybe Wilder will listen to us. We're assuming Conway is involved, of course. I don't see any other explanation that makes sense. Remember, when I was in Conway's trailer I discovered an email to someone named Sergei offering to sell something once the plant was completed. What it was, was not mentioned. But it could be a clue."

"Whatever we get needs to be more than probable," Carrie said. "It needs to be conclusive."

"Absolutely. If we can build a case, a convincing case, she would have to act."

"Where can we start?"

"I think I need to go out to the river site where Lori supposedly was found and look around. Don't know what I'd find but it's worth a shot. Then, maybe go to Atlanta and see if I can find Mom's car."

"I have a long day tomorrow," Carrie said. "I'm working the lunch and dinner shifts so I'll be gone all day. You going to be all right?"

"Oh sure," he said, returning to his doodling.

℮ჟℯჟ

Special Agent in Charge Wilder was at her desk early. Also in her office were two men, Bill Toomey and Charles "Chuck" Dalrymple, field agents for the Georgia Bureau of Investigation. The three agents were meeting before the start of business for the day. The sun was barely on the horizon as Wilder outlined what she wanted.

Wilder brushed a lock of hair from her forehead. "Trinity's mayor, Mr. Bruce Baxter, was brutally murdered in his lavish home the other night. The Trinity police are investigating. Due to the high profile nature of the case, I believe we should involve the Bureau."

"If I may interject," the man named Toomey said.

"Go ahead, Bill," she said. "I'm listening."

Toomey was a man in his twenties, considered hefty by Bureau standards, had straight black hair that he combed back over his tanned head. "Local authorities haven't asked to involve the Bureau, have they?" he said, taking a gulp of coffee from a large mug.

"No, not as yet. But I want to send someone to check it out and report back. The state's Heinous Crimes Act gives us the authority. By all accounts, this was a brutal killing. It certainly qualifies."

"What if they don't want to cooperate?" Dalrymple said. He was an older man, in his forties, with graying temples, Roman nose.

"They will. I know the chief there," Wilder said. "A man named Paley. Alex Paley. I'll give him a call and let him know you two are coming."

Toomey nodded. "You want us both up there?" he said.

Wilder's smirk was unmistakable. "I think the presence of two agents should be enough intimidation to encourage them to cooperate, don't you?"

Both men chuckled.

"In addition," Wilder continued, "I want you to familiarize yourselves with the contents of a report I filed after talking with two of Trinity's residents. A Mr. Collins and his girlfriend. Mr. Collins was fearful that this mother's death in a car accident in Trinity was in some way connected to the nuclear power plant that a large corporation wishes to build there. That her death and the death of several others were orchestrated to prevent opposition to this plant. Mr. Collins also brought in a journal written by one of Trinity's residents before he died mysteriously in a fire. His suspicions aren't evidence. And although not overwhelming or able to stand up in court, they are nonetheless, disturbing. So, before you head to Trinity, check out the file."

"When do you want us there?" Dalrymple said.

"The sooner the better. The mayor's home is still an active crime scene. I think you can offer any assistance our office is able to give such as DNA analysis, latent print identification, fiber analysis, that sort of thing. Chuck, you know how to do this. Offer support and assistance in a professional way but let them understand you are there to make sure that nothing gets screwed up."

"Will do." Dalrymple nodded, took a notebook from his suit pocket, jotted a few lines. He glanced at Toomey. "Well, partner, let's get moving."

Both men rose, waved at Wilder, and left the office.

Alone, the Special Agent in Charge gazed out her window, admiring the sun's soft golden hue. She hoped Special Agent Dalrymple would take his assignment seriously and not just go through the motions. He was a good man and Toomey would learn from him. But Dalrymple had campaigned for her job when the Special Agent in Charge position became open. He had made it plain that he felt he was the most qualified to lead the field office, was visibly disappointed when Wilder was chosen over him. But, to the man's credit, he continued to act in the professional manner for which he was noted, allowing Wilder a huge sigh of relief.

She hoped it would continue.

Chapter 21

The man named Sergei sat across from Conway in the salon of *Sandpiper,* which was moored at the exclusive Isle of Hope Marina. Conway had motored around Tybee Island then up the Wilmington River to the marina southeast of Savannah. Although many boats were harbored at Isle of Hope there was very little traffic in and out of it. Mostly it was a place for the wealthy to party on the weekends.

It was midnight, no one was on the docks. Each man sipped whiskey from crystal old-fashioned glasses, Sergei bourbon, Conway scotch.

"You have a nice boat," Sergei said, taking a sip of his liquor and looking about the cabin. "Very nice indeed."

"It's not a boat, my friend," Conway said, irritated at the man's derogatory description. "It's a yacht."

"*Perdono,*" the man said. "I did not mean to offend. It is a most…how do you say?…luxurious yacht. I am duly impressed. How fast will she go? Twenty, twenty-five knots?"

"Maybe at top speed," Conway said. "But she cruises at sixteen. Bow thrusters and an Naiad stabilizer system as well."

"Communications?"

"VHF radiotelephone, SSB radio telephone, Navtex receiver, EPIRB, radar transponder, triple band GSM telephone, antenna system. All the comforts of home. You are a yacht enthusiast, Sergei?"

"Hardly," the man said, setting his tumbler down on the teak table beside his chair. "Just interested."

"We even have immersion suits in case we have to abandon ship. It's a technologically advanced yacht."

Sergei nodded in agreement.

"Your visit, Sergei, is quite unexpected. You bring information?"

"Yes, of course." Sergei shifted in his chair, his tone assumed a flatness, almost pedestrian. "The cartel I represent are concerned that our agreement may not be progressing as originally scheduled. They—"

Conway held up a hand, nodded. "Their assessment is accurate to a certain degree," he said. "The vote on the plant is behind schedule, to be sure, but the overall timetable for success is still on course."

"My friends will be happy to hear that," the man said, his tone still clipped. "What has led to the delay?"

"Trinity's mayor met with an unfortunate, untimely accident."

The man stared at Conway.

"He was murdered, actually," Conway continued. "In his own home. A tragic turn of events."

A sardonic smile crossed Sergei's face. "How inconvenient," he said.

"As it happened it may have helped our cause. Mayor Baxter's death will allow a more goal-oriented person to assume his duties."

"The cartel will be happy to hear it. They don't take kindly to making deals then having them fall apart, due to negligence or incompetence. Time is growing short, Mr.

Conway, and I have been instructed to emphasize that point."

Conway rose and refilled their glasses. He didn't appreciate threats, even in this tangential manner. "I can assure you and your friends that I am neither negligent nor incompetent." His eyes narrowed. "And I don't like threats, Sergei."

"*Perdono,*" the man said. "It was not meant to insult. But I have to return to the people I represent with a progress report. Things go a lot smoother if they are pleased."

"Tell them this, Sergei—one catches more flies with honey. I don't cotton to being threatened by the folks I'm doing business with."

❧❧❧

A cool breeze blew down the Dogwood River south of Trinity. The sky was overcast with dark clouds billowing low overhead. Grant drove his rental car along the narrow road that paralleled the river casting an occasional glance at each pull-off. He was searching for the place that Lori Spelling had supposedly been found floating face down. From the few remarks that Sergeant Brady mentioned earlier the pull-off in question was next to a steep bank leading to a sand bar near water's edge. At times the road curved close to the river while at others it was fifteen to twenty yards away from it. The trees that grew alongside the road were a dense collection of southern trees—cypress, river birch, swamp maple—all with their branches sporting the ubiquitous Spanish moss.

As Grant continued southward toward the Euclid Street Bridge, he remembered Brady's latest report. Lori's car still had not been located.

He slowed as he approached the bridge and found the

pull-off near it. He eased his rental off the road onto the dirt area short of the bridge, stopped, and exited his vehicle. The bank leading down to the river was a steep rocky one and while there was no path he found he could pick his way over the rocks to the water.

Grant worked his way down the bank using footholds he spotted in cracks. It was slow work but he methodically made his way over the sharp rocks. His course led him across the bank for a number of yards before descending again. It was difficult, sweaty work but after half an hour he found himself at river's edge.

The water at the bridge slowed to a smooth crawl looking more like dark syrup than a fast moving river. At the shoreline, there was a narrow sand bar that allowed him to walk a few yards downstream. Occasionally, a limb would protrude over the bar requiring him to negotiate the obstacle. Nestled in a small eddy of the river was a collection of tree limbs and branches that had gathered around a stump. Grant could see how a body could get lodged among the boughs and not float further downstream.

Probably where they found Lori's body, he thought.

Would a person go walking at night along a steep riverbank? One that was as tricky to negotiate as the one he had just traversed? No, he doubted it for the bank was too steep and dangerous in the dark.

Finding nothing he considered interesting, he climbed back up the bank to his car. He wandered past the vehicle to another wide spot in the road, searching among the rocks and pebbles, the short grasses. He had no idea what he was looking for—anything that didn't belong, he surmised. The asphalt road near the Euclid Street Bridge was in such a state of disrepair Grant wondered why Trinity's residents tolerated such neglect from their city leaders. But now the council had been decimated by recent deaths including the mayor, who, he was learning, was not liked by at least half the town. The nuclear plant had divided the town, to a point that Carrie thought was irreparable. Many of the town's residents were so angry over the thought of having nuclear waste in their midst that the hope of cheaper energy couldn't sway them otherwise.

Grant stooped and picked up a rock, turned it over, watched an earthworm slither away. Located not far from town, this area was isolated, not much traffic along the road. Further south, Trinity's main street intersected with it and provided access to the larger homes along the river. But long this particular stretch there wasn't much, no homes, no traffic.

Continuing to amble along, he reached an edge of the road where the asphalt dropped abruptly to the dirt and gravel. There, he noticed something. He bent down, and picked it up.

A cigarette butt.

In fact, there were several scattered over the ground.

He studied the butt. It rang a note in his brain.

They belonged to the brand smoked by Sergeant Brady.

ↄ৵ↄ৵

Chief of Police Alex Paley sneered at the two men in his office. He didn't appreciate the Bureau of Investigation sticking their noses into his business, and he was, hopefully, making that point unmistakably clear. The two agents had arrived unannounced, although he had received a call from Samantha Wilder notifying him they would be arriving in the next few days. Their fine tailored suits were out of place in a small Southern police station.

They had flashed their identification at his officer in the outer office then she in turn stammered their arrival to Paley.

After the exchange of introductory pleasantries, the three men settled in his office, eyeing each other. He waited for the agents to speak first.

"We are here," the agent named Dalrymple said, "to offer the Bureau's assistance in your investigation of Mayor Baxter's death. We have an entire crime lab at your disposal if you care to avail yourselves of its resources."

"Actually, Special Agent Dalrymple," Paley said, "we have all the bases covered. But thanks for the offer." Paley knew his voice carried a tone of irritation but he didn't care. He didn't like state agents snooping in his business.

"What about latent prints?" Dalrymple said. "Need any help there?"

"Nope," was Paley's curt reply.

"DNA testing? We have a state-of-the-art lab in Atlanta."

"Got it covered."

"Can you fill us in on the case?" the man called Toomey said. "Where it currently stands?"

"You bet," Paley said in an impatient voice. "The victim was, as you mentioned, Trinity's mayor. Bruce Baxter. The perp apparently entered his home through the back door where Baxter confronted him in the kitchen. A struggle ensued and Baxter's throat was slashed. He bled out at the scene."

"Much blood?" Dalrymple said.

"Like I said," Paley said. "He bled out. Pretty grisly."

Dalrymple smiled weakly. "With all that blood on the floor there must have been a footprint or two. Find any?"

"We found one footprint next to the back door. Pointed toward the door as if the perp was leaving the scene. Size twelve, I believe."

"We understand that there is a push to bring a nuclear power plant to town," Dalrymple said. "Any reason to think that it is connected to the mayor's murder?"

"None at this point," Paley said. "You are correct about the plant, but nothing points to DynaTech's involvement. Of course, that could change."

"My partner and I," Dalrymple said, standing. Toomey followed suit. "My partner and I would like to see the crime scene if you can arrange it. You never know, Chief, how extra sets of eyes might be able to help."

Paley was visibly upset at their request, and he didn't bother to hide his feelings. He let out a long, exasperated sigh. "Look, men," he said, his tone crass and impatient. "I really don't have the time to be chauffeuring you about town. But your boss, Agent Wilder, called and asked in a nice way so I don't want her to think that we're not hospitable to Bureau agents here in Trinity. So—"

He pushed the intercom button.

"Yes, Chief?" came a female voice.

"Marge," Paley said, "I want to you run these Bureau boys over to the Baxter place. They can follow in their car. Then get right back here. I have a job for you."

"Right, Chief," was the woman's reply.

Paley turned his attention back the agents sitting across from him.

"Okay, gentlemen, Marge will show you the way. And just remember, this is my crime scene so don't muck it up."

The agents left Paley's office and from his window he watched them drive away. *Christ. What next? Now I've got a couple of state dicks peeking into my business. Great!*

In all his years as chief of police the one thing that got Paley's blood boiling was having to put up with law enforcement jockeys from other agencies. It rankled him that so many of FBI and Georgia Bureau agents walked around as if they had a chip on their shoulder. Sometimes his acerbic manner could put them off—and they wouldn't stay long—other times it didn't. Dalrymple and Toomey seemed nice enough, respectful enough of his turf, so maybe they wouldn't be a problem.

Only time would tell.

Chapter 22

What makes you think finding a bunch of cigarette butts along the river amounts to anything?" Carrie asked the question, not to belittle Grant's efforts but to show him what he found wasn't really evidence at all.

They were at his mother's house. Grant had called and wanted her to meet him there. He was going to look the place over—once more.

"Listen," he said. "Lori was found floating near the bridge. The cigarette butts were found a good half-mile up the road. I'll give you that Brady was probably at the bridge during the recovery of Lori's body but what were those butts doing way back up the road? Answer me that."

"They could have been from anyone, Grant. Someone stopped, had a smoke, and drove on. It could be that simple."

"Smoked four cigarettes during a break, Carrie? I doubt it. Besides, those butts belonged to a brand smoked by Brady. I saw him puffing on them."

"Still, it doesn't put him at that particular spot. And with Lori. What would she have been doing stopped on the river road?"

"Maybe she didn't stop there," Grant said, wandering into the kitchen. Carrie followed and watched as he fixed two glasses of iced tea, handed her one. "How about this? Maybe she was taken there. By Brady."

"In his patrol car?"

"In his patrol car or private vehicle, it doesn't matter. Remember, I found that note at her apartment. River Road, eleven p.m. Remember that? And they've never found her car as yet, don't forget. Brady killed Lori, took her body to the river, dumped it, and returned later when it was found. He did it at night. The road was dark, empty. No witnesses. Problem solved. Over and done with."

"What problem?" Carrie said after a drink of her tea. "Why would Brady kill Lori? What's his motive?"

They wandered back into Helen's living room. Carrie sat while Grant paced.

"I dunno. Haven't figured that part out." There was a pause in their conversation before he continued. "Maybe he killed Lori for Conway. Maybe Conway has the police department in his hip pocket."

"Maybe you can't figure it out because that's not the way it happened. Not the way Lori died."

"What do you mean?"

"I mean maybe, just maybe, the toxicology report was correct. Maybe, unbeknownst to any of her friends, Lori was a coke freak. She was a closet druggy."

"You believe that?"

"No, not really. But I *have* been surprised by people, haven't you? Someone has a secret life you knew nothing about until something happened? Sure you have, we all have. I didn't know her well but I saw her at the diner often enough."

He shook his head. "But she never once gave out a hint she was doing drugs. She had a great job at the college."

"Well, people like that can do cocaine on the weekends, party and whatever, and still make it to work during the week."

"All I'm saying is she never gave out any signs. Can I be positive she wasn't doing them? Of course not. But I'd be willing to bet that she wasn't. So she was killed and made to look like and overdose."

"Why?" Carrie leaned forward on the sofa. "That's the big question. Because she was lobbying against the power plant like your mother?"

"And the rest of those people we have uncovered," Grant said. He set his glass on a table, sat next to her.

"It seems we're right back where we started. We have a theory but no proof. I'm beginning to think we'll never have any."

"It's useless to go see Chief Paley again," Grant said. "He'll just take Brady's side. For all we know, the entire police force is corrupted.

"You don't know that. And you don't have to go to him accusing Brady of this without any proof. But talk to him again with your continued concerns is well within your rights. I would try again. Tell him about the appointment you found in Lori's apartment. What about that email you found in Conway's trailer?"

"It was something about Conway selling something that would bring him a lot of money. There was no mention of what it was but it seemed big."

"Is it possible to find out what it was?" Carrie said as she finished her tea.

"I don't see how."

"Go talk to him. Tell him who you are, that you think your mother was misguided. Get him talking about the power plant. See if you can get him to say something."

"I doubt he would see me," Grant said. "Why should he?"

"He might if he knew your mother was a former lob-byist against his precious plant. You'll never know unless you try."

"I dunno."

"You had the nightmare last night, didn't you? You tossed and turned, moaned, almost cried. I reached out to you but you turned away. Then you finally settled down."

"It's the same dream on Ambush Alley. It won't leave and I think I'm slowly losing my mind. I shouldn't burden you with my problems, Carrie. I probably ought to start staying over here at Mom's. My sleeping with you isn't doing your reputation any good, I'm sure."

Carrie looked at him, tears welling in her eyes, a lump forming in her throat. "If you do that, Grant Collins," she said, "I'll never speak to you again." She forced a weak smile.

"Our relationship has gone further than I ever expected—or planned. I never thought I'd find someone like you, Carrie. It's just that…"

"That what?" she interjected.

"I can't bear the thought of hurting you. Until this problem of mine is resolved, that is what eventually will happen. I'll hurt you terribly and I couldn't bear that. Either that or you'll walk away, unwilling to deal with all my issues."

She reached out and took his hand in hers.

"So many times since returning I have thought my feet were firm on the ground but the world around me seems to spin out of my control. When I take inventory of myself, I find that all I have doesn't add up to much. It's as if I'm locked in a maze and can't find my way out."

"Baby," Carrie said, caressing his hand, "I will help. Together we can work this out. Together."

"What does a person do when they have lost their

way, Carrie? Something happened to me over there in Iraq, and it broke me inside." He felt tears begin to well in his eyes, tried to calm himself. "It's as if I'm a lost person and cannot find my way. You understand? I—I'm not the man I was and it causes me much pain. I don't want to push my problems onto you."

"You don't."

"When I look out at the world, I want to see beauty and grace, not people killing each other. I want that which I see to make my heart sing with joy not tremble in fear. I want to live in a world of peace and harmony not one where small children carry guns to war. Most of all, I beg for God to have mercy upon me for what I did and heal whatever is broken within me."

Carrie placed a hand on his cheek.

"We can't fix all the world's problems, Grant. There are too many of them and on a scale unimaginable. But each of us can live our lives with courage, honor, and integrity. I think it's the best we can hope to achieve."

"I'm glad to have found you, Carrie," he said, wiping his eyes with a sleeve.

"I'm here for you, for as long as you need me. I said that before, remember? It's wonderful to be needed. You don't worry about me. You go do what needs to be done here and concentrate on getting well."

❧❧❧

Special Agent Dalrymple, followed by Special Agent Toomey, stooped under the yellow crime scene tape and ambled up to the Bruce Baxter mansion. There were no police officers on the premises but they found the front door unlocked, let themselves in.

Dalrymple led the way through the expansive terra-cotta tiled entryway lined with marble statues of Greek figures. An immense crystal chandelier hung from the two-story ceiling.

Toomey pointed to it. "Obviously imported," he said after a low whistle. "The man did quite well for himself."

They continued on through the living room, one Dalrymple had to admit, dripped with ostentation. From thick brocaded curtains to the Renaissance artwork hanging on the walls, Baxter had spared no expense in furnishing his home.

"Can you believe this guy?" Toomey said, studying a large painting up close.

"He obviously enjoyed the finer things of life," Dalrymple replied. He continued through the house, down the hallway and into the large kitchen. The blood had been cleaned up but a large maroon stain still remained on the tile floor.

The kitchen was in shambles, the result of a violent struggle, one that ended in Baxter's death. A table lay on its side, legs broken off, while the remains of several chairs were scattered about. Broken dishes were everywhere, on the counters and floor.

The two agents stepped carefully around the mangled clutter poking their noses in every nook, corner, horizontal and vertical surface. Toomey crawled on his hands and knees, inspecting every square inch of the floor while Dalrymple checked the back door and rear garden for evidence missed by the Trinity investigators.

Toomey sang out. "Chuck!" he hollered. "Back in here."

Dalrymple returned from the garden, stood in the rear doorway. "Yeah?"

Toomey was holding up a hand, grasping something with tweezers. "Look at this," he said.

Dalrymple stooped to get a closer look. "What is it?"

"A fiber, a blue fiber," Toomey said. He held the object closer and Dalrymple noticed a small strand about an inch long.

"Save it," Dalrymple said. "We'll give it to the lab."

He watched Toomey pull a small vial from his pocket, open it, and drop the fiber into it. After resealing the vial, his partner stood, stretched his back.

Dalrymple smirked. "That's why I have you, Bill," he said. "I'm too old to be crawling around a crime scene. Good eyes."

"Well, I can't wait till I can have a young strong back to do my grunt work," Toomey said. "By the way, how long till retirement?"

"Fourteen months. Judy and I are going to find a place down in the Keys and spend our remaining days fishing. If the kids want to see us they can find us down there."

"Fourteen months. I envy you, Chuck. I really do envy you."

"It comes quicker than you think, Bill. One day you're up to your ass in work, the next retirement is staring you in the face. I hope I'm ready for it."

"That Chief Paley seemed a real charmer," Toomey said. "These local guys always seem to have a chip on their shoulder."

"You can't blame them, though. We come waltzing in here, and they think we're going to make them look like a bunch of imbeciles. The sad thing is, we usually do. If we're finished here, let's drop by the ME's office and see if we can get a look at the body. Then we'll head back."

At Dr. Samuel Witherspoon's office, they learned the doctor had signed Baxter's cause of death as *homicide* then released the body to the funeral home. No, he hadn't performed an autopsy, hadn't seen the need. The cause and manner of death was obvious. Homicide by multiple stab wounds. After lecturing the doctor on the law and the necessity of an autopsy on homicide cases, the two agents drove over to Trinity's sole funeral home and found the director eating a sandwich.

"I'm Rupert Gladstone," the elderly gray-haired man said after Dalrymple introduced himself and Toomey, produced identification. "You're wanting to view Mr. Baxter's body?"

"We do, Mr. Gladstone. The doctor didn't perform an autopsy so we need to examine it."

"Oh my," the man said, adjusting a pair of wire-framed spectacles. "Gosh, well—er—"

"What's the problem?" Toomey said. "He *is* here isn't he?"

"Oh yes," Gladstone said. "But I have embalmed him already. Did it this morning. I hope I haven't—"

"You're fine," Dalrymple said. "We just need to examine the body."

Gladstone led the two men through a back room filled with coffins of all shapes and sizes and into a small side room he used for the embalming procedure. Filled with a hydraulic embalming table, embalming machine, plastic jugs of all sorts of chemicals, aspirators, and surgical tubing, the room smelled strongly of formaldehyde. Dalrymple rubbed his nose, irritated by the strong odors. A male body lay on the table.

"I was going to dress the deceased but you men take all the time you need. I'll be out front."

With that the men left the room leaving Dalrymple and Toomey alone with the cadaver. Dalrymple approached the body lying starkly nude on the stainless steel table. The glare of a lone surgical light gave the body a glistening unearthly, almost transparent, appearance.

The first thing he noticed was the large incision-like

wound in Baxter's neck that had been sutured closed.

"Almost took his head off," he said, indicating the wound with an index finger.

"Got both carotids in all likelihood," answered Toomey who stood opposite his partner on the other side of the table. "And look at these."

Toomey was pointing to multiple stab sounds over Baxter's chest, narrow in length, maybe at most a centimeter or so.

"Stiletto," Dalrymple agreed. "Not at all the usual weapon favored by most perps."

When finished with their examination, the agents left Gladstone to his work and headed back to the Savannah field office. They stopped at a gas station for coffee along the way.

"What do you think, Bill?" Dalrymple said when they were back in the car.

"Well, the first thing I'd consider is to get the body to Atlanta and have a thorough autopsy done by a competent forensic pathologist. That doctor was a moron."

"It's something to consider. However, I meant your impression of the body. Think it was an execution or a robbery gone bad?"

"Most robbery perps don't take along a knife in case things get dicey," Toomey said. "More like they carry a firearm of some sort. So robbery wouldn't be high on my list. But a premeditated murder? As mayor, I'm sure the man made his share of enemies."

"I can't believe this local ME didn't ship the body to Atlanta for a formal autopsy by a qualified forensic pathologist. That doctor was a joke."

"The mayor could have been killed for any number of reasons," Toomey said.

"Possibly. Maybe that fiber you collected will give us some information."

And it did.

Chapter 23

Grant drove his rental car down Interstate 16 into Savannah, followed the highway as it curved northward, then exited onto Bay Street. He continued into the Riverfront Plaza area that was located across from Yamacraw Bluff, the spot where General James Edward Oglethorpe landed to settle the colony of Georgia. After parking his car off a narrow tree-lined street next to a small courtyard, he walked the half block to Winston Conway's office. The unassuming sign above the door read, *DynaTech Corporation.* He took a deep breath and entered.

There was no one in the office. A single desk occupied the room along with several straight back chairs that were aligned next to a wall displaying several large photographs of DynaTech energy plants. Behind the desk was another door that Grant surmised led to the *inner sanctum*, Conway's private office.

He stood at the desk, contemplating his next move, when a young man in a business suit entered from the rear part of the office. He looked startled upon seeing Grant.

"Uh, beg your pardon," the man said. "Can I help you?"

"Yes," Grant said, "I'd like to see Mr. Conway. I was told he was here today."

"He is extremely busy," the man replied, curtly. "And is unable to take visitors."

"I think he will want to see me," Grant said. He tried to put forth an authoritative air.

"And why is that?" The man seemed irritated at this delay. He shuffled through a stack of papers on the desk, not looking at Grant.

"Let's just say I represent the Citizens Against Nuclear Power in Trinity. In case you haven't heard, it's the citizen's committee lobbying against DynaTech building its nuclear plant in Trinity. Tell him I'm here. I'm sure he'll want to see me."

The man stared at Grant, his expression unchanging. Grant decided to offer a carrot, something other than a simple threat, to entice the man out of his self-made bunker. "Tell him—" he continued, "—tell him I think we can reach a compromise. It would be good business for all concerned. You go tell him that."

The man was hesitating, Grant thought, trying to decide if he should interrupt his boss. "I suppose I could call Commissioner Hayes at the Atlanta NRC office," he said. "May I use your phone?"

"Er, just a moment," the man said. He turned and disappeared through the inner door.

Grant smiled at his ploy. He had no idea whom to call at the NRC. *We'll see,* he thought, *we'll see.*

A few moments later, a portly man in business attire appeared and smiled at Grant. He approached and extended his hand.

"Please excuse, Bill, Mr..." the man said.

"Collins. Grant Collins." Grant said taking the hand. He noticed it was a firm grip, confident.

"I'm Winston Conway. Bill mention something about a citizen's committee?"

"Yes. Is there somewhere we can talk, Mr. Conway?"

The man turned and opened the inner door. "Of course," he said. "My office is right this way."

Grant followed Conway down a short carpeted hallway past a large conference room to a cramped office filled with charts, blueprints, several computer terminals, television, and a tall bookcase filled with musty smelling books. He took the proffered chair.

"You'll have to fill me in on this committee of yours," Conway said after they were seated. "Are you at odds with my nuclear plant coming to town?"

Grant studied Conway as the man spoke, weighing his words carefully. The owner of DynaTech sat behind his enormous desk, looked the part of a successful entrepreneur, probably thinking he would crush Grant with a little finger. The man's eyes flashed as he talked, a definite smirk on his thin lips.

"You might say that," Grant said slowly. "We don't need to be coy with each other, Mr. Conway. I believe you know very well about the Citizens Against Nuclear Power that organized in response to your wanting to bring a plant to our town. My mother was on that committee."

"Oh?" Conway said, eyebrows raised.

"She's dead. Died in an automobile accident. But I have suspicions it wasn't an accident at all. In fact, several other committee members have met with unfortunate accidents of late. All since your announcement of the Trinity plant."

Grant thought he detected a slight shifting of the man in his chair. An almost imperceptible squirm. He's uncomfortable, he thought. *Good.*

"I'm sorry to hear that. Yes, I've been apprised that

there was some opposition to our plans but the mayor has a council vote scheduled in the near future. DynaTech, of course, will abide by the town's wishes. If Trinity turns us down, we will find another location. It will put us behind schedule but if it is necessary, so be it. And please accept my deepest condolences regarding your mother."

Grant felt a hot, acid bile rise in his throat, burn his tongue. He couldn't believe this pompous jerk was actually sitting before him denying any knowledge of his mother's committee, the one he increasingly felt she gave her life for. It was all he could do to keep from lunging cross the desk and take the man by the throat, choke the life out of him, extract a confession. He fought to ignore the burn in his throat and concentrate on the task at hand.

"With all due respect, Mr. Conway," Grant said in a measured tone, "a number of us Trinity residents have a problem with the way DynaTech does business."

Conway's eyes narrowed. "Whatever do you mean?" he said, his voice turning sour.

"Look at it from our point of view. DynaTech announces plans to build a multimillion-dollar nuclear power plant along the Dogwood River in Trinity. A number of concerned citizens, men and women who are justifiably skeptical about nuclear safety, form a committee and begin lobbying against DynaTech coming to town. Then, inexplicably, members of the committee begin dying off—killed in a number of accidents. Accidents at least determined so by the Trinity police and medical examiner. As a result, a city council vote seems likely to ensure that DynaTech will prevail."

Grant paused, allowing his words to have an effect on Conway. "So, I ask you, sir. Does this scenario sound like the ravings of a depraved mind? Like some fantasy found in a crime novel? I think not. On top of that, Trinity's mayor has been murdered, the victim of a home invasion. So you see, Mr. Conway, things are not at all peaceful in our little town. And all since your company announced it wanted to build a power plant near it."

Grant could tell he had struck a nerve. The man struggled to maintain his composure.

"Usually," Conway said in a monotone that signified authority, "when people have issues with one of our plants they bring a bevy of lawyers in here to threaten or plead their case. You don't seem the lawyerly type."

"Not at all, sir. I'm just a citizen concerned that my mother's death may not have been an accident and am trying to get to the bottom of it."

"I'm appalled, Mr. Collins!" Conway said in a loud voice. "I ought to have you thrown out of here this instant. Have my lawyers file suit against you. How dare you insinuate—"

Grant held up a hand. It was his turn to smirk. He had indeed struck a nerve. "I'm not implying or insinuating anything, Mr. Conway. I'm just stating what a number of people are thinking. If you choose to take it personal—"

Conway stood. "We're finished here," he said. "I suddenly have taken quite a dislike to you, Mr. Collins. Good day." DynaTech's owner spun on his heels and headed for his office door. Standing in the doorway he stopped, turned toward Grant. His eyes shot darts. "You can find your own way out," he said, menacingly, then left.

Grant found his way back to his parked car. On the road again, he thought about Conway's response to their conversation. The man was taken off guard by his sudden appearance and insinuations, that much was obvious. What he would do now was anyone's guess. Conway was a man who liked to operate from a superior position, one of power and authority. *He probably treats his employees the way he had just been treated*, Grant thought. But

Grant thought he detected something else in the man's voice, his demeanor. A certain trace of fear, a suggestion that the meeting worried the mighty Conway. If that was the case, he might be tempted to do something foolish, make a mistake that would help Wilder and her office in her investigation.

As he eased his car onto Interstate 16 and blended into the traffic flow, Grant switched on the radio and found a station playing classical music. A Mozart sonata played and its melodic notes slowly eased the tension in Grant's neck. How much longer he was going to be able to stay in Trinity was weighing on him. He was going to have to return to DC soon. He was afraid the power plant affair was dragging on to the point where he would no longer be in a position to continue his personal inquiry.

Carrie was a definite interruption in his life. A short ten days earlier he was living a care free, albeit, troubled existence, unencumbered by a close personal attachment. Yet, here he was, in love with someone he barely knew. It was a distraction he didn't feel he could afford in his current state of affairs. He had no visible means of support other than his VA disability pension, which wasn't much. In addition, his nightmares weren't a problem he wished to inflict on anyone, let alone someone he cared about. Sure, Carrie was saying all the right things to make him feel as if it might work. But how would she feel in a year? Two? Five years?

It was a chance he wasn't sure he was willing to take.

In spite of being in love with her.

He glanced in his rear view mirror and noticed a black limo following him. It had been in the inside lane but as it got closer it pulled in directly behind his rental car. Its windows were tinted so it was difficult to make out the passengers inside.

Grant accelerated and the limo fell farther behind. His

thoughts returned to Carrie and how their relationship would play out. Would she go for a long distance one for a while with him in DC and her still down here? For the near future at least? Until things became more settled with him. They were going to have to talk.

He shot a look at his mirror. The limo was back behind him again, having pulled up nearly on his rear bumper.

Jesus! What's this all about?

Was it Conway or his people trying to scare him? Grant pushed on the accelerator and sped ahead. At the last moment, he turned off onto the Trinity exit, noticed the limo continue on the Interstate. He took a deep breath and drove into the town.

He had no sooner turned onto Main Street than a police cruiser fell in behind, hit its lights and siren. Grant pulled to a stop, watched an officer exit his unit and saunter up to his window. He rolled it down.

"What's the matter, officer?" he said, trying to sound cheerful.

"Driver's license, please," the officer said. His tone was gruff and clipped.

The officer looked at the license Grant offered,

"You Grant Collins?" the officer said.

"I am," Grant said. "Why? What's the matter?"

"Step out of the car, please," the officer said. "You are under arrest."

Chapter 24

Special Agents Dalrymple and Toomey stood under the bright lights in the lab of the Georgia Bureau of Investigation's Division of Forensic Sciences located in the heart of Savannah. Dalrymple's back ached and, from the look on Toomey's face, the man was bored, if not downright exhausted. The two men had been at the lab since early morning watching the technicians perform their tests on the fiber Toomey had found at the Baxter crime scene. Now they were simply waiting for the results.

The Forensic Biology section of the Georgia Bureau of Investigation performed serological and DNA analyses of physiological fluids for the purpose of identification and individualization. The type of material typically examined included, but was not limited to semen and saliva collected at crime scenes or from articles of physical evidence. These types of physiological fluids were frequently generated during the commission of violent crimes such as homicides, rapes or assaults. The GBI's ultimate goal was to identify what type of body fluid is present and then, through the use of DNA analysis, link that material to a specific person.

They also performed routine analysis of hair and fiber

samples with an eye toward identification as well as latent print identification.

During their morning at the lab, the agents listened to Mark Crenshaw, the fiber technician, discus fiber analysis, a dry boring subject to Dalrymple. It was a review he didn't need. His and Crenshaw's path had crossed on numerous cases down through the years.

"A fiber is the smallest unit of a textile material that has a length many times greater than its diameter." Crenshaw seemed to enjoy giving the lecture to a captured audience, even if he knew the agents. "Fibers can occur naturally as plant and animal fibers, but they can also be man-made. A fiber can be spun with other fibers to form a yarn that can be woven or knitted to form a fabric. The type and length of fiber used, the type of spinning method, and the type of fabric construction all affect the transfer of fibers and the significance of fiber associations. This becomes very important when there is a possibility of fiber transfer between a suspect and a victim during the commission of a crime.

"Many different natural fibers originating from plants and animals are used in the production of fabric. Cotton fibers are the plant fibers most commonly used in textile materials, with the type of cotton, fiber length, and degree of twist contributing to the diversity of these fibers. Processing techniques and color applications also influence the value of cotton fiber identifications. Other plant fibers used in the production of textile materials include flax—linen—ramie, sisal, jute, hemp, kapok, and coir. The identification of less common plant fibers at a crime scene or on the clothing of a suspect or victim would have increased significance."

"That's all very interesting, Mark," Toomey said. "But what does it have to do with the fiber in question?" Toomey was getting restless, Dalrymple noted.

"Well, for starters, whenever a fiber found on the clothing of a victim matches the known fibers of a suspect's clothing, it can be a significant event. Matching dyed synthetic fibers or dyed natural fibers can be very meaningful, whereas the matching of common fibers such as white cotton or blue denim cotton would be less significant. In some situations, however, the presence of white cotton or blue denim cotton may still have some meaning in resolving the truth of an issue. The discovery of cross transfers and multiple fiber transfers between the suspect's clothing and the victim's clothing dramatically increases the likelihood that these two individuals had physical contact."

Dalrymple had heard enough. "Listen, Mark," he said, "we know this guy had contact with the victim. The perp killed him for Christ's sake. We also know the victim did not own any blue articles of clothing. So the blue fiber may have come from the perp. We need to know what kind of fiber?"

Crenshaw nodded his understanding. "Chemical analysis can determine the chemical composition of the fibers. In the case of synthetic fabric or carpet, this information can be used to trace the product to the manufacturer using standards databases, further enhancing the probative value of the evidence. In the case of your fiber, we found it was part of a Dutch weave fabric, unusual in American cloth making. Usually found in European fabrics of European manufacture. When we subjected the fiber to spectrophotometric testing we found the dye used was from Hungary."

"The dye was made in Hungary?" Dalrymple said, suddenly alert.

"Yes," Crenshaw said. "Blue-dyeing, or *kekfestes*, is a centuries-old tradition in Hungary, however, only six blue-dying workshops still operate in the country. One of the most well-known of these is that of the Kovacs family, who have been passing down the craft from parents to children since 1878."

"You guys are amazing," Toomey said, laughing.

Crenshaw shrugged. "The family creates beautiful blue textiles with a resist-dyeing method where the white fabric is first printed with a resist paste, using wooden motif blocks or sometimes a block-printing machine. The fabric is then immersed in an indanthrene solution that works much faster than the original indigo dye. The printed areas resist the dye and come out white, resulting in a delicately patterned blue fabric. Blue-dyeing was originally brought to Hungary by German immigrants who came to resettle the southwestern parts of the country after the Ottoman occupation ended. Today this fabric is popular for use in clothing and for quilting and other crafts. Quite lovely, actually."

Dalrymple frowned. "So this fabric was made in Hungary. How common is it?"

"Not very," Crenshaw said. "Probably one can only get clothes or handkerchiefs made with this cloth in Eastern Europe or the Balkans."

As the agents returned to their field office, Toomey spoke first.

"Don't ask me to come here again, Chuck. The guy is an insufferable bore."

Dalrymple laughed. "Crenshaw's all right," he said. "He's just been locked away in that lab of his he's starved for human interaction."

Both men had to chuckle at Dalrymple's description of the fiber analyst.

"So our perpetrator is foreign," Toomey said. "Is that how you make it?"

"Seems like it. If that is true, then he's a pro. Which means the Baxter killing was a professional hit."

"Puts a different light on it."

"Yeah, a whole different light," Dalrymple said.

అఅఅ

The holding cell at the Trinity police station smelled of urine and vomit, not a pleasant odor to Grant's nose. He was the cell's only occupant, a fact that pleased him for his temper was about to get the better of him and he couldn't afford a fit of anger. This was his second arrest in a week. It was getting old. He waited impatiently until an officer came and escorted him to Sergeant Brady's office. The sergeant was typing furiously on his typewriter. He looked up when Grant's escort shoved him into a chair.

"Mr. Collins," he said in a terse tone. "You have used up my patience. Crossed the line."

"Now what have I done, Sergeant?" His voice was loud and spewed venom. "This is bordering on harassment."

"I received a phone call from a Mr. Winston Conway," Brad said. "He claims that you waltzed into his office and threatened him."

"What? Are you kidding? And you believe that jerk?"

"He has a witness. His assistant confirms you were there and that he heard you threaten his boss."

"That's impossible," Grant shouted. "He wasn't even in the office when we had our conversation. If he said that, he's lying."

Brady lit a cigarette. Still smoking the same brand, thought Grant.

"You're saying that it was just the two of you in his office?"

"Of course! Why would I lie to you? I admit I went to see him but it was to talk about his plans for the power plant. I did not threaten the man. Is that what Conway himself said?"

Brady nodded, taking a puff on his cigarette.

"Both him and his assistant. The assistant wasn't physically present but he claims he heard you threaten Mr. Conway in a loud voice. In addition, you left Trinity against my expressed orders to not do so."

"I did not threaten Mr. Conway," Grant said. He was exasperated at this turn of events, couldn't fathom the reason for it unless his presence in Conway's office had struck a nerve. The man was reacting out of fear, he thought. "If he felt threatened, I can't help it. And his so-called witness wasn't even physically present during our conversation. So you really don't have much of a witness do you, Sergeant?"

Brady snubbed out his cigarette, looked at Grant with flashing eyes. "Frankly, Mr. Collins," he said, "I'm getting tired of running you in here. You seem to have a habit of turning up at inopportune times and causing people grief. I could throw you in a cell and hold you until you get a lawyer. A judge would probably toss this charge out the window so I'd be out a lot of unnecessary work and you'd lose a few days doing whatever you do. You might even sue for false arrest. It seems that this is a case of your word against Mr. Conway's, his assistant's testimony notwithstanding."

Grant felt his pulse rise. The sergeant continued.

"So, I'm not going to arrest you. But, I'm warning you." Brady's leaned forward in his chair, his face mere inches from Grant's. His words were menacing. "Don't let me catch you doing anything improper again, you understand? If you do, I'll have you in a cell eating food you won't recognize. The best thing for you to do under the circumstances would be to leave Trinity. However, in the event you don't choose to heed my advice, I suggest you remain on your best behavior." He stopped to allow time for Grant to digest his words. "Do we understand each other?"

"Perfectly," Grant said.

Brady turned to the officer standing next to the door. "Officer," he said, "escort Mr. Collins back to his car."

The police officer nodded, opened the door, waited. Grant left without looking back at Brady. He was fuming.

On the way to his mother's house, Grant could hardly contain his irritation at the Trinity police sergeant. He was being harassed but for what? To what end? Asking questions about his mother's untimely death? About the deaths of other Trinity residents? But why? What was the deal about the black limo following him? Another threat from Conway? The longer Grant stayed in Trinity, the more questions he raised. Maybe the sergeant was right—he should give up and return home.

He was beginning to think the whole town was nothing but one gigantic conspiracy. One designed to thwart all attempts to block the power plant from coming to town. That's how it was shaping up in Grant's mind. There really was no other explanation. So why could not others see it as clearly as he and Carrie?

Unless Trinity's law enforcement and other high-ranking officials, like Dr. Witherspoon, were part of that conspiracy.

Suddenly he became nauseous. He parked his car in his mother's driveway and raced into the house and into the kitchen. He poured a glass of water and gulped it down, took a towel, wiped the cold sweat off his face.

My God, is there no place to which we can turn?

What if the conspiracy extended beyond Conway? To include most of Trinity's leaders? If it did, were they all expecting a financial windfall from the power plant? How big was this thing?

Feeling better, he stumbled into the living room, collapsed into a chair. His mind was a whirl so he closed his eyes, tried to relax his tense muscles. Slowly, as the wave of bewilderment abated, he knew what he had to do.

He was going to have to return to Conway's trailer for a better search. Surely there was evidence he needed in that trailer. But he would need more than a few minutes.

This time he would ask Carrie to be a lookout.

Chapter 25

The luminous dial on Grant's wristwatch read two-fifteen a.m. He and Carrie left Trinity's few burning lights behind as he drove toward Conway's property. It was a cloudless night but the moon was not scheduled to make an appearance for another two hours. A warm salty breeze wafted up off the Dogwood River along the way toward Conway's trailer.

Earlier, when Grant mentioned his desire to return to the trailer, she became argumentative, saying it was unnecessary. He hadn't found anything they could use when he last searched the place so he wasn't likely to discover anything now. But he had persisted, pointing out to her that they were out of options. It was unlikely that Wilder's agents would turn up anything making it imperative that he and Carrie do the dirty work.

She had not been persuaded, however. But she went with him, nonetheless. Why, she didn't know, except she couldn't bear that anything happen to him without her being near.

He donned his black pants and shirt, found his flashlight. They jumped into his car and headed out of town, driving for ten minutes before Carrie spoke. Her voice was tense, fearful.

"You want me to remain at the car and watch for possible trespassers or other prowlers?" Carrie said.

"That's my plan," Grant said. "I need plenty of time to make a thorough search of the place. You're going to honk the horn if you see anyone. Hopefully it will give me time to get out of there."

"I think you're crazy. If Brady catches you, he's going to lock you up and throw away the key. Why take a chance?"

"This whole thing has stuck in my throat like a bad piece of meat. I've got to cough it up or *go* crazy. Sooner or later I'm going to get something on that bastard and I'll have my justice. After my meeting with him, I believe there's a strong possibility that Conway had Mayor Baxter bumped off. Probably because the mayor wasn't delivering the vote for the plant fast enough. I'm telling you, Carrie, there was something evil about the man. The way he looked at me. He had this sinister smirk. It was quite unsettling."

They drove past Pete's Crab Shack. Grant steered off the main road onto the narrow gravel affair that wound up the rise overlooking Conway's property. He slowed, the car's wheels crunching on the soft ground. The road veered to the right then back to the left as it approached the short rise ending in a steep bluff on one side. He doused the headlights and inched to a spot that gave a commanding view of the property below. He parked the car and turned off the motor. The large house under construction lay beyond the high chain link fence. All was dark.

"Okay," Grant said. "Wait here. If you see anyone, honk twice. If I don't return in twenty minutes, lay on that horn."

"Grant—" Carrie said.

"I'll be fine. Just keep a sharp eye out and keep the binocs handy."

With that said, he let himself out of the car, ran down the bluff then ducked into a nearby grove of trees. The night air was balmy, the strong river odor of fish and moss tickled his nose. Frogs and crickets sang their night chorus as he crept toward the fence. Off to his left was the gate and guardhouse.

No signs of anyone about. The guardhouse was dark.

He knew it was a risk leaving Carrie alone in the car unprotected and without a weapon to defend herself. While in Savannah he had thought about purchasing a handgun but didn't know with his mental health diagnosis if he could pass the background check. So he had decided against it. He realized that sitting alone in a car in the middle of the night must be nerve-wracking to her but he needed someone to watch his back. And she wanted to do it. She was more worried about his safety than her own. It was just like her.

Without moonlight the metal fence stood as a dull gray affair against a black background of forest and river edge meadow. He worried that it might be electrified since his last visit but he was committed to searching the trailer. Why wasn't there a twenty-four hour guard at the place, he wondered? The frame skeleton of the house was enormous—it was obviously going to be a three-story mansion having a circular drive in front. The rear of the house faced the river with a wide walkway already in place leading down to the water and a floating dock.

He stood for a moment, allowing the breeze to tickle his face. Noises from beyond the fence reached him, pushing him toward panic but he swallowed hard, told himself the noises were small animals down near the river. His muscles were rigid, tense. He forced himself to think of Carrie sitting back in the car. She was watching.

Her pleadings ran on and on in Grant's mind, a pattern of repetitions with different words all producing the same primal fear in him. She wanted him to give up on this whole sordid affair and maybe she was right, he didn't want to lose her. Standing at the fence, pulse pounding, fearful—maybe he ought to turn around, return to her apartment and let her sooth his frazzled brain. Maybe.

He scaled the fence as before without difficulty, ran to the copse of trees alongside the gravel drive that led to the construction site. He rested, catching his breath and giving his heart a chance to calm its pounding. He swallowed hard, forcing down the lump of cotton that formed in his throat.

Moving as fast as caution allowed, he continued in a wide circle toward the trailer parked to one side of the partially constructed house. His footfalls made soft crunching sounds in the grass and leaves. He stopped, glanced back toward his car and Carrie. It was nothing more than a dark silhouette perched on the rise. He couldn't see her inside. And it wasn't too late to return to his vehicle. But nothing seemed amiss.

At the trailer's small wooden porch he paused while the wind gusted again. An owl hooted in a tree above but otherwise, except for the crickets and frogs, the area was quiet. He was surprised how still his muscles had become.

His watch read two-forty-two.

Remembering the combination to the door lock, he dialed it and after latch clicked open, let himself in. Inside, the trailer was dark, a musty smell greeted him. He retrieved his flashlight and switched it on, following its eerie beam through the darkness. It took a moment for Grant to regain his bearings, remembering the layout from his earlier visit. He followed the light from the kitchen area to the back of the trailer where he remembered the master bedroom was located. Satisfied he was alone he closed the trailer door.

It was not a luxury trailer. Most of the fixtures were cheap metal and plastic, a typical construction site trailer.

Grant began his search in the tiny kitchen where he found a coffeepot, microwave, and a small refrigerator. Dirty coffee mugs along with several forks lay on the counter. *Someone uses the place frequently.* An ashtray full of cigarette butts sat on the table next to the kitchen. The metal cabinets were well worn, a polished sheen shown bright under the flashlight's beam. He opened them one by one, going through them but finding nothing but a few plates, glassware, more coffee cups.

He shined his light on the small table where a large blueprint was spread out next to the ashtray, its corners held down by more coffee mugs. It was a blueprint of the nuclear power plant's core, showing the location of pumps, surge tanks, dissolvers, crystallizers, contamination and waste prep areas, as well as the core itself. None of it made sense to Grant.

He moved on to the living area that contained the leather sofa and two recliners and a television. The electric fireplace was along one wall. Numerous books were scattered about and in a small wooden bookcase. A quick appraisal told him they were federal regulatory guidelines and other OSHA standards. Nothing interesting.

Stepping into the main cabin he found the desk positioned between two chairs. It was an old metal desk with a plastic top. The interior smelled of stale cigars and cigarettes, no doubt from the construction crew that were in and out of the trailer. Somehow, he couldn't see himself in that profession—building mansions for the wealthy. Grant pulled a chair in front of the desk and systematically rifled through its contents. Same as before—mostly contracts and cancelled checks. He held the flashlight in his mouth, then began going through the documents, one by one. The contracts were with various building contractors, bricklayers, cabinetmakers, plumbers, and the like.

The cancelled checks matched the contracts. Fifteen thousand dollars to the bricklayer alone. *This is going to be some house.*

Directing his attention to the filing cabinets, he opened the bottom drawer, the one he remembered containing the email. This time he searched through the drawer's contents more completely. More of the same documents pertaining to the plant and the house.

He found nothing that would incriminate Conway.

The man would have to be awfully stupid, he thought, to leave incriminating evidence lying casually around. *No, he's much too smart for that.*

The honking of a car horn pierced the quiet.

His car horn.

Carrie!

It wasn't two blasts of the horn—it was a continuous, repeated honking.

Then quiet.

Oh God, Carrie!

Grant bolted out of the trailer, crashing over a chair, flashlight off, into the night. He shot a glance up toward the rise and his car but couldn't make out anything. In the distance he heard the squealing of car tires. He swallowed hard. *What the hell was going on? Was Carrie all right? Had she been harmed?* If something had happened to her he wasn't going to be able to forgive himself. It was his suggestion she sit up there to keep a lookout for him.

If she was hurt—

Sprinting to the fence, he lunged at it, lungs bursting and out of breath. He vaulted over as easily as an Olympic high jumper then raced up the bluff to his car. He crashed over the rocks, clawing his way up to the summit. Once, his foot slipped propelling him backwards but with a last-minute effort he managed to regain his balance before pushing on.

Why did I pick this spot to park the car? If only I had left Carrie at her apartment.

The going up the bluff was infinitely more difficult that his earlier trip down to Conway's property. His legs burned with the effort. Sweat trickled into his eyes, stinging, nearly blinding him. His heart pounded in anticipation with what he might find when he reached his car. In the dark it was difficult to see where to step and his feet became snagged on rocks and crevices making the arduous climb more painstaking. What would he do if she was gone? Assaulted? Grant's stomach lurched at the thought of finding Carrie that way.

At last he could make out the crest of the bluff. Just a few more yards.

When he pulled himself over the top he noticed a figure in the front passenger seat of his car. It was slumped forward.

Carrie?

The lone figure didn't move. But closer he could tell that Carrie's shoulders were shaking, her head buried in her hands.

Chapter 26

Special Agents Dalrymple and Toomey were in Special Agent in Charge Wilder's office with news of the Trinity mayor's murder. They had gone straight to the field office in Savannah upon returning from their investigative trip to the small hamlet against Toomey's protests. The man wanted some steamed clams and a beer.

Wilder smiled at her two favorite agents. They were men of the highest integrity and accomplishment, Dalrymple having been awarded Best Agent in the Bureau twice in his long career.

Pairing the two together was her brainchild, one of her better judgment calls. They complemented each other in a way few agents did—or could. Dalrymple definitely had the brains and the experience while Toomey had an innate sense of where a case might lead. His intuitive thinking had helped the pair solve a number of ticklish cases during their five-year partnership.

"So you think the mayor's murderer was a foreign professional?" she said.

"That's what the evidence seems to indicate," Toomey said, slouched in his chair, his tie loosened at the collar. "The fiber we found at the scene was manufactured in Hungary. And the mayor had no clothing that matched it. It had to have been purchased in Europe or the Balkans."

Wilder nodded, scribbled some notes on a legal pad.

"Plus," Dalrymple said, "when we examined the body at the funeral home, the man had been stabbed and his throat slashed with some sort of stiletto. Not just any knife but a thin bladed stiletto."

Wilder continued to write for a moment then she set her pen aside and looked at the agents. "Sounds like East European or even Russian," she said. "More like a professional killing than a random murder."

"That's what we're thinking. There were no signs of robbery, nothing appears stolen from the residence," Dalrymple said.

"It begs the question, though," Wilder said, leaning back in her chair, "as to motive. Why would there be a professional hit of a small town mayor? Probably cost a fortune. You could get a local addict to do it for a lot less."

Toomey shook his head.

Dalrymple shrugged. "Don't have any idea at this point. A local hit might cost less but not nearly as certain. It may have something to do with this nuclear plant you mentioned. Anyway, we're getting s court order to look into Baxter's financial records, his bank accounts, safe deposit box if he has one."

Wilder stood and paced around her office, occasionally glancing out her window. "When that young man, Collins I believe was his name, and his girlfriend were here, they seemed convinced that Trinity's other deaths were not accidental but had, in fact, been killings. Orchestrated to sway the city council's vote in favor of the power plant. However, they had nothing to go on. But you might check into that angle while you're at it."

Dalrymple stood and Toomey followed suit. They ambled toward the door.

"It's late," Dalrymple said. "We'll follow up tomorrow. Tonight I have to help a granddaughter with her homework."

"Where's her mother?" Wilder said.

"Taking a night class," he replied. "Ever since her divorce she's been working on her degree. So one night a week I get to babysit. It's a great job if you'd care to apply."

"Hey," Wilder said, laughing. "I've got one of my own, remember?"

ᏨᎦᏨᎦ

Grant ran to his car and yanked the door open. Carrie sat slumped in the passenger seat, sobbing. She didn't look at him.

"What the hell happened?" he screamed, reaching over the driver's seat and grabbing her by the arm.

She turned toward him. With the car's dim dome light he noticed the tears on her cheeks. She shook her head. "Those bastards," she said, voice quivering.

Grant slid into the seat beside her, closed the car door leaving them in quiet darkness. "Those bastards what?" he said. He could tell she was visibly shaken, a demeanor he had not seen her display until now. "What happened, Carrie?"

"A car drove up and parked next to me," she said in a measured tone. "These two guys hopped out—I had forgotten to lock the car after you left—one jumped in next to me, the other climbed in behind me."

Carrie still had not looked at him, kept staring through the windshield straight ahead.

"Go on," he pleaded.

"The one behind grabbed me by my hair, yanked it around to face the other man. He threatened me, Grant. Said if I valued my health to get you out of town any way I could. Said he knew where I lived and could hurt me bad anytime he wanted. He scared me, Grant." She put her head in her hands, sobbed softly again.

"What did they look like?"

Carrie looked at him with red swollen eyes. He could tell she was scared, really scared. "I didn't get a very good look at either of them but the one next to me had tattoos all over both arms. They both smelled bad."

"Those are the same bastards who assaulted me," Grant said, reaching out to her and putting a hand on her shoulder. "I guess they didn't learn their lesson. This may turn into an all-out war."

"Don't, please," Carrie said, taking a napkin from her purse and drying her eyes. "Let's just go home."

"You okay?" he said. "They didn't hurt you?"

"No. Just threats."

On the drive back to Carrie's apartment, Grant's blood began to boil. Beating him up was one thing but involving an innocent woman was another. Well, the gauntlet had been thrown down and something was going to have to be done with these goons. He glanced at Carrie who sat against her door staring out the window. Not speaking, just staring. He was going to make those bastards pay, one way or the other.

In the apartment, he got two beers and brought them to Carrie's small living room where she sat silent on the sofa. He handed her one and collapsed next to her. She took a long gulp, smiled weakly.

"So, what did you find in the trailer?" she said.

He smiled at her. Some of the sparkle was returning to her eyes allowing him to breath quiet sigh of relief. "Unfortunately, nothing. Just as before. But I don't suspect Conway is stupid as to keep incriminating papers laying about where they could be found. I had to have another look just to be sure."

"Then it was worth it," she said.

"You feeling better?"

"Much. Thank you."

"I'll make them pay, I promise," Grant said. "So help me they will."

"No need," Carrie said, leaning over and kissing him in the cheek. "But the sentiment is sweet. My protector."

The next day, after seeing Carrie off to work, Grant drove into Savannah and purchased a handgun. He decided to take a chance with the background check and to his surprise there were no problems. He bought a Beretta nine millimeter similar to the one he carried in Iraq and a box of ammo. He opted for the clip that held thirty rounds, making the weapon an awesome killing machine. He had no idea what he was going to do with the pistol or if he would even need it but it felt good to have it. He would leave it at Carrie's and show her how to shoot it after she got off work.

He waited at his mother's house for Carrie to get off work. While doing so, he took a legal pad and scribbled the names of Trinity's dead committee members.

Cybil Nottingham who drowned in the family swimming pool. Henry Edison who was electrocuted while working on a generator at his home on the Dogwood River. Olivia Bruckner, a victim of a hit and run driver along the Dogwood River road. Lori Spelling, who died of a drug overdose. Hollister McLain, who died in the fire in his hardware store. Finally, there was his mother, Helen Collins, who perished in an automobile accident.

Six people. Six supposed accidental deaths. All different mechanisms of death.

Grant took a beer from the fridge, sat in his mother's

recliner, studied the list. He took a long pull of the beer, didn't bother switching on the lamp next to the chair. It was afternoon, the sun on its downward arc, which threw the room into shadow. As Grant sat in the dim light, he went over the list, name by name, jotting down what information he had gleaned about them. All six victims had been members of his mother's *Citizens Against Nuclear Power* committee. He searched for clues to possible similarities or a common threat among them.

Cybil Nottingham. Mrs. Nottingham was a member of a family gathering and, according to family members, had been drinking. She apparently fell into the pool and wasn't discovered until it was too late to revive her. Dr. Witherspoon signed her death certificate. No autopsy performed.

Henry Edison. Odd name for a man electrocuted accidentally. Supposed faulty generator. Dr. Witherspoon signed the death certificate. No autopsy.

Olivia Bruckner. Miss Bruckner was struck and killed by a car on the river road. The driver yet to be found. Dr. Witherspoon signed the death certificate. No autopsy.

Lori Spelling. Died of heroin and cocaine overdose. Dr. Witherspoon ordered the blood analysis and signed the death certificate. No autopsy.

Hollister McLain. Death by smoke inhalation in his hardware store fire. Fire apparently started in a pile of oily rags. His wife said he would never be so careless. Dr. Witherspoon signed the death certificate. No autopsy done.

Lastly, there was his mother, Helen Collins. Died by hitting bridge abutment. Suspicious nature of rear end accident in the past. His mother never mentioned she had been in a prior collision. Dr. Witherspoon signed death certificate. No autopsy performed on his mother.

There they were—six names, six deaths. Scanty information about each.

One thing was glaringly obvious.

Dr. Witherspoon signed each person's death certificate.

And he hadn't performed an autopsy on any of them.

Peculiar to say the least.

But the information Grant had wasn't much. Surely there was more to be learned about each one. Carrie had chatted with Mrs. McLain so it was doubtful she could add anything more. As far as he knew, Lori had no family in Georgia so speaking with them would be difficult. Maybe by phone if he could locate a family member. But the Nottingham, Edison, and Bruckner families might be willing to talk, shed some light on what happened. He decided he would look up each family and see what could be gleaned, if anything.

Then he would go see Dr. Witherspoon again.

c∕⊃c∕⊃

Carrie finished her chores at the *Trinity Cafe,* sat for a moment next to the cash register, contemplating what had transpired the previous night. The goons who threatened her and Grant had left a pernicious, haunting impression, and she didn't want to face Grant just yet. She needed some time alone, to think, to consider what her options were.

The thought of dumping Grant left her with revolting sense of shame, something she was loath to do. To abandon him now in his hour of greatest trial would reveal a character flaw she didn't want to admit she possessed. Maybe the power plant wasn't worth all the fighting. All the killing. And she was just as sure as Grant that the Trinity deaths were not accidental. There was always the possibility of more deaths until the plant was a reality.

Was it worth it, she thought? She didn't think so. Not now.

If she could persuade Grant to give up his crusade, maybe they could settle down to a normal, easygoing relationship. As it stood presently, their kinship was based on his fascination with the *why* of his mother's death and her attraction to his brokenness. Once the Trinity plant was behind them they could concentrate on each other's happiness. She knew in her heart that Grant was the one for her. Underneath his nightmares was a strong, sensitive man capable of great things. She wanted to be a part of his life.

If it meant leaving Trinity to be with him, so be it.

She would have to speak with him and get him to see things her way.

Chapter 27

It was late afternoon when Grant pulled up to the modest home of Greg Nottingham, Cybil's oldest son and member of the swimming party on the day of her death. He was nervous but determined to talk about the man's mother and that fateful day. Swallowing hard, he sauntered up the concrete steps to the front door and rang the doorbell. A woman answered.

"Yes?" she said, eyeing Grant as one would a stranger. She wore a flowered apron about her waist.

"Mrs. Nottingham?" he said in as non-confrontational tone as he could muster. "I'm Grant Collins. I used to live here in Trinity and my mother was Helen Collins. I believe your mother-in-law served on the power plant committee with my mother."

"Yes," the woman said from behind the unopened screen door.

"I was wondering if I could have a brief word with Greg. Is he at home?"

She nodded and hollered into the house and soon a husky man wearing a Trinity Power and Light uniform appeared at the door. Grant repeated his request.

"I was hoping we could talk. You see my mother died in an automobile accident shortly after testifying before the town hall meeting. We might have something in common."

"Come in," Nottingham said, holding the screen door open.

He led Grant into a small study and indicated a chair. The smell of cinnamon filled the house. After they were seated the man spoke again.

"You said we might have something in common."

"Well," Grant said. "Where to begin. Your mother and mine were members of the committee lobbying against DynaTech building a nuclear power plant here in Trinity I believe."

Nottingham nodded, smiled. "It was sort of peculiar. What with me working for the power company and telling her it would mean cheap electricity for all of Trinity's residents. But Mom had a mind of her own. She was fearful of nuclear power."

"As was mine," Grant said. "I hate to bring up a painful memory but your mother drowned in the family pool didn't she?"

"A tragedy, to be sure. She'd had a little wine that day but not nearly to the extent the papers let on. By the time my brother noticed her, she was at the bottom of the pool. We gave her CPR was it was no help."

"Was a doctor called?"

"Old Doc Witherspoon came by in his capacity as medical examiner but he said she was too far gone by the time she was discovered. He signed Mom's death certificate if I recall."

"You've known the doctor long?" Grant said.

"Many years," Nottingham said. "But our family never went to him. We drove to Savannah for our medical care."

"How come?"

"Didn't trust the old doctor. There have been stories—"

"Yes?" Grant said. "Please continue." He edged forward in his chair.

"Well," Nottingham said, his eyes darting between Grant and the kitchen where his wife was cooking dinner. "There have always been stories. My family never did trust the man."

Grant shifted, his mouth suddenly dry. "My mother died in what the police called a one car accident but it certainly was not investigated properly. At least that's my opinion. Was it a family party—that afternoon?"

"Family and friends. A few city council members. And the mayor."

"The mayor?" Grant said, again sitting forward in his chair.

"Yes. Mom knew Bruce from her work and we all knew him since childhood. Shocking what happened to him."

"It was. You say your mother hadn't had much to drink that afternoon?"

"Hardly anything."

"She wasn't drunk then?"

Nottingham laughed. "Not at all. I never saw Mom inebriated ever. A glass or two of wine was all she ever had and that only on special occasions."

"Could someone have put something in her drink?" Grant said.

"Like what?"

"I dunno. Something to make her drunk. Something that if she fell or was pushed into the pool she would be too drunk to help herself."

"Gosh," Nottingham exclaimed. "But who—"

"Again, I dunno. But your mother was on a committee fighting to keep a multimillion-dollar plant from being built here in Trinity. It stands to reason that there were people at your party that wanted the plant built. Any one of them could—"

"Wait a minute!" Nottingham roared. "I work for the power company and wanted the plant a reality but I wouldn't dream of doing away with my mother."

Grant held up a hand, smiled. "Of course not. I didn't mean to imply that you would. However, can you say the same for all your guests that day?"

The was a pause in their conversation while Nottingham contemplated Grant's suggestion. He stared at him while he rubbed his chin.

"Listen," Grant added. "There are a lot of people who stand to make a lot of money if and when that plant is built. The lure of big money can do strange things to some people."

Nottingham had a faraway look in his eyes as if trying to remember all of the guests that day. After several moments he looked at Grant, shook his head.

"Wow!" he said. "I can't be sure. I suppose it's possible. There *were* some folks there who championed the plant. But to stoop to murder? Wow!"

"You mentioned that there were stories about Dr. Witherspoon. Care to elaborate?"

"I can't give you specifics," Nottingham said. "They were more like rumors, if you like."

"Like what?"

"People having bad results from the doctor's care. Unnecessary amputations, people dying 'cause he messed up. That sort of thing."

"And to think the man is still practicing in town," Grant said.

"Practicing is probably the correct term," Nottingham said and both men chuckled.

Grant left Greg Nottingham sitting in his chair puzzling afresh the circumstances surrounding his mother's death while he drove to the Edison place. It was out on the river road. He found Henry's widow laboring in her garden.

"Mrs. Edison?" he said, climbing out of his car and approaching the woman stooped over a hoe. She looked up at his approach.

"I'm Grant Collins," he said. "Helen Collins' son. Your husband and my mother were on the committee against the power plant."

The woman stood, leaning on her hoe, wiped her face with an apron, then smiled.

"You're Helen's boy? My, my. Yes, I knew your mother. Come in, come in. I was just finishing up. Ever since Henry died, I have tried to keep up his garden. It was his passion." Mrs. Edison led Grant to the front porch where she took a seat in an antique swing and pointed to a wicker chair. "Henry liked that chair," she said. "I hope you find it comfortable."

Grant nodded as he sat. Mrs. Edison was a graying woman with a tanned, wrinkled face and cheerful blue eyes. He noticed her gnarled arthritic hands as she rocked.

"I hope I haven't stopped at a bad time," Grant said. "If so, I can come back later."

"Oh no," Mrs. Edison said. "I usually sit here for a spell after working in the garden before I go in for supper. What brings you out this way?"

"Well," Grant started. "It's about your husband's death. My mother too, recently died in an automobile accident."

"Yes," the woman said. "I was so sorry. Henry and your mother worked on that committee. You're here about Henry's death?"

"Yes. I don't think my mother's death was an acci-

dent and I was wondering what your thoughts were regarding your husband and the way he died. The paper
mentioned something about a generator."

Mrs. Edison's blue eyes flashed. "That infernal con-
traption," she said, her voice spitting out the words. "It
was a brand new generator. I told Henry to take the thing
back and get himself a replacement but no, he said he
could fix it."

"What happened?"

"I have no idea. It wouldn't start, I do know that.
Henry was out in his shop working on it. I went out to
tell him lunch was ready and found him lying on the
ground next to it. I called nine-one-one but he was dead.
Dr. Witherspoon said he had been electrocuted."

"Did you ask how a new generator could have electrocuted your husband? Sounds unlikely to me."

"You think so?" Mrs. Edison said, her face suddenly
taut with a frown.

"I'm no expert but those things are pretty safe. There
were no signs of anything unusual?"

"Such as?"

"Maybe a struggle. Maybe someone assaulted Henry.
Killed him. There was no autopsy, right?"

"Dr. Witherspoon said there was on need. That it was
obvious how Henry died."

"Was your husband in good health?"

"He was. He took pills for his blood pressure but it
was always normal when he took it."

"Never had a heart attack or anything?"

"No. You mentioned your mother's death, son. She
and Henry were both on that committee. Now you have
me wondering. You think their deaths could be related?"

"I don't know, Mrs. Edison," Grant said. "That's
what I'm trying to find out."

"Why would Dr. Witherspoon lie about Henry's

cause of death? I mean if it wasn't electrocution."

"I have no idea. I can't say for sure their deaths are related. But there have been other strange deaths in Trinity over the past months. And they make me suspicious."

It was obvious his thoughts upset the woman, so Grant decided to leave well enough alone. When he left her house he noticed she was still sitting on the porch. He drove to Carrie's and found her fixing dinner. She seemed in a somber mood so he hesitated in telling her how he had spent his afternoon. After they ate and were sitting in the living room, Carrie wanted to talk.

"I've got a few things on my mind, Grant, and I want you to listen. Don't say anything until I'm finished. Just listen."

Grant's heart jumped in his chest for her tone sounded onerous.

"Last night's experience got me to thinking," she continued. "Why are we doing all this? For what?" Grant started to say something but Carrie put him off. "I said I wanted to get this off my chest, so please Grant, let me do it. Now, as I was saying, what's the purpose? Nothing can bring your mother back, nothing. You've managed to get yourself in trouble with the police, even arrested and will have to appear at a hearing soon. You've been assaulted, hurt, and have broken the law by breaking and entering Conway's trailer. We tried going to the Bureau of Investigation and, although the agent seemed interested in what we had to say, nothing seems to be moving forward on that front. You have your own problems and issues to deal with and, for you, that should come first. I'm not trying to indicate your mother's death that, tragic as it was, is something you should just forget. I'm not suggesting that at all. Please don't misunderstand. But there is no credible evidence to suggest it was anything other than an accident.

"I have my own life to live, Grant. And you know what? It is inexplicably intertwined with yours. I have fallen in love with you, and I cannot bear to see you making yourself ill over this. Or more ill than you say you are. In the long run, the power plant is coming to Trinity. You've got to accept it. The forces aligned with it are too formidable to oppose. If your worst fears are correct, then delving further could endanger both our lives and our future together. I don't know but maybe you don't feel about me in the same way. If you don't, then I'd appreciate you just saying so, and we'll go our separate ways. "I thought I was strong but I guess I'm not as strong as I thought I was. And I'm frightened. Scared that you'll be next, found dead somewhere, or worse, that it will happen to both of us. I don't want to die, Grant. I don't want to lose you, either. If you insist on persisting in this crusade of yours, I'm not sure I can be a part of it. I just pray you can see it from my point of view."

Finished, Carrie collapsed back in the sofa, gazing at the wall opposite her. Grant waited a few minutes to be sure she was through talking.

"Is this an ultimatum?" he said.

She wrapped her arms about herself as if she had taken a chill. "I hope not. I certainly don't want you to take it that way."

"At this point it's a little late for me to be having second thoughts," he said. "I have no illusions about the difficulty facing me in proving mother's death was anything more than an unfortunate accident. However—" And, with this, his tone hardened. "—I have no intentions of ceasing my investigation. Just this afternoon, I spoke with the son of the woman who drowned, and guess what? She wasn't drunk at all as the paper said. A glass or two of wine, that's all. There were people on favor of the power plant at that party. Any one of them could have slipped something into her drink and rendered her unable to navigate properly. And the man who was electrocuted? It was a brand new generator. No reason for a malfunction. He was alone in his barn. He could have been assaulted. He was in otherwise good health. And here's the biggest news flash. Dr. Witherspoon signed each and every death certificate without an autopsy on any of them."

"Grant, I—" Carrie's voice wavered.

"These are not coincidences. The same man signs all these death certificates and, at the same time, rules there was no need for an autopsy. On any of them. He's part of it, Carrie. Witherspoon is part of the conspiracy. I'm going to prove it."

Chapter 28

Grant sat across from Olivia Bruckner's parents, Bill and Cynthia. Photographs of a young girl in golden picture frames sat on the mantle and a small table next to Grant's chair. The girl was dressed in various clothes from a Girl Scout and band uniforms to more mature dresses. She was quite beautiful.

"She was our darling," Cynthia Bruckner said. "I was so proud of her being a college student and standing for what she thought was right against nuclear power. She thought the world of your mother."

"I didn't realize she was on the committee with my mother. She was going to college here in Trinity?" Grant said.

"She was," Mr. Bruckner said. "She was living here at home and was in her senior year."

"Majoring in political science," added Cynthia.

"Please forgive my awkwardness but what happened, exactly?" Grant asked. He felt uncomfortable under the pair's inquisitive gaze.

Mr. Bruckner cleared his throat. "She was jogging. Something she did every day. Helped keep her trim figure, she always said. She was wearing her headphones and I guess she couldn't hear traffic noise. A car ran her

over and kept going. Never stopped or called an ambulance. A passerby found her lying off to the side of the
road and got the paramedics there who called for a heli-
copter. She was airlifted to Augusta but didn't make it
out of surgery."

"What time was the accident?" Grant asked.

"We don't really know exactly. She left the house
around two in the afternoon. We got a call about four-
thirty." Bruckner took his wife's hand, patted it gently.
There were tears in Cynthia's eyes.

"Were they ever able to locate the driver?" Grant
said, his heart pounding in his chest.

"Not as yet," Bruckner said. "The police interviewed
residents along the Dogwood River road but no one saw
or heard anything around that time."

"Whoever it was," Cynthia said, after wiping away
her tears, "left Olivia dying on the road. If they ever
catch the person who did this, I'll—"

"There, there, dear," Bruckner said, again patting his
wife's hand. "Don't say it." He turned to Grant. "We
don't hold out much hope for finding the driver. She was
at the wrong place at the wrong time. Unfortunate."

Grant looked about the room. It was a typical room
for a hard-working middle class family struggling to
make ends meet. Plain, simple furniture, cheap items for
wall hangings, and Olivia's pictures scattered throughout
the house. His heart ached for these people, still grieving
for the loss of their beloved daughter.

"Mr. Bruckner," Grant said, "I'm going to say something that may shock you but I want you to hear me out.
My mother was killed recently in an automobile accident,
one I am beginning to feel was orchestrated to silence her
involvement with the committee against the power plant.
Other committee members have died as well, most under
mysterious circumstances. Is it possible that your daugh-

ter could have been the victim of foul play? Did she have any enemies that you know of?"

"Oh Christ!" Cynthia exclaimed in a gush of breath. "Bill—"

"My God, Grant," Bruckner said, eyes bright and alert. "Never gave it any thought. No, Olivia never had any enemies. Everyone liked her. But I do know that Trinity was about evenly divided as to whether they wanted the plant to come here. So I suppose there might have been people that were opposed to what she was doing. But to resort to murder? Come on."

"Believe me," Grant said. "You're not the first person to have those same thoughts. But I'll tell you what I told them. There's millions of dollars at stake here. So I believe anything is possible."

Bruckner nodded. "Yes, I suppose you might be right."

"Is the plant really that important to Trinity?" Cynthia said. "I mean worth people dying over?"

"Like I said, Mrs. Bruckner," grant said, "when there is so much money to be made people can be tempted to resort to all sorts of evil. The power company, DynaTech, stands to make a lot of money if Trinity's residents allow the plant to become a reality. That's a lot of pressure."

"We've lived her for thirty years," the woman said, "and it's always been a quiet town. Nothing out of the ordinary happens here."

"My sentiments exactly, ma'am," Grant said. "I was raised here. My father worked at the college so I have roots here."

"You live here now?" Bruckner said.

"No. I left home, joined the marines, went to Iraq. I came back for my mother's funeral and found myself embroiled in this power plant thing."

"You think there's a conspiracy here, I take it?" Bruckner's tone had turned dark.

"Yes, sir. More and more with each passing day. I just can't get the police to see it from my point of view."

"You think they're complicit in this conspiracy," the man said. "It would be a far reach I would think."

"I don't know. I hope they aren't. But they don't seem to be very eager to investigate these deaths."

"Our daughter's death, for one," Cynthia said.

"One last question, if you please," Grant said. "Why didn't the doctors in Augusta sign her death certificate instead of Dr. Witherspoon? I mean they were the last to attend your daughter."

"Dr. Witherspoon said he would do it," Bruckner said. "Save them in Augusta the trouble. He had been to the scene of Olivia's accident."

Grant stood, thanked the couple for their patience, then said his goodbye.

So there it was. The deaths of all the committee members and each person dying under suspicious circumstances. Back at his mother's he retrieved his legal pad with all the deaths listed and went over them again. A drowning, an electrocution, a hit and run death, a drug overdose, a store fire, and an automobile accident. Each with a different manner of death. If the deaths were related, why were they all killed differently? And why would the town's medical examiner sign a death certificate when he wasn't the last to attend the patient? Only one answer was possible. It made unraveling who was responsible extremely difficult.

❧❧❧

Grant was going to see Dr. Witherspoon but, before he did, he decided to run by the Nottingham's and see if

Greg was home. Something he had said now struck him as peculiar. Something about never trusting the man. Grant wanted to know more.

Greg Nottingham offered Grant a chair on the front porch as if he didn't want his wife to hear their conversation. Maybe the previous one had upset her.

"Something you said the last time I was here Greg," Grant started, "I remember as peculiar. You said your family never trusted Dr. Witherspoon. That go for your parents as well?"

"Yes," Nottingham said. "As far as I can remember the Nottingham family never used him as their doctor."

"You said there had been stories. You mentioned a few rumors."

Nottingham nodded.

"Is it possible for you to elaborate further?"

The man rubbed his chin a moment while he thought. "Yeah," he finally said. "A lot of stories. None of them good. I'll be frank with you, Mr. Collins. The man apparently is a butcher. And you didn't hear that from me. Botched many operations the years after coming to Trinity. There is no hospital here, so he worked on many folks in his office, doing a variety of procedures. Including what I've heard were needless amputations, bloody abortions, botched plastic surgeries. Supposedly, and this came from my mother, there were a number of deaths that occurred in his office during those surgeries. She used to say that people who lived near doc's office could hear screams at night coming from there."

"Christ," Grant said. "It's hard to believe."

"Well, Trinity was a different town back then. People were simpler, mostly a farming community, very little education, not much television or nightly news." He smiled. "No CNN."

"Still, things like that would be hard to swallow by a

town. Didn't the medical board take any action against him?"

"Don't know if they really knew what all was going on," Nottingham said. "Besides, you know all doctors watch out for each other."

"Not anymore," Grant said. "You said he came by and didn't do anything except pronounce her dead and sign the death certificate later."

"As far as I know. When he was here, he listened to her heart for a while but I could tell it was hopeless. She had that ashen gray look. He was right, I believe. Mom was too far gone when we pulled her out of the pool. There was nothing we could do to save her."

After leaving the Nottingham's, Grant decided to go to the library and see if he could dig up anything in past newspapers on Witherspoon. If he wanted to go back thirty years, it was going to take him most of the evening.

He found a secluded microfilm reader in a rear corner of the library. After asking a young attractive library attendant to bring him old copies of the *Trinity Eagle* dating back thirty years. She brought him a cup of coffee with the first set of reels that she set on the table beside the reader.

The library was quiet, with only a few patrons milling through the book aisles along with several mothers chasing their children in the children's section. Grant fed the first reel of microfilm into the reader then began browsing through the papers listed. The attendant had brought the earliest years Grant requested so, over the next hour, he worked his way forward in time. As he scanned through the various editions he became aware of an extremely interesting fact.

Trinity became a community in the years between the two world wars, settled by immigrant farmers mostly from Alabama but also from Germany and Italy. Grow-

ing peanuts, peaches, and blueberries, they made the bot-
tomlands produce crops as never seen before. Men fished
the Savannah River that brought blue crab, oysters, and
shrimp to the local markets.

On one reel was an edition in the *Eagle* describing
the opening of the community college and a profile of its
first president, Malcomb Painter. Grant was reminded of
his father going to work at the college in its maintenance
department. He would regale his family with tales of
working overtime to keep the air-conditioning going during brutal summers.

Then he hit pay dirt, found what he was looking for.
Looking through the next fifteen years of newspapers
Grant found nine articles on Dr. Witherspoon outlining
patients who either suffered serious complications or died
while under his care. Nottingham was right—most were
surgeries the doctor performed in his office that went bad
or the patient died outright. One woman who was severely injured in an automobile accident was taken to Witherspoon's office where he amputated both her legs. Later,
those in attendance felt the surgery was unnecessary. She
sued the doctor but lost in court.

There were two abortions that subsequently required
further care in Savannah because they were hemorrhag-
ing. One of the women died, the other rendered sterile
and unable to have children.

So Dr. Witherspoon did not possess a stellar reputation. It seemed to Grant he was continuing in his negligent ways in his role as medical examiner. He had never
heard of so many suspicious deaths without an autopsy
performed.

He copied the information, thanked the attendant,
then left the library. On his way to Witherspoon's clinic,
he rehearsed what he planned to ask. He would show the
man the list of deaths and politely ask him why he had

not performed an autopsy on any of them. If the man tried to obfuscate the issue, Grant would keep asking until the man answered or called the police.

This time he wouldn't mind seeing Sergeant Brady. Grant pulled into the clinic parking area was glad to see the doctor's BMW was the only car there. He parked his car, entered the building, and greeted the doctor as he was getting ready to lock up for the night.

The doctor shot Grant a surprised look. It was a look of fear.

Chapter 29

D r. Witherspoon?" Grant said. "I'd like to have a word with you if I could. It's important."

The doctor stopped. He had keys and a briefcase in his hands. "I'm sorry, young man, but I was just leaving. Perhaps if you called for an appointment."

Grant strode toward the elderly man, his blood pounding in his temples. The doctor didn't look as formidable as during their last encounter. "No, doctor," Grant said in a sinister tone. "We'll do it now. Or I'll go to the medical board and tell them about your negligence in the recent deaths here in Trinity. Which will it be?"

Witherspoon's shoulders sagged, a resigned look in his face. "All right, young man. In my office." He turned and Grant followed him through the waiting room, down a short hallway, to his office. Witherspoon tossed his briefcase on his antique desk then sat, letting out an exasperated sigh. He didn't offer Grant a chair. "Now, what's this about?" he said.

Grant pulled his list from his pocket, handed it to the doctor. Witherspoon glanced at the paper not comprehending its significance. "It's a list of the most recent deaths here in Trinity," Grant said. "Deaths you attended in your capacity as medical examiner."

The doctor frowned as he looked over the list. "Your point, young man?" Witherspoon was clearly irritated by the intrusion.

"I am not a young man," Grant said. "I am a marine veteran and my name is Grant Collins. My mother died in an automobile accident two weeks ago. You attended her death as well as the others on that list. The point is, Doctor, that in none of them did you see fit to perform an autopsy. I would like to know why?"

"Mr. Collins," Witherspoon said. "I can assure you I discharge my duties with the utmost responsibility. You have no medical degree or experience in these matters yet you dare barge into my office and accuse me of dereliction of duty. How dare you? Where do you get the nerve? You have no idea, not the slightest inkling, of the duties or difficulties of my profession. Or my obligations as a medical examiner."

Witherspoon had worked himself up into a fury, spittle flew from his lips. His angry look caused Grant to pause, wondering if the man might attack him.

"Doctor, I want to know why, in each of these cases, you did not deem it necessary to conduct an autopsy. The cause of death might have been different than originally thought."

The doctor leaned back in his chair, his appearance harrowing and formidable. "I used my judgment. Something you are showing little of at the present. The law stipulates these cases must be attended by a medical examiner and does not necessarily require a post-mortem in each and every case. It wasn't something I was required to do."

"But I would have thought—"

"You would have thought, you would have thought! Enough of this foolishness. Out with you. I have other more important business to attend."

Witherspoon stood, indicating an end to the meeting. Grant rose, found his way back to the door. The old doctor followed him.

Standing in the doorway, Grant turned, venom spewing from his mouth, "Before I'm finished here, Doctor," he said, "I'll see to it you never practice another day in Trinity—or anywhere else, for that matter."

With that, he closed the door and left.

ℰↄℰↄ

It was early afternoon. Grant needed a nap, for his head throbbed from his meeting with Dr. Witherspoon. Carrie was working the lunch and dinner shifts at the diner and wasn't due home until after nine. He sat in his mother's chair, seething at being summarily dismissed by the doctor. *How dare he?*

Grant didn't quite know what his options were at this point. Maybe Carrie was right—he needed to stop this insane investigation of his and get his own life in order. Since coming to Trinity, he had put his own health on hold, the nightmares becoming more frequent. Losing Carrie was not an option. She was a strong woman, his mother might even have called her headstrong. She certainly knew her own mind, a quality he respected and admired. That day in Ambush Alley, his commander pushed forward when all the signs said go back, retreat. In the end, it was the right decision. Now Carrie was telling him to retreat. *Could it be the right decision now?* he wondered.

During times of deep reflection, he knew she was right. Nothing was going to bring back his mother. She was right also, in that Trinity was no longer his home, so what did he care if the town voted for the power plant? In the final analysis it only mattered if he was to make his home here with Carrie, and she as much told him she didn't care where she lived. As long as it was with him. They could leave and never worry about Trinity again. It might be the best thing for their respective mental well-being.

Grant hated to leave a job undone. His father's mantra was if a job was worth doing it was worth doing correctly. He drummed that saying into Grant and Eric's heads almost daily. Too bad his father wasn't here for some much-needed counsel. How Grant longed for his father's kind word, his mother's gentle touch, her smile.

And Carrie's tender encouragement.

There was a loud knock at the door. Two men introduced themselves as Georgia Bureau of Investigation field agents and flashed their identification at Grant.

"May we have word with you," said the portly one who identified himself as Special Agent Dalrymple.

Grant showed the men into the living room where all sat. Grant waited, pulse quickening.

"Mr. Collins," Dalrymple said, "we are here because we are investigating the murder of Mayor Baxter. This is my partner, Special Agent Toomey. You are aware of his killing?"

Grant nodded, not sure where the question was leading.

"Our SAC, Samantha Wilder, gave us the file regarding your recent visit with her. It outlined your suspicions regarding other deaths in Trinity. Why you think they were not accidents after all."

"SAC?" Grant said.

"Special Agent in Charge," Dalrymple said.

Grant let out a sigh, nodded again. "I didn't think your department was actually looking into my complaint," he said. "I didn't have any evidence at the time," he said. "Still don't, really."

"We may work slow but we eventually get things done," Dalrymple's partner said.

"Did you know the mayor?" Dalrymple said.

"I met him a week or so ago. We talked a while, that's all."

"We are interested in your theories," Toomey said. "Why you think the deaths might have been orchestrated by someone?"

"I dunno," Grant said, squirming. "Maybe it's nothing. I just have this crazy feeling, more of a notion. It turns out that all these so-called accidental deaths were attended by our local medical examiner, but he never performed an autopsy on any of them. That, in itself, sounds suspicious to me. Six deaths and not one single autopsy? I would think the law of averages would dictate there would be at least several. Then, as I told Special Agent Wilder, my mother's car showed signs of a severe rear end collision, as if she could have been pushed into the bridge abutment that killed her. The Trinity police never even investigated that possibility."

"The police take pictures of your mother's car?"

"Sure. I looked at them."

Grant noticed that Dalrymple was taking notes in a small notebook. The man turned to his partner. "Bill," he said, "make a note to check out the pictures of the Collins woman's car."

"Finally," Grant continued, "all these deaths were people that served on a committee that was lobbying against a nuclear power plant coming to town."

"The Citizens Against Nuclear Power?" Dalrymple said.

"Yes. That's the one. It has to be more than coincidence. But, beyond that, I don't have any concrete evidence."

"We might be able to help on that score," Toomey said.

"How is that?" Grant said.

Dalrymple removed another notebook from his suit pocket, flipped it open. "We have reason to believe that the mayor's killer was a foreign professional. That it was a contract killing."

"But why?" Grant said, stunned at the agent's remark.

"We believe we know who the man is. And our investigation has linked him to Winston Conway. You're familiar with the name?"

"I talked with him only last week."

"Threatened him is the more accurate description," Toomey said.

"So the bastard says," Grant hissed. He didn't appreciate the accusation. "And the Trinity police continue to sit on their thumbs."

"The man in question is a Hungarian mercenary the FBI has known about for several years," Dalrymple continued. "We have certain telephone records indicating communication between him and Conway. Recently, I might add."

"But why?" Grant said.

"We don't know at the moment. We do know a few things about Conway's company, DynaTech." Dalrymple stood, stretched his legs, and turned a page in his notebook. "DynaTech is in serious financial trouble. Conway needs cash. It is a serious question whether he even has the resources to build the plant if it is approved by the city."

"So why murder the mayor?" Grant said, having difficulty following the agent's train of thought.

"We don't know that Conway, in fact, had anything to do with it but it certainly is possible. We need more

evidence. Your threatening him might push him into doing something stupid."

"You mean force his hand?"

"Exactly," Toomey said.

"The town is divided as to whether they want the
plant. A vote is scheduled soon," Grant said, thinking
aloud.

"If the mayor was on Conway's payroll," Dalrymple
said, "it might be that he was not proceeding quick
enough to suit him. Or some glitch developed in their relationship. If so, it might explain getting rid of Baxter."

"But it would only postpone the vote," Grant said.

"I must admit," Dalrymple said, returning to his
chair, "we don't have all the pieces yet."

"He has his yacht, the *Sandpiper,* moored down at the
Savannah docks," Toomey said. "Quite a boat."

"He's building a mansion on the river here in Trinity," Grant said. "If he is strapped for money, how can he
afford these luxuries?"

"Like I said," Dalrymple exclaimed, shaking his
head. "We don't have all the pieces."

⣁⣒⣁

A bright silver moon shown through thin clouds
when Carrie got off work at nine. She was the last to
leave the diner, having said goodbye to Deke when he
left a half an hour earlier. She wrapped her sweater about
her shoulders and headed to her Celica, eager to get home
and see Grant. He had spent the past several nights at his
mother's house, and she was afraid they were drifting
apart. He called her at the diner and asked if he could
come by after she got off work.

As she strolled across the asphalt parking lot, a gentle
breeze fluttered through her hair, her heart throbbing with

anticipation. She took her keys, unlocked her car.

Out of the dark two huge men grabbed her, one placed a burly hand over her mouth, the other hissed. Struggling was to no avail, they had her firmly in their grasp.

"One shout out of you, bitch, and it will be your last," one of the men growled. "Understand?"

Carrie nodded her understanding. She fought the overwhelming urge to scream as the man slowly released his grip on her mouth. Rancorous bile belched up into her throat leaving her nauseated while the suddenness of the attack caused her legs to weaken. It was too dark to recognize the men but they were large and smelled of sweat and booze.

Carrie tried to turn her head in order to get a good look at them but they pushed her across the parking lot, forced her into the backseat of a car. The man with the burly hands climbed in beside her. She forced an attempt to calm herself.

"Wha—what's going on?" she pleaded. "Why are you doing this? Where are we going?"

The man behind the wheel started the car's engine, squealed down the road. "Shut up," he yelled over the roar of the motor. "Just keep your mouth shut."

Carrie shot a glance at the man next to her but she didn't recognize him. He was burly, unkempt, sported several days beard growth. He had one eye that was larger than the other—it twitched constantly. The driver, who did the talking, had a strange accent. Like European or Russian. Possibly Balkan. She couldn't place it.

Soon the car's interior smelled of garlic, alcohol, and week-old body odor, causing Carrie's stomach to convulse.

She said a silent prayer, hoping she wouldn't throw up on herself. The driver sped through Trinity then accessed the Interstate heading East toward Savannah. *Where are they taking me?*

Chapter 30

Grant let himself into Carrie's apartment, wondering why she wasn't home from work. It was nine-thirty, well beyond the time it took her to drive from the diner. The apartment was dark so he switched on a light in the kitchen, helped himself to a beer, then plopped in a chair. He had brought his legal pad on which he had written the names of the dead and the notes he gleaned in each of them. He sipped his beer while looking over the list.

He wanted to clear the air with Carrie. After her exhortation the other night, he realized he had been narrow-minded in not seeing things from her perspective. He wanted her to know he understood. And that he still cared for her. But it wasn't going to alter his pursuit of the person or persons responsible for his mother's death. How could he get her to understand that he was sorry for had happened the night while he was inside Conway's trailer and that if she wished he would stay away until the issue was resolved. He didn't want to see her hurt or frightened again. He could stay at his mother's.

His watch read nine fifty-two. Carrie still had not arrived home. He was beginning to get worried. Pacing about her apartment, he worried over what might be tak-

ing her so long. Problems at the diner? A meeting with
Deke? An errand? No, too late for running errands in
Trinity.

At ten o'clock, he was finished with his beer but still
no Carrie. He decided to drive over to the diner and see
what was holding her up. Along the way, he kept a short
eye out for her car but never saw it.

When he turned the corner, he saw the diner's parking lot was empty except for Carrie's Celica. He parked
the rental, hurried to her car. It was unlocked and her
purse lay on the front seat but Carrie was nowhere
around. On the ground next to the driver's front tire was
a set of keys. He stooped and picked them up. They belonged to Carrie.

Grant went to the diner's door, knocked loudly, but
there was no answer. He peered in a side window but the
diner's interior was dark, no sign of life. He returned to
her car and stood for a moment, thinking. Where could
she have gone? He glanced around the vacant lot. Something wasn't right.

At that time of night, Trinity was dead quiet, no traffic to speak of, no pedestrians out walking. All the shops
and businesses were closed and their windows were dark.
Grant slid behind the wheel of his car and slowly made
his way through Trinity's small business section. Keeping his head on a swivel, he glanced up and down the
town's side streets but saw no Celica.

He decided to cruise down to Pete's Crab Shack on
the off chance she went there with friends for an after
work dinner. However, her keys laying on the asphalt
didn't portend well for that possibility. Visions of Lori
Spelling flashed through his head.

Turning onto the river road, he ventured along the
river, window down, breathing the fragrant salty air. The
road was devoid of traffic, he was alone. At the restau-

rant, it too was closed and its parking lot empty. He turned around and headed back to Carrie's apartment where he found a note tacked to her door. It was short and to the point.

Your girlfriend's life is in your hands! She will die unless you leave town immediately. Get out of Trinity before you both die! This is no idle threat! Your friend will be released unharmed but only if you obey these instructions. If you value the woman's life you will do as we say. We mean business! Leave and never return! Do not call the police. Just leave.

Grant's pulse skyrocketed. The note was typewritten on what appeared to be an old typewriter for several of the letters had parts missing. Now, he had really messed everything up.

And Carrie was the new victim.

❧❧❧

Carrie recognized the small suburb of Savannah, Thunderbolt, as they sped along the Interstate. Then it was up and over the Thunderbolt Bridge and she knew they had crossed the Wilmington River and were on Whitemarsh Island. It was part of the greater Savannah metroplex she rarely visited but the roaring tiger mascot on a passing billboard had been unmistakable. Ramshackle cottages lined the river along with lavish estates, their dark silhouettes stately in the distance. Her abductors had settled into a silent routine and seemed content to say nothing as long as she sat quietly and didn't provoke them. They didn't seem to care if she saw their faces for they wore no masks or sunglasses. Several times when they passed under the glare of streetlamp she got a good look at them. They were different from the ones who threatened her the previous night.

The car screeched then lurched to one side as it exited the freeway onto a four lane divided street fronted by high wrought iron fences, trees, and dense shrubbery. There was little traffic on the road. Off the Interstate, the car's driver, nevertheless sped along, leaving Carrie in doubt as to their precise location. After another ten minutes, they rambled over a second bridge and she caught a glimpse of the sign at the side of the road— *Wilmington Island.*

Carrie lost track of the turns. Eventually, they were on a two-lane road colonnaded by palm trees, sea pines draped in Spanish moss, and immaculately trimmed hedges. That much she could make out. An occasional imposing house could be seen in the distance, its dark skeleton barely visible against the black sky.

The car turned onto a drive whose roadside sign announced they were at the Savannah Yacht Club. Carrie could make out that it was very rich, very fashionable. There were quite a number of high-end saltwater boats and yachts nestled in their respective berths that lined a number of piers. In the dark she could see that the club's grounds were neatly mowed. An occasional streetlamp illuminated the drive as it meandered along the piers. The driver stopped at the entrance to a private pier, its gangway leading down to an enormous boat, its sleek white hull riding high in the water.

The man next to her opened the door, grabbed her by an arm, yanked her out. He and his partner pushed her down the gangway toward the boat. It was immense, a yacht really. What was happening? Her captors shoved her into the yacht's rear cockpit then into the main cabin. She collapsed, out of breath, panicked, into a plush overstuffed chair. The two men stood on either side until a man dressed in a black smoking jacket complete with silk cravat entered the main cabin. He smiled sardonically when he saw Carrie.

"That's fine," the man said. "You may go now."

"Yes, Mr. Conway," the man who drove the car said.

The two men made their way off the boat leaving Carrie alone with the man called Conway. Her perplexed stare made him chuckle.

"Please forgive me, my dear. I'm Winston Conway. I trust my friends didn't treat you poorly."

℘℘℘

Grant was nearing a panic state. The note was unbelievable. Why would anyone want to harm Carrie? It spelled the threat out plain enough but it didn't answer the nagging question—why? And who. There was only one person who had the motive and the means to pull it off as well as the obvious meanness. That person was Conway. Winston Conway. The agents said Conway spent a lot of time on his yacht, conducted business there. It didn't take him long to decide he would confront the man, force him to release Carrie. If he had her.

Even if it cost him his life.

Grant stuffed his Beretta nine millimeter into his belt then jumped into his car. He hurried to the Savannah docks across from Hutchinson Island and parked next to the only bar on the short block, the Hook And Sinker. On the way, he worried if he had the strength to use the pistol. What if Conway had bodyguards? What then? What if Carrie wasn't on the yacht? If she was would the Beretta be enough to get her safely off?

Inside, the bar was muggy, thick with stale smoke and there were a few patrons drinking beer in the dim light. A TV over the bar was turned to a baseball game.

He ambled to the bar and nodded to the bartender at his approach.

"What'll it be?" the bartender said, a trickle of sweat across his forehead.

"Just some information," Grant said. "You know a man by the name of Conway? Owns a big yacht around here?"

"Yeah," the bartender said, "I've heard the name. You looking for him?"

"I am. Got word he might have a job for me. Any idea where I might find him?"

The bartender shook his head. "Not around here. Not now, anyway. Used to have his big yacht moored down the block there but he moved it several days ago."

"To where?" Grant asked. "You know?"

"I might," the man said, wiping his brow with his towel. He began cleaning glasses. "But information around here costs money. Got a Jackson?"

"A what?"

"A twenty. You want answers, I could use a little dough."

"Sure," Grant said. He reached in his wallet, retrieved the bill, handed it to the bartender.

"It's called the *Sandpiper*. I heard he moved his big boat over to the Savannah Yacht Club. It's a posh place, right up his alley."

"Where's the yacht club?"

"It's on Wilmington Island where Turner Creek empties into the Wilmington River."

"Where the hell is that?" Grant said.

The bartender smiled, then chuckled. "Not from around here?"

"Trinity," was Grant's reply.

The bartender nodded, waited until Grant pulled another bill from his wallet and handed it over.

"Take the Harry Truman Parkway to Thunderbolt and go East. Can't miss it."

"Thanks," Grant said, and he left the bar.

Learning that Conway had moved the *Sandpiper* to the Savannah Yacht Club irritated him. It wasn't going to be easy finding the bastard.

Using his car's GPS as an aid, he eventually made his way onto the Islands Expressway and headed East. He cut south to Johnny Mercer Boulevard, continued onto Wilmington Island.

The eastern sky was beginning to lighten to a dark gray, a sign that dawn was around the corner. Off in the distance beyond where the rivers dumped their waters into the Atlantic, clouds were building, portending possible rain later in the day. An occasional bolt of lightning shot across the clouds and soft thunder rolled over the island.

What was he going to do if and when he caught up with Conway? If the man was even on his yacht. The note warned him to clear out of Trinity and not return until the city council vote on the plant. As long as Carrie was in danger, it was a warning he was loathe to heed.

He pushed harder on the gas pedal.

Grant thought back to their first meeting in the diner. How captivated he was with her engaging smile, her sparkling eyes, the easy way she chatted with him. The lovemaking later had been unexpected, spontaneous, leaving his head swimming. At first he couldn't understand her involving herself with his problems. Surely there was an ample supply of young men who occasioned the diner to keep her entertained. But as he got to know her, he sensed in Carrie a genuine caring for the hurt he felt over his mother's sudden death and his quandary as to how it could have happened.

He didn't know much about her, which was odd, considering how deep his feelings ran. Beyond the fact that she had almost married a man in Atlanta but left him after he hit her several times, he didn't know anything about her past life. Where she grew up, who her parents were. They had been so involved with what was happening in Trinity and Lori's death, they had little time for such things. A situation Grant vowed to change.

If they survived.

He turned and drove under the arched gate of the Savannah Yacht Club. From what he could see in the dark of predawn, the bartender was right—the club was a place for the idle rich. Yachts of all shapes and sizes lined the numerous piers that were lit by mercury vapor lights along the various gangplanks leading down to the boats. The grounds were immaculate with trimmed hedges, multiple flowerbeds sporting azaleas of all colors and other plants. Concrete walkways that were lined with small LED lights led from the piers to a central yacht club office. There was no one about. The office was dark.

Grant parked in the empty parking lot. He needed to find the *Sandpiper* but with the morass of boats the task would be next to impossible. It was going to be necessary to wait until morning when the office opened and see if they could tell him where the boat was moored. He had driven most of the night. He was tired and hungry.

And it looked as if a storm might be brewing.

Grant settled back in his seat, reclined it, tried to relax. *Maybe an hour or two of sleep will revive me.* When he cracked the windows, the hint of rain filtered into the car. Rain mixed with an ocean scent. A pleasant smell. He closed his eyes.

Carrie was out there somewhere.

Chapter 31

Carrie stared in disbelief at Conway. The pearlescent sheen of his smoking jacket reflected in his harsh green eyes casting him with a diabolical appearance. His forehead was furrowed, his teeth almost pointed. With his widow's peak, she thought for a moment he looked like Count Dracula. Slouching further in her chair, she fought the urge to try and escape, run. Anywhere but aboard the yacht.

"So you're Mr. Conway," she said. "DynaTech's owner. The man who wants to bring nuclear power to Trinity." Realizing she was on the edge of panic, she fought to bring herself under control, refusing to stoop to hysteria.

"I am, indeed," Conway said. "I want you to be comfortable during your stay here, my dear. Can I get you anything? Water? Coffee? Soda, perhaps?"

Carrie shuddered at Conway's continued use of the phrase *my dear*. "No," she said. "But you can tell me why you have seen fit to kidnap me."

Conway crossed the cabin, took a seat opposite her, adjusted his cravat. "As I mentioned earlier, until the council vote is history, you will remain here, unhurt, of course, as long as your boyfriend cooperates. And I must insist on your full cooperation as well."

"Cooperation?" Carrie said, starting to regain her composure.

"Please don't cause trouble while on board," Conway said. "It makes our captain nervous. We will be making a little trip as soon as it gets light."

"Trip? Where to?" Her heart thumped in her chest at Conway's mention of leaving.

"Not far, my dear. Just out into the Atlantic near an island I know. It's just a precaution against that boyfriend getting brave and trying to locate you. I pray for your sake he is more intelligent than to do that. I don't relish the idea of harming you."

"You will go to any lengths to ensure your precious power plant is approved, won't you," Carrie hissed. She watched the man through narrowed eyes. She was scared but the venom in her voice was unmistakable.

"I *will* protect my interests at all costs. You are quite right about that."

Conway rose, went to a teak cabinet, poured himself a drink, returned to his chair.

"That include murder?" Carrie said, a rage boiling inside. "Grant's mother? The other committee members?"

Conway's eyebrows arched and he smiled weakly. His watery eyes looked Carrie over as if he were examining a piece of merchandise. "Oh, is that your young man's name? Grant? I do hope that when he finds the note left for him he acts accordingly with the smarts he seems to possess. Being attracted to a lovely creature as yourself."

"In all likelihood, he'll go directly to the police. You won't get away with this, Mr. Conway."

"The police?" Conway laughed, took a sip of his drink. "The police? Now that is a funny one. The Trinity police are friends of mine, or didn't you know?" He chuckled again. "I don't think the police will give us any problem."

Carrie's heart sank. She looked about the cabin. Paintings adorned the salon's walls while its floor was covered with a rich plush carpet. The door to the front of the yacht was closed.

"We've been to the Bureau of Investigation," she said, after collecting her thoughts. "They know about your schemes."

This revelation obviously took Conway by surprise. It seemed to be something he hadn't expected—or counted on. "Well, my dear," he said in a slow drawl. "It appears you both are more resourceful than I expected." He paused for a moment, thinking. "It is something that will be dealt with in due time. Life, as in a football game, always has certain setbacks, surprises. A mere inconvenience."

Carrie looked out a window. Dawn was near. Streaks of gray caused the water to appear as a slick sheen. But dark clouds were moving in from the East and an occasional rumble of thunder could be heard off in the distance. She muttered a silent prayer for Grant's safety.

Conway finished his drink, pushed a button on the table next to him. Soon, a middle-aged man with graying temples and a trimmed goatee entered. He was dressed in a cream colored suit with crisp seams. He nodded at Conway.

"Tell the captain we'll be underway in an hour, steward," Conway said. The man nodded again, turned to leave. "And bring some breakfast for our guest."

The man left the cabin closing the door behind him. Conway stood.

"Where are you taking me?" Carrie said. "When I don't show for work, my boss will start looking for me."

"Let him look," Conway said. "Now, my dear, I must

go forward and speak with my captain. If you will excuse me."

Conway left through the main door, closed the door behind him, leaving Carrie alone in the main salon. She stood, stretched her aching legs, sore from her abduction. Along either side a bank of windows extended the length of the cabin. Tufted white sofas with overstuffed chairs were arranged around a teak table while a large screen television occupied one end of the salon. Carpeted steps with a chrome railing led upstairs to what Carrie assumed was the bridge. On the end opposite the television was a polished mahogany dining table and chairs.

Carrie ambled about the cabin, running her hand over the finished wood and fine upholstery. The extravagant furnishings of the yacht overwhelmed her.

The door opened. The steward entered carrying a tray of food. He set the tray on a small round table in front of a sofa, nodded quietly, smiled, then left her alone. Suddenly, Carrie was famished. Not having eaten since yesterday at lunch left her with a ravenous appetite. She sat and inspected the tray, which was filled with numerous dishes containing fried shrimp, lobster bites, pasta in an Alfredo sauce. There were sliced peaches in a bowl. A pot of coffee and a bottle of water completed the tray.

She grabbed the water bottle and drank down half of it in one gulp then turned her attention to the food. She attacked each dish with relish, devouring each one completely before moving on to the next. Twenty minutes later, she was finished and sat relaxed, sipping the coffee.

The yacht rumbled with the starting of its engines. A quick shudder ran through the cabin then settled to a dull gentle vibration. Slowly, the boat began moving, leaving its mooring behind. Carrie looked outside, noticed the sky was now the color of slate. Dark clouds, which were occasionally pierced by a bolt of lightning, billowed overhead. Rain was in the forecast.

She rose, ambled over to a window, and peered outside. She could tell they were cruising southeast down the river. Wilmington Island was on her left while southeast Savannah lay in the distance off to her right. This was the isolated region of coastal Savannah, the only things visible were the low clumps of vegetation growing along the shoreline. Now and then they passed a smaller boat. Probably fishermen, Carrie thought.

The door to the salon opened again and Conway entered.

"How was your breakfast?" he said.

"Fine, thank you." Carrie didn't bother getting up from her seat.

"We are underway. I suppose you were able to discern that."

Carrie nodded. "Where are you taking me?"

"As I mentioned earlier, a place where we will be safe from prying eyes," he said, slicking back his hair with the palm if his hand. "A spot in the Atlantic I use for fishing. Quite secluded actually. I don't think anyone will bother us."

"For how long?" Carrie said.

"Long enough, my dear. Now, it's a two hour run so if you care to rest I can show you to your suite. You can freshen up, take a shower if you like, nap."

"Thanks. I do feel a little sticky. A shower would be nice."

Conway escorted Carrie to one of several private suites aboard the *Sandpiper* and after a hot shower and a short nap she felt much refreshed. For the present she was resigned to make the most of her predicament. She found Conway seated in a small office to one side of the main cabin. He looked up and smiled.

"You look decidedly better, my dear," he said.

"Yes, thank you." Carrie didn't know how to act, considering the man's hospitality.

"Would you care to see the bridge?" he said. "It's a technological marvel."

She nodded. "That would be fine," she said. "Why are you being so nice?"

Conway rose, led her up the short stairway to the upper decks. "My dear, I certainly have no intentions of harming you—at least as long as you behave yourself. If your boyfriend doesn't follow instructions, however, I will show him just how nasty I can become. Watch your steps here."

At the top of the stairs, Conway paused, pointed to his left. "Back that way, aft on the boat, is the galley." He turned to his right and continued through a narrow aisle. "And up this way is the bridge, the *Sandpiper's* nerve center."

A wide doorway opened into a broad room fronted by a wrap-around windshield and large side windows. The view was amazing. Along the front was a bank of electronic instruments, all foreign to Carrie. A man sporting a goatee and a typical yachting cap sat in a leather chair. He turned and acknowledged Carrie with a quick nod.

"This is our captain," Conway said. "He is responsible for getting us to where we're going." He pointed to a panel of gauges. "This is the main engine instrument panel. It shows the acoustic alarm, the heating and starter switch, revolutions per hour counter, voltmeter, and oil pressure. Over here," and Conway pointed to a different bank of instruments, "we have the trim gauge indicator, water temperature, engine hour counter, and waste water levels."

Conway seemed enthralled with his yacht and all its dials and gauges. Carrie found her mind wandering but the man continued, pointing to a large screen.

"Here we have our marine GPS and radar, marine VHS radios, single side band radios, and the navigation calculator. All necessary instruments on a boat this large."

Carrie feigned interest in the tour of the bridge but couldn't take her eyes off the approaching storm outside. There was a large red blob on the radar screen. Conway must have noticed her concern.

"Yes," he said. "There is rain in the forecast. I must insist that you remain inside as the seas may become quite heavy. For your own safety."

The dark sky merged with the dark water of the Atlantic creating an invisible horizon. Carrie could not tell where the water ended and the sky began. Tall dark waves swelled around the boat while whitecaps crashed over its bow.

"Out there, somewhere," Conway said, "lies our destination. Cockspur Island. We just passed Tybee Island and are now in the Atlantic heading for Cockspur."

"Why there?" Carrie said.

"I like the fishing around there. Cockspur Island has been of some importance since the founding of the Colony of Georgia due to its strategic location just outside the mouth of the Savannah River. Each month spring tides cover the entire island.

"The first military use of Cockspur was in 1700s with the construction of an earth and log fort near the confluence of the South Channel and Lazaretto Creek. Nearby, on Tybee Island, there was a quarantine station and customs checkpoint. This Fort, named Fort George, protected both the entrances to the city as well as enforcing quarantine and customs regulations. Fort Pulaski was built on Cockspur and belonged to what is known as the Third System of coastal fortifications. Most of the nearly thirty Third System forts built after 1800 still exist along either the Atlantic or Gulf coasts. Wooden pilings were sunk up to seventy feet into the mud was used to support an estimated twenty-five million bricks. Fort Pulaski was finally completed right before the Civil War following eighteen years of construction."

"Nice history lesson," Carrie said. "But I'm really not interested. When the authorities catch up with you, you're going to spend a long time in prison."

Conway chuckled. "But my dear, no one knows you are here with me. And I doubt that boyfriend of yours is going to spill the beans. That is if he cares anything for you."

Chapter 32

Special Agent Dalrymple sat across from Dr. Witherspoon, the elderly doctor looking frail and unkempt. Dalrymple wondered if he had spent the better part of the previous night on an emergency. The man fidgeted nervously in his chair as the agent took a notebook from his suit pocket.

"You have the records on the deaths I called about, Doctor?" Dalrymple said. "As Medical Examiner of record you kept detail records of the circumstances surrounding their demise and your findings, correct?"

"Special Agent Dalrymple," Witherspoon began, "I am not accustomed to having to prove that I performed my duties according to the letter of the law. I—"

"Come now, Doctor," Dalrymple said, irritated by the doctor's stonewalling. "Medical examiners are used to being questioned by law enforcement and also in a court before a judge. Are you saying you've never had that privilege?"

The doctor coughed, fidgeted again. "Quite frankly, sir," he said, "these were the first deaths I attended as medical examiner."

Dalrymple was surprised at this revelation. Surely there had been other deaths in Trinity requiring a medical examiner's signature and opinion. "When we were here before that was information you withheld from us. Just how long have you been a medical examiner, Dr. Witherspoon?"

"Three years."

"You mean that in all the years you've been in practice here you have only been the medical examiner the past three?"

Witherspoon avoided eye contact with the agent, kept toying with a pencil. "That's correct."

"How is that, if I may ask?"

"Dr. Reynolds was the medical examiner before he retired. When he left town, our mayor asked me to perform the examiner's duties. Didn't really have to do anything until recently."

"Are you saying you do not have any records you can produce?" Dalrymple was losing patience with the man. Incompetence always got his temper to flare. And he had very little tolerance for stupidity.

"I was given to understand when I took the job," Witherspoon said, now beginning to perspire, "that a death certificate would suffice in all cases. I complied with that stipulation."

"And who gave you that information?"

"Our mayor, Mr. Baxter."

"You didn't think to contact the state medical examiner office in Atlanta for guidance?" Dalrymple said.

"No, I took it that Mr. Baxter knew the law. I didn't."

Dalrymple returned the notebook to his coat pocket. He was getting nowhere with the man so it was useless to continue. He stood to leave, the doctor followed suit.

"Am I in any trouble?" Witherspoon said.

"No." Dalrymple headed for the door, paused at the threshold. "Poor record keeping is not against the law. But I can sure arrange for your replacement."

❧❧❧

Grant woke with a jolt, a heavy pounding in his head. He was awakened by the honking of a horn, a screaming that tore through his brain like a sharp scalpel. He sat up, looked around and noticed the parking lot of the Savannah Yacht Club had a few more cars in it than when he arrived before dawn. He glanced at the yacht office and saw that it was open so he walked over to it. The clouds were heavier, darker, now pushing a stiff humid breeze ahead of them. No sun was visible.

Inside, a heavy set man sporting Bermuda shorts and a navy Polo shirt was sweeping the floor. He looked up at Grant's footfalls.

"Can I help you?" he said.

"Looking for Winston Conway's boat, the *Sandpiper.* You heard of it?"

"Of course I have," the man said. He stopped his sweeping, tugged at his thinning beard. "It's moored at the end of C pier."

"Where's that?" Grant asked. He looked out the windows of the office down toward the docks.

"Last pier to the north there," he said, pointing.

"Thanks." Grant turned and headed toward the door.

"But I don't think it's there," the man called after him. "I believe I saw it leaving the harbor before dawn this morning. But you might check just to be sure."

Grant strolled down to the docks looking for C pier. When he found it he hurried over the wooden decking to the end of the pier. A sign that read *Sandpiper* hung on a post but the mooring was empty. The boat was gone.

Gone with Conway and Carrie aboard.

Where, Grant didn't have a clue.

His pulse raced at the thought of being this close to Carrie then losing the trail. Where had Conway taken her? Across the Atlantic? Spain? The Mediterranean?

On the way down to the pier he noticed that between pier A and B was a small shack with several boats riding in the water. Looked like a boat rental and fishing business. He wandered down to the shack, found the place locked and empty. It was a small wooden building built on stilts over the water with a short attached dock. Next to the opulent yacht club the little shack looked almost decrepit, crumbling. The wooden structure was weathered and worn, grayed by the years being buffeted by winds, surf, and rains. As he walked along the dock the planking under foot creaked and moaned. Several were missing.

The small boats tied at the dock were Boston Whaler and Carolina skiff center console fishing boats. Nice boats for such a ramshackle business, Grant thought. A sign in the window said the rental opened at eight. His watch read seven-twelve a.m.

Hungry, he ambled back to the office to see if he could find breakfast. The office manager put down his broom long enough to mention a small cafe further down the road so he jumped in his car and headed that way.

He ordered ham and eggs, biscuits, coffee. It was the largest breakfast on the menu. The cafe was half full of patrons most of who looked like they were either yacht owners or fisherman waiting to see if the storm would break. As he ate and downed several cups of coffee in an attempt to clear his mind and curtail the pounding in his head, he worked to formulate a plan to locate Carrie. Conway had taken her somewhere for sure, but where? Up river? If he went up river in the *Sandpiper* he could only go so far due to the boat's size and displacement. West of Savannah the river wasn't navigable much further than Fort Wentworth making it a poor choice if he wanted to hide. East was a different story. Around the mouths of several rivers the Atlantic was home to a number of uninhabited islands so it was reasonable that Conway took Carrie east toward the ocean. Maybe even across it.

So he would try and follow.

He finished his breakfast and drove back to the yacht club this time parking near the boat rental. It was a little past eight so he went inside and was immediately confronted by a elderly disheveled man wearing a tattered sweater. His hazel eyes looked out from under prominent salt and pepper eyebrows. Grant wondered if he was hung over.

"Need something?" the man said.

"You heard of a man named Winston Conway?" Grant said, not sure if he had the man's undivided attention.

"Sure, who hasn't?"

"I understand he took his boat out earlier today."

"Don't ask me," the man said brusquely. "If his boat's not in its slip I wouldn't know where he went."

"It's important that I catch up with him," Grant said, trying to put an urgent tone in his voice. "Any idea where he might have gone?"

"Nope," the man said. He returned to the chore he was doing when Grant entered which was making coffee in a battered pot over an antique hot plate.

"If you have any ideas, it would be worth some money to me to hear it."

The man stopped what he was doing, looked at Grant through leaden eyes. "Yeah?" he said. "How much?"

Grant removed his wallet, pulled several bills out, held them up. "I've got sixty bucks here if you know where Conway might have headed."

The man hesitated a moment then smiled, revealing several missing teeth. He snatched the bills out of Grant's hands. "I know he likes to take that yacht of his over to near Cockspur Island. East of there the ocean drops off significantly and he likes to fish along that wall. The big fish come up from the depths to chase the smaller ones in the shallow waters."

"Can I rent one of your boats and get out there?" Grant said, his heart now racing at the prospect of being back on Conway's trail

"Today?" the man said, frowning. "You kidding? Look out there, man. The weather is about to turn sour. Rain is in the forecast. I wouldn't advise going out to-day."

"But it's vitally important that I catch up with him."

"An emergency? If it is, we can get the coast guard to try and raise him on his radio."

"No, nothing like that. But it has to do with his busi-ness. Like I said, it's extremely important."

"Still, we could try and raise him and get him back here. It would be safer than you going out there in a small boat. His yacht is built to withstand these storms."

"No time, I'm afraid. Can I rent one of your boats? Time is of the essence."

"These boats cost a lot of money. You lose it the storm, well—"

"You got insurance don't you," Grant said.

"Sure, but—"

Grant took out his wallet, smiled at the old man. "Would money help you decide?" he said.

"Of course."

Grant took a wad of bills from his wallet and handed them the man. "It's all I have," he said.

The man took the bills and stuffed them into his pocket, shrugged.

"Okay," he said. "I'll rent you a boat. But I must warn you that it could be dangerous. You lose my boat, and I'll be coming after you. But of course, not if you're dead."

Grant shrugged off the warning, his only thought and concern was Carrie's whereabouts and welfare.

"Thank you," he said. "Now, can you show me where this island is located?"

The man shuffled over to the small counter and retrieved a marine chart. Spreading it out on the counter he motioned Grant closer.

"Here we are," he said, point to the yacht clubs location on the chart. "Over here is Cockspur Island. You'll need to motor down the Wilmington River along this route until you reach its mouth at the Atlantic. Head north around Tybee Island until you come upon Cockspur. You should see the Tybee light off your port beam. Should be fairly easy to find."

"Can I purchase this chart?" Grant said.

"That and I'll give you the GPS coordinates you can plug into the satellite receiver and it will take you right there. Just follow the course on the screen."

Grant paid for the chart and the boat rental and the two men walked down to the dock. The man had suggested renting his Bluewater 355, a center console thirty-five foot boat with three engines. They climbed on board. The man showed Grant how to start the boat, where the necessary gauges and instruments were located, and programmed the GPS with Cockspur Island's latitude and longitude coordinates. After releasing the boat's mooring lines, the man jumped back onto the pier and watched Grant slowly head out into the river's main channel.

Glancing back over his shoulder he watched the man return to his shack and disappear inside. With storm clouds building on the horizon, he was on his way.

Grant pulled his Beretta from a pocket and shoved the large clip into it before stuffing it back into his pocket.

He was glad he had thought to bring his jacket along as the weather continued to look menacing off to the east.

He eased forward on the throttle and the boat responded by lurching forward onto a plane. The river was smooth, the boat forming white foamy waves in its wake. As he sped down the river toward an uncertain future, a thought struck him. Had he made a terrible mistake? What if Conway wasn't at the island? What if he had turned south, headed for Florida or the Caribbean? Or worse, across the Atlantic?

"It's too late for second thoughts," he muttered to himself. Better be doing something to save Carrie than to knuckle under Conway's demands and leave Carrie to face her fate alone. He gripped the boat's wheel until his fingers ached, pushed hard down the river. Ahead, lightning crashed toward the water while the resulting thunder boomed louder. He pushed thoughts of Carrie from his mind, concentrated on keeping the boat on the GPS course line. The wind picked up.

And it began to rain.

Chapter 33

Carrie sat in the *Sandpiper's* main cabin staring out into the gloom and rain. Heavy winds rocked the boat gently but with its anchorage and stabilizers movement was barely noticeable. They arrived at their location an hour earlier leaving Conway to retreat to his suite to change clothes. How long was she going to have to remain here, she had no idea.

Had Grant seen the note Conway left for him? Had he decided to heed its warning and return to DC? She wouldn't blame him if he had. Carrie squeezed her eyes shut, concentrating on Grant, willing him to stay away. A chill shot through her. She hated the cold.

She sensed that it was all over, that Conway and DynaTech had won. And the strange thing was, it no longer mattered that Trinity would get its nuclear power plant. No longer mattered that Grant's mother and others were silenced by evil men. When good men and women failed to act, evil thrived. But Carrie, if she was anything, was a survivor. Grant was a survivor as well. He proved that each day he got up and faced his demons. So, why sacrifice one's life for an improbable cause, one certain to fail? She hoped Grant would come to the same conclusion.

Conway entered dressed in jeans and a long sleeve shirt. He looked at Carrie with an indulgent gaze.

"Would you care for some lunch?" he said, walking toward her. "I was going to have some. I would love the company."

She nodded, without saying a word. He escorted her to the dining table where the steward laid out their meal of lobster fritters, grilled shrimp, conch salad, and black-berries in cream. Carrie picked at her food while Conway devoured his. They ate in silence for a while with the man rarely looking at her. Finally, over his coffee, he leaned back, gave her a soft look.

"My dear, you've hardly eaten anything," he said. "The food didn't agree with you?"

"It was all very nice, thank you," she said. "How long will the storm last?"

"Should be finished sometime tonight. Are you afraid of storms?"

"Not really. I was just thinking about Grant. Where he might be."

"If he has any sense, he should be well on his way back home. You worried about him?"

"Just wondering where he is."

"I hope, for your sake, he is smart enough to return home. Hopefully, your confinement shouldn't last very long. I have heard from my sources that a man has been appointed interim mayor and he plans on calling a coun-cil vote in the next few days."

Carrie sat silent at the news. She didn't want to think about it.

"If the vote goes my way, my dear, you'll be returned forthwith," Conway continued. "You and your boyfriend can get on with whatever life has in store. I don't hold grudges."

Carrie wasn't sure she believed the man sitting across

from her. She looked out the cabin window where the rain continued to pelt the yacht.

Was Grant out there somewhere?

∾∾

The wall of rain and wind hit him like a brick in the face. Grant squinted, trying to see through the storm. The boat pitched wildly in the raging seas as he entered the mouth of the Wilmington River. The Atlantic lay as an amorphous mass in the distance, the horizon blotted out by the downpour. He zipped his jacket to his neck with the hope of preventing the battering rain from chilling him to the bone. The wind had picked up and he was having difficulty keeping his balance on the bouncing deck. He wiped the rain from his eyes and shot a glance at the GPS screen glowing a fluorescent green in the prevailing gloom. Somehow he managed to keep the boat on course.

He shot past the flashing red buoy off to his left, blinking red every four seconds. Ahead in the mist he made out another flashing red beacon which served as his marker where he would begin his gradual turn north into Wassaw Sound and the Atlantic. On the map he recognized a series of breakers where the water was only a few feet deep—a hazard he needed to avoid at all costs. Breaking up or running aground in this storm would most certainly prove fatal. He would have to run east of the breakers, a course that would take him out into the ocean.

The Bluewater 355 continued to chop with ease through the waves. He marveled at the boat's seaworthiness but longed for a windshield to keep the spray from hitting him in the face. In spite of the boat's advanced instruments it still did not have radar so Grant was unable to see the extent of the weather ahead of him. The sky had darkened considerably and loud crashes of thunder assaulted his ears. Spars of lightning split the sky with alarming frequency, their strobe effect painful.

Grant slowed the boat as he approached the vicinity of the breakers. He could tell where the water was shallow for the waves broke upward sending showers of white water into the sky. Keeping the boat on an easterly course, he bounced past the breakers then made a turn to the North directly into the wind. The boat's bow jumped and bucked as it struggled over the seas. With the shallow water behind him, the depth finder on the GPS screen indicated the water underneath him was a good ten to twelve feet deep.

Grant took a deep breath, tried to calm the pounding in his chest. His hands ached from grasping the wheel. He was cold and miserable.

Even though he was heading straight into a rainstorm, Grant's mouth felt parched, it screamed for water. *Should have thought of that*, he mused. But he cleared his mind of his own misery and concentrated on his objective—the *Sandpiper*. Out off his starboard beam he saw a red flashing beacon, punctuating the dark every six seconds, the last beacon before the Atlantic Ocean.

He continued his turn northward and skirted alongside Tybee Island on his left. He found the going somewhat smoother closer to the island so steered a course only a few hundred yards from its coastline. Smoother was only relative, however. Tybee Island appeared as a dim dark shadow, menacing and somber. The coast was a changeable marshland. Uninhabited.

The Atlantic Ocean here was a rolling churning mass of water, dark and foreboding. Large swells forced the boat up and down in seesaw fashion. At the top of a swell he could make out Tybee Island's dark coastline. When he was at the bottom, he saw nothing but water all around the boat. A sense of fear gripped him similar to what he felt that day in Iraq. He choked down the panic and concentrated on keeping the boat on course.

When he reached Tybee Inlet, he saw its lighthouse on his port side thirty degrees off the bow. The light in the tower flashed periodically, a beacon to sailors along the East Coast. Here the water got extremely shallow so Grant steered a course further east. Up the channel past the lighthouse near Horse Pen Creek he noticed the vague outlines of the numerous cottages and cabins that were perched near the water. Probably good fishing up there, he surmised.

As he continued on, he began to make out various buildings along the eastern shoreline of Tybee Island. The ferocity of the rain increased, stinging his face and hands.

"Dammit!" he yelled out loud.

Soon, through the storm-darkened mist, the regular flashing of a lighthouse off to his left front loomed larger. The 140-foot Tybee lighthouse that overlooked Fort Scraven during World War Two was an integral part of the American Coastal Defense System. Now the old fort served its new owners as a scenic overlook on which to build lavish homes.

Grant backed off on the engines slowing the boat to a crawl. He squinted at the navigation screen. Cockspur Island was several miles ahead where it lay at the inlet to the Savannah River. But first he would have to cross the much traveled Tybee Roads, a narrow channel dredged for bigger ships to make their way into the Savannah River docks. The old man at the boat rental warned him of this dangerous area.

Surrounded by shoals that broke the ocean's tides, Tybee Roads marked the entrance into the river proper. Up ahead he noted a series of flashing buoys signaling the south side of the channel. There was a lighted tide gauge on the other side of the channel that he would have to navigate past.

He wiped the ocean spray from his face, motored slowly. Seeing much beyond the boat was nearly impossible. Any ships coming down the channel would run him over if they weren't able to see him. He was in all likelihood too small to be picked up by their radar. It would be a dangerous crossing.

He pushed the throttle forward and the boat lurched back onto a plane. He steered a course between two flashing buoys as the Tybee lighthouse faded from view over his left shoulder.

Grant was soaked to the skin, he felt like a prune. In spite of the balmy weather the storm and rain caused him to shiver. He had read about storms at sea and people dying of hypothermia and exposure in spite of warm weather. The symptoms of hypothermia were lightheadedness, giddiness, dizziness, blurred vision, and then lethargy followed by coma and death. He uttered a quick prayer and pressed on.

As he passed between two red flashing buoys, he realized he was now in Tybee Roads, the main channel. His biggest fear was being run over by a tanker. He pushed the Bluewater boat faster hoping he wouldn't blow an engine. Glancing down at his instruments, Grant realized he was doing close to forty miles per hour, causing the rain pellets to sting like needles as they pelted his face, his body.

The channel was much deeper and the water appeared black. Black as thick syrup. The seas seemed calmer here, something he couldn't figure but it made for a smoother ride. An occasional wave hit the boat's bow catapulting it skyward. He gripped the wheel tighter, an act that caused his hands to become numb. Pain seared both legs from standing on the pitching deck in an attempt to maintain his balance. He was beginning to wear down, fatigue and strain taking its toll on his slumping body.

Grant cursed the rain again and his foolish decision to head out to sea with the weather as it was. The old man had been right, of course. But he was fearful for Carrie and that spurred him forward into a future as uncertain as the weather. The thought struck him that he didn't have a clue what he was going to do if and when he sighted Conway's yacht. Did he think he was going to waltz right up and board her, brandishing his Beretta? And expect the man to give up Carrie just like that? He was beginning to feel the way he did that day in Iraq. In Ambush Alley.

Then he was back there in that place, gunfire exploding all around him. His Humvee veering first left then right as the driver attempted valiantly to skirt the burned out tanks, other vehicles stranded on the road. Then that car appeared, heading straight for his vehicle. That car full of kids bent on killing them all. A flash, a fireball. Suddenly he was momentarily blinded by it. Its concussion rocked him back in his seat.

He blinked. The seas ahead were a dark onerous mass of darkness threatening to engulf him into its waiting arms. The rain pelted his face. He was cold, shivering, weak. "My God! Please help me!" he cried out.

A flashing red buoy up ahead marked the far edge of Tybee Roads, the northern boundary of the channel. It flew past in a blinding moment.

Another lighted buoy in the far distance. As Grant drew closer he could see that it marked a small outcropping of land, not really an island but a definite spit of land forming an obstruction. Good thing there's a light, he thought. *I could have run right into it.*

He skirted the land and continued northward toward

Cockspur Island, now looming closer on the GPS monitor. He peered into the dark ahead but could see nothing. He reduced the RPMs and the boat slowed. He felt for his Beretta, glad to know it was still in his belt.

A large black mass appeared ahead.

Cockspur.

He threw the throttle into neutral, allowed the boat to slowly come to rest in the rolling seas. The island was large, stuck in the middle of the seam between the intercostal waters and the Atlantic. Grant reached in a compartment and retrieved a pair of binoculars. Bringing them to his eyes he scanned the waters in front of him. Off to his right there was a light smudge rolling gently. As he studied it he realized what he was seeing.

The *Sandpiper*!

Studying the yacht, he could tell its interior lights were blazing brightly. No one was about outside. Smart people, he thought. Was Carrie aboard? Impossible to tell. He stood in the rain contemplating his next move. Barging in on them now was an invitation to disaster. He would wait until later. Much later.

For the present, he would motor back to the little spit of land, conceal himself and the boat behind it, and wait.

Then he would rescue Carrie.

Chapter 34

Conway and Sergei sat across from each other in Conway's private suite. Carrie had retired for the evening, gone to bed without eating dinner. Now he looked at the man across from him and nodded.

"I'm appreciative for what you've done, Sergei. It was money well spent." Conway sat back, peered out the suite's window into the raging darkness. His yacht rocked gently, the effect of the storm greatly reduced by the gyro stabilizers. An electronic motion sensor detected even the slightest bit of movement in the water and sent commands to the external hull fins to rotate accordingly. If the boat rolled to starboard, the fins turned counter-clockwise to counteract that motion.

The man smiled. He didn't say much, a trait that Conway appreciated.

"The girl needs to be watched," Conway said. "I don't want her sneaking a call on the radio or trying to signal a passing boat. So please, keep an eye on her."

Again the man nodded. He hadn't said much since arriving on board the yacht but Conway had grown to like the man. He didn't know much about his past, didn't care either. It was all business with Sergei.

The man left the suite so Conway wandered back to

the main salon to fix himself a drink. He poured a snifter of Courvoisier Esprit cognac, his favorite, from a crystal decanter. Settling in a chair he sipped and listened as the wind and rain beat against the *Sandpiper*. He had come a long way since the early days when he had nothing. Those days when he worked for Georgia Power. He gambled in a business of his own and the gamble had paid off. Was he getting too big for his britches? Possibly.

His business was in trouble and he needed the power plant to go up in Trinity. He needed to sell some plutonium to get back on his feet financially and the plant would make it easy to do. Once he had the necessary licenses it would be easy. Only nine pounds of plutonium-239. Nine pounds from the spent nuclear fuel from the power plant. It would solve all his problems. Possibly as much as a billion dollars.

And Sergei knew the right people.

⋐⋑⋐⋑

Grant checked his watch. The luminous dial read two-fifty-three a.m. He looked across the sea toward the *Sandpiper,* noticed it was dark. Everyone must have gone to bed. He had motored to a spot just beyond the small landmass where he had a good position in which to observe the yacht.

The storm had abated, blown itself out, moved on over Savannah. The lightning flashes still occurred but now they were over land and would die out soon. Clouds obscured the stars but the wind had dwindled to a mere breeze. Grant remained soaked but no longer as chilled as he was earlier. He took the Beretta out of his belt, checked the clip, returned it to his belt.

After starting the Bluewater's engines he began a

slow advance toward the yacht. His heart pounded in his temples, his stomach rumbled. Fortunately, while moored behind the bight of land, he had taken some time to sit, giving his legs a relaxing rest. He even dozed for a while. Now, somewhat refreshed, he kept the yacht in view as he approached. The seas were calm, the waves a mere foot or less. As the boat glided through the languid water, Grant wondered how close he should get. If he left his boat and swam to the yacht his Beretta would become waterlogged and possibly inoperable. The man at the gun dealer said it should still fire if it was submerged but should he test it now? Maybe he could hold the gun in his mouth while he swam to the boat.

Closer to the yacht, he slowed to a stop, used the binocs to scan the area. Nothing. The *Sandpiper* was still dark and quiet, its anchor rode extending off the stern at an easy angle. He motored closer, stopping a quarter mile from the boat, killed the engines. He dropped the anchor and sat on the bench in front of the wheel, thinking, waiting.

What if he climbed on board with the Beretta drawn and Carrie wasn't there? How foolish would that be? Conway might just kill him, dump his body overboard. But he had come too far to turn back. Right or wrong he was going to board the yacht. He hoped she was there.

He slipped over the side and into the water, its cool temperature giving him a start. He gripped his pistol with his teeth, hoping to be able to keep it dry on the swim. He began a breaststroke trying to keep the Beretta out of the water. A thought struck him—were there sharks in these waters? He didn't know but what a time to start worrying about them. He could see a big one swimming up underneath him, taking a large hunk out of him, leaving him to bleed out. What a grisly thought. As he swam he scanned the surface for signs of a fin but saw nothing.

The imposing silhouette of Cockspur Island rose out of the waters off the yacht's port side, a dark mass in the middle of nowhere. To his left was the flashing of a buoy. To take his mind off the possibility of sharks he counted the interval between the red flashes. One— Two—Three—Four. Four seconds. He had no idea what the buoy marked, probably an obstruction or shoals.

The yacht loomed larger now. He could make out its name lettered on the stern where there was a ladder was attached. It would make boarding easy. Unless he was discovered. What if there were motion or deck security sensors that would sound an alarm if an intruder gained access to the boat? *Fine time to think of these things.* He would just have to take his chances.

He approached the *Sandpiper* from its stern, stroking silently through the waves. His jaw ached from the effort to clench the Beretta and keep it out of the water. The yacht rode high, its ladder barely skimming the water's surface. Thankfully, the cold water numbed his limbs taking away the pain of effort. Grant concentrated to each stroke, methodical, regular, as he got closer to Conway's yacht. His mouth burned from lack of water. But he continued on.

Grant maneuvered to the boat's rear, paused at the ladder to catch his breath. Hearing no sounds, he began the climb. As soon as he was out of the water, the breeze hit his wet body, causing a chill to shoot through him. He shuddered. Standing on the ladder, he stuffed the Beretta in his belt and slid onto the deck.

He shot a quick glance around the yacht. Still, all was quiet.

He looked back over his shoulder in the direction he had swum. The sea was calm, dark, no sign of his boat.

The yacht's open deck was a large affair with several all-weather chairs around a metal table. Beyond the table he noticed a sliding glass door that allowed entrance to the boat's interior. Drawing his pistol from his belt, he moved across the deck to the glass door and tried it. It slid open without much effort.

He took a deep breath and stepped inside.

The main cabin was dark illuminated by a single night light along a far wall. Grant took a moment to catch his breath, orient himself to his new surroundings. He listened for any sound that would indicate someone was up but heard nothing. He had a firm grip on the Beretta, its cold metal feeling strange in his hand. He advanced into the salon, noted the stairs to his right, then skirted around the dining table. He thought about resting in one of the overstuffed chairs and wait for Conway to appear. What a greeting that would make. He climbed several of the stairs only to find that they led to the bridge, which was currently unoccupied.

Back in the salon he crept toward the forward door. It was open. On the way he stumbled into a small cabinet containing a number of liquor bottles and crystal decanters. Above the cabinet a dozen wine bottles lay in an ornate rack. When he bumped the cabinet the decanters rattled, piercing the stillness. He stopped, gun at the ready, waiting for someone to appear in the shadows but no one did.

To the right of the salon and through another doorway he recognized the galley full of pots and pans hanging from hooks swaying slightly with the boat's gentle motion. A coffeepot sat on a narrow counter.

Grant moved to the far door, keeping his footfalls to a muffled shuffle. A short hallway led beyond the salon to what Grant surmised were the staterooms. Several nightlights glowed with a soft yellow light along the carpeted aisle. Four closed doors fronted the hallway, doors Grant thought must open into the bedrooms. Was Carrie asleep in one of them? Was Conway? How was he to know which one? It was hard to fathom that he had made it this far without being detected or some alarm going off. Maybe Conway felt safe enough out here in the middle of nowhere to not arm the security alarms.

Grant decided to return to the salon and wait for someone to wake and move about. He turned and took a step. A deep voice bellowed behind him.

"Stop where you are! Throw that pistol down and raise your hands!"

ℰↃℰↃ

Special Agent In Charge Wilder looked at Dalrymple and Toomey with a satisfied smile. Both men sat across from her, Dalrymple with his notebook in hand. A gentle rain from an overcast sky beat on Wilder's window.

"So, I believe we have enough evidence now," Dalrymple said, "to get an indictment against the chief of police, the deceased mayor, and Dr. Witherspoon."

"On the charges of—" Wilder asked. She knew the answer but it needed to be said, discussed before going to the US Attorney in Atlanta.

"Willful negligence in the performance of official duties, fraud, accepting bribes, malfeasance, intimidation of public officials, to name a few," Dalrymple said.

"And Conway? What about him?" Wilder leaned forward, elbows on her large mahogany desk.

"We're on a little shakier ground there," Dalrymple said, glancing at his notebook. "Extortion and possibly murder. We need to bring him in for questioning. Put some pressure on him."

"He'll just get his lawyers down here and raise a ruckus," Wilder said.

"I think we can stand the heat," Toomey interjected. "He needs to explain a few things."

"Such as?" Wilder picked up a pen, adjusted her legal pad.

"Why DynaTech is in financial trouble, for starters," Dalrymple said. "Especially in light of his wanting to expand and build the Trinity plant."

"Don't think those questions will fly, gentlemen," Wilder said, tapping her pen on her desk. "Without more concrete evidence of law-breaking, his lawyer will claim invasion of privacy and advise Conway to not answer. He would be on firm legal footing, I'm afraid."

"Any suggestions?" Dalrymple said.

"I think questioning him is a good idea. However, we can't expect too much in the way of cooperation. You have anything that can link him to the Trinity deaths?"

Dalrymple shook his head. "Unfortunately, no. We are still tracing the Hungarian fiber we found at the scene of the mayor's murder. Might turn up something there."

Wilder leaned back, clasped her fingers together. "Well, go bring him in. We can at least do that. Do you know where he is at the moment?"

"He's either at his office or condo in Savannah or aboard his yacht. We can find him."

"When you bring him in," Wilder said, "I want to be present for the questions. I have a few myself."

Chapter 35

Grant's knees turned to jelly. His heart pounded. He threw the Beretta on the salon floor.

"Don't move," commanded the male voice behind him.

The man shoved him into the main part of the salon, pushed him into a chair. Grant looked at the man and saw someone with Russian features holding a pistol on him.

"So," the man said in a decided Eastern accent, "we have a prowler."

Conway burst into the salon, his eyes wide with obvious surprise at the noise.

"What's this?" he demanded. His voice was cold, hard.

"I caught this prowler, Mr. Conway. Found him in the salon here."

Conway shot a look at Grant, suddenly irritated by what he saw.

"You!" he shouted angrily. "Collins! What the hell are you doing here? You sonofabitch! How dare you!"

Just as Grant was about to answer, Carrie came stumbling into the main cabin, rubbing her eyes as if she had just awakened.

"Grant!" she exclaimed. "What on earth?"

"My sentiments exactly," Conway said, his voice tempered now. "Please tell me, Mr. Collins, to what do we owe the honor of this unexpected visit?"

"I came for Carrie," Grant hissed.

"Do tell," Conway said. "What made you think this venture of yours would succeed? I am interested to know."

"It doesn't matter," Grant said. "I had to do something. After all, you killed those people in Trinity, including my mother. I wasn't about to let the same fate happen to Carrie."

"You had a gun. Were you planning to kill me?"

Grant didn't answer the question. His eyes locked with Carrie's. Their looks spoke volumes.

"Sergei," Conway said, "lock them in the woman's cabin. If they escape, it will be your hide."

The man pushed Grant and Carrie down the hallway into her stateroom. Grant heard the key lock the door. Carrie collapsed on the bed, crying softly.

"Why, Grant? Why did you do this?" she said, tears running down her cheeks.

"Why?" he said. "You can ask *why*? There was no way I was going to let this happen to you. How did it happen?"

"That man named Sergei and another man grabbed me after I got off work, pushed me into a car. I wound up on this boat."

Grant seethed, clinched his fists in anger. "That asshole hurt you?"

"Not at all. In fact, he has been the perfect gentleman. Keeps calling me, *my dear.* He said after the vote was over and the plant was voted in he would let me go. He seems to think he's above the law."

Grant made his way to the cabin's window, tried opening it but found it locked. Outside, the night winds had calmed, the rain all but over. "We need to find a way off this boat," he said. "Before it gets light, if possible."

"Sergei will kill us," Carrie said, wiping her eyes with a sleeve.

"I don't trust Conway," Grant said. "That bastard can't leave any witnesses behind. He'll kill us and dump our bodies overboard. No one would ever find us."

"How can we do it?"

"I dunno. These doors can't be all that strong. Maybe I can force it open and we make a run for it. Jump overboard. Swim to the boat I brought out here."

"Is it far?" Carrie said. "I'm not a very good swimmer."

"A quarter mile or so. I have it hidden behind a small bit of land south of here,"

Carrie rose off the bed, put her arms around him. "Oh, Grant," she sighed. "If only we could."

"We will," he said. "Just leave it to me. If I can save you, that's all I care about."

"How did it come to this?"

"We started asking questions, that's how. Conway has a lot to hide, most of all those murders. I think his actions of late pretty much defines his guilt."

"I'd like to see the bastard hang," she said.

"We'll wait until it quiets down. Then we're getting off this damned boat."

The two of them rested on the bed for an hour. Grant was exhausted, having been up all night fighting the storm and swimming to the yacht. He managed to doze a few minutes while Carrie stroked his cheek.

At five-thirty, Grant rose and peered out the window. A dull slate sky was forming in the East, portending a dawn within the hour. He crossed the cabin, stood with an ear to the door, then nodded. Carrie bounded off the bed and stood behind him. He tried the door.

Still locked.

He pushed his frame against it. Nothing happened.

He struck the door with his full weight.

Nothing.

Again, he crashed into the door.

This time it punched open.

Grant stared into the hallway, praying no one heard the sound. When Sergei or Conway didn't appear, he took Carrie by the hand and led her into the salon after closing the door behind them. He thought he heard someone moving around behind him.

"Hurry," he said in a hushed voice. "Out onto the deck."

Grant opened the sliding door to the main deck and was immediately greeted by humid salty air. For a moment it felt good to out of the yacht's air-conditioning. Along the yacht's gunwale a row of fishing poles rested in their holder. A shelf held other tackle. Several spearguns stood alongside the poles. He grabbed one.

For a moment, he and Carrie stood at the side of the boat, Grant wondering if the risk was worth it. Inside the cabin a shout was raised. It was now or never. He took Carrie's hand in his.

"Jump!" he yelled. "Now!"

⌒⌒⌒

Conway heard two splashes, ran out the salon onto the main deck. In the distance, he saw Grant and the girl swimming, heading for Cockspur Island, a hundred yards in the distance.

"Sergei!" he yelled. "Out here!"

The man arrived at Conway's side. Conway pointed to the pair, already halfway to the island.

"There," he said. "Get the rifle. Shoot them!"

Sergei disappeared inside the cabin and returned in a short minute with a high-powered rifle with attached scope. He aimed at the receding pair of swimmers, fired two shots in quick succession. Both missed.

"Dammit man!" Conway hissed. "Kill them!"

Sergei shot twice more without hitting either swimmer. His clip was empty. He threw up his hands in exasperation.

"Go get them!" Conway commanded.

"It will take time to lower the dingy," Sergei said.

"Not in the dingy, stupid! Swim after them. Go now! Kill them!"

Sergei checked his survival knife in its scabbard, shot a look at Conway that said, *Are you nuts?* then dived overboard. Conway watched the man for a few minutes, then satisfied that he would overtake them before they reached the island, returned to the salon and closed the door.

Even though dawn was just breaking and it was earlier than his usual drinking time, Conway poured himself a healthy glassful of scotch. He ambled back to his suite and sat in the dim light, gulping the liquor.

This was the moment, he thought. The moment when all his planning and conniving would pay off. When the couple was dead, he would have Sergei take their bodies in the dingy far out into the Atlantic and dump them overboard. No one would ever know. It would cost him more money, but it would be worth it.

He tried to relax in a chair but his racing heart made that impossible. Conway took another drink and waited for Sergei to return.

෴

Carrie was giving out. Her arms could no longer

place one in front of the other. A cramping pain shot through both legs. She looked at Grant, and he nodded. As seawater lapped over her face, he moved in closer to her.

"Rest your arms on my shoulders," he said. "I'll push you the rest of the way."

Glancing back over his shoulders, she noticed a form swimming and splashing toward them. "Someone's behind us!" she screamed.

Grant hesitated, turned, and saw the form gaining on them. Carrie stared at the man, who looked like the one called Sergei, making a fast line behind them, getting closer. Without uttering a word Grant resumed his swimming. Could they make it to the island before Sergei reached them? She saw what looked like a large knife clutched in the man's mouth.

"Hurry!" Carrie shouted. "He's got a knife!"

She felt Grant's legs kick harder while he picked up the pace of his strokes. They needed to reach the shoreline before Sergei caught up with them. The knife only meant one thing—he was intent on killing them both.

Carrie could tell it was difficult for Grant to swim while at the same time holding the speargun. It made for an awkward pairing. Her, struggling to remain afloat, despite being exhausted and, Grant, fighting to get them both ashore while holding on to the speargun, their only means of defense. In the far distance behind Sergei, she spotted Conway pacing the deck, peering at them through binoculars.

What was going to happen if they reached the island? Grant had one spear in the gun, one shot at Sergei. What if he missed? Then, she reasoned, they were doomed. She looked toward shore. It seemed as if they had not made any appreciable progress although she knew that wasn't possible. Grant was swimming hard. But maybe the tide was pushing them back. Pushing them back out toward the yacht and Conway.

Oh, dear God! Please not that!

Somewhat rested, she resumed swimming on her own. She noticed that they were making progress, slow as it was, and Sergei was no longer gaining on them. He was still behind them but he must be tiring as well.

Her foot bumped something.

The bottom.

She was able to stand while Grant supported her. They stumbled onto the narrow shore, Carrie out of breath, her chest heaving. Grant grabbed her arm and pulled her into the dense foliage, stumbling as he did so. With his eyes wide and red, he had the look of a man possessed, one intent on living.

"What should we do?" she said, pulling on his arm.

"Get as far inland as we can before that bastard makes it to shore. Then we hide." He raised the speargun. "If he finds us, I shoot him with this."

"You think we have a chance?" she said, stumbling over logs and roots.

"As long as we are alive, we have a chance."

They crashed through the thick island vegetation, bumping into fallen tree logs, stumbling over vines and roots that caught their legs. Carrie's arms and legs were bleeding from the myriad scratches she got along the way. Blood oozed down one arm. Grant didn't look much better, his clothes tattered and bloodstained. She checked each clump of vegetation for places to hide but didn't spot anything suitable.

Grant stumbled onto a narrow trail that led deeper into the island. She followed him at a trot, her lungs burning. She gasped for breath.

She caught her foot in a stump and went tumbling, landing on her side, her foot at an odd angle. Pain shot through her entire body, searing her brain. She cried out for Grant. "Help!"

She watched as he stopped, glanced over his shoulder, then returned to where she lay grasping her ankle.

"What happened?" he said, stooping over her, inspecting her injury.

"I twisted my ankle on a stump," she said. "Dammit!"

"Rest for a moment," he said. "Then we'll see if you can stand on it."

She massaged her mud-splattered ankle, shot a look behind them. "I better be able to 'cause that bastard's gonna come crashing right down on us if I can't."

"Wanna try and stand?" Grant said, placing an arm under hers.

Carrie stood and put her weight on that leg. She winced as a bolt of pain shot up the leg. "Shit," she exclaimed.

She tried hobbling around on the foot and found the pain was less intense and that she could walk. Not very fast. But she could move.

Carrie turned an ear to the shore, listened for sounds of Sergei coming through the foliage after them. For the present, all was quiet.

Grant supported her and together they made their way down the trail farther into the island's interior. Every few minutes, Grant stopped, peered back behind them, and listened for Sergei. But there was nothing.

The trail led to a small rise then down into what looked like a sinkhole, a circle of clear dark water surrounded by cattails and short green grass. Grant led them around the water and deeper into the island's interior. He took her hand with a rough grasp and helped her along.

Up ahead, Carrie saw a small clearing that abutted a steep rock formation. Like a small butte. She was dying for a drink of water and a rest. Grant pulled her closer to the rocks. As they approached what was a rock wall she spied a small indentation—a tiny cave. Grant saw it also and pulled her toward it.

It was just big enough for the two of them if they huddled together. The wind picked up and whistled past the cave's entrance. Carrie collapsed on the ground with Grant falling beside her. He pulled her close to him, wrapped his arms about her, warmed her with his body.

Together, they waited for Sergei to arrive.

Chapter 36

Grant and Carrie squeezed into the small cave, their backs against the limestone wall, peering out into the darkness beyond. Both shivered and Grant felt himself getting lightheaded, the first sign of dehydration and hypothermia. They were miles from any sort of help, with no means of communication, cornered on an uninhabited island as their executioner stalked somewhere behind. He was exhausted, totally spent. Huddling next to Carrie, he placed an arm around her, felt her shiver, saw the terror in her eyes. God, she looked beautiful. Her auburn hair was a mass of tangles, her body was covered with numerous cuts and bruises, and there were large patches of caked mud and sand stuck to her clothes. But still, she was beautiful. He realized that, if he was to die in the coming moments, it was right to die alongside her.

But what was he thinking? He had the speargun and clutching it in his hand renewed his hope that all might not be lost. Somewhere in the depths of his character his Marine Corps training rose to the surface, a mental attitude that, as long as they were alive there was hope.

He refocused his attention on what lay beyond the cave's opening—death or life. Inspecting the speargun, he noticed it was a wooden gun and constructed out of what appeared to be African mahogany. The arrow shaft was stainless steel. An awesome killing machine. But how Grant longed for his Beretta.

Carrie's shivering was worse. Her lips were blue and she appeared to be disconnected from their present situation, a sign, he knew, that didn't portend well for her survival, even if he managed to kill the man behind them.

Grant heard rustling in the bushes beyond the pocket-sized rock shelter in which he and Carrie were hiding. He gripped the speargun with aching fingers, pulled the band back toward his chest to cock it, and watched for any movement. Carrie huddled behind him, he felt her warm breath on his neck.

"If he finds us in here," she whispered, "shoot the bastard."

Grant adjusted his position to ease the cramp in his legs. "Don't worry, I will."

The rustling grew louder, closer, then Sergei appeared in a small clearing in front of the cave. He was covered with bruises and scratches from his foray through the island's vegetation. He paused, looked around, not seeing the pair huddled together in the cave. He took a step forward.

"Hold it right there!" Grant shouted from the confines of the small enclosure. He noticed that Sergei had his survival knife in his right hand.

Sergei looked around, as if he was trying to locate the source of Grant's voice. He took another step.

"One more step and I'll shoot," Grant commanded.

A cynical smile formed on Sergei's face. "Shoot me with what?" he said, a sinister tone in his voice.

Grant exited the cave and crouched, facing Sergei, the speargun pointing at the man's chest.

"With this," he said. "And at this range, I can't miss."

Sergei stepped forward again, brought the knife up into the ready position.

"Please," Grant shouted to the man. "Don't make me do this. I don't want to shoot, but I will if necessary."

Sergei paused. Grant was suddenly transported back to Iraq and Ambush Alley. The car with the kids were coming at him. He hesitated. He heard someone talking.

"...you're both dead," Sergei was saying.

"Grant, please!" Carrie screamed behind him. "He means it!"

Grant shook his head, tried to clear his mind. No, this wasn't Iraq. What the hell was the matter with him? The war was over and he was no longer a marine.

Sergei let out a yell and sprinted toward him, his knife looming larger as he approached Grant.

"Noooooo!" Grant screamed.

He pulled the speargun's trigger releasing the steel shaft. It pierced Sergei's chest to the left of his breastbone. A shot direct into the man's heart.

Sergei stopped abruptly, stood for a moment as if stunned that he had taken the arrow. He remained motionless, his eyes wide in obvious horror. Then he fell forward to the ground pushing the shaft deeper into his chest. Blood spurted from the wound forming rivulets in the dirt. He grunted several times then was still, not breathing.

Grant stooped over Sergei, turned his body over while Carrie made her way to his side. The man's watery eyes stared upward, no recognition in them.

"Bastard," Carrie exclaimed. "Now what?"

"I want to go back and confront Conway. Make him pay somehow."

"Are you crazy, Grant? He'll kill us both if we go back there."

"The only other option is swimming to the boat I

used to get out here. It's a longer swim than back to Conway's yacht."

"But it's safer." Carrie wandered back to their cave shelter and sat.

Grant followed her. "Okay," he said. "We'll do it your way. When we get to my boat, then we can decide. Head for Conway or head for Savannah."

They began swimming for Grant's rental boat he left on the far side of the landmass south of the yacht. Overhead, the thinning clouds allowed a few rays of sunshine through, bathing the sound in a soft light. Grant's muscles warmed and loosened, the swimming became easier. He was still thirsty, his mouth felt like it was full of cotton. Carrie swam alongside, her strokes clean and rhythmical. In the far distance, he could see the undersized bit of land barely protruding out of the water. He renewed his determination and stoked harder.

Along the way, Carrie had to rest, so they did as before with her holding onto his shoulders while he propelled them through the water. He knew he was dehydrated and hoped he wouldn't cramp up before reaching the boat. To put his mind on something else, he chatted with Carrie.

"Back there," he said, "when I faced Sergei, I momentarily was back in Iraq. It was so strange. I saw the car full of kids heading straight for our Humvee, their rifles pointed at us. It was bizarre. I thought for a moment I was losing my mind."

"You weren't losing your mind, honey. You had a horrible experience while in Iraq. No one should have to experience that kind of fear. But you did. It's understandable that your mind revolts at that sort of thing. Perfectly natural. We don't have control of what tricks our minds play on us. We just have to hope for the best."

"I was scared in that moment. I didn't know if I could pull the trigger. Just like in Iraq."

"But you did," Carrie said. "Just like you did in Iraq. You saved your men then and you saved us today. I'm glad."

Grant thought he could see the boat in the distance and, after a few more minutes, he was sure of it. It appeared as a small white speck behind the spit of land.

In a half hour, they were at the boat and Grant crawled aboard then helped a fatigued Carrie. They collapsed on the deck, totally spent.

After resting, he started the Bluewater's three engines, retrieved the anchor, and sat idling in a calm sea. He felt his pulse racing in his neck, a vein in his head pounded away. He looked northward toward where the *Sandpiper* lay anchored, weighing their options.

"You're going back, aren't you?" Carrie said. "Going back to face Conway?"

"Dunno," he said, spitting out the word. "I can't decide. Like that day in Iraq, dammit, I can't decide! God help me."

"Grant," Carrie said, standing next to him at the wheel with a hand on his shoulder. "Whatever you decide, I'm with you. That bastard killed your mother. Let's go get even."

Grant swallowed hard, clinched his jaw, shoved the throttle forward. The boat leaped onto a plane and soon they were racing toward the yacht and a rendezvous with an uncertain future. The clouds, which earlier had been dark and foreboding, had disappeared and a bright sun beat down with a veracity known only in the southern Atlantic. The wind whistling through Grants tattered shirt cooled him as they flew toward the yacht. He had one arm around Carrie's waist and she rested her head on his shoulder.

On the northern horizon, Grant made out a hazy silhouette and figured that was Hilton Head. A long day's journey away. He wondered how he had managed to swim this distance in the middle of the night and avoid being eaten by sharks. Just lucky, he guessed. He had read that the great white sharks patrolled the Georgia and South Carolina coasts so it was just pure luck that he had avoided them.

A siren wailed in the distance. Off his starboard beam he saw a coast guard vessel plowing through the seas at a high rate of speed. It was a hundred-foot Fast Response Cutter and its course was taking it directly toward Conway's boat. Its siren pierced the otherwise quiet of the waters off Cockspur Island.

Grant backed down on the throttle, allowing the cutter to move ahead as it raced northward. When the *Sandpiper* came into view, he shoved the throttle into neutral and drifted to a halt. The coast guard cutter kept on its course until it came to within fifty yards of the yacht when it slowed its speed and began circling it.

He and Carrie watched with fascination as the cutter closed its distance from the yacht. A voice on a loudspeaker called to the boat but Grant couldn't make out what was being said. Some sort of command. He grabbed the binocs and saw Conway standing at the glass door. It looked like he held a pistol in one hand.

The loudspeaker on the cutter kept issuing commands. The cutter stopped behind the yacht and Conway emerged from the main cabin still holding the pistol. It looked like he was shouting at the coast guard vessel. What it was couldn't be heard.

"He's got a gun," Grant told Carrie who was still clutching him by an arm.

"Just give up, Conway," she said.

But Conway didn't give up. He stood on the stern

deck of the *Sandpiper*, yelling with a raised clenched fist. coast guard personnel ran forward manning the twenty-five millimeter auto-cannon and the fifty-caliber machine guns.

More commands from the loudspeaker. The coast guard was obviously commanding Conway to lay down his weapon and surrender.

He did not.

Instead, he raised his pistol, pointed it in the direction of the coast guard cutter.

There was a barrage of machine gun fire and Conway went down. The salvos continued long after he was down. Grant saw that the back of the yacht was covered in blood and bullet holes.

"Oh my God!" screamed Carrie. "They killed him!"

The roar of a cannon boomed and the round hit the yacht directly causing the back of it to explode and erupt into flames. Grant stood transfixed by the sight. It was as if he was back in Ambush Alley, the sounds familiar to his ears.

Then, the entire yacht exploded in a giant fireball, the shock of the concussion nearly knocking Carrie out of their boat. Thick black smoke billowed skyward as pieces of the yacht fell into the sea. Grant panned the area with the binocs. Nothing much more than the skeletal remains of the yacht's hull remained, the rest of the boat vaporized in the explosion.

The cutter advanced on what remained of Conway's boat. A dingy was lowered and a handful of men left the cutter and motored back and forth over the scene. As if looking for survivors. It was obvious to Grant there were none.

He turned the boat toward Savannah and headed home.

Epilogue

Grant and Carrie stood at his mother's grave in the Trinity cemetery. The day was warm and bright, the sky filled with large cumulus clouds. They were there to view the headstone Grant had ordered. It was next to his father's, a rose-marbled affair with Helen's name engraved on it. Tears filled his eyes and for a moment he was transported back in to a time when she taught him to dance before his first prom. He remembered her laughter as she showed him the steps.

"She was a great lady," he said softly. "I miss her already."

"She knew you loved her, I'm sure," Carrie said, squeezing his arm.

"At least we brought some justice to her death," he said. "That was important to me."

"You going back to DC right away?" she said.

"I dunno," he said. "My counselor at Reed said I was much better. I sure missed you."

"You know you can stay here for as long as you want. I need you in my life, Grant."

"Don't worry, Carrie. You're not getting rid of me.

After all that's happened, I'm just not sure Trinity is the place for me. Or you either."

He turned away and they walked back to his rental car and drove to Carrie's apartment. Arriving, he noticed a dark SUV parked in Carrie's driveway so he parked in the street and got out. A woman exited the SUV. She looked familiar as she approached.

"Mr. Collins?" she said. She showed an identification card. "I'm Samantha Wilder with the Georgia Bureau of Investigation. Remember me?"

"Oh yes. Of course. You remember my friend, Carrie."

"Of course," Wilder said, smiling.

Carrie nodded. "Won't you come in, Agent Wilder?" she said.

The three of them sat in Carrie's living room where Wilder continued.

"As you know, Winston Conway decided his own fate by not surrendering to the coast guard authorities. It is unfortunate that three possibly innocent people lost their lives due to his foolishness. His captain, cook, and steward. Whether or not they had a role in the Trinity murders is still the subject of an ongoing investigation. The governor has appointed a special panel to lead the investigation into their deaths and whether the coast guard acted appropriately. In addition, the chief of police, Sergeant Brady, and Doctor Witherspoon have all been brought up on charges.

"Of course the lives of the committee members here in Trinity can never be brought back but you can hold your head high, the two of you, knowing that your contribution helped solve the riddle of their deaths. As such, their families are sleeping better tonight. On behalf of the people of the State of Georgia, I want to thank you for your courage and perseverance in seeing that justice was finally done in this case."

"What about the man left on the island?" Carrie said. "The man Grant killed."

Wilder nodded. "He was a Yugoslavian killer. An international assassin hiring himself out to the highest bidder. Where Conway found him is still uncertain at this point. Fibers from his clothes matched the one found at the Baxter murder scene."

"So he killed the mayor?" Carrie said.

Wilder nodded again. "What's new with the two of you?"

Grant looked at Carrie, felt his face flush. "We haven't decided."

"Well," Wilder said, standing. "I wish you both the best."

After she left Grant sat with Carrie while she stroked his cheek.

"What made you change your mind?" he asked Carrie.

"What do you mean?"

"Once, you said you didn't know if you could continue with me or not. In the end, you did. I'm asking what changed your mind?"

"You, Grant. You changed my mind. I realized I couldn't face my future without you. Pretty simple, really."

"I see."

"What are you thinking?" she said.

He thought for a moment, then smiled, took her in his arms and kissed her. "I'm thinking it was a long way back but I'm finally home."

About the Author

Richard Edde was born and raised in Oklahoma. After graduating from Central State College, he attended the University of Oklahoma College of Medicine, where he earned his medical degree in 1971. After spending a few years in family practice in two rural Oklahoma towns, he completed a residency in anesthesiology. Following a long career in academia and private practice, he retired to devote time to writing. His first novel, *The Photograph*, was released in 2014. Dr. Edde resides in eastern Oklahoma with his wife.

www.ingramcontent.com/pod-product-compliance
Lightning Source LLC
Chambersburg PA
CBHW070625260626
47161CB00007B/2584